Fantasy

CW00659708

WACOOH

HARRISON V. PERRY

WARPED
AND TORN

First published in the UK in 2023 by Warped and Torn

Copyright © Harrison V. Perry, 2023

The moral right of Harrison V. Perry to be identified as the author of this work has been asserted in accordance with the Copyright, Designs and Patents Act of 1988.

All rights reserved. No part of this publication may be reproduced, distributed, or transmitted in any form or by any means, including photocopying, recording, or other electronic or mechanical methods, without the prior written permission of the publisher, except as permitted by copyright law.

This is a work of fiction. All characters, organizations, and events portrayed in this novel are either products of the author's imagination or are used fictitiously.

Book cover by Tommy Hardman
Edited by James Anders Banks

Published by Warped and Torn

first edition paperback 2023
ISBN: 978-1-7384007-0-6

www.warpedandtorn.io

WARPED
AND TORN

To Mum, Dad, and Dec—for never backing favourites.

WACOOH

PART ONE

"I have no greater joy than to hear that my children walk in truth."

— 3 John 1:4

BLOOD, LIES, AND A FLOWER

– NEW HAVILAH –

He must have grimaced because nurse Iskra said to him, 'I thought the Immortal Man felt no pain?'

The hypodermic needle hurt more than he remembered from the last time. Quinton stared at the vial as it filled rapidly with his blood. It's all alright, he thought, there's plenty more inside me. He swallowed and told her, 'That's a New Havilian rumour. The sort of talk you'd hear in the pub.' He met her eyes, properly, for the first time since entering the surgery that day, and noticed that they were mottled by beautiful green flecks.

Iskra looked down at the vial, evasive. 'I don't know where I heard it then, because you won't find me in a pub.' He thought he saw her smile. 'But all these years you've never once screwed up your face like you just did, Gospodin al-Zoubi.'

'Perhaps I'm changing, Iskra, perhaps I'm getting ready to move on.' I'm long for this world. Tired of waiting.

Their eyes met again. Iskra smiled and he did too. Then she blinked, a thin translucent membrane closing vertically across her eyes.

One of her tentacles slid the needle from his arm, a second pressed a bundle of cottonmoss over the bleed. He was rather grateful that it was finished. All these years they'd been taking his blood, checking it, searching for the source of his immortality, finding nothing, growing more frustrated with him, maybe they would give it up, and let him live his life.

As he went to sit up, Iskra pushed him back down, saying, 'No, no, I need to take a second sample.'

There was no use trying to fight her suckers. So he lay back and said, 'Another sample?' And here he hoped they'd given up on him.

'It will only take a minute,' she said.

One tentacle gripped his arm, a second held his chest down, and the rest packaged up the first vial of blood and prepared another needle.

'What's going on?' he said. 'Why are you taking two samples?'

'That's what the procedure protocol is asking of me,' she said, working deftly on the next needle.

'Yes, but ... there must be a reason.'

Iskra looked over at him, her eyes uncertain, the green flecks mocking. 'The protocol has changed, and I follow the protocol. Keep still.'

Follow the protocol, he thought to himself. Take no responsibility. 'But why did the protocol change?'

She raised a few of her tentacles and shook them, as if to say, Leave off!

'Iskra,' he said, pleading, 'how long have we known each other?'

She held the fresh needle and vial up to the light and checked them over. 'What's it matter?' she said. 'If all New Havilians were immortal like you then there'd be no sadness.'

There's still plenty of sadness.

He struggled against her tentacle on his chest. 'Years,' he said, 'years and years, all this time a single test. And you don't want to tell me why things are changing.'

'I don't know what to tell you,' Iskra said. 'Would you stop wriggling.'

Her cheeks had turned blood red.

'How about the truth?'

She clicked the needle and vial into one, laid them on the silver tray next to him. 'I don't like your tone.' Her eyes shifted, taking turns staring into his.

'It's Lady Jupiter, isn't it. She's put you up to this.'

Iskra shook her head, and a few of her tentacles. 'Don't you think we should try everything?' she said. 'You really can't imagine all the good it would do if we unlock your secrets?'

'You want to live forever?' he said, still struggling against her.

'I never thought about it, not properly at least. But who wouldn't?'

'You might think you'd want to,' he said, 'but when you never die, you sure see everyone else do it. It gets hard to go on.'

She wiped his arm. 'You don't have something to live for?'

He remembered, way, way back, his mother making him noodles, the rising steam warm on his face. They would sit together and eat and he would try and suck up the longest noodle he could find before she pinched it from his lips.

And you'll see her again, Quinton, Sophia whispered to him. *She's on her way back from the stars.*

Iskra shoved the second needle into his arm. 'Well, then, don't you have something to live for?'

'Of course I do.' But this time he didn't let himself think of his mother, he shut her out.

4

Maroon liquid trickled into the glass vial and sent his stomach turning. 'Are you not going to tell me?' he said, as soon as he was sure he wasn't going to throw up. 'What's Lady Jupiter want with an extra vial of my blood?'

'I don't know answers to those sorts of questions,' Iskra said. 'Why don't you ask her yourself?'

I think I might.

A few moments later Quinton stood at the surgery's reception desk, surrounded by New Havilah's sick and needy, hoping that none noticed him. A man sat hunched in a chair, one of his horns had grown in a curl from the top of his forehead and into the underside of his chin; a lady sat next to him, her green skin covered in red radiation burns; and a boy, only about six, sat with his father, the boy's breathing raspy and struggled, phlegm bubbling up from the air-holes around his neck. The lot of them must have come all the way out from Gamma Valley. Hopeless, unless they can make it to Waters.

It was the boy's father who noticed him. He patted his son on the head, and slithered over to Quinton. He left a trail of slime along the floor, ignoring the posters on the surgery wall: 'No secretions inside!' The man, judging by the way he smelt, was a hempmoss collector. It took him a long time to find the courage to say, 'Y-you're ... you're the Immortal Man.'

Quinton nodded. Gestured for the man to keep his voice down.

'My son,' he said, 'my son's breathing ... it ain't right. It's my fault. I have to take him with me to work. He's got no mother.'

The boy's face lacked colour, and the air-holes around his neck

5

were most certainly infected: puss, yellow scabs, dried blood. Which was worse? I'd take that infection over motherlessness any day.

'Can you … can you please help him?'

Quinton shook his head. 'There's nothing I can do.' No exceptions, no favourites. 'Make sure you both take Waters at the Summer Solstice.'

The father did not go back to his boy. His antennae extended, holding up his eyeballs, and swivelled them about in a panic.

'Listen,' Quinton said, 'I can't help you, please—'

'We can't wait that long, he doesn't have that long.' His antennae shrivelled back to his head. 'That's a week away, please, I'll … I'll do anything.'

Quinton took the man's hands and lowered them. 'Take Waters.'

The man ripped his hands away. Coughed up phlegm and spat it onto Quinton's chest, and slithered back to his boy.

How many have I let die?

'There we are,' Iskra said, appearing at the other side of the reception desk. 'You're all good to leave. We'll let you know if the lab makes any … discoveries.'

Quinton forced himself to smile. He plucked tissues from the desk and wiped the spit from his chest.

'Gospodin al-Zoubi,' Iskra whispered, leaning slightly over the desk towards him, 'I don't want to be rude, but would it be OK if I asked you a question?'

You're allowed questions and I'm not? The man's spit smelt exactly like onions. How he missed onions. Iskra didn't seem to notice.

'I was wondering,' she said, a tentacle curling into a spiral, 'do you ... do you really not know what made you the Immortal Man?'

His thoughts were on the man, on his boy, on the extra blood vial, on the smell of the spit.

'Gospodin al-Zoubi?'

He shook his head, chucked the tissue into the bin. 'No idea,' he said. 'I've no idea whatsoever. The radiation? I was there in the Old World. When the Bombs first fell.'

She blinked a few times but did not go all the way back to her side of the desk. Her many tentacles played about on the stone desktop.

'It's not an easy life, Iskra.' And he walked out of the surgery to go find his bicycle, the boy's raspy breathing the last thing he heard inside.

'Ganymede Geiger Counters!' cried a Maskirovka trader, stationed right outside the doctor's surgery, hawking Ganymede Manufacturing products. 'Don't leave town without 'em!'

Quinton worked quickly, unlocking his bicycle. Snow fell as soft powder only to turn to slush on the show-shovelled road, ready to make trouble for his hard tyres. The smell of roasted mushrooms, seasoned with salt and powdered bark beetle, filled the air too, setting his fasted stomach a-roaring.

The trader had spotted him and closed him down. 'Gospodin,' he said, addressing Quinton formally. Maskirovka traders and their sham etiquette. He kept his eyes on his bicycle.

'Travelling outside the city?' the Maskirovka asked.

'On a bicycle?' Quinton said, wrapping his bike lock over his shoulder. He got a look at the trader: a prosthetic ear dangled from his head, half torn off, revealing his ear-hole. He'd fake lips too, which were split and leaking their filler, half covering a mouth that opened and closed like a sphincter. Probably why he's down here and not up the mountain. Can't keep his face on.

The trader pulled a Geiger counter from the box strung about him. 'Finest bit of engineering in all of New Havilah.'

'Go bother the Subsolumers,' Quinton said, and hopped onto his bicycle.

'If only I could, Gospodin. But they're light on tradable goods at the moment—and if you don't have a licence to trade them for heat and power credits... I ain't got even a *nybble* in my pocket! No cabbage, no wheat, nothing!'

Quinton squeezed his brakes, the strain making his recently punctured arm throb, and said, 'They aren't trading *crops*?'

The Maskirovka trader spat on the floor. 'Nothing, Gospodin. You look like a man who goes outside the city. Here—' he held out a Ganymede Geiger counter '—listen to that click-click-chirp.' The counter crackled and clicked infrequently, the radiation being as near to nothing in town.

They must have their reasons not to sell to the Maskirovkas. It can't be as bad as all that. He set off down the Corridor, pedalling as fast as his worn body would let him. The Subsolumer fields can't be collapsing. Not yet.

'Thanks for nothing!' yelled the trader behind him.

Quinton cycled through knots of people, past market stalls,

8

towering buildings, and a bleached white wall graffitied with the message *Lady Jupiter Leads*. He pedalled beside the tram lines, over snowy slosh and grit; and he even managed the uphill portion to reach his building.

What has she done with my blood?

He stashed his bicycle in Hotel du Soleil's basement, fanning his way through the plumes of geothermal steam rising from vents as he walked back outside. He headed into the lobby, decided to take the stairs—avoiding Jed the elevator operator and his endless prattle on the *Lucha Libre*—and soon shoved his key into his rooms' door.

As he walked in, the centuries old floorboards creaking, he stepped on a letter. He shut the door softly, hoping to not draw the attention of his neighbours or, if she was still about, the postlady. He picked the letter up, blazoned by the stamp of Lady Jupiter's Resource Council and marred by some icky black glue—that shining postlady gunking up my letters again!—and finally sliced the letter open with his fingernail:

Gospodin Quinton al-Zoubi,

The Resource Council requests your expert opinion on a Subsolum trade agreement. Arrive promptly at the Sun Church for 11:30 today.

Humbly,
Lady Jupiter,
Resource Council of New Havilah

He read it as quickly as he could.

9

She is after me. A trade with Subsolum? There weren't any big trades lined up with Subsolum. They took years to negotiate. Maybe this was why that Maskirovka was having trouble. Lady Jupiter's bungled some trade talks, Subsolum isn't happy, and now she needs me to rescue her. But why in all that's Bright has she taken another vial of my blood? Who is getting desperate?

He tore up the letter and chucked the shreds on the coffee table.

'Sophia!' he called, as he stripped off his heavy coat, hung it on the wall peg. From the coat's pockets he fished out his pipe and lighter, and then made for the living room.

In the living room, Sophia stood as a silhouette against the big windows which overlooked the New Havilian townscape. On top of the Corridor's buildings were teams of people draping Summer Solstice decorations over the limestone balustrades. Lanterns, knotted and dyed red hempmoss rope, and—Quinton had to squint—what looked like quilts of patchwork with holiday messages stitched into them. 'Brightness,' Quinton said to himself, sticking his pipe into his mouth, 'it can't be the Solstice yet.' But he remembered what the man had said in the surgery, the solstice was only weeks away. And I'm getting worn—tired. My bones might as well be chalk. He needed his *Zed*. Every year it got harder.

Sophia had her arms crossed and didn't budge an inch at his presence.

'I miss her,' he mumbled around the pipe. 'I miss her, I do, but it's been so long and I'm so—*beaten*.' He tried to light the pipe but realised he'd no tobacco in it. He unscrewed the lid from the jar on the living room table and took a pinch from that. 'And now

10

Lady Jupiter's after me, Sophia. There's no other way to put it.'
The tobacco crackled in the pipe bowl as he lit it. 'Taking an extra vial of my blood!' He snapped his lighter shut, the metallic click familiar and grounding.

Sophia whispered, *You're so close,* but didn't take a look behind her. *You'll be off this rock and in the stars soon, Quinton. Forget this place.*

Exhaling twin jets of smoke from his nostrils, he headed over to the stone table outside the Flower room. He smoked the last dregs and then set the pipe down on the table, the stone yellowed over the years by tobacco leaching from the pipe. His hand lingered before the doorknob to the Flower room, where he waited a few moments to see if Sophia had anything more to say. She didn't, so he went in.

The room's heat brought the blood to his face and set his fingers tingling. He sat himself down on the stool and swivelled the sun-lamp to one side.

The Flower's ten petals glowed brightly and white. A bead of *Liphoric Zed* clung to the tip of the stigma. Quinton reached up to the shelf and found a washed pipette. In careful and precise movements, so as to not touch or disturb the petals, he sucked up today's *Zed* with the pipette, marvelling as it glowed brightly.

What in sunlight is Lady Jupiter up to? *Two* samples? Uneasiness crept upon him. What would she do with the extra vial? Try to drink it? It wouldn't be the first time someone's tried to drink my blood. He shivered. She'll be slicing bits off me in no time...

He unlocked the safe beneath the worktop and grabbed the

11

bottle of *Liphoric Zed* from inside.

Almost full.

The viscous liquid glowed and shimmered inside its bottle, chucking out its soft, green light. Without looking, he pulled his logbook from its cranny and laid it on the worktop beside the Flower. He opened the log book and double-checked yesterday's reading against the bottle's current reading. Happy that the two levels matched, he unstoppered the *Liphoric Zed* bottle and squeezed out today's extraction into it. The open bottle perfumed the stuffy air with fruits of the Old World. The smell reminded him terribly of Sophia, of those days right before she left.

But I never left.

He squinted at the scale on the side of the bottle and noted down the new *Zed* level, then locked it back up.

And that was when he saw it.

A throaty yelp slipped out from him—followed by a momentary blackness. He trembled. It couldn't be? But he reached out and delicately pinched the tip of the petal to take a look at its underside, hard to do with his shaking hand. But there, as clear as the dust in the sky, was a yellow blotch.

A yellow blotch.

For a few moments all he could do was sit there, staring at the blotch, praying that it might disappear.

He pushed back from the worktop, gathered himself as best he could, and took in everything around him: the hydroponics arrangement and loop, the bulb shape and wattage, the humidity, the temperature of both air and the nutrient solution, the growth medium—he gathered this all up and speculated: It has to be heat stress. The big bulbs in the nursery were a lot better than what he was using here. Taking on Billick as an assistant all those years ago had forced him to move the Flower to his rooms. I should have known sooner or later that this would happen. Heat stress and poor air circulation. It's all taken its toll.

He stared at the yellow blotch, at his beautiful Flower. 'I need to move you,' he said aloud. 'Brightness me.'

γ

As he entered the *Al-Zoubi Plant Nursery*, the means and methods of how he was going to move the Flower were on his mind: Will the transport case be light enough to take on foot? Or will I have to get the tram? Are my designs even ready? How long can it be off water and nutrient solution? Isn't the design going to be too bulky to be carried *discreetly*? Do I even *need* to move it? How can I be—

The perfume of one hundred and fifty densely packed strawberries put an end to all this thought. It was as if Summer Solstice decorators had broken in and had a go at dressing the growing platform up for its day in the Sun Church. Vivid reds streaked across dark greens in a haphazard style—the fruit and leaves perfect substitutes for paint and dye.

A while back, when the bright red flowers had first burst out from their buds, Quinton suspected that that was all they would be getting—some wonderfully pretty strawberry flowers, the rarer red type too. But then the fruits had come, and they didn't stop coming.

Now, those delicious fruits dangled from their plants taunting his hungry stomach. *Why didn't I eat at home?* And then he remembered the blotch on his Flower, and went back to staring at the strawberries, albeit miserably now.

He couldn't believe Billick had managed to grow them, let alone so many. When John Ganymede had told them that he'd found an Old World seed vault, Quinton and Billick both thought that he either didn't know what a seed vault was or, if he did, all the seeds inside would be dust. But Ganymede had been right.

For the first time in over a hundred and fifty years, strawberries were back on planet Earth.

And Quinton was totally forbidden to eat any of them.

Ganymede wanted them for Lady Jupiter, and had paid Billick and Quinton handsomely for their labour and the exclusive rights—they were Ganymede's seeds after all.

Quinton sniffed the air. The sweet scent drew out an ancient memory: him and his mother huddling in a bunker eating dried strawberries as the Bombs fell above. He did his best to stuff the memory deep back inside his mind. He'd been thinking of her enough today.

'The strawberries look about ready, Cap'n,' Billick said. 'Over ripe, if you ask me.'

Quinton heard the botanist, but couldn't see him. 'Where are you?' Marching past the strawberries, he crossed through the ribboned threshold to the exotics growing room—where he thought Billick's voice had come from. On the exotics platform were two juvenile cacao trees, no fruits; five *coffea robusta* plants all in good health, plenty of cherries; and a single tobacco plant, flowering.

A *slap*, *slap*, *slap* sounded from the other side of the exotics table. 'You're barefoot again,' Quinton said sharply.

Billick rounded the corner of the exotics table, and smiled up at Quinton, baring fangs. 'You were out,' he said, trying to soften that gravelly voice of his, 'and I had the radio on. I was dancing as I labelled the strawberry containers.' He danced a little jig.

'Dance with shoes on then!'

'No soul, Cap'n. No soul that way.'

Quinton didn't have the patience today. Pressing his fingertips to his forehead, he said, 'Why are the strawberries not in the containers? I want to get the plants into a grow house. We're behind as it is.'

Billick shrugged, squashing his round chin into his round body, and lifting his spindly arms up.

'You don't know?'

A little flustered, Billick padded over, and Quinton sat on a stool. 'Ganymede hasn't telephoned to say he's collecting them,' Billick explained. 'He said he would. I don't want to harvest them as they'll go bad off the plant, and we can't freeze them—'

'Why not?'

'Because Ganymede wants them fresh—and where are we gonna keep them?'

Quinton scratched at his beard. 'Brightness, these two are worse than roaches.' Lady Jupiter wants my blood, and Ganymede wants my livelihood. He rose. 'I don't give a hoot what John Ganymede wants. We need to clear the growing platform. Pick and pack all the strawberries into the containers, take them out the back and cover them. They should freeze outside.'

'He don't want them frozen, Quin,' Billick said.

'I'll never understand Ganymede. Strawberries—' he jutted a thumb behind him—'have not been seen in over a hundred and fifty years and he doesn't want to pick them up? What's he got wrong?'

Billick searched about the room and then padded over to his wheely cart. He climbed in and wheeled back over to the exotics growing platform. High enough now, he inspected the young *coffea robusta* plants. He looked like a school boy at the *Museum of the Old World*.

'He's married, aye, Cap'n? That's what he's got wrong with him.'

'You think Lady Jupiter is delaying him?' *When will she leave me alone?*

He shrugged again.

After a lapse of silence, Billick said, 'How was the nurse? They sell your blood, I bet. The Immortal Man's blood makes for fine booty.'

'They aren't selling my blood.' *He hoped.* 'It was fine,' he said, heading back to the strawberry room, 'but she took two vials.' He stopped short of the threshold to the strawberry room and looked down: a tiny tray of about five portobello mushrooms on a worktop. The tray worked on its own hydroponics loop; its growth medium had been stained white too. 'What's this?' Quinton said.

Billick jumped from his wheely cart and padded over, only to hop up onto a stool to bring himself level with the worktop and

16

tray—and Quinton's jutting finger. 'It's not what you—'

'I told you,' Quinton said. 'No experiments. I have it under control.'

'Aye, yeah, but— I wanted to wait until after we'd shipped the strawberries,' Billick said, his tone still trying for softness but failing, 'But—' he tugged at a pointed ear '—a whole rack in grow house four went Black last night.'

'You're sure it's Black Rot?' Quinton said, going for his pipe, then, suddenly conscious he couldn't smoke in the nursery, started clawing at his beard.

'Aye, Cap'n. No doubt in my heart.'

Quinton said, 'No one saw it, did they?'

'No, no one knows a thing, but for Syd and Dobromir.'

'Good,' he said. 'It's *spreading*, then.'

'Aye, and fast, Cap'n.' Billick tapped the ceramic tray which held the mushrooms. 'I had the potters knock me up a bright white tray and give me some of that white perlite. I could spot the Rot as soon as it set in. These 'shrooms are being overfed. Want to see if that's it.'

'Pack it up. I don't want any experiments in the nursery. If you drag the Rot in here— Well, what will happen to our business?'

Billick hopped down from the stool, waved a hand, saying, 'Yeah, yeah. I'll do it, but I know a hempen halter when I see one.'

'A what?'

'A noose,' he said, this time making no effort to soften his voice: it came out in the usual deep, gravely tone. 'The Rot's a noose around our necks, Cap'n.'

'Yes, I get it, very clever.' The clock at the top of the exotics room said 11:46. He was late for the Resource Council meeting—from one disaster to another. 'I need to go,' he said. 'No more experiments.'

'Aye,' Billick said, 'and if you see Jonny-boy, tell him to give me a dingle on the telephone, or I'll give away the surprise to Lady Jay.'

Quinton rolled his eyes, picked out one of the portobellos from Billick's experiment and ate it. As he chewed, the unslippable thought returned to him: Why has she taken two vials of my blood?

γ

Snow creaked under Quinton's boots. Though he was late for the Resource Council meeting he took his time walking along the Corridor, towards Lady Jupiter and her Sun Church. He hoped to find John Ganymede too, and try to convince the man to take his strawberries. There's something I never thought I'd have to do.

A tram rattled past him. From its glassless windows projected the barrels of roach hunter shotguns. The roach hunters would be heading up the mountain—their grim, weather-worn faces still as the mountain rocks. Part of Quinton wished to be a roach hunter. In another life he'd been very good with firearms. But, he thought, no matter how many roaches those hunters kill, they will *never* come back down the mountain with coffee or tobacco. And they don't keep this town alive like I do.

He tucked his chin into his collar and pressed on, a smile on his face.

As he drew nearer to the Sun Church he was bothered more and more by Lady Jupiter's Sun Priests. They wore bright red painted faces (the same colour as the strawberries), and were chanting at anyone who came within earshot.

A group of three—hooded by their black and tattered robes of real, Old World cotton, but so ancient that they were threadbare and half falling off—were storming towards him, the two without hooves had feet blue from cold, wearing nothing but open toe sandals. The three locked hands and claws and began chanting, 'Ooo, ummm, sttzhz.'

Quinton said, 'Get off!' and tried to walk around them. The church loomed large and close—it's rusticated bottom nearly within his reach.

'Hey!' one of the priests said. 'It's the Immortal Man!'

'Got any coffee?' another said. 'It's been months.'

'What about a lick of Waters?' the third said. 'I've had a burn in my throat since the last Solstice!'

Quinton had to stop. He looked the one who mentioned Waters dead in her single, cycloptic eye, and said, 'Lady Jupiter 'll string you up from the church tower for asking that.'

'You're in a foul stink,' the third priest said. 'What's the Immortal Man got to be so miserable about? Don't you know you've made it. You've cheated death, Gospodin.'

All three leant backwards and faced the sky. The third priest continued. 'Soon,' she said, 'the Sun shall part the stratospheric dust and grasses and plants shall grow on the lands!'

As all their eyes were skyward, they didn't see him slink off.

He reached the Sun Church, the heavy wooden door twice his height, and grabbed the iron knocker. Just as he was about to strike the door, it swung open, and he had to jump back to avoid a blow to the face.

'John— Would you wait a moment? Brightness! Johnny!' came Lady Jupiter's bellowy calls from inside the church.

The great and powerful New Havilian leader, John Johnny Ganymede, strolled out from the doorway, ducking slightly so as to not hit his head.

'John,' Quinton said, a little surprised to see him.

'Al-Zoubi,' the giant nodded, his eyes containing a bolt of that Sun-awful lightning. Quinton often wondered how the man slept when he had lightning bolts in his eyes.

Ganymede made to walk off.

Quinton said, 'You don't want your strawberries?'

The giant shook his head and swiped the air in a dismissive gesture. 'Not now, we can do this later.'

'Johnny!' came Lady Jupiter's calls, closer now.

'But the strawberries are—'

'Later!' His eyes glowed a bright electric blue. 'And shut it.'

Lady Jupiter burst out from the Sun Church door. 'Johnny,' she said. 'Where are you going? Ah Gospodin al-Zoubi! You are very late, but that's not a problem.'

Quinton smiled and watched the theatrics.

'Juju,' Ganymede said, 'I do not want to argue.'

Lady Jupiter grabbed Ganymede's two massive hands with the four of hers (two apiece) and stared up at him. 'Then don't be so dismissive. If we don't do something soon, the pipes will be

20

seized!'

What is going on in Subsolum?

'I am not getting involved in Subsolum's politics,' Ganymede said. 'Do not try me.' He pulled his hands away from Lady Jupiter's and rubbed his stubble. Ganymede's face always looked to Quinton like granite covered in radiotrophic moss. The giant, shaking his head, walked off.

Lady Jupiter clasped her hands together and shook her head too. She said to Quinton, 'Come on then, let's talk,' and headed back inside.

He followed her into the church, one of her Sun Priests closing the massive door behind him.

Between pillars, great patchwork quilts had been hung. Guttering paraffin candles lined every ledge, shelf, and flat horizontal surface Quinton set his eyes on. He could hear the candle wicks burning. Where has she got all this paraffin from? Motes of dust floated in the air, billowed about as Lady Jupiter crossed from one row of pews to the other.

'Well don't stand there and gawk! What do you think?'

'That's— There's quite a few candles.'

'Yes, yes, yes!' she said, seizing a prayer-cushion from a pew. 'We may not have the Sun, but we do have the flame.' She smacked the prayer cushion and dust plumed into the air. 'Don't you think it's marvellous?' When he didn't reply, she stopped running around and stared at him. 'OK,' she said. 'I'll forgive you for being late, but your underwhelming reaction to my decorations can never be forgotten.'

'Are you sure I'm late?' he said. 'I don't see everyone else.'

21

'You are the only other person required.'

'I see.' His fingers curled ever so slightly. What are you up to, Lady Jay? He sat himself down in a pew. At least he had found Ganymede and mentioned the strawberries. And if he doesn't collect them by the day after tomorrow, we'll set up a stall in front of the nursery and sell them. I don't care if he's paid up already, he can't clog up the nursery's capacity like this.

He ran his hands over the wooden backrest of the pew in front. Mahogany. He longed to see trees grow again—to build something with his hands.

'Nevertheless,' Lady Jupiter said, strolling towards him, 'here you are.'

'Here I am.'

'Shoosh over.' She fanned at him with all four of her hands. He slid down the pew. It creaked under Lady Jupiter's weight as she sat. 'I have been good to you.'

'You have,' he said, not looking to start arguments yet.

'I have been good to you, and now you must do the same.' She turned, the pew creaking some more, and looked directly at him. She didn't have any eyelids, and so never blinked. They sat there in silence, candle wicks burning, her big gelatinous eyes peering. He hated those eyes. 'Will you do the same? Will you be good to me?'

Quinton turned away, watched as a candle snuffed itself out. He decided to jump ahead a few lines, and said, 'When Ganymede was leaving, you said to him there were plans to seize the pipes. I hope what you want from me has nothing to do with that.' Certainty he couldn't afford, but he knew, at the least, that

22

whatever was going on, the two heads of New Havilah were in disagreement.

Lady Jupiter smiled, lifted her head. 'All this here,' she said, sweeping an arm through the air, 'all this decoration and pageantry, is an attempt to hold on to hope. And I need you to help me do it.'

'A Maskirovka trader earlier today told me that Subsolum were trading fewer power and heat credits. That they aren't selling wheat or cabbage.' He wasn't about to be swept up by her theatrics, however alluring. 'He said he didn't have even a nybble.'

'Don't pay any attention to those false-faced idiots,' Lady Jupiter snapped. She plucked at the folds in her skirt, worried a loose thread out and tore it off. 'We've made a trade,' she said at last. 'That's why they aren't selling to the Maskirovkas.'

'What sort of trade?'

'We got every last ounce of their paraffin, as you can see.'

This was most likely the last paraffin in all the world—at least until an industrious New Havilian figured out how to plumb the Earth for oil again.

'And in return,' Quinton said, 'what have we given them?'

She clapped both sets of her hands together, snuffing the nearest candle with a blast of air. 'That's where *you* come in, Gospodin al-Zoubi.'

Behind her eyes, sat the truth. And I'm not seeing it. I'm the outsider, looking in, unaware of how she's manipulating me.

'And in return, we shall provide training to a Subsolumer agronomist.'

23

He swore the church bells tolled.

'The Subsolumer is to live and work in New Havilah, to retrain as a hydroponicist, teaching delivered by *you*. It would appear that their ecology—'

'Excuse me?' His heart, he was fairly sure of it, had stopped.

One of her big eyes darted about in its socket. 'Yes. You've tried all this before.'

'And it *failed*. Subsolum will never turn from the soil.'

'Times have changed, Gospodin al-Zoubi.'

He said, 'It doesn't make much sense. If they are so devout, why send an agronomist for me to train?'

'They are all on rations. Desperate.'

There is something else here, something she doesn't want to tell me, but what?

'The time has finally come,' Lady Jupiter went on, 'for Daniel Marston to abandon the soil.'

'What does Ganymede think of this?'

A long, wet tongue, about as wide as two of Quinton's fingers, slipped out from Lady Jupiter's mouth and wetted each of her eyes. Once the tongue had withdrawn back into her mouth, she said, 'John doesn't have to think anything of it.'

'He seemed angry.'

'He's a complicated man.'

'Obviously, he doesn't agree with you, or with this trade.'

'No,' she said, 'but his focus, his jurisdiction, is domestic.'

'Mhmm.' Quinton breathed out heavily, a yearning for his pipe rising up inside him. 'I don't have a decision to make.' If Subsolum is finally ready to move away from the soil, to truly embrace a proper cultivation technique, it would bring the two societies much closer together. Something I've wanted for almost as long as I have lived. But I've heard all this before.

And it was no wonder Sophia had no words for him right now.

Lady Jupiter licked her eyes again.

Over by the altar, where a clump of candles burnt brightly, a painting, one Quinton hadn't seen in a long while, caught his eye. It was called *The Fall of the Bomb*. A massive warhead fell towards the ground many miles below. I am that bomb. I am on my way down. He tore his eyes away from it. And found Lady Jupiter standing in the aisle.

'I must be getting on,' she said, 'the Summer Solstice ceremony does not prepare itself. I shall have a black book prepared for you, with all the instructions and details of this operation. Understand that this is a highly delicate operation, Gospodin al-Zoubi. I expect your utmost compliance.'

'One last thing,' Quinton said. 'My annual blood exam was today.'

The tip of her tongue poked out from her mouth. If she had had eyelids, her eyes would certainly have narrowed.

'It went a little differently,' he said, 'to the last twenty or so times.'

They stood in silence: candles burning, dust motes drifting.

'You aren't going to explain?' he said. 'You don't want to tell me what you're up to with my blood?'

The tip of her tongue slid back into her mouth. 'Oh,' she said, 'did Nurse Iskra not explain?'

'No,' he said.

'We've developed another test. Well, John and his lab have. It looks rather promising. We'll be unlocking your mysteries before Summer Solstice is over, I'm sure of it.'

IT MUST MOVE

– NEW HAVILAH –

"It is to the plant's great distress that it cannot uproot itself and run."

— Doctor Conrad Kilkenny

That evening, over by the big bay window which looked out on the town, where the usual gloom of orange light spilt in from the streetlamps, Sophia stood and stared and did not say a word. She had been in that posture for—Quinton wasn't sure—months, and he thought that it was time he adjusted her. Radiator pipes rattled as the Earth injected its geothermal warmth into the building. A release valve hissed outside, and steam rose through the orange light, where it coloured to look like poison gas. The orange light—light Quinton had often fallen asleep to—no longer steadied him, it terrified him. A poisonous gas cloud—that sounded right to him. Lady Jupiter was a poisonous one too, and so was the Black Rot, and so was his mother. Why had she gone? Left him on this irradiated planet so he could fight in an endless war—to watch person after person die and perish and not once know him. He clung to her promise like life clings to the planet: desperately, and at all costs. He found the courage to walk across the living room and put his hands on Sophia. She did not flinch. After he was sure he didn't feel her stirring, he gently unfolded her arms, and let them hang at her sides. She looked more like herself this way, and a lot less cross. He lifted her chin slightly, and then turned her head so it pointed directly at the Sun Church. So you'll see all the good I'm planning to do, he told her. No reply came back to him and he thought that a good sign. The Corridor couldn't be seen from the window, and he wanted badly to see it, to see it ticking along in its regular way. He had sacrificed so much for this little town—for his home—but he was starting to worry that it might all fall apart anyway.

But this *isn't* your home, Quinton.

He stepped back from Sophia and helped himself to the last mushroom puff on the dinner table.

Your real home is beyond the stars with your mother, not here on Earth. She promised to come back for you.

'And I have waited,' he said, settling into his armchair.

You have waited a very long time, and she will surely be proud.

He crossed his legs, trying to get comfortable, and, by ancient habit, he held his hands up to the wall expecting to feel the heat of a crackling fire, but instead there came the faint heat of the radiator. I miss fires. I miss trees and creatures and insects— Can you believe it, Sophia, when I was young people would whack spiders dead, clobber them with rolled up newspapers. Now none of that exists. Everything is dead. If people saw a spider today they would stick it in a spider-sanctuary and we would pay to come and visit.

She didn't want to talk. And he knew why. Daniel planned to send another Subsolumer. They were getting on the merry-go-round again. The last time it happened, he fell in love, so nearly abandoned his mother for her, for Sophia. But not this time.

He got out his pipe and started smoking. What if she doesn't come back? What if she died on the way to Proxima Centauri? Got herself eaten alive by a gamma ray burst or crashed into space debris? There's been no message, no sign whatsoever, it's been … so long, Sophia, I don't know if I can keep this on. He puffed away. I'm happy here. They need me here. I keep their mutations alive. And I bring into this world the small luxuries that make it worth living in. Coffee and chocolate and tobacco—no one else can do it. Well, Billick could. He could run the place. If it wasn't for Bill, we'd all still be eating bark beetles and have no mushrooms. These people are real, Sophia, and they are here, unlike my mother who *isn't*, who *left* me with nothing but a Flower. Tobacco smoke rose past his face smelling rich and warm, reminding him of the many smokes he had shared with Sophia.

What if I give up? What if I say I don't want to wait for her anymore? What if I say she can stay wherever it is she is, and never come to get me? What if I say I don't need her?

Sophia had no answers for his questions.

He curled forward and held his head in his hands, letting his pipe drop to the floor. Tears came quickly, and he did his best, at first, to not let them take him over, but tears have their way, and soon he was crying.

He was back in the Bombs, back when the they burst and rattled your skull. His mother stroked his hair, whispered to him: 'Everything's going to be alright, it's all going to be alright.' He was six years old when the Bombs fell. And when the sky went dark, he remembered his mother saying, 'That's not the last time you'll see the Sun, it's going to be bright when we burst through

29

in our starship. We have a new home, Quin, a new home much better than this one, so don't cry, don't cry about the Sun.' And she would scoop the tears off of him with a crooked finger.

He rose up from the armchair and wiped the snot and tears from his face. 'I want to see her again, Sophia. I don't want to die here.'

Then what must you do?

I need to manage my business, I need to prepare for the Summer Solstice, I need to know who's got my blood, and ... He hesitated.

And?

'And I need to move the Flower. It mustn't die.'

γ

'I know, Bill,' Quinton said into his telephone, the white, morning cloudlight straining his eyes, 'but there's nothing I can do about it. Don't freeze them. If he doesn't pick them up today, we're going to set up a stall outside the nursery and sell them—I decided yesterday. I've got a feeling Lady Jupiter isn't ever going to accept them.'

'I knew they were for his lady.'

'Quite the gesture, yes.'

'When you getting in?' Billick said. 'I can't get out to the grow houses and start the new coffee batch and check on the production house; there's cacao beans fermenting which need to come out, and I've got a hundred other odds to do.'

'I'm sorry, this is Resource Council business,' he said, studying his drawings on the table. 'I'll be as quick as I can. Get over to the production house today and start the chocolate. Chocolate strawberries at the Summer Solstice sound good to me.'

'Oh, aye aye, Cap'n.'

Billick rang off and Quinton was connected to the switchboard operator again. 'New Havilah Connection,' the lady said, 'number, marker, or name please.'

With his finger, he traced a line on the drawing. Is that right? Will the inflow tube fit it?

'Hello?' croaked the switchboard operator. 'You aren't the only body who has calls to make, you know.'

'Sorry, sorry.' He pulled away his hand. The drawings are good, sound. 'I need the blacksmiths next to the al-Zoubi Plant Nursery, marker twenty-two.'

'A moment.' The line hissed, and then:

'Meta's Metalsmith,' answered Darleaner Meta. 'How can I be of service?'

'Darleaner, it's Quinton. I need—'

'You can quit it with the needs, buddy. I'm hanging up.'

'Wait!'

'Those bicycle frame repairs—do you remember those? The ones you said you'd pay me a *kilo* of coffee for? I told my husband this was too good to be true, but he said it was the Immortal Man, says that someone who lives that long can't get away telling lies, says that they would have caught up to him by now.'

Quinton held the telephone against his chest and glanced at Sophia. Whatever he was searching for, he didn't find there. 'Oh,' he said to Darleaner, 'they most certainly do catch up to you— you simply tell better lies.'

'*Helvíti*, that your idea of a joke? What do you want? I'm very

31

busy.'

'I need you to make me a portable plant pot—but it needs to house everything, not just the roots. It's to be tall and protective, rad-proof as well, and I need it to meet the same specifications as my hydroponic loop in the nursery. It needs out-flow and in-flow sockets and a chamber for growth media.'

'I'm hanging up,' Darleaner said.

'I've got two kilos of tobacco, 300 grammes of chocolate, and a handful of Old World fruit you've probably never even heard about.' If she makes this plant pot, the Flower's safe. I'll have to figure a way of paying when I can.

All he heard was breathing. Then a ruffle, then, 'Bill's been chatting in the pub, you know this? Says he's got 150 bright red Old World fruits—strawberries, he calls them. Says they are sweeter than chocolate.'

'Much sweeter.'

'Also says they are exclusively for Ganymede. So you can go take a walk in Gamma Valley for all I care, Quin. I'm not taking goods that don't belong to me.'

'Ganymede is expecting 100. We've overproduced.'

'Overproduced.'

'That's right,' he said, 'much too many. We're very good at our jobs.' He had her, he could feel it in his bones. 'You'll do it?'

'When do you need this by? I've got parts due on a tram this week.'

'Tomorrow.'

'I'm hanging up.'

'Wait!'

32

'Quinton, I can't make all that,' she said. 'I'm not smelting time. Do you have designs?'

'I can drop them off right this minute.'

'And it needs to be rad-proof?'

'Yes.'

'Do you want it plated gold too, huh? What are you but trouble.'

'Please, I won't forget this.' I should have made this up years ago—I should have known I would need to move the thing—again. Last time I took too many risks. It's got so delicate over the years.

Darleaner sighed and said, 'Make it three kilos of tobacco, a half kilo of chocolate, and two handfuls of the strawberries.'

He swallowed—he did quick sums, visualised his pantry and the production house, the drying room; he had the tobacco, but not the chocolate.

'Alright,' Quinton said at last, 'that's a deal. I'll see you in a minute.'

He quickly rolled up his drawings—at least he had the forethought to design the plant-pot, rushed out of his front door, and collided into Lady Jupiter. He yelped.

Her, in this building? In Hotel du Soleil? Go back, he wanted to yell. You don't belong here! There's nothing to see here. Sophia's not for you!

In her lower two arms she carried a black book. Quinton gripped tightly onto his rolled up drawings.

'Sorry to shock you,' Lady Jupiter said, 'but it's good you are here. When I telephoned the building, the elevator operator told me you hadn't left for the day, so I thought I'd deliver this myself—I don't dare trust the post-service with a sensitive item such as this.'

'No,' he said, uncertainly. Sophia! he cried inside himself. I'm sorry! This wasn't my idea. She's a conniving, long-tongued trickster! He shuffled the rolled up plans to hold them under his sweaty armpit, and locked his front door, the keys rattling in his shaky hand. The hallway was empty. Next door hadn't had anyone in it for some time now, and the couple that lived in the rooms at the end worked in the turbine factory and were always there, never in. But he still didn't feel entirely comfortable talking in the hallway. The thought of letting anyone into his home, let alone Lady Jupiter, had him plotting wars to rival the Old World wars. No one we find you, my love.

Lady Jupiter's lidless eyes twitched, as she noticed his drawings, but she didn't mention them. Perhaps that's what made you a head of state, you don't ask questions when you don't need to.

'You aren't sick, are you?' she said. 'You're white as the sky. Have you got radium fever?'

'What are you doing here?' he said. 'I ... I don't take visitors. First you take my blood, then you make deals without me, and now this, invading my home.' He headed for the stairs, and would have words with Jed, the elevator operator, about letting anyone into the building without him knowing. The bicephalous fool, you'd think with twice the brains he'd never get a thing wrong.

Lady Jupiter, pursuing him, called out, 'This is your briefing book, Gospodin al-Zoubi. The Subsolumer agronomist, Ken Wu, is to be picked up from the Subsolum entrance tomorrow.'

'At the top of the mountain?' he said, stopping right before the elevator. 'I don't have time to take a trip up the mountain.' Nor did he want to very much.

She held out the black book. 'I don't know what to say to you other than, Do your job.'

The elevator doors chimed and opened.

Jed, the elevator operator, said, 'Ground floor, Miss Jay?' And Lady Jupiter waited for Quinton to take the book before stepping into the car.

He took the black book, said goodbye, and headed back to his rooms, trying hard not to shake or shiver or give any sign that she had struck a blow.

My home, he kept thinking, she's come to my home! What if she saw you, Sophia? What then?

γ

Jed was talking to himself as the elevator car rode steadily towards the ground floor:

'The Squid of the deep,' Jed's first head said, 'does not know how to work over a crowd.'

'Exactly,' the second head said. 'She is in lack of pageantry.'

'But the Hydra? Now there's a wrestler who stirs crowds, who fills auditoriums with cheers and cries, who doesn't give the audience room to—'

'Please!' Quinton snapped. 'Both of you, please. I've … I've not got the patience for it.'

'Sorry, sir,' the first head said, 'but it's nearly the season and …'

'... and you know how we like the *Lucha Libre*,' the second finished.

'If Lady Jupiter ever tries to come inside the building again,' Quinton said, 'you have to warn me.' He looked at both heads in turn. 'Do you understand? I don't give a damn if she is the wife of Ganymede and the head of the Resource Council, she has not got the right to be here uninvited.'

'Yes, sir,' they both said, 'we're sorry, sir.' The elevator car juddered to a halt and Jed began turning the wheel to open the doors. 'It won't happen again.'

Quinton took the tram from Hotel du Soleil to the Corridor, no time to bicycle.

'...ain't it always so?' came New Havilah Wireless over the tram's speakers. 'I sure think so. There's uprisings, coups, rebellions— Hey, do ya think we're getting too political? I sure think so. How's about a tune to soothe those radiation burns? Here's one I'm sure you'll love, a love song.'

Quinton stepped out from the tram as the song ended. It had filled him with ideas about how to give Sophia a bit more love. Perhaps we'll dance this evening? No, no, he reasoned, there's no way she'd go for it.

In the Corridor, people hovered around open-air stalls, sampling foods and haggling prices over their Summer Solstice dresses and suits; snow-sweepers hurried people out of their way; a band played on the low balcony a few buildings down, the five-neck guitar handled by the only ten-armed person Quinton knew.

He took all this in uneasily. The Subsolum's soil was sure to fail, and the Black Rot was growing worse. What happened when it took out a whole mushroom house? Or, Sun forbid it, his Flower? Goodbye! he wanted to yell. See you in the next world!

A snow-shoveler knocked him off balance, saying, 'Get out me way! Loitering on the pavement like that. Who do you think you are, the Immortal Man or something?' When he looked up, he froze for a moment, then, 'Oh, Brightness in the sky! Forgive me!'

Quinton went to go around, but the snow-shoveler lifted a feathered arm, blocked his way. 'Oh, kind, Immortal Man, my mother is a moss-collector, out in the Gamma Valley, she's got the radium fever, got rashes all over, can you—'

'Get her to Waters,' the Immortal Man said, and barged the man out his way. No favourites. How many have I let die?

He came to the low wall outside Darleaner's metalshop, next door to his nursery, and squeezed his rolled-up plant pot drawings. There must be some other way to treat the Black Rot. But he'd tried everything. He didn't need Billick to experiment because he'd done it all himself. He could never find the cause, and had had to resort to destroying what was infected or sparing what he could of his *Liphoric Zed* to help rejuvenate the infected plants.

If only I could grow another Flower.

He walked up the pavement towards the blacksmiths' door, keeping his head low, in case Billick had popped outside for air or to haggle a street vendor on a roach meat skewer.

And I've tried, tried and failed, to grow another.

A poster, slathered on the marble of the blacksmith's front wall, read: *New Havilians are Rad Proof, Subsolumers Ain't!* with Lady Jupiter's bold visage hanging underneath, sending shivers up and down him.

He knocked once on the blacksmith's door, and then headed in. Darleaner was standing over a bright red metal pole. Huge black goggles clung to her face. 'Oh, hey, you're only an hour late, huh?'

As he set his rolled up design down on a three foot wide anvil, he realised that the pole was a section of tram handrail. 'Ganymede pays you well?'

She dunked the top of the handrail into water, steam hissing and screaming as fierce as any geothermal pool. Once the water settled down, she pulled off the goggles, and said, 'At least he shows up on time.' She walked over to Quinton, black soot falling away from her, a floating trail forming up behind. She took the plans and unrolled them, read them over and tutted. 'By the end of today?' she said, not looking up.

'I need to go up the mountain tomorrow,' he said, 'so yes, this evening at the latest.'

'How's the bicycle?' she said, not taking her eyes from the drawings. 'It'll hold up all through next winter. Some of my finest work. I could have made it in the Old World, you know? Would have rivalled any bicycle manufacturer.'

'I'll have your payment over to you this evening.' And he headed back out to the Corridor.

γ

After returning home, checking on the Flower, extracting the daily dose of *Zed*, and breakfasting with Sophia, Quinton arrived at the nursery to find Billick plucking and snipping strawberries from their stems. A pirate sea shanty played over the speakers. Quinton lifted the needle from the record, startling Billick, who nearly fell out of his wheely cart. 'What do you think you're doing?' Quinton said. 'I never told you to pick them.'

The scaly man said, 'You didn't, Cap'n, but John Ganymede did.'

Quinton pulled off his coat and threw it onto a worktop. He rolled up his undershirt sleeves and said, 'What?'

'Ganymede came by as I got back from the production house—beans fermented good, by the way, should have a nice chocolate batch for the Solstice.' He went back to snipping strawberries from stems.

'You were saying?' Quinton said.

'Yeah, Ganymede, he came to collect, but I told him, "We haven't got them off the plant yet," and he goes, "Then get them off the plants," and I say, "But Gospodin al-Zoubi isn't in ... I can't do something like that without him," and he tells me he doesn't care, tells me to get on with it.' Billick frowned.

Quinton pressed his fingertips to his forehead, and fought the urge to scream. Thank the Sun I came back now. 'OK,' he said, 'we'll harvest them. But we keep aside two-handfuls—my sized hands, not yours.'

The shears in Billick's (small) hand snapped shut, but missed their target. 'We'll do what, Cap'n?'

'I need to keep back two handfuls,' he said, 'I've had to pay over asking for a project.'

'Ganymede won't like it.'

'I don't have a choice.'

Billick set the shears down on the growing platform, spun his cart, and wheeled it over to the worktop behind him. Small ceramic pots lined the worktop. Billick lifted the lid from one of these, revealing a bunch of strawberries. He closed it, and said, 'About two of your handfuls here.' His eyes would not meet Quinton's. He held himself in a hunch, frowning slightly.

'What's the matter with you?' Quinton said. 'You're surrounded by fruits of the Old World— And that reminds me, what are you doing running your mouth in the pub? Darleaner told me everything, you—'

'What's wrong with me?' Billick said. 'I don't ask too many questions, I'm good like that, but you're not here. We've got Black Rot—which I keep secret for you—and you're not doing rounds, we've got beans in the production house and you're leaving me to do it all by myself. You're not here. You're on secret projects, snooping around to talk to Lady Jay, *stealing* Ganymede's strawberries. What are you playing at, Cap'n? It doesn't make any sense. What are you keeping from me? I don't know if I can keep on like this.' He breathed a deep breath and met Quinton's eyes.

'I didn't know you felt all this,' Quinton said.

It doesn't matter what he thinks, Sophia whispered. *He's a means to an end.*

I can't have this argument here, now.

You should never have brought him to the nursery. He takes and he takes. Always wants more from you.

'I don't like to tell you these things,' Billick said. 'I don't like to

40

because I know how you are. You and your privacy, and I don't ask any questions— When I catch you talking to yourself, I don't ask any questions. But I'm worried, Quin, I'm worried more'n I've ever been.'

'It's about to get worse, too,' Quinton said. 'Lady Jupiter wants us to babysit a Subsolumer agronomist.'

' *We've* got that job?' Billick said.

'I'm afraid so. I might be the Immortal Man, but getting on the wrong side of Lady Jupiter is trouble neither of us can afford right now, not with the Black Rot closing. We are to teach the Subsolumer the art of hydroponics.'

I've been here before.

Billick, who no doubt knew parts of Quinton's history through pub talk, kept quiet, not wanting, at least to Quinton's mind, to make a tense moment any *more* tense.

Sighing, Quinton took a step towards the strawberry plants, reached over to a strawberry on its stem, and plucked it off.

'Quin!' Billick said, and then snatched the strawberry from the air.

'Eat it,' Quinton said, plucking one for himself. 'We've earnt this.'

Billick's forked tongue lashed the fruit. 'It's so sweet. I've been sniffing these for months.' He held it close, his eyes beaming brightly yellow. 'Blow me down! And the colour, when they first started growing, I said to myself, "I've never seen colour like this." Could make dyes from it.'

'Come on,' Quinton said, the strawberry tucked into his cheek, unchewed, 'let's pretend for the moment we're in the Old World.'

Billick popped the fruit into his mouth. Chewed. His eyes watered, and he had to steady himself against the worktop. 'It's so sweet,' he said, 'sweeter'n chocolate. I didn't know anything could be this sweet.'

'There used to be a thing called sugar,' Quinton said, 'which was even sweeter than this.'

'Aye, I've read about it. Don't believe it though.'

They stood in silence for sometime, enjoying the strawberries, savouring every last molecule. And when they were both finished they looked at each other, the same thought on their minds: Can I have another? But they couldn't. He'd already stolen two handfuls.

'I'm going to be honest with you, Bill,' Quinton said.

Don't.

Billick stiffened.

'The reason I've been all over the place is because a special possession of mine is ...'

Quinton, the more you tell him, the harder it gets. You can't trust a soul on this Earth.

What choice do I have? The Flower is dying in my rooms, Sophia. It's going to die if I don't bring it here.

'How do you say?' Quinton said aloud. 'It is ... it's dying.'

You're a fool. What would your mother think?

'It's a plant?' Billick asked.

'Yes.'

'One I've never seen?'

'That's right and—and it's very special to me.'

'You said that.'

42

'I did, yes. I did say that. What I'm saying is, I've had to take care of this very special plant in my rooms, because I didn't want anyone else to see it.'

'What's so special about it?' Billick said, wheeling back over to the strawberry plants, where he resumed snipping strawberries from their stems. 'We're going to have to keep some seeds,' he said. 'Another crop of strawberries—'

'I would like to very much, but Ganymede owns the lineage. If we want to grow more, we have to pay him.'

'*Pay him!?* How can you own—'

But Quinton didn't have time for this. 'Look, Bill, don't worry about that right now. I need to tell you about my plant.'

The shears snapped. 'The Immortal Man's special plant, aye? The roots, I wonder, do they dangle in the fountain of youth?'

'It's a flower,' Quinton said, ignoring the question for the moment. He'll know when he knows. And I'll have to accept it. Then came her whispers: *And he'll steal it, kill it, take away your chance at seeing her again. Of ever reaching the stars.* 'It's as old as me.'

'Oh! It's from the Old World.'

'Yes. A Jaborosa. Ten bright white petals. It glows.'

'Glows? I've never read about a flower that glows,' Billick said, twisting a strawberry flower to take a look at the petals' underside.

'Not vividly,' Quinton said, 'only slightly. And I need to move it, move it into the nursery where we can take better care of it.'

'Right.'

'I'm trusting you, Bill, to not tell anyone about this flower. If you thought keeping the Black Rot secret was important, then this

43

is—I don't know—in lots of ways this is far more important.'

γ

'Just a minute,' Darleaner said, and then pushed a thumb against one side of her nose and blew hard. A stream of black snot shot out from the opposite nostril. The sight reminded him of the boy and his father in the doctor's surgery, a memory he'd done his best to let go, but one he couldn't seem to slip. I'm here doing what I can to keep everyone alive. There have never been favourites.

She shot another string of snot from the other nostril. 'I should've worn a mask.'

'Why not make up for it now and use a tissue?'

She shrugged, and found a stained rag on a workbench.

There were few Subsolumers living in New Havilah, fewer still who thrived, and Darleaner was one of these—not merely a survivor, but a thriver. To his mind she was more New Havilian than most New Havilians. She never complained, hated anything to do with Starships, and swore that roach meat would hold its own against any of the Old World meats. Rad sensors and air-recyclers were installed throughout the workshop, not that they were necessary, but they droned in the same way that Subsolum droned: a monotonous up and down cycle. They were here, he guessed, to remind her of her old home.

'I don't know if you've got enough chocolate for what you've cost me,' she said, wiping the snot up with the rag. 'That case is a work of art.'

Quinton set down the strawberry-filled ceramic pot, the big

parcel of tobacco, but no chocolate—and admired Darleaner's work. The case was art. A foot high, metallic cuboid sitting on top of a stubby cylinder, which had two valves bolted into it for in and out-flow pipes, making it connectable to his hydroponic loop in the nursery. Whilst its shapes were primitive, the joins, welds, and rivets, all so flawlessly done, forced anyone to admit her skill.

'Snap open these,' she said, flicking open clips at the top of the cuboid, 'and it'll open up.' The sides fell away. 'You'll be able to load whatever growth media you want in there. Any trouble, you call me.'

'It's rad-proof?'

'It's a laminate of tantalum, tin, steel, copper, and then aluminium. It'll absorb whatever stray gamma emissions you find around town—no alpha particles are going to get in whatsoever, nor beta. It's as rad-proof as possible.'

'I can't thank you enough.'

'But you can pay me enough.' She lifted the lid from the ceramic pot and looked in. 'So these are strawberries?'

'Try one, they're ... other worldly.'

She pinched one. 'It's fleshy.' She held it up to inspect. 'What're you made of?' she said to the strawberry. 'And you just eat it?'

'I'd take the green stem off.'

'The colour is incredible.'

'Yes, it's as if it were a new colour we thought we lost.'

'Like this?'

'That's it. I would keep the stems and use them for fertiliser—the humus collectors will happily take them as well.'

'And I eat it, eat it as is?'

'You can do all sorts of things with them—'

She popped the strawberry into her mouth, chewed away. First there was silence, then there was a faint moan, then a breath was let go, and her whole body shuddered. She stared blankly at him. Fruits of the Old World. He smiled. She blinked a few times, ran her tongue over her front teeth.

'You forget, don't you?' she said. 'Forget that there was an Old World.'

'Yes, we do,' he said.

'There were once a lot more people. Our language didn't come from us. Food was more than fuel. There was a Sun. You forget.' She looked about her workshop, lifted a pile of metal offcuts from a chair, and sat down. 'You forget.' Her head fell into her hands and she started to cry.

He hesitated. 'I'm sorry,' he managed to say. 'I didn't think … I didn't know that…'

'It's alright,' she said, her head still in her hands. 'This is why I can't read the Old World books anymore. I get so angry.'

'Angry?'

'They're like spoilt children.' She sniffed. 'Stupid spoilt children who couldn't learn to get along—who couldn't compromise.'

'You can't hold it against them.'

'Of course I can. They killed our home. All those wonders, Sun made wonders, and they blot out the sky. Turn it into dust. And then radiation-bomb each other.'

Should I hold her like Sophia does me? He shifted about, smoothed down his coat. He wanted to. Do it. Though instead of doing it, he said simply, 'But all that gave birth to us.'

46

Her face came away from her hands, and she looked up at him, her eyes red, tears running down her cheeks. '"Blessed are the meek: for they shall inherit the earth." I know what the books say, but I don't care. We didn't inherit the Earth. We survived it.'

'Darleaner, I...'

'I'm OK, Gospodin al-Zoubi, the Immortal Man is in my presence, eh?' She stood, wiped tears on her sooty sleeve. Where's my chocolate?'

'I don't have it.'

'I can see that. Even when I've tears in my eyes I can still see you trying to cheat me.'

'Understand that I—'

'No, I don't. I don't give a roach's arse who you are. You can't come in here and rob me. I need to live. You've put me behind on Ganymede's tram parts.'

His gaze flicked between her and the flower case.

'Uh uh,' she said, 'I'm not letting you take it without payment.'

He stepped over to the case, and tried to pick it up. It was heavy, too heavy for him to run out with. He was like a roach in a hunter's trap, desperate. This is my own doing.

Darleaner stormed across the metalworks, yanked open her office door. 'I'm calling the *politsiya*.'

'Darleaner!' He rushed over to her, nearly knocked his head against a pulley dangling from the ceiling.

In the small office, she picked up the telephone and started dialling. He heard the switchboard operator say, 'Number, marker, or name please.'

'Put it down.'

'Yes,' she said into the receiver, 'I need the *politsiya* at marker—'

Reaching across her desk, he thumbed down the telephone hook, and said, 'Listen to me. Can you listen to me.'

'You can't keep bullying me,' she said. 'Time and time I let you get the better of me.'

'I have never got the better of you. I have always paid you, always sent customers to you, never uttered a wrong word. I need this case because New Havilah depends on me.'

'And the town doesn't depend on me? I've made half the parts in all the trams—made crutches, prosthetic limbs, spades, shovels, roach spears! It goes on and on!' She sat back in her desk chair, hung up the telephone receiver. 'I'm tired, Gospodin al-Zoubi, I've never been more tired in my life.'

'How old are you?'

'Thirty—fucking—two. What's it matter?'

'How old do you think I am?'

She looked up at him, looked him hard in the eye, as if she were planning an attack. 'How old's the Immortal Man, he says. I don't know. You look fifty.'

'I'm two-hundred and six years old.'

'What do you want me to say? That you've got it worse than me?'

'I'm tired too.' He sat on the edge of her desk. 'I'm tired of worrying about cockroaches and food shortages. I'm tired of worrying about our little town, the last town, worrying if it will see tomorrow. I don't want to come in here and take from you, but I don't have a choice. I must keep this town alive and the only

48

way I can do that is by taking that case.'

'Do you know what it feels like?'

'I have had many people take things from—'

'No—' she leant forwards, her eyes beaming—'you're older than the Bombs, you must have seen the Sun.'

He was stunned. The room, her breathing, it steadied. 'Yes,' he said. 'I haven't just seen it, I've felt it.'

'And what did it feel like?' She nudged forward, looking up.

'Warm,' he said with a wry smile. 'Though a novel I read long, long ago, said, "There are things beyond description, of which the sun is one."

'But the most precious part,' he went on after a pause, 'is that you took it for granted. No matter how bad the day before was, it would always return. Until it didn't.'

'Until it didn't,' she repeated. 'I couldn't live underground. I read too many books, too many descriptions of wind and snow and oceans. I had to get out. But the one description I loved the most, the most beautiful, it's not here. Sometimes, when I have the welding torch burning, I take off my mask, close my eyes tight, and pretend the heat and light are the Sun. Isn't that stupid?'

'We do what we have to to cope.'

They both sat for some time. His pocket watch ticked, ticked, ticked. He wanted to check it, he wanted to get to sleep, knowing the journey up the mountain the next day would take much from him, but he needed to move the Flower, so he needed that case.

'I want more strawberries,' she said at last, 'when you grow your next batch, I want another two handfuls.'

'You'll have them. Along with the chocolate.'

49

And it was the truth.

Gloomy street lamps lit his way. He towed the heavy Flower case along the street using one of Darleaner's carts, alternating burning forearm for burning forearm. The rhythmic racket distracted him from his thoughts—most of his thoughts—but others clawed their way into his mind. He couldn't understand how he had got here. How had he let himself slip, to let the Flower wither? *Maybe I am tired. But Sophia is so sure I don't need help, other than hers.* But she couldn't stop him from looking: he looked about the empty Corridor, peered down alleyways and into windows, but there was no one, no one coming to help, no one coming to save him. *It's just us, Sophia. It always has been.* Ever since his mother left the planet on a starship.

Gulping for air, sweat trickling down his spine, he lugged the Flower case and cart up the hill towards Hotel du Soleil. He went in through the lobby doors, called the elevator, and hoped that Jed hadn't gone home for the night. *The one time I want to see him, and he's not going to be here.* But the floor indicator above the doors started to count down and when it stopped at 'G' the car doors came apart.

'Oh,' Jed's first head said, 'we were getting worried, sir.'

'We've never known you to be out so late at night,' the second head said. 'We thought it best to stay back a few hours after lock up, make sure you arrived safely.'

The two faces, neat caps on their heads, smiled toothy smiles. A warmth built up inside him. It swelled like a blocked geothermal vent slowly building pressure—it was friendly, companionable. And he hadn't felt it in so long. 'Thank you,' he said. 'I ... I ...' I needed help today. He stumbled and caught himself on the wall.

'Easy there, sir. Is everything alright?' Jed took the cart handle from him. 'You've worked yourself ragged.'

I'm getting weaker and weaker, Sophia. Maybe this Solstice is the last time. Maybe I'm not meant to go on.

Nonsense.

'We'll get all this into your rooms for you, sir, no problem.'

Could he trust Jed? At least Jed couldn't break the case, even if he tried.

'Thank you.' He hobbled into the elevator car, a tight squeeze with the Flower case, cart, himself, and Jed. The elevator climbed up towards his rooms, screeching under the heavy load.

'It's no problem, sir. You must remember we're here looking out for you.'

'That's right,' the other head said, 'we New Havilians are good at that.'

ESTABLISHED THRONES

– SUBSOLUM –

Katherine snapped on the radio. 'Good afternoon, New Havilah! This is New Havilah Wireless Radio. Bark beetle soup is hot, records are spinning. Mhmm. It's good to be alive.'

'You still listen to that Overworlder nonsense?' Tiffany said, squeezing through the narrow doorway and into the room.

'Stay crouched,' Katherine said. 'And close the door behind you.' Katherine had gone nearly six months without showing a soul—without wanting to—but now she had something to show off, she couldn't help herself. And Tiff will see, she'll know right away. This is it. This is how Subsolum survives.

Tiffany glared, outstretched a hand for the radio controls. 'So this is where you've been hiding, a mouldy and mossy cubby hole? I guess it's not on anyone's rota.'

'It's an old storage room,' Katherine said, wondering how she would fare if she slapped Tiffany's hand away from the radio controls. Probably not well.

Tiffany mashed the radio off, kicked the door shut, and then sat down on an upside-down perlite box.

'If you can convince my father to spend the resources on fixing Subsolum's radio station,' Katherine said, 'I'll happily switch over.' She turned the radio back on. 'But until then, it's New Havilah Wireless. The news is about to start.'

The radio presenter continued in his relentlessly jovial way: 'The Resource Council have agreed a deal with Subsolum in an act of co-operation. A Subsolumer is to live and work in New Havilah. Ain't that marvellous?'

Tiffany snorted.

Katherine shushed her.

'If you spot someone who's symmetrical, who looks like they're *made* for all our old and magnificent buildings, well,' the radio presenter went on, 'wave a friendly hello! And if you don't have arms ... figure something out! This is New Havilah Wireless Radio, the weave in the cultural fabric. Here's one for the lonely-hearts: we're crying, you're crying, let's dance.'

A love song played from the small speakers. Katherine imagined the song playing as she took her first steps on the surface—I will dance under the sky. Look towards the endless horizon. Let the breeze run over me. Free from the womb.

'That's gonna be me,' she said.

Tiffany laughed. 'You're mad, Chick. You'd have been told by now.'

'I'm not sure.' Tiff wouldn't know.

'Our cautious president might let someone up there, but you? His daughter? He won't allow it, you're mad to think he'll let you up there.'

Katherine turned the radio off. The love song gave way to the drone of air recyclers. She tried to look serious and confident. I'm not starting this fight again. 'You want to see why I brought you down here or not?'

Tiffany glanced around the small room. She shrugged. 'So you've taken plants from the fields? This some agronomist's lair?' She was pointing at the neat row of four potato plants, their vivid green leaves bursting up from a blend of perlite granules and New Havilian moss.

Katherine shuffled over to the nearest box and took the plant's stems. 'This is *my* lair,' she said, and dug up growth medium until she could pull her harvest free: a single, fist-sized potato dangling from the stems.

Tiffany shot up from her seat, nearly hitting her head on the ceiling. 'You grew that? In this tiny room?'

'Yes.' Katherine could barely hold back her smile.

'I haven't seen a potato in ... in years.'

'You can thank hydroponics for their return.' Katherine gestured at the ramshackle hydroponic loop, grinning, heart-thumping. She'll get it. And everyone else will too. Even Dad. Especially Dad.

'All this time I thought you had got a boyfriend.' Tiffany leant forward, peering over the tubes, cases, mounds of perlite, lamps, metal buckets, pumps, circuitry, and sensors, until she said, 'Or a girlfriend... You really built all this?' an eyebrow raised.

'Yep.'

'What the *helvíti* is that?' Tiffany extended a beefy finger, pointing at one of Katherine's optical transducers.

'That's a sensor which measures the amount of nutrients in the nutrient solution, all in real time.'

Tiffany narrowed her eyes—one didn't move as much as the other since her last fight. 'Real time?' she said after staring for a bit. 'As opposed to fake time?'

Katherine tried not to laugh. But if the roles were reversed, Tiffany would be cruel enough to laugh. I deserve a laugh.

Katherine opened her mouth to say something like, No, you tit, it means as it happens, but Tiffany crossed her big, sinewy arms and frowned, and the thought remained firmly a thought.

'You've shown your dad?' Tiffany said, breaking the silence.

'Not yet.'

'Good.'

'Good? What do you mean, "Good"?'

'Don't show it to him, Chick.' She shook her head, walked a few paces around the cramped, rock walled room, muttering, '*Helvíti*, I wish you'd got a girlfriend.'

Katherine stripped the potato from the rest of the plant, and chucked the greens into a compost bin. 'This is what Subsolum needs, not more rationing.'

'He's not going to let you up there.' Tiffany shrugged. 'Especially if you want to go and learn how New Havilians grow their food.'

'How do you know?'

'Well, one,' Tiffany said, 'you're his daughter. Why would he ever risk you? Two, because he's had years to ask New Havilah for help. We've had food shortages all this time and only now does he want to send one of us up there? It doesn't make sense. But three, my father knows otherwise.'

Katherine sat down on an Old World carry case and studied the potato's patchy skin. 'He isn't stupid,' she said, but didn't know what else to say. What more could she say? She had no idea why her father was making this sudden shift to send an agronomist up to New Havilah. The Pipeworkers were on half rations now, and his own health had never been worse, especially these past few months. He was always coughing up his lungs, puking up phlegm into a bucket.

She shivered.

What Tiffany had said processed, and Katherine asked, 'Your father knows what?'

Even though they were in a tiny room with the door shut, Tiffany still looked over her shoulder before leaning in towards Katherine. 'At the last senior Pipeworkers meeting, my father explained that President Marston refused an escort for the agronomist going up to New Havilah. The Pipeworkers offered to carry equipment, provide protection, and even assist in the training. But your dad refused it all.'

'I didn't know that.'

'Because he doesn't trust you.'

Katherine's body went tight, but she wasn't about to blow up at Tiffany, and make everything worse. Not yet, anyway. She stayed level, and said, 'But that doesn't mean he isn't trying to solve the problem.'

Tiffany sighed. 'The Pipeworkers don't know what he's up to. But he isn't being honest.'

She's never liked him. 'Once he sees what I've achieved here, he'll have to send me.' To trust me.

Tiffany shook her head. 'He'll take one look at your kit here, sweep his arms, and go, "No! Not in my town!" and that'll be the end of it. He'll make you pack it down, worried it'll catch on. He's never going to change.'

Green mould grew on the sweaty rock walls. After a couple weeks working on her hydroponic project, on the very bottom level of Subsolum where the air-recyclers didn't work hard enough, Katherine had noticed a tightness in her chest. Even with its rock walls, air filtration, and geothermal water and heat, Subsolum couldn't keep rot from setting in. *It's rotting from the inside.* She squeezed the potato—threatening to break the skin. *He'll listen to me. Tiff doesn't know what she's talking about. She's scared, but won't show it. I'm the only one who's worth sending.*

Tiffany, like one of the bears from the stories Katherine's mother used to read to Katherine, pawed through the other growth cases, searching for more potatoes. 'Do you mind? I'll leave you some. But your father's not got plans to redouble the Pipeworkers' rations, has he? He doesn't understand how essential we are. He'd let us starve if he could. You ever try to crawl through a half-metre water pipe, sweating puddles, on an empty stomach?'

'I've got this one anyway,' Katherine said, and waved her potato about. 'I'm sure one will be enough to inspire him. Why don't you ask him to double your rations tonight?'

'Tonight? At the play?'

'Yeah, give him an earful then.' When it looked like Tiffany still wasn't following, Katherine added, 'You are sitting in the box tonight?'

'Not with the way your father's treating us now. If the other Pipeworkers saw me up there, I'd never live it down. They'll think I'm eating good,' she said as she pulled potatoes from their plants.

'Your dad's sitting up there,' Katherine said. 'Isn't that going to send a message? It's a tradition.'

Tiffany paused a moment, ran a perlite granule between finger and thumb. 'It's his job, his job as Chief Pipeworker, to keep the peace.' She looked at Katherine. Her slightly swollen eyelid gave her a squint, as if she were trying to stare through her. Stare right into my soul. 'Our fathers differ in one crucial way,' Tiffany said. 'Yours is a traditionalist, unable to change, and mine isn't.' She went on stuffing her overalls with potatoes. 'You need to see them for who they are. Your father's never going to let you up on the surface; he's never going to let you do this either. It's always been soil and earth. As much as I don't like the New Havilians, your father hates them. Realise it and move on. The Pipeworkers have.'

Katherine let the air-recycler drone fill her mind for a moment. None of this had gone the way she had thought it would. What was I even expecting?

'What do you mean, the Pipeworkers have?' Katherine said.

Tiffany no longer met her eyes; she kept her arms and elbows in, and hunched forward slightly, trying to make herself small. Three distinct lumps bulged out in the front pocket of her overalls. She patted these carefully. 'The Pipeworkers aren't afraid of change. We have had to learn to adapt countless times. As aquifers shift, as the rock slips, as pipes burst, as the hydro-turbines crack.'

'I still don't understand—'

'If you really want to help your home, Kath, don't bring this science experiment to your father, bring it to mine. Let the Pipeworkers control this. They will see you get the resources to save our home and people.'

A ringing flooded her ears. Katherine, holding tightly onto the potato, couldn't do much more than that. She watched as Tiffany headed for the door. 'I … I— Do you really think I could do that? I would be going against my father.'

'As soon as you show him this,' Tiffany said, 'he'll shut it all down, Chick.'

'But to go to the Pipeworkers with it… I'd be betraying my father. I can't do it.'

'You've already brought it to the Pipeworkers,' Tiffany said, and tapped the insignia over her heart: the wrench crossed by a pipe segment. She opened the door but stood at the threshold. 'You know, by letting your father shut this down, the real betrayal is to every other Subsolumer. Don't hesitate, Kath. I think you've already made up your mind.'

γ

In her father's office, the long run of floor to ceiling windows drew out those cherished childhood memories of hers. Katherine rested her forehead against the glass. 'I remember,' she said, 'when Mum was too sick to look after me and I'd come here, to sit while you worked.'

Her father, sitting at his desk, coughed into a fist and then adjusted his glasses. 'Are you going to sit?'

Katherine walked the length of the windows, overlooking the dying subterranean fields. Memories filled in the patches where the crops had died. 'I remember,' she said, 'when you could see maize, wheat, potato, carrot, cabbage, and onion growing. I would try and count the yield from here.' She pointed down at his carpeted floor—the only carpet in Subsolum.

Her father dabbed his mouth with a handkerchief, licked his lips, and made the exact same adjustment to his glasses. 'Kathy, I am a busy man.' Open on his desk was the latest harvest report. Katherine knew it well, having spent the past few months—aside from her hydroponics project—on compiling it. As her father looked the report over, his forehead lined deeply.

'You work too hard,' she said.

He grunted, waved a hand at the chair on the other side of his desk. She sat down, the smell of his recently oiled, ebony desk hitting her with all its might—the only wooden desk in Subsolum. She buried her hand in her pocket and grasped the potato. Tiffany doesn't know what she's talking about. She's a Pipeworker—all she knows is how to crawl through pipes, nothing about politics or growing food. Katherine inhaled, went to speak, but was cut off.

'You want to know who I am sending to New Havilah,' her father said, turning a page in the harvest report.

'Not just that. I—'

'Don't you know there are eight foot cockroaches, clouds of radon gas, and destitute wanderers up there? Each of those things so deadly, Katherine, so evil.' He looked up from the report, the light from his desk lamp catching on his lenses.

She dug her fingernails into the potato.

'They are unbelievers too. They do not await salvation nor do they want it.' He held a stare for a few seconds, before breaking

60

into a cough. He coughed so much he had to take his glasses off and wipe the sweat from his face. His face contorted and he spat phlegm into the metal bucket he kept beside his desk.

'You shouldn't be working, Dad.'

Hands trembling, her father got his glasses back on his face. 'Daniel Marston—take a day off? I don't think it's right. What would your mother say? She'd call me a lazy bag of bones and send me right back here. Your mother only took days off when she couldn't lift an arm. When she needed help to eat. I am fine. It's only a cough.'

For all his faults, he has a work ethic—he loves his people. He'll understand. Tiffany doesn't. I know I'm right about this. The Pipeworkers aren't the future.

Katherine took the potato out of her pocket and set it on the desk. They both stared at it. He divided glances between her and the potato. She was six again, showing him one of her drawings.

'Where did you get that?' he said, covering his mouth in anticipation of a cough.

'I grew it...'

'It looks healthy.'

'... hydroponically.'

A racking cough came: as if he were battling a demon. He bundled up his handkerchief and coughed into that. Sweat gleaming on him now, he rang the handbell on his desk, whipping it as hard as he could. The office door opened and Ólafur popped in. He glided across the office, nodded at Katherine, and then said to her father, 'President Marston, sir, how may I help?'

Her father gestured at the drinks cabinet. Ólafur bowed and set about fixing a drink. Their wordless communication bothered her. As if he knew her father better than she did.

And soon she found herself saying, 'He doesn't need a drink.'

But Ólafur wiped the desk and laid down the gin for her father. 'Sir,' he said, 'is there anything— Oh a potato! It is good to see the crop yields are recovering.'

Her father shook his head. 'Out you go, Ólafur.'

He bowed and made to leave.

'Ah, wait. Replace the bucket.'

Ólafur eyed the silver bucket full of her father's spit and mucus, and nodded, smiling. 'Yes, my president, sir, I would be honoured.' He took the bucket and left.

Her father drank down his gin, sucked on his teeth, and smacked his lips together. 'Hydroponically?' he said. 'You grew the potato hydroponically. Where did you learn a skill like that?'

'A New Havilian book I got from a Maskirovka trader. It came from the Great Library in New Havilah.'

But that wasn't quite the truth. It was her mother's book. And if Dad ever found out—that Mum gave it to me, that she made me promise her I'd learn it, and never tell him about it—I don't know what would happen. But it would yank open the already growing rift between them.

Her father's eyebrows rose as if remembering something. 'You built a completed loop?'

She nodded, a little surprised he was familiar with the terminology.

'What are you using for the growth media?'

'Let me show you.'

62

'Katherine, no. If you are using your rations to grow plants I'll have them taken away. You'll go hungry.'

Katherine's mouth went dry. The more I see him, the more I realise I have no idea who he is. She wanted to say, But dad! and suddenly caught herself. I'm not a child. 'All I want is to replace the poorest field with a hydroponic system.'

'A field!' He rapped his knuckles on his desk. 'I wouldn't risk a field.'

'It doesn't make sense, Dad,' she said. 'These are artificial fields we've created—there is so much degradation in the soil now. We can buy the growth media from New Havilah—the radiotrophic moss and fungus. They farm it. I think that's what they use to grow their—'

'Stop it, Katherine. We will *never* turn away from the soil.'

'But it's dead, Dad. There haven't been any earthworms in it for years now. Cultures all come back the same. No fungi, no bacteria, no protozoa, and no nematodes. The soil is barren.' She shouted the last sentence.

He adjusted his glasses, and said, firmly, 'I will not be dependent on New Havilah. Do you understand? We aren't going to move from the soil.'

'But you had to trade the paraffin *to* send someone to New Havilah, to learn hydroponics!'

Her father hefted shut the harvest report and pushed his chair back. He rose, and hobbled towards the plush seats at the centre of his office. Katherine wondered what her mother would think of him now.

'Sit with me,' he said. His knees popped as he sat down on one of the centre chairs. 'Isn't it magnificent—' pointing at the fields. 'Whilst the world was busy warring, we sheltered in our home.'

Katherine crushed her eyes closed and breathed. He'll understand. It'll be painful but he'll understand. There's no other option. She opened her eyes to see her father gawping out at the fields. The huge lights that shone down from the rocky ceiling were slowly dimming, in a mock setting of the sun.

'Come on, Kathy.' He patted the seat next to his. She grabbed the potato and walked over. 'Are you sure you don't want a drink? I know there is not much left in the common circulation. There is whisky and gin and even beer, *real* beer here, not that mushroom stuff. I'll call Ólafur.'

'No, I don't want a drink. Stop it.' She sat down, crossed her legs, and shook her head. 'You know what I want.'

He smiled, said, 'Yes,' and sighed, the breath raspy and weak and smelling strongly of gin. Finally, he looked up at her to say, 'You have all the best parts of your mother, you know this?'

'I don't want your flattery. I—'

'But all your worst parts, they come from me—' he tapped his chest '—and I know them well. Listen, will you? Sit and listen a moment, please, Kathy. Will you do that, do that for me?'

She nodded, biting her tongue.

'New Havilah is a dangerous place for a Subsolumer, but I shouldn't have to tell you this.'

When she was speaking with her father, there seemed to be a law of physics that stated that the probability of bringing up Mum's death increased exponentially with conversation length. But all she had to do was fight it, ignore it.

'The New Havilians,' her father said, 'are hardened—more or less—to those dangers. Though the world up there it does get everyone, eventually ... except the Immortal Man.'

'That's New Havilian folk tale.'

'It isn't, Kathy.'

The Subsolumers and their Starships, the New Havilians and their Immortal Man. Why can't we just save ourselves?

'I will not deny that we are desperate,' her father said, 'but New Havilah has its own problems, you see? And this is our time to shift the power balance. To create more equal societies.'

'Then let me replace a field,' Katherine said. 'And we can restore—'

'No! Katherine, no, you aren't listening to me. We will *never* turn from the soil. New Havilah would have far too much control over us.'

Her hands balled into fists. She wanted to shout and scream at him. She wanted to make him understand. Tiffany isn't right. I know my own father better than she does. I'm not going to betray him and go to the Pipeworkers.

'I am sending someone to New Havilah because the power balances are changing there. Yes, an agronomist will train in hydroponics, but it is political. The leading hydroponicist in New Havilah may have a way for us to restore the soil—but it isn't a new method of growing.'

'Then what is it?'

Her father stared at her. 'A way to fix our soil, Katherine. To get Subsolumers off of the rations.'

Talking to him made her doubt her own sanity. Had they gone

around in circles? 'But what is it? A technology? A *fokking* fertiliser?'

'I'm not at liberty to say.'

'You're the president. You can take whatever liability you like.'

'If only it were so.'

At length she said, 'And you won't send me?'

He squeezed her thigh. 'No, Kathy. It is too dangerous. You'll be chased down by giant roaches or ... or left irradiated on the mountain.'

I'm still a child in his mind. 'Then who are—'

'Ken Wu.'

Did I hear right? 'Ken Wu?' She gritted her teeth to stop herself from shouting. She imagined explaining this to Tiffany. If my father, the smart, kind, and caring man that he is, who can see any threat even beyond the horizon, thinks Ken Wu is best, then Ken Wu is best. And Tiffany will say to me, 'Ken Wu? The man who destroyed a field?'

Katherine's head dropped.

'He may have made mistakes in the past, but that was because he had just lost his wife and daughter. He wants to atone.'

She shook her father's hand off her leg.

'Kathy?' he said. 'Are you—'

'I don't understand.' She looked up at him, at his misty glasses, his red face. 'What can Ken do that I can't?'

'Follow orders.'

She ignored it. She wasn't about to let him bait her into overreacting. 'What do you need the hydroponicist for? You aren't going to save the soil by employing a hydroponicist.'

66

'I can't tell you that.'

'Why not?'

'This is the end of the conversation, Katherine. You have fields to attend to and I—'

'Have gin to drink.' She rose, holding back everything that was trying its hardest to burst out from her, and stepped towards the door. 'I'm getting to the bottom of this.'

'Out,' he said, pointing at the door.

'You're going to destroy our home.'

γ

Despite the half-rations, people were working as hard as ever on the *Stjörnu Farartæki* play. Katherine had to dodge her way through the crowd in the Great Hall, her heart still racing from the conversation with her father. I don't understand why it has to be hard. It's all so simple to me. We're starving. We have to change.

Huge swells of eager-audience members stood in her way. Stage hands rushed about carrying props, set pieces, costumes, lights, and cables. There were even people holding out sacks, asking for food donations for the performers and riggers. She dropped in the hydroponically grown potato, much to the stage hand's surprise. '*Þakka þér!*' the man yelled, eyes wide as could be.

Katherine slogged on through the crowd, passing the nearly completed stage. When she was a little girl the anticipation of the play each year nearly killed her. The endless waiting, the fading memories of last year's play, the food, the dancing, the singing, the laughter. Subsolum felt like one giant family back then, especially when Mum was still alive. I remember her. Sort of? Every time I think of her I get scared the memory will fade more.

Get it together, Kath.

Those good years grew distant, the play became stale and outdated, the mood shifting from revelling in hope to enduring a struggle.

She stuffed her hands into her pockets, kept her head down, and took the ramps to the Service level. He isn't going to get the better of me.

Late for the agronomists' evening meeting, she opened the door as quietly as she could and nabbed an empty desk at the back, unseen.

Until Eva, at the podium, said, 'Ah, Katherine, you've made it.' And the entire room of agronomists turned their heads to take a look at her.

She blushed, nodded and smiled, and said, 'Don't stop for me.'

'Where were we?' Eva said, her thick, grey eyebrows low over her eyes. 'Yes!' she said, her eyebrows shooting up. '*Biohazards!*'

Katherine searched the room for Ken Wu. He usually sat at the front, but she couldn't see him. Has he left already? There was a chance Ken had been sent to Medical to get shot up with anti-rad drugs. So nauseated he can't work— Maybe I'll find him there. Though what she wanted from him, she had no idea. Everyone knew Ken as the guy who screwed up, who destroyed a field. Maybe he thought following her father's orders was his only chance to make things right. The leading hydroponicist is subject to our political interest. That's what her father had said. No matter how she tried to make sense of it, she couldn't. There were so many people better suited for this than Ken Wu. Ken could barely keep up on his rota— Ken *fokking* Wu!

'...that room is still off limits due to radiation contamination and is now to be considered a biohazard. As for crop rotations, fields: *Holtasoley, Hvonn, Mosi,* and *Lupina, must* be worked again, already. Those of you who belong to those fields are required for double-shifts. You will be given extra rations.'

There was a collective groan from the room. Katherine's field wasn't on the list because it was one of the better performing ones. At least she could take some pride in that. Some.

'Yes,' Eva said, 'we're all under the thumb. But don't let the times suffocate you—you are Subsolumer agronomists! Two hundred years of worn hands and sore knees. We will get through, as we always have.' She scanned her notes on the podium. 'That's about it this evening.'

After a bit of discourse on the crop rotations and the *Stjörnu Farartæki* play, Eva ended the meeting, and everyone flooded out to their posts for the evening shift.

Katherine sat alone in the empty room, breathing steadily and trying to make sense of her father, when she heard the door creak. She looked up and saw Ken Wu stepping into the room.

'Oh, sorry,' he said. 'I thought everyone had gone.'

'No ... I'm—' she got up, nearly knocking her chair backwards '—what are you after?'

'Peace and quiet,' he said, and strolled over to his usual desk at the front of the room and sat down.

Katherine went over, noticed he'd closed his eyes. 'What's the matter?' she asked, trying to keep the tension from her voice.

'Nothing's the matter,' he said. 'I'm praying.'

'Praying?'

'Yes.'

'Praying— yes, alright,' she said, 'I'll leave you alone.'

He opened one eye—his good eye—and said, 'Be seeing you.' His knees were bouncing underneath his desk.

She wanted to say to him, It doesn't matter if you pray, the radiation is indifferent. But instead she stood there, not saying anything. I will get to the bottom of this.

Annoyed, Ken opened his eyes, and said, 'Can I help you?'

She looked about the room, made sure there was no one in the doorway. 'I don't know,' she said. 'You're going to New Havilah.' She said it flatly, directly, right to his face which twisted up in a grimace.

'No, no, no,' he muttered. 'I don't want to talk about that.'

'I don't understand. Do you want to go?'

'Leave me alone,' he said, 'I want to pray.'

'Ken—' she reached out and took his arm '—I'm in a position to make this right. Whatever my father's said to you, I need to know it.'

He pulled his arm free. 'There's nothing to say. I have a duty to Subsolum and I can't ignore it.'

'Do you know anything about hydroponics?'

He smiled, shaking his head. 'You haven't been told everything, then.' He shut both his eyes, and set his elbows on his desk. 'It doesn't matter what I want. I lost everyone's trust a long time ago and now I've been given a chance to get it back.'

It was like talking to her father in disguise. 'What do you mean by that?'

'My duty?' he said, eyes still shut.

'No, you smiled and shook your head, when I mentioned hydroponics.'

'Forget it,' he said.

'Ken, do you want—'

He slammed his open palms on the desk. 'I said forget it!'

She stepped back, bumped into a desk.

Ken sat hunched over the desk, muttering the *Fable's* Common Pray: 'Take us, Blessed Ones, who took themselves to the Stars.'

'Do you know how large the cockroaches grow up on the surface, Ken?'

He stopped the prayer mid-sentence. With a fingernail, he scraped rust from the desk. Eyes still closed, he said, 'I told you to forget it.'

Katherine dragged out a chair and sat down. This is what Tiff would do. 'Don't you understand?'

'Understand what? There's nothing for me to understand.' His eyes were open now. His left eye was cloudy and blind and didn't move in its socket. A dead bit of jelly. She looked directly into it. Ken had curled himself like a dying leaf, and was trying to keep his blind side from her, but she hunted it down. 'Y-you want to tell me I've got a choice.'

'Of course you do,' she said. 'My father can't force you. What you need to understand is that this is more important than the individual. We need to fix our crop production. But sending someone up there, who doesn't want to go, is the wrong way to do it.'

'I'll right all my wrongs,' he said, and tried to smile. 'Bring back honour to my name.' He sat up, but almost immediately curled again. 'President Marston was right to choose me.'

'Do you spend time listening to the Maskirovka traders?'

'I can't look them in their fake faces, the rad heads.'

He can't go up there.

'You should listen to them,' she said. She shuffled the chair forward. The legs screeched against the floor. 'They talk about the roaches.' She waited for him to see the roach, to imagine it. 'Those giant roaches that burrow in the snow.'

'I know them!' His leg bounced harder under the chair. 'You can't scare me.'

'The roaches squirt you with their juices, to pre-digest you. The green and yellow juice puffs up your skin, and then, when your skin is soaked through, the juice gets into your bloodstream. Did you know that?'

A tremor passed through him.

'Once their juice is in your blood it attacks your nerves and it paralyses you. Did you know that?'

He shook again, clasped his hands until the skin turned bone-white.

'Then, when you can no longer move, they eat you, feet first. Those chomping mandibles work like machines, mashing blood and bone into pulp.'

'I don't need to hear this.' He tried to turn away, but Katherine grabbed his arm.

'You need to know the risks,' she said. 'Even though you're

72

paralysed, the Maskirovkas say, you still feel everything. The hot roach breath on your exposed muscles and guts, sharp teeth stripping away your tendons. You feel it all.' She sat back. Ken squirmed, sweated.

'Why are you telling me this?' he said.

'Because my father didn't tell you everything, Ken.'

All of his shaking and trembling and squirming reached its apex: he jumped up from his chair, scurried backwards until he knocked over a desk. 'Get out! I don't want to hear it! He's sent you here to torture me, to make me pay. I know I don't have a choice, so don't ... don't make me hurt more. I deserve that at least.'

'He's forcing you?' she said.

'You know what he's doing to me.' He eyed the door. 'I'm not letting his daughter torture me too.' And he ran.

γ

After the evening shift, Subsolumers bustled like New Havilian bark beetles before a bunch of dried mushrooms—all in anticipation of the Stjörnu Farartæki play starting. The Great Hall, near to bursting, reverberated, roared. Katherine marvelled at the crowd from her high perch, a box seat raised by scaffold to tower over the commoners— No, the people who need my help.

The stage consisted of thousands and thousands of pipe offcuts, twisted and riveted and welded together. Its towering proscenium arch—the tallest she had seen—swept across the Great Hall, a patchwork stage-curtain dangling from it. The stage was a symbol. It reminded everyone that their society could still construct, could still build something. We don't need to starve. If he lets me up to New Havilah, I'll learn it all. I'll come back and replace a field and we'll never go hungry.

Her father, sitting next to her, snapped his fingers and Ólafur appeared, gin in hand.

'This telling,' Einar Laxness said, who had the honour of sitting at her father's right-hand side for the show, 'will be the greatest in all the two centuries.'

Between sips of his gin, her father said, 'And they told me it would be impossible to put on a performance with the rationing.'

Katherine snorted. 'They had food donations set up.'

'Yes, Katherine,' Einar said, 'that's what needed to happen. The Pipeworkers donated much of the food. We even helped rivet the stage frame together.'

'It's a shame your daughter didn't want to join us, Einar,' her father said.

Einar gripped the handrail running along the top of the box barrier. He nodded at the crowd, saying, 'Tiffany's happier down there, with her people.'

Her father coughed into the crook of his elbow, Ólafur ready to bound over with handkerchief and bucket, but he waved him off.

'Are her people not up here too?' her father said.

A silence between the two men. Einar slowly ran his hand through his knotted beard. He laughed, slapped her father on the thigh. 'Daniel, there's three of us up here, thousands down there! Tiffany's got her numbers right.'

Tiffany would sooner go up to the surface, naked, than bow to my father by sitting up here. But maybe if she would spend time listening to him, she would understand him more. As her father lazily drank his gin, she realised she didn't understand him. Is he trying to protect me or does he think I'm incompetent? Can he fix the soil or is he a fool? She held her stare, unknown to him, and soon saw the man who raised her after her mother died, the man who kept her society together singlehandedly. She wanted to grab the gin glass from him and smash it. She shook and she wasn't sure why. Subsolum was approaching a precipice, but her father didn't seem worried.

The lights dimmed, the stage curtain drew apart, and the crowd below fell quiet. Hushed voices shushed others. Excited whispers of 'It's starting!' and 'Hush hush!' filled the floor.

Einar smiled and clapped like a boy, running counter to his Iron Baron reputation. No matter how many times Katherine had asked Tiffany if the rumours were true—if Einar had cemented a thief into a section of pipe, if he had dropped a Maskirovka trader into a boiling pool of geothermal water, all for trying to trade bad steel as if it were good steel, no matter how many times Katherine had asked, Tiffany's response was always the same: People thinking he's like that is good for business.

A twelve-foot, bright red prop starship, three tail fins and a long, pointy nose cone, slowly rose from the stage floor. Her father smiled and giggled. Katherine whispered to him, 'I spoke to Ken,' and the giggling died away faster than rations could be eaten. 'I know you're forcing him,' she said, keeping her voice low, 'but you can send me. I'm volunteering.'

On the stage, the First Subsolumer struggled to get the door to the starship open. Between attempts, he would look at the crowd and ask, 'It still ain't working, any ideas?' and the crowd would shout back, 'Pull harder!'

'Why would you do something like that, Kathy?' His breath reeked of gin.

'Why?' she shouted, turning a few heads in the crowd below. Quieting herself, she added, 'Because I didn't have a choice.'

The First Subsolumer had finally flung the prop starship door open—the crowd cheered, Einar clapped away—but, standing in the doorway, already inside the starship, was an army general. She wore a ceremonial blue dress uniform: a peaked cap, golden frilly epaulettes, a blue tunic, silver badges dangling over her heart, skirt and tights, and shoes no Subsolumer would ever get the chance to wear: real leather polished to the point of reflection. 'What the devil are you doing?' she said to the First Subsolumer. 'There's no room for you in here.'

'Katherine, I won't have this conversation again,' her father whispered. 'I've told you, it's too dangerous. Wu is not going up there to learn hydroponics, he's going up there to...'

'To what?' Katherine whispered furiously.

'It's better for you not to know, Kathy, please. Can't you trust me?'

Trust him! He wants me to trust him? It cuts both ways, Dad. She thought about getting up, leaving, but she was trapped. To leave now would only cause a scene. She glared uncomprehendingly at the play.

The army general went back inside her starship, yelled, 'One moment,' then returned, jangling some keys.

'What are those?' the First Subsolumer said.

'These?' the General said, and motioned at the crowd.

'Yes, those!' the First said.

'These?' the General said, jangling the keys even harder.

The crowd, Einar and her father, all yelled: 'Yes, those!'

Katherine whispered to her father, 'The Pipeworkers have approached me. They want my hydroponics set up. They believe in it.'

'*Helvíti*, Katherine! You fool.'

Einar looked over and said, 'The both of you must shut it!'

On the stage, the Army General, from her starship, said, 'These are the keys to your future!' and she chucked them at the First Subsolumer. He looked down at them, confused.

'But what do they unlock?' he called up to the Army General.

She swept her hand down and a great quilt fell from the rafters. The First stared at the quilt, oohed and awed along with the crowd. Stitched into it was a depiction of the first tunnel boring machine used to burrow into the mountain.

'That's what you'll need to do: burrow and wait!' The General closed up the starship, and bright flames started to ignite at the thruster.

Katherine leant over to her father, and said, 'And I'm tempted to go along with them.'

As the starship rocketed off (pulled up by wires), so did her father. He threw his empty gin glass onto the floor, shot up from his seat, and stormed from the box.

Katherine met Einar's eyes, but she wasn't sure what it was she saw there.

HE'S BEHIND YOU

During the *Stjörnu Farartæki's* intermission, while stage-hands prepared the stage for act two, Katherine stood at the fringes of the red-curtained refreshment area, watching the Subsolumer elites mingle amongst themselves, indulging as the rest of their people starved.

She drank a mushroom beer, her thoughts on her father, and how many more of his tantrums she was going to have to endure. And he wanted me to trust him? He can't even keep himself together.

She spotted him. A gaggle of bulb makers were chasing him around, trying to squeeze out what truth they could.

'When will we be off the rations?' one asked him. And, before he could answer, another asked, 'There's been no food shipment from New Havilah. I thought you traded them paraffin? For *rations*, yes?' She could only just hear them over the din of everyone else.

'When I say so,' her father yelled. 'I'm in constant contact with the head of the New Havilian Resource Council, Lady Jupiter.'

'Can you confirm you traded our paraffin for rations?' another bulb maker asked.

'We'll be off the rations soon,' her father said and charged off, only to be waylaid by tunnel engineers, asking all the same questions. Despite his running off, and his obvious cough, he carried himself like a leader. No one seemed too concerned about him; he didn't look flustered. He fended off questions, batting them back as if they were playing a game of caveball.

She knew she had hit a nerve threatening to take all what she knew to the Pipeworkers. And she wouldn't apologise for it, either. If he trusted me I wouldn't need to play these games.

'Katherine.'

The deep voice shook her from her thoughts.

'You like mushroom beer?' Einar said. 'I miss real beer.'

Einar belonged to a different age, an age where it was common to wear a sword or an axe, where ram-raiding villages provided for your family, where the warrior was king. Katherine always anticipated a horned helmet or war-paint, and when they never showed, an uneasiness lingered around Einar, as if he were hiding his true self.

'But your father made sure we never tasted it again.'

Katherine looked around: no one had heard him over the chit-chat and murmurs. Before she could say, How dare you, he continued,

'My Tiffany told me you showed her something. And, I won't lie to you, Katherine, I overheard much of what you and Daniel were ... discussing. Before he ran out, that is.'

Einar Laxness, leader of the Pipeworkers, standing right in front of her wanting to know more, what more could she want? This was her opportunity to feed Subsolum—to ensure hydroponics took Subsolum forward. But am I betraying my father?

'I have no idea what Tiff is thinking of,' she said.

The Pipeworkers leader smiled. He put a hand on her shoulder and squeezed. 'Little Kathy,' he said, 'you have always been smart ... but not so tough.'

The hardest part was that she wanted to tell him. But what if I can change Dad's mind? What if I hang on for a few more days? And let Subsolum creep closer to starvation...

'Am I supposed to take offence?' she said.

He smiled again, his two golden canines glinting. 'Your father has always dreamed of rescue. Starships returning from a distant planet no one has ever communicated with, a two hundred year promise which is no more than myth and legend now, no more than a mere pantomime. Daniel is blind.'

'He is still our president,' she said firmly.

'But you agree he is blind.'

Katherine dropped her gaze.

'How long will Subsolumers let a blind man lead them, Katherine? How long will our leader suppress innovations like the one you have developed? How long does Subsolum have? We don't value your people enough. The agronomists have worked dead fields all their lives and I want to change that.'

She remained silent, thinking, as the swell of Subsolum's elite slowly suffocated her. Bulb makers drank, tunnel engineers laughed, traders danced, but where were the agronomists? Einar was right. Where was Eva? The glamorous bar, shielded from view by a thick red curtain, didn't belong to them—the soil pushes.

Maybe it is time our status was updated. But it's Einar Laxness. She looked up at the brute, at that angular, soulless face. Pupils as dark as the abyss. Golden teeth and golden ear hoops as if he were royalty. He isn't a leader, he's ruthless. He'll run Subsolum like an army, like he does Pipeworks: insignia, ranks, orders. A tyrant king. But was her father any better? He has let Subsolum's fields die, has let his people starve, guided us towards our slow and sure collapse. And when I suggest a way out, he won't hear it. She was stuck—Subsolum was stuck—between two old men clinging onto their legacies, racked by their addictions to power.

'If I were in charge,' Einar said, 'your secret project would not be so secret.'

A tremble ran through her. Briefly, she saw every field remade into gigantic hydroponics loops. But then came her father, crashing down on it, clawing all her hard work to bits. Could she ever convince him? If we don't do it, we all die. Maybe the only way through this is playing them off against each other. But she wasn't political like that. I don't have it in me.

'You two should be mingling,' her father said, appearing from the crowd, sweat gleaming on his forehead. He carefully unfolded his handkerchief and wiped his head. 'The bulb makers haven't given me a moment; they've brought the sweat right out of me. I had to get Ólafur to run them around.'

'Your lovely daughter and I were just discussing how the New Havilians endure the radiation,' Einar said, not a hint of his conspiratorial tone left in his voice.

'Is that right?' her father said.

Katherine bit her lower lip, nodding. She could count on a single hand the lies she had told her father.

'I've heard that it's their genetics,' Einar said, 'the only people in the world who had a tolerance for radiation, and so they inherited the Earth.'

Her father adjusted his glasses. 'Sounds plausible.'

'You must know more than us, though, Daniel. Your wife, after all, did spend much time up there.'

'Yes,' her father said, his voice uncertain, his face pinched in a blend of confusion and suspicion. To Katherine he said, 'How are you finding the play?'

We aren't going to talk about your tantrum, father? Just like that, all's forgotten?

'You must be curious,' Einar said, as Katherine opened her mouth. 'Those New Havilians have cured their own cancers. Wouldn't that be a wonderful feat? Especially for a person in your condition.'

Her father smiled weakly.

'I would gamble,' Einar pressed, even daring to take a step closer to her father, 'that's your reason for sending Mister Wu overground.' Then, in a low voice, he added, 'To save your own skin.' He patted him on the chest.

'You have to do this here and now?' her father said. 'You can't let one night go—one *fokking* night—without pressing me?'

She studied Einar, to bring up her father's cancer like that, to use it as a weapon against him.

'All the people want,' Einar said, 'is to eat.'

'And you would have us bend over to the New Havilians and let them control us,' her father said.

'Dad, let's go back to the seats.' She reached out to take his hand to lead him away. I don't need to hear this now. Her father shook his head, keeping his hand from her reach.

'Then why are you sending Wu,' Einar said, 'he is going to learn hydroponics, no? But you want to keep to the soil? It doesn't add

82

up, Dan. There are tunnel whispers you're losing your mind. That the pressures of your illness have gotten to you.'

Her father coughed and pulled off his glasses. She stopped for a second, thinking how Einar's question was identical to hers— It didn't make any sense. Why was Ken to learn hydroponics when her father so resoundingly rejected ever using it in Subsolum? It's political.

He rubbed his glasses clear, rubbed them so hard she thought the lenses might crack. He got them back on his face, and said, 'You Pipeworkers have an inflated sense of self—you're short-sighted.'

Ólafur had noticed them, and had paced over, his face bleached white. He made glances at the crowd, hoping, she guessed, no one would notice the two men arguing.

Her father stuck a finger into the much larger man's chest. 'We can't live up there, but they can live down here. You see? As soon as our survival is so dependent on theirs, they have the option to come down here, wipe us out, and run the pipes for themselves.'

'Please,' Katherine said. Though the truth was she wanted this to play out to its bitter end. Why is he doing this? It doesn't make sense. It's political, Katherine—that's what he had said. Out of filial duty, she begged: 'Both of you, please, stop. This isn't the place.'

'Not anyone can run the pipes,' Einar said, trying to stand up taller. 'The skill has been developing for centuries—through the heart and spirit of the Pipeworkers.'

Katherine cut between them both and took her father by the shoulders. His face had gone bright red, his hands white fists that

83

trembled with rage.

'Forget it,' she said, gazing into her father's wild and furious eyes. 'Not here, Dad, please.' His heart thumped through his suit jacket. 'Please,' she said again.

A breath escaped him, and his balled hands opened up, one taking Katherine's. They started back to their seats.

'You're a coward, Daniel, you always have been,' Einar yelled after them. 'A coward who speaks in contradictions!'

They moved through people drinking and laughing, discussing the play and the stage, joking about the dying fields and the rations. At every overheard joke and jibe, her father twitched or tensed, the simmering anger inside boiling over but never quite erupting.

γ

Einar didn't rejoin them in their box seats.

The stage lights clunked on, revealing an excavation project. Subsolumers wore helmets and high-vis jackets, and swung pickaxes at giant rocks.

Katherine's heart pounded so hard she felt it in her teeth. *We should leave.* She caught a glimpse of Ólafur in the corner watching over both of them. *He's thinking the same thing as me. They nearly came to blows.*

The audience cheered on the actors as they burrowed deeper into the rocks that would become Subsolum.

'We don't have long!'

'We can't wait around!'

'The world is dead!'—the three chorused as they swung their picks.

'He's a dangerous fool,' her father whispered to her. 'And so is his daughter.'

Katherine closed her eyes and breathed. 'What is going on?'

The three actors broke into song, swinging their picks as they went:

> *We don't have long*
> *We can't wait around*
> *The world is dead*
> *Oh hum, oh la, oh do!*

Sparks flew each time their picks struck the rock. The crowd sung along, and soon the rocky walls reverberated with Subsolumers' sing-song.

Her father leant over to her and said, 'You don't need to know. Keep away from them both. That means Tiffany too.'

The stage lights died abruptly, leaving the stage and the audience in darkness. The sing-song quickly faded. Was this a new part of the play? Had the rationing forced rewrites? Murmurs and whispers snaked through the crowd.

'Dad?' she whispered.

Then, quietly at first, but steadily rising to a crescendo, were chants: 'Oust! Oust! Oust!'

'Dad, is this part of the play?' She gripped her armrest.

'Oust! Oust! Oust!' cried a section of the audience.

'I ... I ... I don't think so.' He traded looks with Ólafur.

'Sir, we should move to your office.'

Katherine stood and held the handrail to look right down at the audience. Everything was so dark, she only saw silhouettes.

'Sir,' Ólafur said. 'Sir, we ought to get going.'

Dark red lights clunked on, illuminating the crowd and the stage. It looked like the actors had run off, leaving the stage empty. But a person was running over to it. Who is that? She squinted, then she realised. 'That's Ken.'

'What?'

'Look—' she pointed '—he's running to the microphone.'

'Oust! Oust! Oust!'

'Sir, I really think—'

'Would you sit down for a moment!' her father yelled, and yanked Ólafur into the empty chair left by Einar.

The darkly red lights grew brighter, shining on Ken Wu and a microphone.

He licked his lips and took the microphone stand.

'What is he doing?' her father muttered.

Ken, Katherine said to herself, remembering him as he prayed.

'My family,' he said, the microphone screeching. 'My family is dead because President Marston wouldn't let us buy medicine from New Havilah.'

'Lies!' her father said.

'My family starved because President Marston refused to agree to the New Havilian trade agreement.'

The crowd booed. Someone called out: 'He's hoarding all the food!'

Ken, drenched in blood-red light, a demon from the Starship

Fables: a post-nuclear wanderer, haunting the unsaved.

'My family is dead because President Marston refused to provide them with the correct protective equipment. The radiation ate my wife, my daughter.'

Boos and hisses. 'Drunk on power!' the crowd roared.

'Helpless, I am to be forced up to the surface all for President Marston's selfish gains.'

The crowd were up on their feet, stomping the ground, yelling: 'Where's all the food? We don't want your rations!'

'And they have the nerve to bully me, to sit up there, high above us all, looking down on us as if they were the Saviours themselves!' He pointed at her, and a bright white spotlight nearly burnt out her eyes. 'But there are those who choose to fight against our president! Those who have saved me from my torturers. Rise!' Ken Wu cheered. 'Pipeworkers, rise up!'

Ólafur yanked Katherine's elbow and brought her away from the edge, just as a stone smashed into the handrail.

'Sir,' Ólafur said, 'it is time to go.'

But her father was fixed in his chair, thinking.

Stones and bottles crashed into the box. Soon broken glass littered every inch of the box floor.

'They are going to block the stairwell, sir.'

I am trying to save you!

The cries of 'Pipeworkers rise up!' shook the Great Hall.

As stones and bottles flew through the air, smashed and crashed against the box and scaffold, Katherine stared at her father. Over and over, he adjusted his glasses, and the thoughts she had held back for so long began to slowly seep into her head, like the noxious fumes of a gas pocket in the rock. Is this him? Could he murder Ken's family? Would he think of no one but himself? Not my father, not Dad.

'There's no time!' Ólafur screamed. Bottles broke all around them. The stench of mushroom beer rose from puddles of broken glass.

Her father shook and looked over, red light in his glasses. 'My office, now.'

They sprinted down the stairwell. Stones clattered all around.

The echoes of 'Oust! Oust! Oust!' chased them up the ramps.

γ

Katherine couldn't get her thoughts to align or her breath to slow down. Oust! Oust! Oust! went the cries in her head. She gulped for air. Will they come for us? Oust! Oust! Oust!

'You kept this from me,' she said to her father. 'I thought these were rumours—but they really want you out.' I haven't been paying attention. But who cares who's in charge when there's nothing to eat? She paced around his office, circling his desk.

Oust! Oust! Oust!

'Sit down,' he said, and coughed into the crook of his elbow. 'You're working up my chest.'

She collapsed into the chair across from him. They would have torn us apart. '... torn us apart and chucked us into the world— no rad suit or mask.' Would Tiff do that to me? She tried to warn me. This is happening. They're about to storm through the office door.

88

As she had the thought, Ólafur dropped a metal bar across the office door and locked it into place.

This is my fault. Einar knows he can use me to grow food. He'll give me everything, let me do what I need to, but he'll be the one in charge, not Dad.

'We're fine, Katherine.' Her father reached across his desk to pat her arm clumsily. He's drunk. 'Security will get things under control— Ólafur! a drink.'

'He doesn't need a drink,' Katherine said, glaring at Ólafur. He needs to start fixing this mess before it's too late.

'Ólafur, a drink.' He stared Katherine down like the little girl he knew her to be. His little girl. 'Ken Wu has dug himself a hole too deep to climb out from,' he said.

So have you.

'He's reckless and a coward. I gave him a chance to make up for destroying that field and he does this to me.' He shook his head, grimacing. 'Pathetic.'

Botanical scents drifted up from the gin Ólafur set on the desk. A slow and somewhat steady consumption of Old World gin seemed to be the last thing her father did with any passion. He slurped it up greedily, and slapped the empty glass down.

'This isn't about Ken,' she said, 'they're going to tear that door down. This is a coup. You have taken too long. You've got lazy.'

'Nonsense. I am their president and the people—'

Clung!

The office door pealed—a death knell.

All three held their breath and looked on hopelessly at the door.

Clung!

Tiffany tried to warn me. I could have sided with her there and then and saved myself.

The blood had drained from her father's face, leaving it as white as bleached cottonmoss.

Clung! At the battering, he trembled.

'Get away from the door, Ólafur!' her father cried. 'Get behind the desk.' As Ólafur ran over, he grabbed Katherine's arm and pulled her to the other side of the desk.

Shuffles and shouts from behind the door.

Ólafur swiped the desk clear and flipped it over. They huddled behind it—the only wooden desk in Subsolum, nothing more than a thin fortification.

This can't be happening.

Clung!

'Where is Security?' her father whispered, and stifled a cough. Blood vessels snaked across his cheeks and nose and looked about to explode.

They steeled themselves for the next battering at the door, but what came in its place was the soft bell of the office telephone. Sat huddled behind the overturned desk, they listened to the ring.

'Well answer it!' her father barked at Ólafur.

Gingerly, Ólafur crept out from behind the desk, keeping low to the ground, and answered the telephone. 'Hello?' He straightened himself up. 'Yes … Ah. Yes, all fine, perhaps a few cuts … Y-yes … No, I understand … Thank you.' He hung up the telephone. Katherine, who had been peeking around the desk, watched, numbed by fear, as Ólafur strolled towards the office door.

'Ólafur,' she said, 'who was it?'

He paid her no mind, and marched on to the door.

They've made a deal! He turns us over and goes free.

Seeing Katherine, her father got to his feet. He followed her gaze and trembled again. 'Ólafur,' he said, 'what is this? Do not open that door.'

But Ólafur calmly unlocked the metal bar.

'Think how I've treated you,' her father said. 'You have never missed a meal! Not once!'

What about the spit buckets? The endless orders for drinks?

None of it had any affect on the servant, nor did she think it would. *I would do the same, if I were him.*

He worked the metal bar up and gripped the door handle.

Will they kill him?

The door swung open. Ólafur jumped out of the way and dropped his head.

This was it. It had happened in a flash. One moment she was sure she could rescue her home, rescue it from her father and from the Pipeworkers, but in the next all had been stripped away from her, and left her a prisoner.

A long, quivering breath escaped her. She gripped the edge of the desk, dug her fingernails into the wood—the only wood in Subsolum.

Einar Laxness walked through the door.

'This is how you seize power,' her father said, 'at the *Stjörnu Farartæki*!'

Einar held up both his hands. 'Come out from there,' he said. 'No one is seizing anything.'

'Look at the mess you have— What?' her father said. 'Y-you aren't...' but he broke off.

Einar flashed Katherine a look. Can you believe him? she imagined him saying. This is our leader? She stared into the carpet.

'Daniel, you created this. Your insane devotion to the soil. Your reluctance to trade with the New Havilians. You have let Subsolumers die for it— for what? A blind allegiance to tradition? What good is tradition when the world we live in changes so often? We must adapt.'

'And you will lead then? You will lead us right into New Havilah's traps—into the irradiated world.'

Einar shook his head.

Katherine was only slightly shocked that Einar sounded the more reasonable. But when he's in charge, how long before critics and non-conformists start disappearing? I must be near the top of his list, once I've given him everything I know.

She wanted to say something, to jump between them again. But every action, every choice, seemed like a fight against the inevitable. This needed to reach its end, and she wasn't going to get in the way, even if that meant her father losing. Whatever that means.

'I saw to it that the people did not riot,' Einar said. 'You are hanging on by sinew, a severed arm dangling.'

Ólafur swallowed, his giant Adam's apple rising and falling as if he'd tried to swallow one of her potatoes whole.

Einar looked around the office, sniffed the air, and shook his head. 'Living like a roach in its hovel, watching over your dying

92

fields as the people starve to death. Subsolum needs better, Daniel.'

He didn't wait for her father's reply, he walked back to the door, his footfall heavy, his gait confident, but before leaving, he flashed his eyes at Katherine.

The heavy office door creaked and then slammed shut.

And he was gone.

Her father kicked his upturned desk. 'That bastard! The nerve he's got—' he looked at Katherine '—I should have crushed the Pipeworkers when I had the chance. Your mother—' an accusative finger jutted out from his fist '—your bloody mother stopped me from doing it. I told her. I told her this was going to be—'

He kicked wildly at the desk.

'Dad,' she tried, but soon realised there was nothing to do but get out of his way.

'S-sir,' Ólafur said, but knew—probably better than she—there was little chance to stop him.

He wailed and kicked at the desk until he was coughing and his face was bright red. Exhausted now, and in a fit of coughing, he stumbled over to his desk chair and fell into it.

Her mother's words filtered through her mind, He needs you as much as you need him.

'Dad,' she said and moved to hold him. He pawed her away. His face was as red as blood itself—he coughed so hard she thought he might vomit up his lungs.

'You've worked yourself up,' she said. 'You've let Einar get to you.'

He tried to say something but couldn't catch his breath. Coughs and wheezes took their holds.

'Have some water, Dad.'

Ólafur appeared behind her, glass of water in hand, completely unperturbed by their certainty of his betrayal.

Her father fell from his chair and sprawled out on the floor. Coughs and wheezes morphed into retches. Blood bubbled up and ran from his lips.

She knelt beside him, her hands shaking, but she managed to push him over so he was on his side. He spluttered and she caught a face full of his blood. 'He's dying!' She wiped the blood from her face and stared at her trembling, bloody red hand. He can't be dying. He was fine ten seconds ago.

'Bear a moment, miss,' Ólafur said, and fiddled with a cabinet.

'Dad,' she whispered, 'Dad.'

Blood dribbled from the corner of his lip. His breathing grew raspier. Short, staccato breaths were all he could manage. An artery in his neck thumped against her fingertips. His eyes searched her. 'I'm here,' she said, 'I'm here.'

'M-my ... my little Kathy.'

Tears stood in her eyes.

'Move aside!' Ólafur said brusquely, and dropped to his knees. 'Hold his head up and keep his mouth open.'

'What are you doing?' Katherine said. 'What's that?'

'Keep him still!' Ólafur said.

She shuffled around so her father's head rested on her lap. Tilting his head up—his skin clammy—she watched as Ólafur unstoppered a glass vial of a dark red liquid. 'Is that blood!?' she said, and nearly dropped her father's head.

'Be still!' Ólafur carefully held the vial above her father's mouth. His short breaths had stopped, the heaving thumps in his neck now nothing more than a flicker.

'He's dying!' she cried. 'Ólafur! do something!'

Ólafur dribbled the red liquid into her father's mouth. 'Keep his head up.' The coppery scent confirmed what she thought. Blood! He's pouring blood.

Tiny particles suspended in the blood shone brightly as they left the vial. Green fluorescent particles.

The tip of Ólafur's tongue poked out between his lips: his eyes were narrowed and his head steady. Half the vial had been emptied into her father's mouth. Even near unconsciousness he still swallowed the blood greedily. He's dreaming of gin. Ólafur sighed and stuffed the stopper back in.

'Are you going to tell me why you've poured blood down my father's throat?'

Droplets of sweat clung to Ólafur's overly long eyebrows. He got back to his feet and stood there for a moment.

In her lap, her father started to stir, he groaned and tried to roll over onto his front. 'Help me get him up— He is going to be alright, yes?' How many times had they done this?

Ólafur licked his lips. He stared down at the glass vial in his hands and said, 'I should think so.'

Together, they got her father onto the long sofa, and draped a blanket over him. He promptly lapsed into snoring.

Ólafur righted the desk, and then poured two small glasses of gin out for the both of them. 'To living another day.' They drank silently, sitting at the desk.

The clatter of bottles and stones, the stench of spilt mushroom beer, the chants Oust! Oust! Oust! seized her until her chest was so tight she struggled for breath. Why didn't Einar do it? He's waiting for something.

'Immortal blood.'

'What?' Katherine said, startled from her thoughts.

'He drank the Immortal Man's blood.'

She set her glass down. 'How— The New Havilians test his blood. And it is a myth ... I mean ... he's not really immortal, he has good genes, but he's not immortal, that's why they never discover anything.'

An impossibly deep and resonant laugh burst out from Ólafur and his narrow body. 'The New Havilians stopped testing his blood years ago. They sell it to us now, completely in the dark about what your father does to it or with it. He calls it "coaxing the magic". But more importantly, the Immortal Man has no idea either. It's one of my better clandestine operations.' Ólafur drank down the rest of his gin. His hands shook and a cheek twitched. Stands from his greasy, swept-back hair dangled over his forehead. She had never seen him so shaken and unkept before. He was the polite and obedient servant, always well dressed and quiet.

'Is he going to be alright?' she asked.

Ólafur nodded, but then said, 'For the moment at least.'

'How many times have you had to do this? I can't believe I never knew.'

'Last year we used all the blood, this year we bought an extra

96

vial. The New Havilians weren't happy about it. We are on borrowed time.'

'But why does the blood not cure him completely? That's what the Immortal Man has, immortality.'

Ólafur shrugged. 'Your father has his theories. I dare say—' But he cut himself off, shuffled on his seat. 'I don't know what to tell you, Miss Marston. Tomorrow, I'm sure, your father shall speak with you. Ken Wu has chosen a side. It seems to me you are all that's left.'

WORLDS ON TOP OF WORLDS

– SUBSOLUM–

A banging at her door woke her.

Soft and rhythmic steel drums tumbled from the radio in the nook above her bed. Groggy, she blindly reached up and groped to turn it off. She must have fallen asleep with it still on. Anything to drown out the faint echoes of Oust! Oust! Oust!

The door-pounder had no mercy for her door. It's not them. *Oust, oust, oust* echoed again and again and again. I'm safe. I'm safe. Though her shaky legs would say otherwise.

'Katherine!' the voice called—her father. A personal visit from the Subsolum president. When was the last time a president made their way to this level?

'Katherine, open up!'

At least he's alive. Though he did seem destined to kill himself in a fit of rage. You have lung cancer, she wanted to scream back at him.

She swung her legs from the single bed, padded the five short steps to the door, unlocked it, and slid it open.

'About time.' He was dressed in an Old World suit, trying to call forth a vague notion of ceremony. Or trying, desperately, to convince her that he had himself under control. The stricken, half-dead face she had clutched the night before had gone, replaced by a florid, controlled visage. 'I don't know why you insist on living down here,' he said. 'There are—'

'I'm too tired for a lecture,' she said, rubbing an eye. She wanted to mention the blood. Was it even possible? She was certain it was a New Havilian myth.

Ólafur, equally well dressed, looked on in horror.

That's right, I am not going to put up with any of this. I will interrupt whoever I like.

Nerves had worn deep lines into the servant's face. He seemed about ten years older than the night before. My father will do that to you.

But all her father did was take a breath, step back, and say, 'Get changed.'

They took her to a private lift she had never seen before. There were so many hidden rooms, stairwells, ducts, doors, and passages in Subsolum, Katherine had stopped finding it surprising when she found another one. But to come to a lift? And a fine, brass-fixtured one at that, did surprise her.

They climbed up through Subsolum, the lift cage rattling, the brass buttons and levers shiny under the single light. Both men were calm, their breathing steady. For her father not to say anything, not to try and fill the empty space... Einar must have lied. He *is* going to overthrow my father, and this is a sending off. They're getting me out, before it's too late.

The lift doors parted onto a wide passage, almost twice the diameter of any regular Subsolum passageway. They walked. Old style lights lit the way, not the daylight mimicking lights she had grown up around. They reached a set of heavy granite doors. A bronze plaque, inset in the wall, read NÚLL HERBERGI. *Room Zero.*

Ólafur unlocked the doors and pushed them open. A draught of snow smelling air crashed into Katherine. *We must be right below the surface!*

Ólafur motioned for her to enter.

Grand paintings hung on every wall, photographs too, all depicting the creation of Subsolum. The largest painting, directly in front of Katherine, was of a mountain-sized tunnel boring machine, a Goliath over its tunnellers, these stern looking men, their faces black from rock dust and red from exposure. Huge, gilded, ornate frames held each painting and photograph, running counter to everything she knew about her home. The only lavishness she had any experience with was her father's office, everywhere else everything was pragmatic and practical, function over form. But she realised, staring at an Old World military uniform kept immaculate in a dusty glass box, that this room's function was its form. It was decorated to impress and intimidate, to make the occupants feel smaller than they were, to make them realise that they were part of a larger organism, more important than themselves.

A metal table stood at the centre of the room. Ólafur pulled out chairs and indicated for her to sit. She sat and, in the quietness, noticed new sounds. She held her breath. Wind howled above. Roaches scratched and scraped as they burrowed into the tundra. Her hand trembled ever so slightly.

At the front of the room was a rusty metal locker, stamped in Old World insignia. There were plenty of them deep in storage, put there by her ancestors, who filled them with various supplies. *What are they planning?* Ólafur scurried over to the locker, opened it, and fished objects from it: rucksack, sample collection kits, drugs canisters, ration packs, a gas mask and radiation-suit (a type she had not seen before), thick Old World leather boots.

He isn't sending me up, she told herself. He can't be, he was so sure he wouldn't.

'This was the first room ever carved out from the rock,' her father said, sitting across from her. He spoke in sombre tones, trying to channel the room's authority. 'The founders of Subsolum met here, before the Bombs fell, before the Sun faded, and decided who and how many should be saved.' He stopped for her to reply, to acknowledge the reverence the room demanded, but she kept her mouth closed. He reached for a drink, but there was none there, so he quickly folded his arms, hoping, she guessed, that she hadn't noticed. 'Very well, Katherine.' He sighed. Shaking his head, he said, 'I cannot trust anyone but you.'

'You don't trust me.'

'What is this?' he said, leaning forward. 'Of course I trust you.'

'Then why choose Ken to be the envoy?'

'I chose Mister Wu because I wanted to give him the chance to redeem himself—not only in my eyes, but in the eyes of the agronomists and of all Subsolumers. It is clear now he did not see it this way.'

'*Vitleysa*!' she said. 'Utter rubbish.'

Ólafur froze, a radiation counter in his hands.

Her father looked off to one side, shaking his head again.

'You choose Ken because he couldn't refuse,' she said. 'He made a mistake days after his wife and daughter died. And—'

'Tread very carefully, Katherine.'

'—and you were the one who let that happen. So you exploited

101

it too.'

Her father adjusted his glasses. 'Think what you like,' he said.

Ólafur, in the corner, had started packing the rucksack with the locker contents. How does he survive under my father? Why does he do it? And so obediently.

'I will,' she said. 'I know what's true.'

'Ken is still distraught about the field,' her father said. 'Meili and Bo died, yes, and it was a tragic accident which precipitated another. After the field was lost, Ken came to me and he begged me for a way to atone.'

'You're lying.'

'I'm not, Katherine. These are the facts. His speech was written by my political enemies, by Einar Laxness and his Pipeworkers. It is slander, designed to soil my image. I have spent heavily on protective equipment. I have never refused medicines from New Havilah. And—'

'But you have rationed us,' she said, 'to near starvation for most.'

'This is about survival, Katherine. Ken doesn't see it, doesn't understand it, is blinded by his loss. He won't cooperate. He wants revenge, not atonement.'

Her father leant back in his chair. Paused to breathe. Behind him, a painting of heaped piles of rock and rubble, of Subsolumers digging for their lives and their descendants' lives, looked down on him. They had no idea what their shelter would become. That its leader would turn on his own people, and starve them as he gets drunk on gin.

'Kathy,' her father said, 'I chose Ken for another reason...' he

102

faltered, cleared his throat. 'Ken isn't *you*. New Havilah is dangerous and I won't lose another person to the surface.'

'But now you're out of options,' she said, 'so you sacrifice your own daughter.'

He breathed deeply again, sliding his fingers under his glasses to rub his eyes. Ólafur worked diligently, packing the rucksack.

'What does it matter to you, Kathy, you're getting your way.'

Her mouth twitched, fighting back a smile. He doesn't get to see me happy when he's doing it for the wrong reasons.

'Our fields are failing,' he said, 'and we have had to resort to rationing. The people are starved and tired and they won't take much more. We must fix our fields.'

'Fix them?' she said, meeting her father's eyes. 'There is no fixing them. The soil is dead. The only solution is to do what New Havilah do and use—'

'If the next word from your mouth is hydroponics I will...' He checked himself. 'We are not giving up on the soil. The first Subsolumers invented the closed-system of soil management and it has kept us alive for two hundred years.'

'Which it was never supposed to do. If you read the original works you would know that, Dad. No one thought that this would last this long.'

'But we are here.'

'Only barely.' She sat upright. Trying to match the postures of those in their regal portraits on the walls. 'If New Havilah had never appeared, we would be dead. Do you understand that? They saved us from starvation.'

'Katherine, they can't be trusted. Once we are of no use to them, they will do as they please, slither down here and work the pipes for themselves.' He looked over at Ólafur. When he turned back to her, his eyes were more focused, his pupils narrow. But his face was pale, like a man sentenced to death.

'"Do you understand that?"' her father mimicked, his lip curling. 'You sound exactly like her.'

'Don't...'

'And do you know what your mother did?'

'I don't want to hear it.'

He slapped his hand on the table and she shook. 'Of course you do! Because you're desperate to walk her path. Desperate to go up there—' he pointed upwards '—ill prepared, hastily, naivety in your heart and head. Don't lose your mind like her, Kathy.' He breathed, the madness, the death stare in his eyes, and he went on, 'I can't think what I would do if I lost you too. If you never came back.'

'You're sending me up there, but for what? If you don't want me to study hydroponics, then what?'

'You are to go to the surface,' he said. She heard it slowly, as if he was on half-speed. 'New Havilah has something that rightfully belongs to Subsolum. And I need you to take it.'

'What has that got to do with food? Subsolum is starved.'

'Katherine—' he chewed his lower lip, calmed himself, fiddled with his glasses. 'What you are about to take will enable us to revivify the soil, to restore ill Subsolumers to full health, perhaps one day *we* will be able to walk around on the surface without concern.'

Ólafur flicked a glance at her. He licked his lips in the same way he had done after pouring the Immortal Man's blood down her father's throat. She wondered if there were more to his glance, if he were trying to warn her.

She narrowed her eyes, focused on her father, trying to understand him. 'Y-you want me to take the Immortal Man's blood? You're crazy.'

Her father gestured at Ólafur, saying, 'What is this? No. I want you to take his *fokking* flower!'

She waited—listen to the howl above in the quietness. She had spent all this time defending him to Tiffany, to anyone who challenged him. And now this.

'A flower?' she said. 'How is a flower— You're losing *your* mind, Dad.'

'I've never been more lucid, Kathy.' He stood, walked over to Ólafur, and took the packed rucksack from him. 'Quinton al-Zoubi,' he said, 'the Immortal Man—'

Quinton al-Zoubi? It was the name of the author of her mother's hydroponics book. *He* is the Immortal Man? All this time?

'—he runs a plant nursery and you are to go there and be taught by him.'

Her father walked towards her and dropped the rucksack, like a sack of her potatoes, at her feet. 'But that's not your goal, Kathy. The goal is the flower—his flower. It is the key to his immortality. A beautiful white flower, almost incandescent, glistening, like the stars.'

'Why would they let a Subsolumer into his nursery?'

He sat back in his chair, leaned forwards, elbows on the table, chin on hands. 'Because they think we are changing to their methods of growing. Don't you see?' He wrapped his knuckles on the table. 'Their power structure is changing. New leadership is a good time to make friends, and that's what we have done. Every last ounce of paraffin has been traded away for this opportunity.'

'For us to steal a magic flower? You're insane, Dad.'

'You haven't noticed?' he said. 'Ólafur, have I coughed at all today?'

The servant's Adam's apple rose and fell. 'No, sir. Not once.'

'Have I wheezed, sweated, or in any way betrayed my illness?'

'No, sir. You have not.'

Grinning now, her father said, 'And why is that, Ólafur?'

'The Immortal Man's blood, sir, is coursing about your veins. It has rejuvenated you.'

'You haven't coughed,' she said, only now realising. No fogged up glasses, no clutching at his chest. 'I believed it last night. We helped you—I watched you nearly die. You coughed blood into my face and I felt your pulse go weak.'

'Then you understand,' he said, 'you understand what it is that man has been hiding. He is selfish. Keeping it all for himself. It doesn't just work on him. I'm sure I can modify it, and help regrow the soil's biome. Katherine, this is your opportunity to do a great service for your home. Don't waste it.' He rose from his chair, gestured at the rucksack. 'This is your field kit. Ólafur can take you through the equipment list.'

The servant nodded. 'It shan't let you down, Miss Marston.'

'I have arranged for you to be escorted from the top of the mountain. When you reach New Havilah, I cannot say who you can trust. The New Havilian Resource Council Leader, Lady Jupiter, is our ally—but since the delivery of the paraffin I've not heard anything from her. The four armed monstrosity is a nuisance I have had to tolerate, but if you succeed, Kathy, then she'll be of little bother, along with the rest of the Overworlders. Once you have access to the nursery, you must find his flower, and take it.'

'They won't leave me alone with it,' Katherine said. *Am I really indulging this?*

'That's why I am preparing a distraction, during the New Havilian's Summer Solstice. You'll have your opportunity then. And once you have the flower, Ólafur here will be there to pick you up from the New Havilian tramstop.'

The servant, somewhat reluctantly, bowed his head at Katherine. *Are we both cowards? This isn't how we fix the fields. But she didn't have to go up there and steal. She could go up there and learn.*

Her father, slumping back into his chair, 'This flower, Katherine, it won't just heal the soil, it will heal me too. It will flush out this cancer.'

If she hadn't seen the blood do its work she might have laughed at him. *I don't have a choice.*

'I have much else to attend to,' he went on. 'Come along and get yourself in order to travel. You leave this afternoon.'

γ

Katherine, the heavy rucksack on her back, walked down the

ramps until she could go no further. A dense crowd blocked her way through. They were right by the exitway that led towards the canteen and food market. Mixed in with the muttering and quiet sobs were occasional yells. She asked a lady who was holding a toddler what was happening.

'They've cut our rations down,' the lady said. 'They've spent the lot on the play! I swear that's what they've done.'

The toddler babbled, and his mother kissed him on his hollow and starved cheeks.

Katherine scanned the crowd—most held children, either in their arms and pressed to their chests, or by the hands. These were the mothers, she realised, the current group of mothers. And her father had cut their rations. He hadn't even told her, hadn't dared mention it to her.

A canteen worker appeared from the passageway. He clambered up a railing and yelled over the crowd: 'You have had your entitlement. There's nothing left to give.'

The mothers and nursery workers shouted back, demanding more, and at all the shouting, their babies cried.

The canteen worker yelled louder: 'Clear out or I'll have to call security.'

Katherine crouched, swung her heavy rucksack around, and unzipped it. Digging around inside the rucksack, she called softly, 'Here, here, eat all this.' But no one heard her.

'Clear out?' a woman cried. 'I've had nothing to eat today.'

Face after face of crying babies, toddlers sucking their thumbs, mothers desperate, panicked. Their sour breath and sweat easily overpowered the mouldy air.

She found the silver ration packets, had them halfway out from the rucksack when a hand grabbed them and ripped them from her.

'She's got rations!' another lady screamed.

The mothers swarmed Katherine as she struggled with the rucksack. 'Get off me,' she shouted. 'I don't have any more!'

The woman who had snatched the rations from her hand must have tried to run, as all the other mothers—clutching their children—bounded around Katherine in a chase.

On her feet, she traded a glance with the canteen worker, who stood gawping at the scene. The whole group had charged off down the tunnel. Their voices and shouts faded until all she could hear was the up and down drone of the air-recyclers and her own ragged breathing.

'We're no better than roaches,' the canteen worker said. 'And it's all your father's doing.'

γ

The door to her cubby room lab was wide open. Shadows played on the wall opposite: the figure searched and handled objects, clumsily dropped them back into place. Katherine held her breath, pressed herself against the wall, beside the door, and carefully peeked into the room.

Tiffany!

The monster woman was pawing through growth media buckets. More thieving, more proof we're no better than roaches.

'You want more potatoes?' Katherine said. 'Learn to grow

them.'

'I've been here for hours,' Tiffany said, keeping her eyes down. 'Want to tell me what's going on?' She found a perlite box and sat down on it. 'Rumours are, you've got your wish—you're going to the surface.'

'How do you know already?' Katherine looked over her shoulder, stepped into the room, and shut the door behind her. She reached for one of the finger-sized optical transducers and unplugged it.

'These caves echo, Chick.'

The gurgle of nutrient solution filled the silence. Katherine worked free the microcontroller too, bundled all the wires up. 'I am going up there,' she said, and swung her rucksack around to her front. They ripped those rations right off me. I was trying to do good. 'I don't know how to feel about it.'

Tiffany gestured at the equipment, saying, 'What? About all this? You're leaving it all here.'

'I'm taking what I think I'll need.' She stuffed the sensor, the wires, and the logic board into her rucksack. 'I'm not sure if I could build these bits up in New Havilah.'

Tiffany ran her tongue along the inside of her lips, then shook her head, and finally got up, hunching under the low ceiling. 'You don't seem very happy about it.'

'That's what I'm saying,' she said. 'I don't know how to feel about it. I don't know if I can leave.' And it had just come out. But that was the truth. Right, Katherine? What's the matter with me? She quickly found another sensor to detach. 'I don't know,' she said. 'I feel as if...'

110

Tiffany tried her hardest to smile.

'I feel like I'm abandoning everyone. I— I just walked through a group of mothers trying to get enough to eat— he's rationed them! I tried to give out some ration packs I had and they all turned into animals.'

'He's rationed everyone, Chick. Don't worry about them. We're all animals. You need to think about what you can do, and that means going up there and … and I don't know what your dad's got planned for you, but it's a plan. And you trust him enough?'

She zipped the bag back up, remembered the book, and unzipped the bag again. The book lived here, in her hideaway cubby room, in the radio set's secret drawer. Beside the radio, Katherine fondled the knobs, remembering all the hours she spent listening to it as she worked. It was a lifeline, to the world above hers, it was good company, a distant friend. She pulled the metal tray open from underneath all the knobs and her book, *Hydroponics in The New World* by Quinton al-Zoubi, sparkled, the golden *Ganymede Publishing* stamp on its cover like a beacon—to what? she wasn't sure. But it never faded. Not even a little bit. Mum would be proud. She pulled it out, closed the tray, and stuffed the book in her bag.

'I … I only had good memories of the play, you know? I remember watching it with my mum. I felt safe.'

'I'm not happy about it,' Tiffany said. She looked down at her feet. 'I tried to convince my father not to do it. I didn't know exactly what they wanted to do, but when Ken Wu walked to the stage, I got it. They were taking a shot at your father, using him.'

'Politics,' Katherine said, getting the rucksack on her back. She pulled the straps tight. 'I don't have long.'

'With you gone, your dad won't be listening to anyone now.'

'He never listened to me,' Katherine said.

'I think they both do,' Tiffany said. 'I think they try their best in the only way they know how. I've been doing a lot of thinking—'

'That makes a change.' She had said it with a smile, and when Tiffany looked at her, she smiled too. The little thrill she got from jabbing at Tiffany never seemed to wear off. It was gambling. You never knew if she would blow up on you.

'You're lucky,' Tiffany said, 'lucky there's this table between us.'

'You've been thinking.'

'Yeah.'

'And?'

'And I think that when it comes to it, they really do listen. Both our fathers—they have the same lives, really. They grew up together, both have daughters, both lost their partners, both hold all this responsibility to the people. But they are insulated now, they don't see the whole picture anymore. I think it comes a bit with age. You can either grow wiser, or you grow narrower, more focused.' She shrugged. 'All I thought though was, It's our role, as their daughters, to bring them out of their focus a bit, or refocus them.'

A little taken back, Katherine said, 'You have been thinking.' And for the first time in a while, Tiffany looked flattered, holding her gaze down to the rocky tiles, shrugging her shoulders as softly as she could.

'What do you think?' Tiffany said.

'I hope you're right.'

Υ

Standing on the freight lift, breathing hard in her radiation suit, Katherine thought that she didn't want very much to be a thief. She had never liked stealing things. Even going back through her mind, she couldn't think of a single thing she had stolen. Yet here she was, the weight of her people resting on her, everyone depending on her to steal a flower from the Immortal Man.

Helvíti, my father might actually be insane.

From the freight lift controls, the operator gave her the thumbs up. Ólafur, stood at the operator's side, paced over, calling, 'One last thing!'

And she thought that this was going to be the Sorry For Not Seeing You Off, from her father, but instead Ólafur reached her and said, 'Whatever you do, when you get up there, don't dare look up. Keep your gaze on the ground, Miss Marston. Firmly fixed on the ground! Good luck!' And he bolted back to his station behind the lift controls.

The sliding door dropped from above. Gears and chains rattled. The whine of electromagnets shifted an octave.

The freight lift climbed.

She was on her way.

THE MOUNTAIN

– NEW HAVILAH –

At some point, so exhausted, Quinton must have made the makeshift bed in the nursery and laid down.

Now, as he rose from the bed of his coat and rough hempmoss canvas, the torture of last night's ordeal thumbed its way back into his thoughts. Over and over he had gone, measuring every metric he could. Had the Flower taken to the new environment? Was the temperature correct? Were the petals discolouring further? The roots, 'The roots!' he had cried, were they rotten and soggy? Did the petals look like they were curling? Did he see the Black Rot on the tip of the stigma? Over and over he went. Was the nutrient solution pressure correct? Did the growth medium need replacing already? Was the metal of the case affecting the acidity alkaline balance? Hundreds of questions and metrics. Yet all of them, every single one, he was able to answer— and he found no fault. He still could not explain that growing yellow patch underneath a petal.

Shaking out the memories from last night as best he could, he collected the coat and canvas from the nursery floor, and was about to set them down on a worktop, when he saw all the pots of strawberries laid neatly across it. He and Billick had finished harvesting the strawberries whilst Darleaner was working on the Flower case, but Ganymede never showed. The man's more elusive than the Black Rot.

He set down the bundle in his arms on a stall and checked the wall clock. It was about nine, so Billick would be here soon. And his Flower, for the first time in so long, will be seen by someone else. You were the last, Sophia.

He circled the exotics table, passing his tobacco plant and its small pink flowers, his coffee and cacao trees. Extractor fans whirled above him in their familiar, soul-soothing way, easing the tensions from the night before, letting him know he was home. Finally, he reached the section of the table where he had connected his Flower and its case. The white petals glowed dimly under the sun bulbs above, the nasty yellow patch faintly visible from the top side of the affected petal. Billick can help. Darleaner's case shined too. On the high growing-table, the top of the case came nearly to his chin. Faint gurgles travelled up from its stubby cylindrical bottom, the sounds of roots being squirted by nutrient solution.

The front door crashed open, slammed shut, quick pitter-patter footsteps followed, then a gruff voice saying, 'Ahoy, Cap'n!' Billick passed through the ribboned threshold of the strawberry room and into this room, found his wheely cart, and hopped in.

'You're late,' Quinton said.

Billick glanced at the wall clock, said, 'That clock's fast. Don't tell me you're never—' He stopped as if he were about to sneeze. From where Billick was (the other side of the growing platform, slightly hidden by a tobacco leaf) there was no way for him to see the Flower. But he smelt it. 'What is that?' he said, and sniffed the air. 'That's ... that's new pollen, eh?'

'Come over here. I need to show you something important.'

There's still time, Quinton. One last moment to stop this. You can't trust him.

115

He shut her voice out.

Billick wheeled himself around. Quinton stepped to one side, and let Billick take a good long look. He blinked a few times, slapped his cheeks in astonishment. His mouth fell open and then morphed into the widest grin Quinton had ever seen on a person. 'It's beautiful, truly, Cap'n, a delight. An Old World de—' His sharp fingernail pointed at the yellow patch. Quinton's guts twisted themselves into knots. He'll speak to it, he'll whisper to the Flower, ask it what's making it sick.

And if he can't?

What other choice is there, really, my love?

Billick patted his overalls, pulled his well-worn bronze magnifying glass from a pocket. He stared and studied, lifting the edge of the petal with his fingernail to expose the yellow patch. 'It looks like heat stress,' he said.

'That's what I thought. I think the bulbs I have in my rooms aren't right.'

'But it ain't,' he said. 'It's the Black Rot.'

Quinton stood unmoving, Billick's words echoing in his head. Was he still asleep? Had he not woken from that bed of coat and heavy hempmoss canvas? He rubbed his eyes, shook his head, but he was still here. He was still in the stifling nursery exotics room, surrounded by a proud and true tobacco plant, strong juvenile coffee trees, with the scent of strawberries as yet unclaimed by Ganymede lingering in the humid air.

Billick peered at the Flower through his magnifying glass, tutting and muttering to himself.

Brightness, I'm not dreaming. This is real. The Flower's got the

116

Rot. Taking a few uneasy steps backwards, Quinton said, 'Are you sure?'

'I know the Rot when I see it, Cap'n.'

'Well, how do we stop it?' Could he dose the Flower with its own *Liphoric Zed*? It might start a negative feedback loop. It could taint the Flower. It could jeopardise New Havilah. His hands began to shake.

'Now you want to stop it?' the scaly leather ball of a man said, looking up at his boss. 'You don't want to burn it and dump the ashes? Surprise, surprise. Maybe if you let me run a few experiments I'll discover a way to treat it.'

The edge of the growing platform served Quinton well as a brace. He held firm to it and didn't dare let go, in case he might fall from shock. Inky blobs had masked his vision, and beat as his heart did. My body is trying to retreat. A stress induced somatic symptom. He pulled out his pipe and held it between his lips; the taste of stale tobacco gave him momentary relief. I've not even planned how to take the *Zed* from the Flower when it's here. Is it even going to be good to use now, with the Rot on its petal? How long before the infection, before the Rot, puts a halt to it? He found his lighter and said rapidly, 'I'm going for a smoke.' A few steps towards the doorway, he added, 'Then we can talk about your experiments. The Flower cannot die, you understand, Bill?' If it dies … he couldn't finish the thought. Sophia would never again see all the good he was doing at the Sun Church. He might not reach the stars.

You've made your path now. I suggest putting Billick to work.
'Aye, Cap'n.'

'And get these strawberry pots into my office. They'll turn to mush in this heat. If Ganymede doesn't show by—' he checked his pocket watch '—10:30, we're doing it, we're taking them out on the Corridor and selling them, and if they don't sell, we'll freeze them for the Solstice.'

It was on the word 'Solstice' that a powerful *thump* sounded at the nursery door. Quinton's pipe flew out from his mouth. He swatted it a few times before catching it.

'Sink me!' Billick yelled. 'He's here.'

'Good. Close up the Flower's case. I don't want him to see it.' Once he'd witnessed Billick shutting the case, Quinton smoothed down his clothes and entered the strawberry growing room, which still housed the plants, though sans their fruits.

'You going to tell him you've nabbed some of his strawberries?' Billick shouted from the exotics room, and then broke into a cackling laugh.

He doesn't know the trouble he gets me in, Quinton thought to himself, chomping down on his pipe stem. He passed through the ribboned strawberry room doorway and into the lobby. The drying room was on his right, the stairs up to the front door on his left. *Thump, thump, thump!* went John Johnny Ganymede at the door. Those poor hinges. Peering into the drying room, Quinton found some peace in the leaves of tobacco that were turning a wonderful deep wood brown. *Thump, thump, thump!*

He groaned.

Ganymede's had all this time to collect. Why now? Quinton charged up the stairs, grabbed a hold of the door handle, and pulled the door open. Blue filled his vision: Ganymede's dark blue

118

skin, the powder blue electric light trapped in his eyes, and a large, navy blue bag thrown over one of his shoulders. Quinton had to look through his own eyebrows to meet Ganymede's face.

'Al-Zoubi,' the giant said. 'I've come to collect.'

In an instant, Quinton processed a few consequences of his thievery and did his best to forage for sensible reasons as to why he was short two handfuls of strawberries. Maybe he won't notice? came one voice in his head. Of course he'll notice! came another. But whatever the cost was to save his Flower, he was willing to pay it.

'Yes, collect,' Quinton said wearily, directing Ganymede down the stairs with a limp hand. 'We've got them in my office. You've left it late, John.'

Ducking under the door frame, Ganymede said, 'I collect when I need to.' The wooden stairs creaked under the bulk of the New Havilian leader.

'Strawberries rot regardless,' Quinton said.

'That's your excuse, is it?'

Quinton's ears pricked up. At the bottom of the stairs, he kept his side to Ganymede and faced the warmth of the drying room. He stared at a tobacco leaf, curling up on itself, and couldn't help note how much he felt like that leaf. 'I don't know what you mean,' he said at last. He was about to pass through into the strawberry room when Ganymede grabbed him hard by the arm.

'Wait. Is your botanist here?'

'He's in the exotics room.' Quinton tried to free himself, but Ganymede's grip worked like steel fetters.

'Can he hear us?'

'No.' What was this all about? 'Will you let go of me?'

'You've put one of my engineers behind on her tram parts,' he said, and let Quinton go. 'I want to know why.' Bolts of electricity danced in his eyes, fighting for escape, hoping to electrocute yet helplessly trapped inside the jelly.

'I needed to save a juvenile tobacco plant,' Quinton said. 'It looked as if some radioactive source had got into it. I needed a shielded casing. Darleaner is very good at what she does.'

'I know,' Ganymede said, 'that's why I employ her to build tram parts. She told me she was paid in strawberries.'

A few unintelligible syllables found their way out from Quinton's mouth. He was lightheaded, nauseous, and was fighting off shakes.

'Is that right, al-Zoubi? You delay one of my best engineers, pay her with strawberries you've stolen from me, all to save a juvenile tobacco plant?'

You knew this could happen. But he'd never guessed that Darleaner would let on how she was paid. But then if she were late with parts, the strawberries were a perfect way to pass on the blame.

Get yourself together, Quinton. Lightheaded? Nauseous? You've had much worse throughout your life. He thought about Sophia, standing at the big bay windows in his rooms, looking towards the Sun Church, waiting for his annual miracle that might not ever come again.

'Yes, I did all that,' he said. 'Tobacco is an expensive crop, to let even a single plant die is … negligent. I will reimburse you for the strawberries.'

Ganymede looked into the drying room: leaves and leaves of tobacco hanging from string, browning and curling under sun bulbs. 'You don't seem to be wanting,' he said.

'There's less in there than you think. And at the rate I'm smoking—' he patted the pocket he kept his pipe in, laughing nervously '—you see?'

Ganymede adjusted the bag slung over his shoulder, waited a beat, then parted the ribboned doorway. 'I do not.' He stepped into the strawberry room.

Brightness! Quinton chased after the big man.

'You've not started another crop yet?' Ganymede said, as he walked a slow loop around the growing platform. Harvested strawberry plants fluttered in his wake. 'Shouldn't these adults be moved to a grow house?'

Quinton hadn't had time. All the running around for the Flower, the trade Lady Jupiter had forced him into, those two vials of his blood, Summer Solstice preparations. 'Yes, when I've the time.'

'When you've the time? What are you doing today?'

'We're travelling up the mountain to collect the Subsolumer.'

Ganymede paused and stared blankly at the fruitless strawberry plants. 'So she's really going to try it,' he said. His glowing eyes looked at Quinton now. 'Your office, you said?'

'Yes. At the back.' And they walked through.

Quinton wiped dust from the top of his desk and from the two badly fraying hempmoss chairs. Ganymede took one look at the chairs and shook his head. He flipped over a metal crate and sat

121

on that. Billick had lined the strawberry filled ceramic pots up against the back wall, but Ganymede didn't seem very much interested.

'She's sending you to collect the Subsolumer?' he asked.

'Yes,' Quinton said, settling into his desk chair. Grime and dust rubbed off onto his legs. He lit his pipe and started smoking, the ring of the metal lighter lingering in his ears, like he'd taken a punch.

'Has she asked you to do anything else? Pass on information?'

'No. She's said nothing.' Quinton drew on the pipe and then thought suddenly, saying it with smoke still in his mouth, 'She's made the trade for the paraffin. I'm to train a Subsolumer in hydroponics.'

'I'm aware. Like old times, eh?'

Quinton smoked, taking the rhetorical question for what it was.

The lights in Ganymede's eyes danced. His tremendous bulk heaved a sigh and he said, rather flatly, 'I don't need to count the strawberries to know that you've stolen some. I could force you to pay me, or have the *politsiya* lock you up for a while.'

Quinton smoked until he was mostly sucking on ash.

'But what I need from you is information on Ju— Lady Jupiter.'

'Spy on your wife?'

'Yes.'

'I don't—'

'She has got herself involved with Subsolumer factions. I need to know why.'

'For New Havilah, I suppose.'

Ganymede growled, just loud enough for Quinton to hear it. 'I

122

hope so. You understand the Pipeworkers and the government, down there, they haven't agreed on much for a time. And it looks like the rationing is threatening what peace there is. The Pipeworkers have made empty threats to seize the pipes, to shut them off—no heat, water, or power. But my focus isn't Subsolum. Juju is the one responsible for maintaining a healthy relationship with Subsolum. I think they've got to her.' Ganymede stood and started to collect the pots of strawberries into his bag. 'I don't know which faction she's working for.'

'Are you sure she isn't working for New Havilah?' Quinton tapped the ash from his pipe, and stuffed it again with loose tobacco he had floating in his pocket. 'Her goal, as far as I can tell, is to get Subsolum growing their food hydroponically. Which would mean our moss farmers supplying them with organics.'

Ganymede set his bag on the floor and turned to Quinton. 'You and I both know Daniel Marston. He won't let Subsolum grow more dependent on New Havilah. He won't give up on the soil either. I don't know what he's up to, letting a Subsolumer come up to the surface. Especially when it's all been tried before.'

'And into my nursery,' Quinton added, ignoring that last sentence.

'I was surprised you went along with it.'

'What choice do I have? I can't refuse Lady Jupiter.' This made Ganymede smile. Quinton thought it a strange sight, a pained and troubled smile, but a smile nonetheless.

'I suppose you can't. She's good at making trouble for those in her sights.'

Quinton liked Lady Jupiter for all the wrong reasons. She never inspected his grow houses, or the production house, or the nursery, and never asked many questions. When the myths around him and Waters reached a great height, she quickly put her Sun Priests to work spreading a different narrative. One about mountain minerals and their restorative properties. How much she knew about his Flower, he wasn't sure. But I've never been pressured there by her.

All this had its cost, though: when she came knocking, he couldn't refuse.

'Are you sure there isn't anything you can tell me?' Ganymede said, and placed a strawberry pot into his bag. 'There must be something.'

'My annual blood test,' Quinton said after a pause. 'This year I had two samples taken. Which was unusual.'

Ganymede worked silently, filling the bag up, leaving Quinton's words in the air, to drift. Finished, he slung the bag over his shoulder, the pots inside clacking loudly. 'That is unusual,' he said, 'very unusual, considering we haven't been testing your blood for a few years now.'

'Not testing it?'

'No, it was getting too expensive. And—' he shrugged '—we weren't getting anywhere. You are an enigma, Gospodin al-Zoubi. Our technical sophistication is not likely to change soon, so why waste valuable time and supplies on you? Immortality seems to want only you, if I am to understand it correctly.'

'So what in Brightness is she doing with my blood!?'

He shimmied the bag higher up on his shoulder and made for the door. 'A good question, one I want you to find the answer to.'

Standing before Quinton's office door, Ganymede stared back at him, and made his eyes glow bright blue. 'Remember, you are deeply in my debt. Those strawberries were worth a hundred tobacco plants. I expect a marvellous Summer Solstice, Gospodin al-Zoubi.' The blue glow dimmed and he left, the door clicking shut.

Quinton closed his eyes and rested back into his office chair, only to be disturbed by the *slap slap slap* of Billick's bare feet on the concrete.

'What do you want?' Quinton said. 'How did you open the door so quietly?'

'Bad news, Cap'n.'

He opened his eyes. Billick's overalls were covered in the crumbs of his breakfast: soupy bark beetle slime over mushroom bread—it smelt of the Baking Sands oven and twisted his stomach in hunger pains. 'You've eaten Baking Sands bread!'

'Aye, Cap'n. There's some— We've got a problem in grow house six. Syd telephoned, tells me they've found the Rot.'

'Oh.' Perfect. 'But we need to go up the mountain today.'

'Eh? Why?'

'The Subsolumer?'

'Oh. Can't it wait? We *need* to get over to grow house six.'

Quinton checked his pocket watch. 'You go. I'll meet you there, I need to check over my Flower.' And try to take what *Zed* there is to take.

Billick opened his mouth but quickly shut it.

Quinton inhaled the warm, earthy, air, and looked down from the suspended metal pathway that ran the interior perimeter of grow house six. His two most trusted harvesters were at the base of a vertical rack, carefully picking out rotten and black mushrooms from their growth media. The Black Rot had eaten two other racks in the house and, had Syd not caught it, would have eaten the rest of this rack.

The sight of the ugly rotten mess shunted his heart into his mouth. Not much longer and it'll consume everything. Every mushroom, coffee plant, tobacco tree. And then what?

Billick hopped up onto the railings and pointed downwards at the racks. 'It's getting worse,' he said. The botanist's narrow, string o' pearls pupils glistened under the Sunlamps. 'It doesn't make any sense. Where's it coming from? I've heard *nothing* in the Blue-Headed Goat. There ain't a rumble. Seems like it's only us. We can't keep it hidden for much longer. We're going to have to start experimenting. Otherwise, Cap'n, it'll eat everything.'

Even my Flower's got it.

The planet is fighting to keep you here, Quinton. It wants you to dissolve into a puddle of slime.

And I won't let it.

But the death knell was sounding, a chime he never thought he would hear.

An infected mushroom exploded down the chest of Dobromir. Syd ran off, quickly returning with a hosepipe.

'Don't hose him down, Syd!' Billick yelled. 'You'll spray

126

particles everywhere. Use the rags and dilute some bleach!'
Billick's pencil thin arms waved about like he'd lost control of
them. His green, scaly skin flushed red, and his fangs threatened
to come out. It took him a few moments to steady himself. He
looked up slowly at Quinton. 'We need this contained. What you
playing at, Cap'n?'

'I've been busy.'

'You've been busy?' He twisted his whole body back and forth,
as if to shake his head. 'I've been running around all the grow
houses, checking on the production house, snipping strawberries!
Where have you been?' His slitted nostrils flared. 'Prancing about
with your glowing flower, that's where.'

The stifling grow house heat had stuck Quinton's clothes to his
skin. On those bitterly cold winter days, when all it did was snow,
and all there was to feel was the cold seeping ever deeper into his
bones, Quinton liked to walk the warm and humid grow houses,
where the heat squeezed the cold from him and restored all his lost
warmth. But under an assault from Billick, all he could do was
sweat and twitch.

Quinton pulled out his pocket watch, opened it up, and stared at
the time, though he couldn't focus enough to read the hands.
Inside the lid of the pocket watch, the photograph of his mother
stared at him. She would never be in this mess. It's unique to me.
I've got careless in my old age.

Billick slapped the metal walkway railing and twanged out a
note.

'Ahay! Matey! Are you listening? I don't ask too many
questions, but this is getting impossible. You put the kibosh on

127

my experiments, then you drag the Rot in the nursery anyway! What's that Flower worth all this for?'

Quinton snapped the watch shut, said, 'We've got to go,' and charged off towards the door.

I can't keep hiding.

You'll tell him your secrets, Quinton? Sophia whispered to him. *Tell him New Havilah's secret?*

I've already shown him it. It's time I told him everything—told another everything.

'We're not even halfway done!' Billick said, padding after him.

'Syd and Dobromir can take care of the rest.'

'What are we doing?' Billick said.

'You two,' Quinton shouted over the railing. Syd and Dobromir looked up at him, wiping each other down with bleach-soaked rags. They both had sets of eyes that sat on top of crowns of exposed bone. It always gave Quinton the shivers when they stared at him together. He wanted to ask if their bones were cold. 'Make a sweep through the rest of the houses. You're on your own.' Then to Billick he said, 'We're going up the Mountain to meet our Subsolumer, Mister Ken Wu.'

γ

'Good morning, New Havilah! This is New Havilah Wireless Radio, the friend you just can't say no to. We've got deep cuts of pre-boom jazz for you this morning, but first the news.

'A Gamma Valley moss farmer was killed and eaten by a roach yesterday—we can only hope in that order. Keep your guns loaded and your wits about you.

'Chaos erupted at the Subsolum Stjörnu Farartæki—am I pronouncing that right?—play last night when a group of Pipeworkers charged the stage, chanting "oust oust oust". Subsolum has denied it taking place. Ain't that curious?

'The Summer Solstice Celebration is right around the corner. Have you got your red threads?

'Now let's have some music. How about a dance?'

Pre-boom jazz drifted through the tram cabin. Quinton tapped his fingers, watched snow-covered buildings, market stalls, and coat-wrapped New Havilians go by. Children, off from school for the Solstice, were out tying red lanterns to street lamps and shop awnings. The smell of mushroom bread made him realise he hadn't eaten today. The clatter of the tram kept him in the world, kept him from screaming. All this as Billick's stare bored through the back of his skull.

Where do I even start? Quinton ran his hands through his long, snow sprinkled hair, twisted it into knots. 'Bill,' he said, and glanced around the tram. Besides the driver and the conductor, who were both seated at the front, the tram was empty. 'I need to explain a few things.' A thumping in his chest rose and did not let up; by degrees it continued to rise, and he thought it might burst him apart. 'Bill...'

Billick, sitting across the aisle, stared patiently, a finger holding his place in his book on teak trees. The rattle of the tram made it hard to speak. They both bobbed up and down. Quinton thought briefly of Darleaner, wondering what parts, if any, she had made for this tram.

He swallowed in a dry throat. Billick shuffled nearer. 'The Flower...' he said, almost tasting the word, bitter and metallic, so much like blood, '... it's ...' But he couldn't.

No, you can't, Sophia said.

Then what do I tell him?

Lie, Quinton. You're so good at it.

Billick, biting a long fingernail, seethed in an anger about ready to boil over, held back by sheer discipline. After a few mushroom beers, Quinton knew all too well, the botanist would lose his resolve and let forth an endless barrage.

The tram clattered on.

'Do you remember,' Quinton said, shoving Sophia from his mind, 'the day your parents let me bring you to New Havilah?'

Billick put his book down, shuffled closer along his seat. 'You don't forget days like that.'

'Your Gamma Valley burns were bad.'

Recalling it now, it reminded Quinton of the boy and his father, who he'd refused to help in the surgery. A parent's desperation to do right by their child captured everything that he loved about humanity. It was both selfless and selfish. An evolutionary mechanism, but one that came bundled with compassion and love. One he'd been swayed by only once.

'Weeping scales, crusted over eyes,' Billick said. 'You don't forget it.'

Billick's parents, both moss farmers who had lived far out of the city, on the border between Gamma Valley and Radon Ravine, were old friends. They had been supplying Quinton with organic matter for his growing operations for many decades. The work in

130

the valley was tough and long and required a specific anatomy. At birth, Billick was not much bigger than Quinton's palm. It took him ten years to develop the leg strength to walk and it was twelve before he could climb stairs or pull himself into the moss harvester cab.

He would never be a farmer.

'I remember showing you my moss collection,' Billick said. 'And my baby roach farm.'

'It impressed me. You had—have—the gift. But you were sick. Never even taken Waters.'

The New Havilian townscape glided by as the tram hissed and clattered down the line. The mountain grew larger in the windshield.

'I didn't know what it was. Waters. It was town-folk talk.'

'I brought you back, showed you around the nursery.'

'It was all coffee and chocolate and tobacco back then, no mushrooms or mint!'

'All your doing, those last two,' he said, smiling. And he'll never let me forget it. 'After I showed you everything, we went into my office. Your burns were itching.'

'Aye, I remember.' Billick, sensing something, a taste of truth, drew nearer still.

'I gave you a drink.'

'Yes.'

'And the very next day?'

'My burns,' he said, 'they were gone.'

Quinton drew long and hard on his pipe, exhaled a grey cloud, closed his eyes. 'That drink, it healed you. That drink was

131

Liphoric Zed, Bill.' He opened his eyes. 'It comes from the Flower.'

After checking and rechecking that the driver and conductor were unaware, Billick narrowed his eyes, and said, 'This ain't a lie?'

'Bill, I am the Immortal Man *because* of the Flower. And when I saw you in your room, showing me all your mosses, knowing you'd never be a farmer, that you'd most likely die in the Valley, I knew I needed to save you.'

Dumbfounded. Speechless. Lost.

'It's a lot to hear,' Quinton said. 'I've kept this from you for good reason.'

'*Good* reason?'

Quinton hunched forwards, whispered, 'Imagine if everyone *really* knew, if I played favourites like that all the time? The myths would be *truths* and I would be set upon.'

'So you keep it all for yourself?'

'Of course not.'

As the last sentence came, the tram cruised past the Sun Church, where in a few days everyone in New Havilah will take Waters. Where I'll do my miracle and stop the mutations from ripping them apart.

'We're sick, us New Havilians, and no one knows it.' Quinton said, nodding at the Sun Church. 'I give what's necessary at Waters, Bill. That Flower is our lifeline.'

'We're *sick*?'

The tram's brakes hissed as it slowed at the mountain tram stop. Quinton rose to get off before the gaggle of perlite miners got on.

'There's a lot you don't know, Bill. But I think that's enough for now.'

γ

They waited at the mountain tram stop. They were scheduled for the two-thirty roach hunter tram and would meet the Subsolumer Ken Wu at the Subsolum entrance, right at the top of the mountain, for four. As they waited for the tram to come back down from the mountain, they both stared up and marvelled at the sheer scale of the snow-covered, bulbous monster. Quinton tried to imagine the Subsolum network buried deeply inside it—where they slept, where they ate, where they tended to their underground fields. All of this buried under so much rock.

A steam hydrant hissed as the moustachioed Kani—the best roach meat vendor in town—jacked his cart into it. He tightened the seal with his claw hands, and then set about steaming the first batch of roach meat skewers, just in time for the droves of first shift perlite miners trundling back from the mines for their lunch.

Quinton watched the miners and wondered what would happen to them when they didn't have enough food to eat, when the Flower succumbed to Rot, and the Rot spread through everything. They'll steal and then they'll kill.

The miners bought their skewers and ate happily at the side of the road. Street performers playing steel drums, bored Maskirovka traders looking to gamble, and Sun priests hoping to proselytise, all seeped from the back-alleys of the road and started their day's work on the miners. Harassing, haggling, and bartering.

The mountain tram arrived, bringing with it the smells of roach blood and juices, of gunpowder and sweat. Much like the miners who had walked down, these roach hunters hobbled out from the tram, their faces elsewhere and vacant. Five hunters carried a single roach hide, the monster's foot long mandibles still slick and slimy, its fat body segments pocked by shotgun blast.

Billick elbowed Quinton and said, 'All this roach meat is making me hungry. What about skewers when we get back down? The Subsolumer won't know what sunk him.'

Quinton, who would normally never hesitate when it came to roach meat, found that he had no appetite. But it wasn't the dead roach that had done it: Billick knows. He knows my secret. And maybe that's not so bad. Am I vulnerable and violated? Or free and unburdened? Has all this secrecy served a purpose, or just left me bitter and lonely?

Lonely? Sophia said.

When I am back, he told her, we will have words.

The roach hunters who did not carry meat, carried traps, buckets of unfired ammunition, guns.

And they'll be alright, if the Rot eats all the crops. They'll have their roach meat. But what then? When the barrel borers all starve? Or the cartridge packers and the weavers who made their nets, what then, when they all starve?

He needed to get out of his head.

The last of the roach hunters disembarked and the tram conductor gestured at the growing line of second-shift hunters (plus Quinton and Billick) to begin boarding.

134

The moment the tram left off up the mountain, Billick began singing his sea shanties:

> *'Oh, what do we do with a drunken sailor?*
> *Throw 'em out the long boat or make 'im bail 'er!'*

Quinton furiously shook his head and tried to hide himself in his coat collar. He'll get us killed! These types aren't the ones to sing! But Billick leapt up and stood on his seat (at the front of the tram) and looked back towards the grim-faced roach hunters. He sang on,

> *'Oh, what do we do with a drunken sailor?*
> *March 'im up the mountain like a Maskirovka trader!'*

The roach hunters cheered. He's never going to shut up now.

> *'Oh, what do we do with a drunken sailor?*
> *What do we do with a drunken sailor,*
> *Eer'lie in the morning!'*

Just when Quinton thought it couldn't get any worse, one of the roach hunters pulled out a fiddle and bow and began playing along to Billick's singing. Soon the entire tram was bellowing Drunken Sailor—all to Billick's conducting.

Quinton, reluctantly, with nowhere else to go, retreated back to his thoughts. Billick knows most of the story, and I need to accept it, despite Sophia's disapproval, and simply move forwards, but what traps lie ahead?

It seemed like more than a coincidence that as he moved the Flower to his nursery, Lady Jupiter found a way to move a Subsolumer there too. But he couldn't see what Lady Jupiter was after—other than his blood. He thought back to the argument she and Ganymede had had at the Sun Church. It was more than a marital spat. Ganymede was suspicious of her, wants to spy on her. Vials of his blood, too. She isn't even testing them! There wasn't much use for it other than for giving his heart something to pump. Who would need two vials of his blood? Maybe it's nothing more than an item of intrigue, a knick-knack. But Ganymede had said they'd stopped testing his blood years ago. Whatever it was being used for, it had been that way for a while.

He let the threads go. Even as Billick and his chorus of roach hunters sang their songs, he found enough peace to drift off to sleep.

He dreamt of his mother, of strawberries, of bombs exploding in the sky.

The tram shuddered to a stop. A jolt to the head woke him. Wind howled behind the metal blinders thrown down to keep out the cold. He checked his pocket watch and saw that they had been journeying for hours. This must be the top. The roach hunters were restless: they shoved shells into shotguns, withdrew blades from sheaths, unfurled tarps and nets.

'Alright,' the tram conductor said, 'this tram leaves in fifteen minutes. Last tram back down the mountain today is the ten o'clock. If you aren't there, you're freezing.' He jerked the door release and the door hissed open on pneumatics. The wind howled and snow started settling in the tram. 'Get outta here!'

The roach hunters piled out, each nodding to Billick on their way, until only Quinton and Billick were left.

'Did you really have to sing?' Quinton asked. 'Why do you always have to sing.'

Billick pulled his coat hood over the top of him and said, 'You always have to sing.'

They jumped out into the blizzard. Wind whipped their coats and scarves and froze the blood in their faces. Billick clambered up onto Quinton's back, his short legs no match for the deep snow.

'I haven't seen a blizzard this bad since we were caught out in the moss farms all those years ago,' Quinton said. Each word came out with a puff of white breath.

'Aye, Cap'n,' Billick said. 'It be a blizzard's blizzard.'

Quinton plodded along the barely recognizable path, until a bright yellow figure raised a rifle at him.

'Stop! Don't take another step closer. We're closed to trading during a blizzard.'

Behind the Subsolumer was a concrete building and a pair of heavy, radiation-proof doors, the only way into and out of Subsolum. A rusty sign read:

VELKOMIN Í SUBSOLUM

'That's great,' Quinton said. 'We aren't here to trade. We're here to pick up a Subsolumer.'

The rad-suit wearing guard, white breath pouring from his gas mask filters, lowered his rife. 'You're part of Lady Jupiter's entourage?' he shouted.

Quinton nodded his head. Entourage!? he wanted to yell back. I'm no part of that!

The guard started to turn, but then quickly raised his rifle again. 'I only see one.'

Billick climbed up Quinton's back—the man was so light he could hardly feel it—and poked out.

'*Helvíti*!' the guard said. 'You brought a kid up here!?'

'Where is our man?' Quinton shouted over the wind. 'We don't have time for this.' The tram was leaving in fifteen minutes and they'd already blown through five.

Apprehensive, the guard said, 'One minute.'

'Blaggards, these dirt-divers, the lot of them. They don't have urgency, Cap'n.'

The Subsolumer walked back to the doors, pressed a button that opened them, and then disappeared inside. About thirty seconds later, another figure joined him. He walked with his face to the sky, swaying, going forward on uncertain steps.

'Blow me down!' Billick said. 'He's scared of the sky! The bloody landlubber ain't got his sea legs!'

Ken Wu, apparently, had never left the rocky warren before. He kept trying to bring his head down, but it would spring back up again. Quinton approached cautiously, doing his best to keep Billick hidden behind his back. If he had never left Subsolum before, chances were he'd never seen a New Havilian in the flesh—and the Subsolumers weren't known for their quick understanding.

Close now, the guard gave Quinton a thorough looking over, and concluded, 'You have to be the Immortal Man, up here without a rad suit on! You know how much radiation you're taking right now?' But Quinton ignored him. He was trying to make sense of what he saw through Ken Wu's mask.

'I don't mean to be rude,' he shouted at Ken Wu over a sudden gust of wind and snow, 'but you look awfully like a lady.'

PART TWO

"When you tire of living, change itself seems evil, does it not? for then any change at all disturbs the deathlike peace of the life-weary."

— *A Canticle for Leibowitz*, Walter M. Miller Jr.

WELCOME TO NEW HAVILAH

'...but you look awfully like a lady,' the long haired man said to her. At least that's what she thought he said. The wind wouldn't let her hear much more beyond her own breathing, her feet kept sinking into the snow, and she was fairly sure she was about to throw up in her mask too. Why did I look up? But who wouldn't look up? After twenty-three years underground, never once going up to the surface, anyone would start to wonder about the sky.

She put her hands on her knees and leant forwards, breathing steadily for the first time since she had stepped outside.

The entrance guard put an arm around her shoulders. 'It's alright,' he shouted at her over the wind. 'You'll get used to it. Try to keep your eyes on the ground and breathe deep breaths, at least three seconds in and out. If you feel yourself panicking, try and think happy thoughts.' He slapped her on her rucksack. 'Good luck.' And he strolled back to his post at the doors.

Happy thoughts? Her home was starving and its fields were failing. There were no happy thoughts to be had.

She got herself upright.

Faintly, so faintly it might have merely been an illusion, the horizon line revealed itself through the blizzard. That's the ocean. She cursed the blizzard—the first step on her journey in that complicated relationship humans have with weather.

The long haired man—the Immortal Man, Mister—*Gospodin*—al-Zoubi—seemed to be in full conversation with himself. Tiffany isn't right. They aren't all crazy up here.

'We don't have a choice. We can't leave her up here, Bill.'

Al-Zoubi had his back to her, and was apparently debating leaving her behind, but she couldn't figure out why. She managed a few shaky steps towards him, reached up to tap him on the back, when he stepped to one side to reveal a green, scaly man, who was as round as a ball and about as tall as her shins. He smiled at her. He had fangs and long spindly arms. His coat had epaulettes on it, much like the Army General from the *Stjörnu Farartæki*. But over his heart (she assumed that that was where his heart was), stitched into the coat, was a skull and crossbones insignia.

I hope these two aren't imposters—aren't pirates.

'Ahoy,' he said, clambering up al-Zoubi, 'do you enjoy dallying or shall we get to our ship?' He clung to al-Zoubi's back. 'Snow's too deep for me, lass!'

They set off at a pace, and she did her best to follow. Whorls of snow twisted all around her, lifting powdery particles from the hard packed ice. If she kept her head low, and pretended that there were walls either side of her, the nausea subsided enough for her to walk.

Every now and then she heard a distinctive screech—so sharp it cut through the rumble of the wind. What is that? She wanted to ask her two guides—or kidnappers, she wasn't sure yet—but even thinking about looking up and raising her voice made her sick.

Further down the mountain, they came to a huge boulder claimed by thick and dense hempmoss fibres. Hempmoss, cottonmoss, and a few rag weeds were all that could grow on the surface. She had seen the occasional bundle hauled into Subsolum by traders, but had never seen it growing in the wild.

She stopped at the foot of the boulder—it towered about eight feet over her—and fingered the strong fibres. Tiny hairs covered each fibre, and as she ran her fingers down the length of it, the hairs stuck themselves to her fingers. But it wasn't resinous. It's looking for warmth—a thermotropism, she figured. And even through my gloves it senses my warmth.

She went to lift off her mask, the thick lenses making it hard to see anything in detail, but then remembered where she was. *Fokk.* She let go of the fibre, a few hairs breaking off, and turned back towards the path.

The two New Havilians were gone.

Whiteness filled her vision. Searching the ground, she saw no footprints. She wasn't even sure that what she was searching was the ground. Her palms turned slick and sweaty inside her gloves. Saliva began filling her mouth in anticipation of vomiting. She dropped to her knees and took two great fistfuls of snow. Ground, that's the ground. She couldn't bring herself to look up. It's all white. There is nothing but white. They had left her. Rushed off to let her die. She started to wonder if maybe this was her father's doing? Maybe he wanted to get rid of her. He wouldn't do this to me. He wants that flower.

A piercing screech forced her to cover her ears. Snow rained down on her as a brown blob burst up from underneath the surface. It scuttled past her, only to dive back under again. *Helvíti!* Was that a roach? The tale she had told Ken, she didn't really believe herself. It was the Maskirovkas telling stories. She tried to get to her feet but was overcome by nausea. She was on her arse, her legs stretched out, supporting herself on her arms. Right between her legs, the roach burst up from the snow again; it screeched and splattered spit and mucus over her mask. Her scream drowned out its screech.

The foot-long roach suddenly stopped its screams. It stopped moving altogether. Driven through its segmented abdomen was a metal fence pole. She followed the pole up until she saw the hand that gripped it. No gloves. It was the Immortal Man, his long white hair blown about by the wind.

'Try not to get lost,' he said, and yanked the pole from the roach. 'And, oh, welcome to New Havilah.'

γ

The tin-metal electric tram rattled down its tracks.

Al-Zoubi and Bill sat across the aisle, glaring at her, not saying a word, steadily swaying as the tram rode round gentle corners on its descent down the mountain.

Her mask rumbled as she breathed. She didn't dare to take it off—especially since that roach had squirted its mucus all over her. The mask kept her safe, like a shield to this new world.

The roach carcass leaked its juices over al-Zoubi's lap. The evil and alien creature, pulled straight from a nightmare, brought into the world only to terrorise. Its screech echoed in her head, punctuated every now and then by the *splunk* of the metal fence pole driven through its flesh by al-Zoubi. In the time it had taken her to walk from the Subsolum entrance to the tram stop, thirty metres or so, she had got herself distracted, become lost and snow-blind, and then narrowly avoided being eaten alive by a baby roach. When her father had warned her of the dangers on the surface and when she had tormented Ken Wu with Maskirovka stories, the realisation that any of it was real, that anyone had actually suffered under those horrors, completely escaped her. But now, like some long, slow-burning fuse finally reaching its stick of dynamite, she understood that it was all real, that there was a world above her world, and that she did not belong to it.

Her head dropped. *He's right about me. I am just his little girl.*

'I can't imagine,' al-Zoubi said, 'what Lady Jupiter would do to us if we brought you back as a body, or if we never brought you back at all.' A long lapse of silence, and then he said: 'I'm sorry, that wasn't part of our plan. I should have kept my eye on you. But, you see, we were rushing because the tram was leaving. These tram drivers are more punctual than clocks.' He laughed nervously. 'I hope we can start over.'

'It's my fault,' she said. 'I was staring at the hempmoss.'

Bill stood up on his seat, gripping the backrest. 'The moss is pretty,' he said. 'It gets lonely up there, not a lot going on. No surprise it caught your eye.'

The tram rattled onwards.

'Lonely?' she said. 'It's a plant.' *I hope these two aren't insane—haven't had their heads fried by the radiation. Helvíti, I'm sounding like Dad already.*

Bill jumped across the aisle and into the seat in front of hers. His pupils were like five tiny black glass beads strung on a thread.

'Plants get lonely, sad, afraid, happy. They feel everything, lassy.'

'Bill, come on, don't annoy her—she's just been attacked by a roach.'

She wondered if this was New Havilian hazing. Or maybe they were trying to scare her off.

'You hear the plants cry when they aren't right. Their cries tell you what they need. You must have heard that hempmoss cry, otherwise you wouldn't have stopped.'

'Bill, you're going to have her rushing off up the next tram!' He reached to grab Bill's hood, the baby roach on his lap flopping about lifelessly. 'Sorry,' he said to her, 'he's not the most personable.'

'Ahhh!' Bill yelled. 'I ain't your pet, bucko!' He freed himself from al-Zoubi's grip and moved a few seats further away. After he'd found his breath, he went on again, 'She knew that hempmoss wanted warmth.'

'It's freezing up here,' she said, 'everything wants warmth.'

'But you felt it, eh? Deep inside yourself you heard its siren call.'

'Bill, that's enough,' al-Zoubi said. 'As much fun as it is, there are more pressing issues.' A penetrating stare came her way.

She stiffened, adjusted her mask, and thought how much she must look like her father, adjusting his glasses over and over. There was no plan for this, she thought sourly, so be honest.

'You aren't Ken Wu,' he said to her.

'No.'

The wind howled outside the tram. Metal blinders pulled down over the windows clattered and threatened to break themselves open.

Her father had told her very little. How was she going to explain away why she wasn't Ken?

'What do we call you?' al-Zoubi said.

'It's Katherine,' she said. 'Katherine Marston.'

Al-Zoubi's mouth fell open and did not close. She realised what she had done the moment the words slipped out: Yes! That's me! Subsolum's very own presidential daughter.

'Any relation to Daniel Marston?'

He knows. She eyed the dead roach. He's really asking if I'm the type to try and lie. 'He's my father.'

Al-Zoubi blanched. His head dropped and he swayed as if a bomb had just gone off. After staring at his feet, he straightened back up, and swept back his long hair to brush out the flecks of snow. 'I didn't know he had a daughter.'

The tram brakes hissed, and all inside tilted forwards.

Al-Zoubi shuffled nearer to her. More snow fell away from him and his tatty coat. He moved the dead baby roach to one side and shoved a hand into a pocket and brought out a wooden pipe. Wood! That's at least a hundred years old. A sharp, tangy scent caught her by surprise, and turned her stomach over. Al-Zoubi had opened a small jar of tobacco and was stuffing it into his pipe.

She had never seen tobacco, let alone smoked it. Subsolum wouldn't allow it and its potential havoc on the air systems, but mostly what kept it out of Subsolum was its price. New Havilians would rather smoke it than sell it.

Lighting the end, he puffed out a cloud of dark blue smoke and then smacked his lips together. 'Last of this batch,' he said. 'Very good batch.'

She settled herself in her seat, peeking at Billick as she did. He was reading a book a few seats down, having lost interest with her a while ago. Her mask was beginning to irritate her. She had swallowed pills which would stop her bones from soaking up any radon that happened to get in her body, but it didn't lend her much confidence. The thought of becoming sick like her father beat out the thoughts of discomfort. The thought of dying like her mother killed whatever was left.

After a few more puffs of his pipe, al-Zoubi looked at her. 'And your mother?' he said carefully.

That was when she remembered her book, her mother's book. She grabbed her rucksack and unzipped it. 'My mother,' she said, 'died when I was young. She always had a soft spot for New Havilah.' She took the book out and handed it to him. 'This was hers, and I think before that, it was yours.'

Al-Zoubi, in a daze, as if she'd just slapped him across the face, held the book, hugged it, as if it were his child.

'You *are* its author?' she said.

Startled, he opened the book and flicked through its golden trim pages, saying, 'You've read all this?'

'More than once.'

'Then there shouldn't be much left for me to show you.' He shut the book, and she took it back. 'How did your mother die?'

'The radiation,' Katherine said. A little taken aback by the bluntness of his questions, but grateful to not have to answer questions on why she wasn't Ken. 'I don't know much. I just remember her being ill.'

The tram bounced on its suspension, the metal blinders rattling.

Her ears were aching too—they were going down.

'Did she ever say much about me?' The question carried such an innocence, it was as if a boy had uttered it.

'I don't think so,' she said. 'All I ever knew of you was the name on this book. But my mother made me promise I'd read it—that I would study it.'

I shouldn't be telling him this. What if Dad finds out? But after all these years it sure felt good to share one of her secrets, like she was somehow closer to her mother.

He smiled and smoked more of his pipe.

'Did you know her?' Katherine asked.

His eyes narrowed and his jaw clenched. Smoke bled from his nostrils like a Tunnel Spirit. He's deciding whether to lie to me.

Al-Zoubi knocked the ash from the pipe, pocketed it, and checked his pocket watch. There was a mouldy photograph of a woman inside the lid of the watch. He stared at it for a few moments, then snapped it shut. He twisted his knees to face the tram aisle, and then adjusted the baby roach so it lay neatly over his lap, drool dripping from its mandibles onto the metal floor. 'You must be hungry,' he said, looking up at her now. 'The rationing, you look half-starved.'

She hadn't thought much about it. About getting half her calories for months on months. But she had been dropping weight, everyone had. 'I am.'

'Oh, lassy,' Bill said, his arm slung over a headrest, 'then we have a treat for you.' He mimed eating a stick or a ... could it be a New Havilian skewer? Tummy rumbles: hunger, hunger. She didn't have to know everything, not right away: food could come first.

The electric tram screeched to a halt.

Katherine's heart thumped and rattled her chest, and she thought that maybe if she asked nicely the driver would take her back up the mountain. But before she could utter a word, al-Zoubi slung the roach over his shoulder, and threw open a metal blinder.

Daylight, or cloudlight, as the New Havilians called it, a uniform light, no flickering, no patchiness, no artificialness, poured into the tram like the novels said it would. Smells and sounds fizzled into her awareness. She heard voices, for the first time in her life, that had no trace of an echo. She smelt, even only faintly, smells she had no words for, smells that warmed your soul.

Al-Zoubi stared. 'Are you alright?' he asked. 'You must tell me if you're finding it difficult.'

She waved him aside and clambered over the seat of the tram, following her nose, and stuck her head out from the open window. Breathing as hard as she could, she still caught only faint scents. She grabbed her mask, went to pull it off, but hesitated.

A person made entirely of squishy pink ropes stood beyond her on the opposite tram platform. No legs or arms or anything like that. Like a big ball of hempmoss fibres. She blinked a few times, frozen stiff.

'Oi oi, Gospodin Rubber,' Bill yelled, by her side now, 'have ye seen thy Kraken?'

'Fuck you,' the man made of rope said—a mouth somewhere. 'I'll see you in the pub, Bill, got to pick up a few kilos of salt right

150

at the end of the Corridor.'

'Calamari is it?'

'Fuck you again!' He flicked a few appendages about, like meaty whips. 'My book, Bill, says you owe me.' Suckers reached out, and stuck to the ground, and then dragged him forwards. 'I'm laying on the opening fight,' he yelled. 'Two-Headed Hydra is three-to-one.'

'Here you are offering me threes on the Hydra when I'm already in your book!' Bill yelled. 'You no good, Dice Man.'

'Enough, Bill,' al-Zoubi said, and yanked his coat. 'We don't want to scare off our guest—' he held a weak smile, his cheeks dimpled, all tinted tan by her mask '—at least not yet.'

She laughed, tried to, but the respirator muffled it.

Juices ran down his front from the dead roach. 'Let's get on,' he said, 'you have a world to see.'

They trundled out of the tram and onto the platform. At least she was on concrete, she knew concrete. She didn't dare look up. Snow was already collecting on her shiny boots. Those flakes are falling from the sky! It's snowing. It's really *fokking* snowing! Her hands shook. Snow from the *fokking* sky! There were no walls here—nothing to reach out towards, no hand holds or cabling or rattling pipes. Eyes down, she focused on her steps, but her knees would not stop wobbling. Balance, Kath, you can do it.

A tremendous hiss to her right froze her in place. Oh *fokk*! A mist drifted past her, carrying a warm, spicy scent that even penetrated her mask. Across the way a steam-hydrant leaked vapour as a man worked open the valve with claws, claws that worked like a wrench. He looked like a Subsolumer except for the claws, right where his hands would go. Working at his cart now, he cranked a handle and rotated spits of meat. Skewers.

Bill had found his way from the tram platform and was running over, craftily avoiding the deep piles of snow.

'Insatiable,' al-Zoubi said. He took her hand. She tried to pull it free. 'It's alright,' he said, 'let me guide you. It'll take a few days before you're comfortable. I'll tell you about buildings.'

He'll tell me about buildings with a dead baby roach slung around his neck!? 'Buildings? I know buildings.'

'But have you felt them?' He took both her hands, and met her eyes. 'I want you to try and look a little higher. Go above the roach meat cart.'

Fingers twitching, legs a little shaky, she tilted her head upwards. Directly behind the claw man and his cart, great towering buildings stood tall and proud. Up and up her gaze went, and the buildings did not stop. Nothing like the novels. These were giant, they had large cut stones, the bottom stones bigger than the upper stones. Busks of New Havilians lined the stonework. These blocks were bigger than her! It was a style. A big, bold style. He was right. She hadn't felt buildings before. She knew the words, rusticated stone, roughed up at the bottom ten or so feet, then all the way to the top the stones became smoother, smaller, but she didn't know the feeling, the intimidation, the triumph of a monstrous building.

'Fine baroque architecture, this,' al-Zoubi said. He guided her line of sight with his finger. Ornate ledges, balustrades, and window frames. 'New Havilah was once a great city, it was known as a place of wisdom, filled to the brim with scientists, philosophers, artists, craftspeople, musicians, farmers and bakers and—it was a bohemia. The mountain, you see—' he gestured towards the mountain, she turned, and her entire being fell out of her body. She dropped to the ground like one of her potatoes, cracked a knee on the cold concrete.

'Hey, hey, hey.' Al-Zoubi crouched beside her. 'A shock, yes. But a good one! Take some deep breaths.'

It was like breathing when the air-recyclers were playing up. 'This *fokking* mask,' she said. Her mind held tight to the mountain, the shape and size, the outside of her home, and only let it go when the cold concrete and her sore knee became too much. That is home, huh, Kath? She fingered the mask straps, tried to worry it loose a touch. You've seen it now, seen it from the outside, so maybe we go back? Get a roof over our head again? She grunted, tried to get to her feet, then al-Zoubi looped an arm under her shoulder and lifted her.

'As I was saying,' he said, brushing snow from her, 'the mountain, your burrow, it acted as a shield against the waves and eddies of fallout—this part of the world isn't radiated.' He met her eyes, and even through the mask his stare penetrated. Inside his eyes she saw a life longly lived. A tired life.

When he stopped his staring, stopped looking into her eyes, she got her thoughts back, and said, 'Say whatever you want, but I won't take this mask off.'

'Oh, but you will,' he said, and let go of her shoulder. He smoothed down and neatened his long coat, and adjusted the dead baby roach so it hung over a single shoulder. 'You've been fed a dish of lies, Katherine.' He pointed at the rucksack. 'Did they give you a rad counter?'

Lies? I've been fed more than lies. 'Yes, I have a rad counter.'

'Why don't you test it out? What's that suit made from? It should stop heavy alpha particles, but betas and gammas, no, they'll rip right through it.'

'There's plenty of alpha activity out here,' she said.

'Prove it.'

She swung her backpack off and opened it up. The thick radiation suit had clumsy outsized gloves. It had kept her warm at the top of the mountain, but here, in New Havilah, she was starting to sweat. She found the rad-counter. It looked a lot like a seeding-gun, only it had a glass valve sticking up from the top. She snapped a switch on it and the gas inside the valve began to glow green.

'Oh,' al-Zoubi said, 'you've got yourself a valve counter. Subsolumers really do live underground!'

Ignore him. The counts are high outside the tunnels. You know this.

The rad-counter had no display, just three different audio clicks: a clip for alpha, a chirp for beta, and a tsk for gamma:

Chirp, tsk, tsk, tsk, clip, clip clip ... went the counter.

Plenty of alpha particles. She swung the device around. *Clip, clip clip* it went. Rads drenched the whole place.

'Worried?' al-Zoubi said.

'The moment I breathe the air here, I'm doomed,' she said.

Slipping something from a coat pocket, al-Zoubi smiled. 'If you trust your counter, that is.'

'What do you mean?' She raised the tubular device, the glass

154

valve glowing bright green. 'It's perfectly good.'

'If you're going to be my student,' he said, 'then you better get used to knowing the truth.' He handed her the device—a rad counter—he'd taken from his pocket. Much sleeker in design than hers and no glass valve on top. The little speaker attached to it was silent.

'It's on?'

'It is.'

'And,' she said, 'that's the speaker.'

'That's right.'

She brought it close to her ear. Nothing. She waved it around like she'd done with her's. Still nothing.

He's *fokking* with me.

There was no way the radiation was this low on the surface. You just needed to *look* at the New Havilians to know that. And how many Subsolumers had perished by going up to the surface?

She handed him back his rad counter, and stuffed hers back into her rucksack. She wasn't here to be a student. She was here to steal his flower.

As al-Zoubi took back his counter, 'Are you going to take it off?'

She shook her head.

'Even with those low counts?' he said.

'I'm not taking it off.' She worked the straps tighter. 'Your counter is clearly broken.'

He raised an eyebrow. Spit and drool and blood all over his coat, leaking from the baby roach. 'You sound sure.'

'I am,' she said.

'Let's go eat,' he said, patting the roach, 'you'll have to take off the mask then.'

γ

Claw Man sliced open the baby roach's belly. He dropped the guts into a metal bucket and clawed great hunks of muscle out from the carcass. Piercing the chunks on a metal skewer, he said, 'You know we don't have any spice left, Immortal Man?'

'I'm aware.'

'It'll be good, but not—' he knocked his two claws together, the sound hollow and ceramic. 'Ah, you don't need my doubts. Doubts lessen the food.'

'Aye,' Billick said.

Doubts lessen the food?

The Claw Man locked the skewer over the cart vent and worked the crank. He eyed Katherine, saying, 'Hey, you must be the Subsolumer, eh? "Wave a friendly hello!" the wireless tells me— Hello, there, Subsolumer, nice to meet you.' His slow, steady cadence reassured her, but the waving claw... *Helvíti*, Kath! You're better than this.

She cleared her throat. 'Hi,' she said, and quickly fell silent, caught off guard by a new smell, gripping her stomach. It set her nose tingling too. She looked over at Billick.

'That's mint, lassy,' he told her. 'When rendered well, the roach acid tastes of mint and turmeric. At least we're pretty sure it's turmeric.' He squeezed his head into his body, lifting his arms up in what looked like a shrug. 'We had a little mint, not long ago,

156

so we know what that tastes like.'

The cart hissed, a wisp of steam swirling into the air.

'We haven't ever been able to grow turmeric, though,' al-Zoubi said, sighing, staring off down the cobbled street. 'We go by the cooking book profiles left over from the Old World. And a few vague memories of mine. We're pretty sure it tastes like turmeric.'

Had she ever tasted turmeric? It wasn't a smell she knew. All she knew was the wheaty paste and mushroom tea that came in the ration packets. She'd long forgotten what bread, cabbage, onion, and carrot tasted like. To even see food being prepared came like a dull shock. The sheer amount of food revolving in front of her was almost too much to comprehend: I could take this back home and feed seven people.

There was so much meat on the skewer she had to grab the edge of the cart to keep herself upright. How many times had she finished eating her rations, only to still be hungry, and march down to her hydroponics room to begin the game of staring at her baby potatoes? She would stare and wonder if eating one would ruin her shot at selling her ideas to her father, all the while letting the hunger grow in her stomach like a tumour. Little did she know that, in the world above her world, there was Claw Man, cranking away at his handle steaming meats. What has gone so wrong?

The roach meat lazily revolved, steaming to tender perfection. You nearly killed me, she said to the meat, and smiled inside the mask. Tiff would be impressed— *Impressed that he saved you, Chick?*

'All I've got is some bark beetle powder,' the Claw Man said, whisking her from her thoughts, 'a fine garnish, don't get a man wrong, but its no—'

'Aye,' Billick said, 'we don't judge.' Then, with a nod to Katherine, added, 'Look at that skeletal frame, eh? She won't mind!'

Katherine's ration starved stomach rumbled. She couldn't muster the energy to snap back a retort. The journey had been long and had played on her enough.

Bill, standing on the steam-hydrant, licked his lips with his narrow, forked tongue. Eyes fixed on the meat. 'We're close now, lassy.'

The screech of the crank handle reminded Katherine of Subsolumer sliding doors. She wondered if her father was coughing right this moment. Or if he was necking gin. Or plotting how to— Stop it! You are up here now. You have a job to do.

'Here we are,' the Claw Man said, sprinkling powdered bark beetle and crunching chunky salt crystals onto the skin. He handed the skewer to al-Zoubi, who quickly handed it to Katherine, much to Bill's protest.

'Have the first one,' al-Zoubi told her. 'You'll be OK, taking off the mask.'

'I am not taking off my mask,' she said. The rad counters on her counter were right. Her father wouldn't do that, give her modified one, to hide and fake the real counts. Would he?

Holding the skewer, the smell infectious, the steam whipping off it like a fledgling Tunnel Spirit, she wondered if cancer was worth it.

'Katherine,' al-Zoubi said, 'I don't want to tell you the obvious, but—'

'I know.' She held the meaty delicacy up, turned it over, salt and fat dripping and running over her gloved hands.

'—but there's no way to actually eat that, without—'

'It's alright, lassy, take a bite!'

Biting her lip, gently at first, but then more firmly, she fought back a memory of her mother: covered in radiation burns, coughing and wheezing behind a leaded window.

My father's not a liar. Though she couldn't figure out what al-Zoubi had to gain by letting her get cancer. It made more sense that her father was the liar.

She gripped the mask, played a finger over the strap buckle. More fat dripped from the skewer. The expression on Claw Man's face read disappointment. Be a good guest, Kath, be an explorer.

She shook her head. 'I'm sorry. I can't take my mask off, at least not outside.' She held out the meat for Billick to take.

'You hear the calls of the hempmoss, eh? These lands, these lands they are on your side!' He thrusted the skewer back. 'Eat!'

The Claw Man knocked his claws together. 'Otherwise it'll catch a chill,' he said, 'and there's no refund on a cold skewer.'

The last pair of eyes to find her were al-Zoubi's. They softened her, almost by their tiredness alone.

You wanted to be up here. You wanted this. How many times have I caught Dad in a lie? He's got me lying right now. He doesn't want me learning hydroponics, he wants me stealing magic flowers.

She took a deep breath, the respirator rumbling, and snapped the buckle open. She pulled the mask off and dropped it into the pile of snow collected around the Claw Man's cart. Cold air kissed her—her forehead, her cheeks, her nape, and she gulped it down into her lungs, where it chilled her insides. The spicy, unfiltered scent of the meat tickled her nose and made her knees weak.

A real breath, she thought. If the radiation was going to get her, it was going to get her. She might as well enjoy herself. Tiff would be proud.

When she exhaled, her breath turned to mist right before her eyes—a ghost white. The *Fables* had many pages on ghosts, on the Tunnel Spirits: they haunt the collapsed tunnels, searching for a body to possess, but the body, pinned in the tunnel collapse, is stuck, so all the Spirits can do is make the dead eyes of the body glow a bright white.

Was her breath escaping her like a fed up Spirit? Was she—

'My goodness,' al-Zoubi said, his face as white as the blizzard. 'You look just like her.'

She let that comment go, at least until her stomach no longer hurt, and busied herself with the meat. Teeth sank in, fat juices jetted, meat melted.

After a few mouthfuls, she noticed al-Zoubi, Claw Man, and Bill smiling at her—grinning. Was she breaking some New Havilian custom? What is so *fokking* funny? Am I eating it wrong? *Helvíti*, when was the last time I ate meat? And who do I look like?

'You eat so fiercely,' the Claw Man said. 'Never seen a thing like it! Not even the perlite miners eat like you!' He set about cutting more meat, his sharp claws effortless in their endeavour.

'Like you've missed all your meals!' Bill said.

'It's the rationing,' she said. 'The last time I ate meat must have been—'

'Ohhh! Hello there! *Dobur den*!' A four armed lady waved frantically at them. Bright green hair, long and wound into bouncing curls, a tremendous bulk for a body, like a mountain rock. Katherine felt a little mean, eyeing her up like this. She met al-Zoubi's eyes and saw a hint of panic in them.

'Lady Jupiter: self-proclaimed Queen of New Havilah,' Bill whispered behind Katherine, before breaking into a cackle. 'Can't get enough of Captain Ganymede, and likes to think she runs a tight ship.'

Al-Zoubi held out his hand, only for Lady Jupiter to bat it to one side. 'Where is he?' she demanded.

'May I introduce—'

'I came over as soon as the tram arrived,' Lady Jupiter interrupted. 'The tram operator telephoned me, you see. What good is having a copperline if you don't use it? Even pedestrian things, such as being informed about a Subsolumer arrival, that is a marvellous use for a copperline, don't you think, Gospodin al-Zoubi? You might think about using one some time.'

The Claw Man paused his work to nod solemnly at Lady Jupiter.

'Well?' Lady Jupiter said. 'I shan't give you all day. Where is this Mister Ken Wu?'

Al-Zoubi rubbed his chin. 'They didn't tell you.'

'Tell me? Tell me what? I've been told everything. Everything, Gospodin al-Zoubi. Not even the smallest of roaches can skitter through these streets and remain unconscious to me.'

Behind Katherine's back, Bill sniggered.

Had no one told her? Why would her father do that? He has lost his mind. The thought came to her in Tiff's voice.

'Lady Jupiter,' al-Zoubi said, 'let me present to you Katherine Marston.' He stepped to one side and gestured at Katherine. 'She kindly agreed to step in when Mister Wu ... when he became unavailable.'

Lady Jupiter squinted, bashed al-Zoubi out the way, and grabbed Katherine's shoulders using her upper arms. 'You ... you ... you delightful person—a Subsolumer on the shores of New Havilah! Oh, you were tucked away there! I couldn't see you!' She embraced her, squeezing her tighter than the mask. 'And in this act of cooperation,' Lady Jupiter proclaimed, arms still wrapped around Katherine, New Havilians in the distance pausing and turning to see what was what, 'we mark a momentous shift! Subsolumers and New Havilians shall cooperate, shall feed themselves by the same process.' She pulled back from the embrace. 'And you have already taken the mask off, Misses Marston, *takk fyrir*!' she exclaimed. 'That's how you Subsolumers say it, yes? *Takk fyrir*!'

'Thank you very much,' Katherine said, translating.

'You are most welcome!' Lady Jupiter said, leaving Katherine a little confused. 'I look forward to seeing you in the al-Zoubi Plant Nursery, amongst our marvellous grow houses also. We have much to share.'

'We don't want to rush her,' al-Zoubi said, 'she has—'

'Aye!' Bill yelled, and snapped his fingers at Claw Man. 'I saw that nibble!'

'We can't rush her,' al-Zoubi said again. 'I'll take our guest to

162

her rooms, to get her settled in. Your black book tells me she is to stay above the Turbine Factory at marker fifty-two.'

'No, no, no! That was my intention for Mister Ken Wu. Had I known beforehand that President Marston would send his very own daughter, I would have prepared her rooms in the magnificent Hotel du Soleil. Yes, I think it pertinent that President Marston's daughter gets our most luxurious of offerings. And, what's grander, she'll be right next to you, Gospodin al-Zoubi.'

His eyes went down, head shaking ever so slightly.

'It would be a great honour,' Katherine said. 'I've come here to learn and—'

'And so you shall!' Lady Jupiter bellowed. Over on the tram platform, New Havilians jolted. So even they never get used to her yells. Lady Jupiter trampled back the way she came, proclaiming, 'So you shall! Now, I must telephone that two-headed Jed and tell him to give up the keys to the rooms next door. Copperlines, Gospodin al-Zoubi, aren't they marvellous!' and she disappeared down the cobbled street.

'Fuck me,' Bill said, 'talk about wind in your sails! She's as blowy as they come.' He hopped down from the steam-hydrant and rapped his knuckles on the cart. 'Come on, matey, I'm hungry.'

A ROACH IN HIS ROOMS

– NEW HAVILAH –

He ate his skewer as they walked back to the tram platform, the meat, as ever, incredible. Made tastier still by his having killed the bastard roach. Maybe he could be a roach hunter after all. When the Black Rot had eaten everything, all he needed was some pointy metal pole and a lot of will.

Katherine was the spitting image of her mother. She looks just like you, Sophia. Don't you have anything to say? All this time you had a child, a daughter, and I never knew.

How she managed to keep that to herself, he had no idea. They were—are—in love, and don't you share everything with your lover?

He grunted, lit his pipe.

The three of them reached the tram stop, waiting for the tram to take them to Hotel du Soleil. Another perturbation to this rather stressful endeavour. She'll be right under my nose.

A couple of perlite miners were sitting on a bench and staring at Katherine. They had metal lunchboxes and helmets at their feet, pickaxes were slanted against the bench. Katherine's bright yellow radiation suit, the emblem over her heart, those shiny black boots, and of course her completely mutation free body, she looked like she'd come from another planet, let alone a few hundred feet below ground. He worried that maybe the miners would say something. They had long horns, curled at either side of their heads, ready for butting. You don't belong here! he

164

imagined them shouting. But who really did?

'Can you tell me about the hempmoss?' Katherine said, pointing at Billick with her skewer, all the meat already devoured.

'The moss?' Billick wiped his nose. 'You start on a question,' he told her. 'Ask the plant, "How do you survive? What are your tricks?"'

Katherine crouched in a feet-flat squat, level to Billick. The squat indicative of a life working the fields. Without her mask on, Quinton could see her eyes grow and shrink—they were wide at the moment and he could see in them the fire, the passion. At least she has that, he thought, clamping the pipe tight in his lips.

It seemed only fit that, as the Flower caught the Rot, he, too, would catch a form of Rot: his black rotten past, leeching back into the present to help send him on his way to death, guided, no less, by the daughter of his lover. He smoked more, thinking how much Katherine was like her—even in her movements and mannerisms.

Billick was saying, '... of course they talk back. Are you daft? The plants are alive and communicate through pheromones— distress, nutrient deficiency, boredom, happiness, it's all squeezed out into the air. If you have the nose for it, you'll have the ears for it too.'

'Can anyone learn?' Katherine asked. She had rocked back on to her bum, sitting in a pile of snow. 'I don't know if I have the nose,' she said.

'I've seen the way those skewers caught you,' Billick said. 'You're teachable.'

The rails made their warbles as the tram arrived. The two

miners collected their belongings and made for the second carriage, offering only a few quick glances.

Quinton blew out a cloud of smoke, tapped out the ashes, and pocketed his pipe. 'Come on,' he said, 'our ride's here.'

As they rode through the town, he pointed out more buildings to Katherine. The New Havilian Library, the Sun Church, the turbine factories, the bark beetle farms. He told her their stories. He told her what they had been before the Bombs too: the government buildings, the centres for currency, nation-state embassies, the university.

Katherine never took her eyes from the townscape, from the people, and he never took his eyes from her. Why had Sophia never told him? Maybe this was the reason she never came back, the reason she broke her promise. She was living down there, being a mother, loving her daughter. All this time I've been forgotten.

I have never forgotten you, Quinton, Sophia whispered to him.

Billick had settled under a carriage light and was reading up on teak trees. It must have been his fifth or sixth go through the book and it was a wonder there was anything left in it for him to learn. No matter how many times Quinton had asked to see Billick's pet project, he had always been refused. By now, the tree would be at least five or six feet tall. Most likely the last tree on Earth.

Quinton smoked his pipe. The grey smoke puffs, rising and swirling, caught in the cones of carriage light. The conductor would kick off anyone else for smoking, but not the Immortal Man.

'There's so much red,' Katherine said. 'The decorations and the flags. And everyone is wearing red too.'

'It's almost Solstice,' he explained. 'The longest day in the year.'

Katherine sat back from the tram window, and looked at him now. 'In Subsolum a day is always the same length. I heard about the Solstice on the radio. The whole of New Havilah is stuffed into the Sun Church.'

'That's right,' Quinton said, 'we do it twice a year. Once in winter and once in summer. But the Summer Solstice is the special one. You'll need to get yourself something red to wear for it.'

'I'm allowed to go?'

'I don't see why not.'

They cleared the Corridor then, and grow house one streamed by, big in the window. 'Look,' he said, 'that's where we grow our mushrooms.'

'It's massive,' she said, 'the same size as a field.'

'And there's fifteen more just like it.'

'All filled with mushrooms?'

'We grow coffee, tobacco, and chocolate as well. We've recently harvested our first strawberry crop.'

She jolted in her seat. 'Strawberries? The fruit?'

He smiled. 'That's right. I hadn't eaten a strawberry in one hundred and fifty years.'

As soon as he'd said it, he knew he'd made a mistake. He wanted to wait for her to bring up his immortality, not heavy handedly bang right into it. Her mother would have told her a lot, he could afford to wait for Katherine to ask her own questions.

'I've never eaten a strawberry,' Katherine said.

'I'm sure there's something we can do about that.'

'No Subsolumer has.'

Relighting his pipe, he puffed away. The tram gently swayed as they rounded the last corner and started the short ascent up the hill to Hotel du Soleil. The blizzard at the top of the mountain hadn't followed them back. All that was in the sky tonight was the stratospheric dust.

'Next stop,' he said, 'so you can pull that cord.'

Katherine reached up, grabbed the tram cord, and tugged it. A bell rang from the driver's cabin, the driver unfurling a tentacle in acknowledgement.

'It's civilised up here,' she said. 'My father told me New Havilah was a wasteland.'

Quinton leant forwards, in the corner of his eye he saw Billick looking up over the top of his book, and he said to Katherine, 'I told you, your father's a liar.'

γ

Marble entrance way, bronze railings, walls lit by glowing orange lights, some damp and radiotrophic fungus flavouring the air: home. All he wanted was to peel off his shoes, sit deeply in his comfy chair, nibble on mushroom puffs, and smoke his pipe until he could really feel it in his head.

'Where is that elevator operator?' he said, and marched across Hotel du Soleil's lobby, to ring for the elevator.

Katherine, dallying behind him, said, 'This is your home? There's so much space.'

'This is the lobby,' Billick said.

The elevator call button glowed, but there was no mechanical whirring to convince him it was on its way. The brass dial above the doors read 10.

'My cube,' Katherine said, 'could fit in one of the corners.'

'You think you've got it bad?' Billick said. 'Sometimes I sleep in the nursery.'

At the mention of the nursery, Quinton flinched. There wasn't a chance he could let Katherine into it. The slowly forming plan was to keep her busy in one of the grow houses. At least until he and Billick could figure a way of treating the Flower. He couldn't let her see it. Once it was out of the nursery, there wasn't a reason not to show her his methods. The more she knew, the greater the chance Subsolum would adapt and change. Who really knew what they might achieve? But all he'd shown her mother seemed to have come to naught.

'Oh! Hello, sir,' Jed's first head said, as the elevator doors parted. 'We were having our supper.'

An ear piercing scream escaped Katherine, so loud both faces of Two Headed Jed winced. 'Blimey,' one head said. And then they both craned their necks either side to look around Quinton. 'Ah,' the second head said. 'It's the Subsolumer.'

'Sorry to give you a fright,' Jed's first head said to Katherine.

'Never seen two heads on one body before?' Jed's other head said.

Quinton faced Katherine: her hands shook and her eyes beamed. She looked about ready to bolt from the lobby and back up the mountain. He stared back over to Jed. 'You two have a room for her?'

'Lady Jupiter has informed us of Miss Marston's requirements over the copperline,' he said. 'Very happy to help in this noble mission.'

'Say hello,' Quinton said to Katherine. 'They're a lot friendlier than that baby roach.'

She stumbled forwards, holding a trembling hand out in front of her, her legs wobbly. 'I'm sorry,' she said, 'I've never s-se—'

'A two headed elevator operator before?'

'A twin headed building manager?'

'A dicephalus caretaker?'

'A doub—'

'That's quite enough,' Quinton said.

Katherine's chin quivered.

'One head for going up!'

'And the other for going down!'

'I said enough, you two.'

'Sorry, sir, you know we like an audience.'

The wind howled, heating pipes rattled, and the elevator suspension system droned and creaked: Anything, Hotel du Soleil thought, to keep away such an awkward and uncomfortable silence.

'N-no,' Katherine said. 'Never have I seen a two headed person before.'

After a few smiles, Jed finally grabbed her hand and gave it four strong up and down pumps. 'It's a pleasure, Miss Marston. Do you know you're the spitting image of your mother?'

'My mother?' She looked down, suddenly stricken.

'We were just a boy when she lived here. She was wonderful.'

170

Jed scratched a head. 'She used to give us roach jerky!'

Quinton said, 'That's enough, I don't want to dig up the past right this very moment. It's getting late and I have work to do in the morning. I'm very sorry you don't get enough jerky now, Jed.'

'My mother lived here? In this building?'

'Has she not told you all this?' Quinton said.

Katherine, unable to look him in the eyes, shook her head.

Another long and lingering pause. The more he fought this slow unravelling, pressed upon him by Lady Jupiter, the quicker it seemed to do just that: unravel. He had half a mind to go to the nursery now and tear up his Flower and get ahead of it all.

'Let's go to your rooms,' he said, and stepped into the elevator car.

Billick padded in. 'Come on,' he said, 'I want to see what a Subsolumer is given to live in. You know I can't afford to live here? This is fine accommodation.'

Katherine, still a bit shaky, and still vacant, stepped into the car. Sophia had been the same way, Quinton recalled. Her shock quickly turned to intense interest, into an insatiable curiosity. To his memory, the only Subsolumer who didn't bat an eyelid at their first sight of a New Havilian was Darleaner. She didn't bat an eyelid at much. And will be knocking at the nursery door demanding her chocolate any shining moment.

'On the telephone,' Jed said, 'Lady Jupiter warned us that a Subsolumer was coming, you see. So we've put on our tolerance caps.' Both heads tipped their caps at Katherine. 'Come on, Miss Marston,' they said in unison, 'let's show you to your rooms.'

171

The elevator car doors began to close.

γ

'Absolutely not,' Quinton said. 'Under no circumstances— In fact, pretend as if I don't live here.' Jed, the intolerable being that he was, had decided to give Katherine the set of rooms directly beneath Quinton's. Every stomp, door slam, floorboard creak, cough, sneeze, fart, and yell: heard by her. What was he to do when Sophia demanded he shout out to her? Would Katherine press an ear against the ceiling and snoop?

'But if we're together,' Katherine said, setting her rucksack down on a sofa embroidered in swirling golden patterns, 'then we can spend more time figuring out how to stop my home from starving.'

'No shared meals, no tea-time, no popping-overs, none of that. You live here and I live up there.'

'You're starting to sound like my father.'

Quinton paced back and forth: the floorboards going like a squeaky choir. He wasn't sure what bothered him more, Katherine living beneath him or knowing that she was Sophia's daughter.

'There're pots and pans and sundry kitchenware in the kitchen,' one of Jed's heads said. 'The bedroom—' he raised an arm towards a door—'has the finest bed and mattress.'

'Sheets,' the other head said, 'Miss Marston, so soft, you'll wonder if you are floating on the stratospheric dust itself!'

Putting a halt to his pacing, Quinton said, 'That should be all

172

for now, Jed.'

'Heat and water run fine,' the second head said.

'Sewage too!' the first head said.

Katherine walked over to the window. It wasn't big like Quinton's bay ones, but you could still see the Sun Church steeple and tower, the corner of the library.

'I like the view,' she said.

'Very good,' Jed's heads said. 'I better get back to the elevator, those levers don't work themselves. Call upon us if you need anything. Good evening.' He bowed and left.

'I can't believe it,' Katherine said, gazing out the window, 'I've a New Havilian home.'

'Yes, well, let's hope we can satisfy whatever it is you hope to achieve here and have you back on your way.'

'You have a plan?' she said. 'I've brought my optical transducers; they give you quantitative readings on nutrient contents.' She tested her weight on a floorboard. 'You use electronic circuitry, yes?'

Billick pattered around, whistling at an ancient wooden dining table. 'I could break that down into a fine vessel.'

Mould grew up in the corners of the walls, around the radiators, anywhere the geothermal heat was plumbed in. It leant the air a sweet scent.

'Circuitry?' Quinton said. 'No.'

'Then how do you know what your plants need?' Katherine asked, almost mockingly.

'By the colour of their leaves, or by their shape. Root structure and development. Sizes of buds and all the rest— and Billick.'

Billick pointed to a great patch of hempmoss growing above the cornicing. 'That moss is very happy.'

'You mean you don't have a single sensor?'

'No,' Quinton said. He ran his fingers through his beard. Sensors? What in Brightness is she talking about? 'Now,' Quinton said, making for the door, 'you have been collected from the mountain and housed. I have a lot of work to do in the morning.' He walked back over to the front door, gripped the handle. 'Good evening, Katherine.'

'Wait,' she said, 'we really don't have a plan?'

'For the moment I think it's wise you settle in first, get your rooms in order, then we can think about a "plan".' He yanked open the door, 'Bill,' he said, with a nod.

'Night, Katherine. Keep an ear open for roaches.'

They left Katherine and took the stairs down to the lobby.

His questions about her mother—about Sophia—could wait at least a night. Because I don't want to know? Because the Sophia I do know might be destroyed?

γ

Outside the lobby, underneath the door's awning where icicles were already forming from the day's snow melt, Quinton and Billick sat on a bench that looked right down the hill. A tram was rounding the corner, packed full of last shift perlite miners on their way home, all looking forward to a warm broth of mushroom soup seasoned by crushed bark beetles. The luckiest of the lot might have roach meat, and fewer still chocolate and tobacco for afters.

And he had enabled it all. Yes, the bark beetles and roach meat weren't directly his doing, but he kept those, whose doing the bark beetles and roaches were, very much alive.

Every other thought that flashed into his head was an image of the Flower: white petals curled, black and rotten, dripping apart like one of Lady Jupiter's paraffin candles. He couldn't shake it.

The dry mountain air had worked his lips sore and rough, and the relentless pipe smoking left his chest full of razor blades, but he still pulled out his pipe and thumbed a great nugget of tobacco into the pipe bowl. The lighter flame danced in his fist as he singed the tobacco delicately. 'For Brightness sake, Bill,' he said, 'all day my Flower's been in that nursery, rotting away, and she's had me up the mountain.'

'She seems alright,' Billick said.

'Lady Jupiter?'

'No, the Subsolumer.'

'We'll see.' A cloud of smoke escaped him. 'If she's anything like her mother, this isn't going to be easy.' Sophia saw right through him, knew the instant he was lying, or trying to stop her from getting close. But you worked your way into my soul, didn't you.

'Your magic flower's been on my mind too,' Billick said. 'If the Rot's only on that petal, we take that petal.'

Quinton shook his head. 'It's no good,' he said. 'It needs all ten petals, otherwise it won't produce the *Zed*.' Back before the Bombs had finished blasting everything, at the university, when he had hundreds of Flowers, he had shown that ten petals were the only possible combination. The variants with more than ten produced *Liphoric Zed*, but it was resinous, sticky, and lacked its liphoric property. Any less than ten petals, and the production ceased completely.

'She's a real hempen halter,' Billick said.

Quinton smiled, blew smoke through his nostrils. 'She be a spirit sent to beguile, to cast men adrift, to pick the riches from their soggy bones.'

The botanist nearly fell off his seat.

'Oh, don't look so surprised. I've read a few adventure novels in my time.' He tapped the ash from the pipe bowl. 'But don't ye dare tell a soul.'

'Aye, aye, Cap'n.' Billick hoisted himself up. 'Should have a few hours yet before the pubs close.' He faltered there, waited, a tiny fang peeking out from behind his upper lip. 'I don't suppose you want to get a drink? After today's voyage, a mushroom beer, maybe even beetle venom, that's how you close out.'

Quinton raised his pipe. 'You go.' The soft evening air, drifting through the gloomy orange streetlights, a faint hint of summer warmth in it, was all the companionship he sought tonight. 'I think I'll stay up a while and smoke.'

After a few paces, Billick stopped and turned around. 'We'll figure this, Quin. If we can grow strawberries, we can do whatever we want.' And he walked down the hill, expertly dodging the deep piles of snow.

Billick long gone, Quinton filled his pipe, and then fumbled about in his coat pocket for his watch. He carefully opened the lid and stared at the photograph. His mother stared back at him. She was still out there, rocketing back from Proxima Centauri, coming to rescue him like she had promised. Sophia's voice tried to get inside him, but he shut her out. He wanted to be alone with his mother, especially now that he knew Sophia had been lying to him all this time. Had he never learnt about relativity, he would have given up long ago, but he knew that his mother would be safe as long as she travelled at great speed. Much like him, she had a responsibility to humanity, and he knew that she didn't have a choice, she had to go with the Starships, she had to leave him behind. She trusted me to keep everyone left behind safe.

And I've done just that. It can't be over, can it?

HOME IS A FOREIGN LAND

– NEW HAVILAH –

T hrough the bedroom windows, where the hempmoss curtains hung soft and delicate, a blooming light poured in. Lying in the comfy New Havilian bed, her toes not even reaching the bottom, the light feathering her face, she held her eyes closed and tried to focus on the light's warmth.

Warmth falls from the sky here.

She fluffed up her pillow and rested herself back, folded the bottom of the duvet over and under her feet, and stretched out. It was these blissful few minutes, granted to her most days, that Katherine savoured more than anything else. For in these moments she wasn't Katherine. There was no Subsolum or New Havilah, no rations, no father, no Tiffany, and no Pipeworkers: all she knew was the comfort of her bed.

And this warm light.

But, like all good things, this comfort ended. She tried to fight it. She tossed and turned, brought the duvet high over her head, screamed into it. But soon came the inexorable return of her consciousness.

They're all starving and you're eating roach meat.

She squeezed the duvet until her fingers cracked.

You're sleeping in when you have a job to do. Find a flower. Steal a flower. Learn, learn, learn.

She flung the duvet off her. The cold air found her skin and she was quick to ball herself up. The radiator at the bottom of the bedroom rattled, so she guessed it was on and giving out heat, but her teeth still chattered.

All that's keeping the world out is that thin pane of glass.

Get up.

She set her bare feet on the cold floorboards. A draught ran from underneath the bedroom door and chilled her ankles. She unrolled a ball of socks, put them on.

The light above her, a big brass fixture like fingers dangling from a limp hand, gently swayed as a tram passed the building outside.

She unrolled her jumpsuit and put that on too, already warming up. The cloudlight pouring in from the window had grown even brighter. She found her jumper, put it on over her jumpsuit, and began the staring match against her radiation suit. It hung from the back of the bedroom door like a skin pulled off a corpse. Bright and yellow, the suit would single her out as the Subsolumer, everyone would know it. But I'll be protected.

From what, Chick? Tiffany said to her. From the non-existent rads the Immortal Man showed you?

Katherine took an arm of the suit, ran her hand down it. 'It could have been a trick.' How insane was this? Talking to an imaginary Tiffany. It was one thing hearing her voice, another completely to talk back.

You don't need it. The Immortal Man was right, your father is a liar.

'Shut up,' she said, dropping the rad suit arm. 'You aren't even here.' She had let al-Zoubi say it, let him trash her father's name, call him a liar because it was easier to keep her thoughts to herself, for now. But al-Zoubi didn't have a reason to lie to her, at least

179

not any reason she could see. Her father certainly did. All the stories he'd fed her about the irradiated Overworld, the godless monsters, the demons who'd abandoned hope and were never going to be rescued. He'd told those stories all her life, to control her. To explain her mother's death. Was that a lie too?

She sat back on the bed and pulled her legs to her chest. The radiation suit hung limply, and she half expected it to move on its own. She breathed. Another passing tram rumbled the building, shaking her softly, swaying the big light above. Whatever the case, she knew not to draw any attention to herself. Going around accusing people—people she barely knew—of being liars wasn't a great way to earn trust. She resolved to make an impression, earn a place. Al-Zoubi didn't want her, because, well, there was clearly more to her father's deal than she knew. Maybe al-Zoubi knew why she was really here. Maybe he knows I'm here to steal his flower. Or he at least suspects it.

She got up from the bed, pulled open the door, and left the rad suit behind: like the shed skin it was.

In the living room, sitting there, on the golden swirl embroidered sofa, was Lady Jupiter. Two robbed figures stood behind her, their faces painted blood red.

A scent caught Katherine, made her stomach grumble in hunger-throes.

'Hello,' Lady Jupiter said, sitting herself more up right, patting the empty space on the sofa. 'Oh, don't stand there and gawk. Sit yourself down. I can tell you're hungry. Are you picking the mould off the sweaty rock walls down there yet? I hear things have got rather brutal.'

All the questions that Katherine had—the whys, hows, and whens of this welcoming—fluttered through her, never to be asked, because all that she could think about was where that infectious, tantalising smell was coming from. It was unquestionably food.

Her nose twitched.

'Ah,' Lady Jupiter said, 'so I must lure you over, is that it?' She clapped her two upper hands: one of the robbed figures jolted, marched around the sofa, set a steaming bowl on the vacant sofa cushion, then promptly returned to behind the sofa. 'There now, that's right. That's for you.'

Katherine didn't need much more convincing, she walked the two short steps to the sofa. Two puffy looking balls floated in a brown broth. She scooped up the bowl, and sat, slurping away.

'Have you lost your voice?' Lady Jupiter said, flicking her bright green hair behind an ear.

'No,' Katherine said, 'I wasn't told about breakfast.'

'And I,' Lady Jupiter said, 'wasn't told that you would be replacing Mister Wu.'

'I don't know what happened with Ken,' she said. The gooey ball broke open in her mouth, bursting with flavours she'd long forgotten. The starving mothers and their children: their gaunt faces stared at her. Aren't you going to share? they said.

'Is that so?' She picked at the hem of her frilly skirt, then nodded at Katherine's soup bowl. 'I promised your father I would place a Subsolumer in Gospodin al-Zoubi's nursery. I didn't think it would be someone so ... so *close* to him.'

One of the red faced robed figures had rounded the sofa at Lady

Jupiter's nod. They stood before Katherine, their face littered by swimming eyes. Each one housing a reflection of Katherine, and her gawping mouth. The acolyte and all their swimming eyes bent down, seized Katherine's half eaten bowl of soup and dumplings, and returned to their station behind the sofa, a wisp of steam eddying behind them.

Katherine, her stomach gurgling, said, 'You're trying to get information I don't have.'

'I'm trying to have a conversation.'

'Ken Wu chose to work for the Pipeworkers. That's all.' Is that all, Kath? Tell her about your father's devotion to dead soil. His love for drinking gin and the Immortal Man's blood. Tell her why you're really here.

Lady Jupiter waved her hands at the robed figures. The one who stole her bowl handed it back, and then they both plodded out to the hall. Once the door was fully shut, she turned to Katherine and said, 'The Pipeworkers? Why would they not want Mister Wu to be sent up to New Havilah?'

Between mouthfuls of broth, Katherine said, 'The Pipeworkers and my father don't agree on how Subsolum should be run.'

'Like any good nation, there is disagreement at the top!' She rose from the sofa, and walked over to the big window. 'What are they in disagreement over?'

'The soil, I suppose.'

'And what do you think?' Lady Jupiter kept her stare out the window.

'I'm here, aren't I?'

'That's what I don't understand.' She faced Katherine. A long wet tongue slid from her mouth and patted her eyes. Once it slithered back inside, droplets of spittle falling and dancing in the air, she said, 'You're going to have to acclimate, my darling. You're shaking like a caged roach.'

Katherine's hands did tremble, but she thought she'd hid it. There was no hiding: she was in an alien world, filled by alien people.

'Your father, as I understand him, would never, ever, give up on the soil. Agronomists' tales of conquering it over the centuries even find their way up here.' Saliva gleamed on Lady Jupiter's lidless eyes. 'And it surprised me that he would send anyone, especially his daughter, to come and learn our ways.' She sat herself back down, brushing her skirt flat, those eyes meeting Katherine's, the stench of her spit on them, like rotten cabbage. 'Our ways forgo the soil, Misses Marston, they do away with it! Can you believe my shock when your father offered to send an agronomist to New Havilah? He had never sounded so desperate.'

The less she said, the better. There was a trap here, somewhere, and she didn't need to set it off. 'We are desperate.'

'Mhm, yes. You didn't think it was unusual, your father's betrayal of his devotion? It makes me wonder if there's something else he is after?'

The taste of those dumplings lingered in her mouth. Her stomach never stopped growling. 'The soil is failing,' she said. 'And my father knows it.'

'So what is it that the Pipeworkers disagree about?' Lady Jupiter lifted her top arms up. 'I'm trying to get it all clear.' She shook the raised left hand. 'Over here, we have your father: devoted to the soil.' She shook the right. 'And over here, we have the Pipeworkers.' The hands clapped together, startled Katherine.

'They think it should have happened sooner,' Katherine said. 'That's all.'

'And what finally convinced your father?'

'I did,' she said. 'I suppose.'

'Do you think he can keep the Pipeworkers under control?'

She thought for a moment, recalled her father snivelling and coughing up blood in his office, chased from the play by an angry mob, only to be saved by Einar. 'Yes,' she said, 'he's very good at keeping things under control.'

Lady Jupiter let a breath go. 'And what does he expect you to achieve?' she said.

'All he wants is for me to learn as much as I can.'

Lady Jupiter's hands clasped over her stomach. She stood, staring for a little while, perhaps wondering whether to say anymore, but then, as if shaken from a daydream, she said, 'I hope you enjoy your first full day. We all look forward to what you shall achieve.' And she left, thumping the door shut behind her.

Once the footsteps in the hallway had fallen silent, Katherine grabbed the empty bowl and licked it clean. She'd thought about breaking open the rations Ólafur had packed, but remembered where they went. The starving mothers and their children would haunt her for the rest of her life.

As she sat there on the sofa, the spotless bowl on her lap, hunger lingering, she wondered why Lady Jupiter was so concerned about the Pipeworkers. If they shut off the pipes, New Havilah will be powerless. Is that why she wanted all that paraffin? She must think that Pipeworkers are going to do it. Her father couldn't let that happen.

She slumped down on the sofa. It smelt of hempmoss: sweet, floral, delicate. Getting caught in these political spats gave her no thrill. It was complicated, but not complicated like a soil culture, or a poorly performing crop, or a fungal infection. These were complications of people playing silly, pointless games. Don't they see how close we are to extinction? If we could set aside our differences and simply work together, we could create a world worth living in, something to be proud of.

And where the *helvíti* was al-Zoubi? It must've been well past nine in the morning. He should be here.

In the kitchen, she put the licked clean bowl in the sink, admiring it as the first bit of New Havilian crockery she'd ever used. Quickly, back in the living room, she found her boots and gloves, donned them, and went out into the hallway to call the elevator.

The dial above the doors slid towards her floor. If she was going to get caught in the middle of all this politicking, she was certainly going to eke out whatever knowledge she could from al-Zoubi and Bill, learn what she didn't already know, then steal his flower. I'm as bad as Dad. Part of her wanted to be convinced to *not* take it. Convinced by the people here, convinced that her world had got things very wrong, and that she was better off living up here.

The doors parted. Two Headed Jed wore a black suit, a golden chain ran from his waistcoat and into his pocket. Both necks had blood red scarves tied around them, and the caps had what looked like metal sun rays, beaming out from their tops.

'Good morning, Misses Marston,' his first head said.

'Did you sleep well?' the other head said. 'We must admit, we didn't hear a peep out of you.'

'Not a complaint! You must be the Hotel's only guest to not take issue on their first night.'

Both heads leant towards her, and in a whisper they said: 'Most of New Havilah's wealthy are rather spoilt, you see.'

'Where is al-Zoubi?'

The two heads glanced at each other. Both throats struggled in their swallows. 'Have you checked his rooms?'

'Take me up there.'

Jed shook his heads. 'I can't do that.'

'No— It would violate the Hotel code of conduct.'

'Then why offer?'

'So as to not violate the Hotel code of conduct.'

'"Assistance must always be offered, but may not be rendered if said assistance violates the Hotel code of conduct,"' the other head said.

'You won't tell me where he is?'

'Let us fetch you breakfast, Misses Marston.'

'How's about Baking Sands bread wrapped in boiled hempmoss?'

'Or mushroom fra-tartar—' he leant forwards again to whisper '—it's a New Havilian delicacy, scrumptious.'

Her stomach growled and groaned but she would not be bought. 'They've brought me up here,' she said, 'so I can learn how they grow their food. Why are you two making it impossible for me to do that?'

Resettling their caps on their bald heads, Jed said, 'You've got to understand—'

'—it's not that we don't want to tell you where he is—'

'—because, really, we do. But—'

'—Gospodin al-Zoubi is one of our most … *cherished* Hotel guests.'

The hallway carpet, lush and bright red, all the brass and finery in the elevator car, the wood floors and doors, it led her into the belief that this Hotel du Soleil was a refuge from the unkind world, a place where she might make friends, relationships that would blossom as the two societies drew closer together, but behind all that opulence was nothing more than the same old *skítt* she found in Subsolum.

She stepped into the elevator car. 'Take me to the lobby,' she said.

'Yes, of course.' Jed wound the brass wheel, shutting the car doors, then worked the brass levers, sending the car in a descent. The bowels of the elevator droned and screeched, filling the silence between them. The golden sun rays, affixed to Jed's caps, caught in the interior lights of the elevator car. And all Katherine could imagine were her father's glasses, gleaming in the light of his desk lamp. I'm no little girl, not here. But she knew better, she knew to pick her battles. Both sets of Jed's mouths opened and closed as if to say something, to offer up a feeble excuse for the lack of al-Zoubi's presence, but she wouldn't hear it. He squeezed the car breaks, and they juddered to a halt; the metal cables above them, hidden from view, twanged.

The doors parted and she left off wordlessly. Two Headed Jed tipped his caps, closed the doors, and she was left alone in the lobby. Wind rattled the glass doors at the front. Snow had collected, piling up against the glass, working loose the memories from yesterday: the terror of the roach attack seized her and she took an involuntary gulp of air.

Her footsteps echoed along the hard marble floor.

She had spent the better part of her life trapped in a tunnel populated by plenty of people she struggled to get along with. Tuning them out had become, by painful degrees, a skill she had mastered. Gripping the lobby door handle, she tuned out Lady Jupiter and she tuned out Jed. If neither are going to help me, why worry about them. I'll do this all by myself. I'll find my way.

She pushed open the door, wind and snow chilling her, and took her first unaccompanied steps in this foreign land.

The snow covered slope, hemmed between great baroque buildings and sliced in two by the tram tracks, led all the way to the Corridor. At least that's what she remembered from last night. Blood red drapes hung loosely from many of the windows and ledges. Blazoned up high, near the top of a building, but underneath a statue of a many faced New Havilian, strobed an electric sign: **HAPPY SUMMER SOLSTICE!**

She nearly lost her footing on the icy path staring at it. They are freer, up here. My father would never let a sign like that go up in the tunnels.

Further down the slope, in a gap between the buildings, children played as their parents sat around on benches. Katherine crossed the tram tracks, headed towards them. It was about a twenty metre square gap, the footprint of a building that no longer was, and in

188

its centre stood a ramshackle structure that the children climbed on.

All this space.

The children wrestled: some strangled with tentacles, others butted horns, others slithered about: but all laughed, except for one, who sat alone, wrapped around a swing, feebly trying to get it to move faster. When the play fighting got too serious, one of the adults got up and settled the matter by separating everyone. The lonely child wheezed and coughed, slime ejecting from holes about his neck.

In all her staring, Katherine hadn't realised she'd reached the fence of the play area. A parent, whose eyes dangled from antennae a foot above their head, fixed her with a glare: the antennae stretched towards her. 'Can we help?' the parent called in a rough, hoarse voice. If she were going by body types, this was the parent of the child on the swing set.

Another sharp inhale. Katherine clasped her shaking hands behind her back. 'H-hello,' she said. 'I was admiring your children.'

What the *helvíti* was that, Kath? Admiring your children?

The parent laughed. 'That makes one of us!' The antennae holding his eyes up telescoped back to his forehead as he slithered towards her. 'You don't look like you're from around here.'

The other parents all stared in their various ways.

'No,' Katherine said, and swallowed dryly. 'I'm from Subsolum.'

'An Undergrounder? Brightness!' He stopped at the other side of the fence. An air of onion hung around him. Katherine breathed

189

it in, savoured the smell, remembering the onion soup her mother had made for her when she was a little girl. 'Ahhh,' the New Havilian said, 'I know who you are. The wireless told me. "Wave a friendly hello." You're here in exchange.' His lips were thin and long and seemed to wrap around the entirety of his face. His nostrils were silts which dilated as he breathed. He wore a loose fitting jacket, but there were no arms to go into the sleeves, and his legless bottom half was completely exposed. He laughed. 'I don't wave much,' he explained. 'But I suppose I can say hello.'

'Thank you,' she said. Behind him, the children still played, and the other parents had lost interest in her. 'You're aware of the trade deal?'

'I'm aware of what I need to be.'

'Do you know where I can find Quinton al-Zoubi?'

Those thin lips curled into a manic grin. 'The Immortal Man—' he spat a great lump on the snowy ground. 'That man thinks he's New Havilah's saviour, but none of us can find him when we want to. And if you do, he'll tell you to get lost. Don't waste your time on him.'

'And why would you want to find him?'

'You really aren't from around here, eh?'

The child on the swing shuddered, hacking up more slime, then shooting it all over the swing set. The other children chorused: 'Gross! Billy's thrown up again!' The father extended his antennae and looked behind without turning from Katherine.

'That's why we want to find him,' he said. 'He'll take our suffering away. He's done it before, but only to those who he likes.' The rest of his body twisted around to face the direction of his eyes. 'It's a few days yet, till the Solstice, and I don't know if my boy 'll make it. We've come all the way from Gamma Valley.' He craned an eye back around at Katherine, waved it side to side, and set off for his child.

All the other children played happily, but the poor slime covered child cried softly, as his father slithered over.

Behind her, a tram clattered past, tooting its horn, red streamers fluttering like exhaust fumes. Katherine wanted to go ask the man more questions, like who al-Zoubi had saved before, why he didn't save everyone. He can't save everyone if it means giving up his blood. But she followed the tram, headed for the Corridor, someone there ought to know where to find him, or know where his nursery was.

It wasn't long before she was barely able to walk a step without bumping into a New Havilian.

Market stalls ran either side of the boulevard, thick knots of New Havilians congregating in front of each one. Huge boiling pots chucked out sweet smelling steam. Bright red clothes and fabrics, fanned about by the passing trams, were snatched from their lines to be tried on or packaged up for sale. Musicians played their instruments: many necked guitars, steel drums, flutes that needed more than a single mouth to play. Baby roaches rattled their cages as New Havilians haggled over their price. Powders and spices piled feet high were scooped and sniffed and sorted into baskets. From the towering buildings came the whine of motors and the singing of a choir. In every direction: tentacles, horns, scales, stone, beaks, feathers, and claws. All the creatures of the Old World blended until they were the radioactive glob that was

New Havilah and its people.

It's not like Subsolum. This place is *alive*. It's more alive than anything I've ever seen.

At the nearest stall, a stone-faced woman, ragweed growing out from the cracks in her cheeks, stirred boiling water in shiny silver pots with her bare hands.

'I'm trying to find Quinton al-Zoubi,' Katherine said, gripping the stall. 'I'm lost.'

'It's a nybble for an ounce, my dear,' the stone-faced lady said, 'or—' she pointed up at the row of metal buckets hooked on the stall awning '—you can have a bucket for a byte.'

'Excuse me?' Katherine said.

'But you must return the bucket.'

A bright green blob, vaguely shaped like a person, appeared from the crowd, dropped a few coins on the counter, and unhooked a bucket. The blob bowed, tipped the boiling contents into itself, belched, and hooked the bucket back up, then disappeared into the crowd.

I'm out of my mind. This place is...

'If you aren't going to buy,' the rock-faced lady said, 'get out of the way!'

'I'm asking for directions,' Katherine explained.

'Directions? This is a shining boulevard. It's left or right, dear. Up or down!'

'Do you know where I can find the Immortal Man?'

'Bah! You can fi—' For the first time she looked at Katherine. 'You're a bloody dirt-diver! Look at you! A bloody dirt-diver at my stall! I thought you were a Maskirovka trying it on, but you

192

really are a shining dirt-diver! Piss off!' She smashed her rock fists on the stall counter: coins flying, buckets spilling. 'I ought to bash your brains in!' She lunged for Katherine, who managed to dodge out the way, but straight into another New Havilian.

'What's all this?' the second New Havilian said, righting Katherine up. His skin was completely transparent, his heart and lungs on full display. He wore a cap and badge, and she recognised it as the New Havilian police emblem.

'You can piss off too, you bloody nudist!' She ripped off her apron and threw it over the stall.

'I'm not here to start—'

'Shuddup!' she said.

The transparent police officer bolted.

Rock lady gripped Katherine's jumpsuit, lifted her a few feet off the ground, choking her. Blood roared in her ears. Her breathing slowed. Words struggled to find their way out. 'Please...' she said.

'Stinking dirt-diver!' she said, the rock cracking at her cheeks.

'I-I'm trying to find the Imort—'

Katherine's legs spasmed, and all went black.

γ

An air recycler warble filled her consciousness. Footsteps, chains jiggling, a sneeze. Where am I? She tried to move, but it felt like a roach had eaten her neck, and she shuddered stiff. Rock breaking ... crumbling, metal buckets ... a translucent policeman ... a giant green blob.

193

'Try not to move,' a voice said, soft and caring. 'You were purple when I got to you.'

'Who are you? Where are you?' She opened her eyes, but everything was still dark. Even after blinking, nothing appeared.

The continuous air recycler drone: it sounds like home.

'You picked a fight with the wrong woman,' the voice said. 'Stone Hands Dragana. She's got about the shortest fuse I ever knew.'

'I didn't pick a fight,' Katherine said. 'I asked for help.'

'Wrong person to ask for help, that's for sure.'

The air smelt burnt, choking, and reminded Katherine of the time she'd spent in her lower level cubby room, welding together the bulk of her hydroponics system. 'Why can't I see?' She went to lift her hands to her face, but the sharp tension in her neck stopped her.

'Can you relax?' the voice said. 'You really nearly died.'

'There was a police officer,' Katherine recalled. 'I saw his beating heart.'

'Oh, that's Lyubomir. If you're reporting crime, anything that's got to do with thievery, or tax, or a crime where no one's bashing anybody, then yes, you'd do yourself a favour by finding Lyubomir. But if bashing's your injustice, that man 'll run for Gamma Valley!'

Biting down on her lip, Katherine wiggled, fighting the pain in her neck. 'Are you— What are you doing to me?'

'I told you to stop moving. You were as good as dead when I got to you. Last thing I want is you to break your own neck.'

A machine rumbled into life: high-pitched screeching followed, and grunts. A burst of sweetness tickled her nose.

'You've hurt your neck real bad.'

A nerve in her neck pinched and her legs twitched. *Fokk*, this is it. I'm getting chopped up for New Havilian broth. Gathering strength, she twisted as far as the pain in her neck would let her. The blackness vanished, orange lights bloomed. She blinked. On the floor was a dirty, damp rag. The machine stopped.

'I told you,' the voice said, 'not to move.'

Holding out a metal cup, a sweetness pouring from it unlike any other Katherine had ever sniffed, was a Subsolumer.

'I'm— I'm back in Subsolum,' Katherine said.

'Pah!' the lady said. 'I'd never have that. Take it.'

The proffered metal cup, water condensed on it, wisps bleeding from it, inches from her nose and dry mouth, could not be further from her: she strained to reach for it but the burning in her neck wouldn't let her lift an arm.

'Ah,' the Subsolumer said, 'you got the squeeze real bad.'

Buckets filled with black water lined the floors. Flames flickered in a furnace at the other side of the room. Bits of scrap metal, dotted about the place, threatened to trip or take an eye out. The Subsolumer darted around.

'Who the *helvíti* are you?' Katherine said.

Her captor threw a bunch of papers off a workbench—technical drawings—and sat down on it. 'Darleaner Meta,' she said smiling, 'émigré.' She swung her legs, large black boots going like pendulums. 'And you must be Katherine Marston. I've heard a lot about you.' The cool cup of drink still very much in *her* hands.

Katherine said, 'I've not been here long.'

'Bill doesn't need much time to gossip in The Blue-Headed Goat.'

'The what?'

'The pub. Here, drink this—' she passed Katherine the chilled cup, this time stretching all the way to meet her '—that'll pick you right up, or put you back down… Dragana had you hanging like a lantern.'

Red pulpy mush, ice cold, and sweeter than ration pack candy. She gulped it down.

'Careful, you'll give yourself a head freeze. I'm calling it a Red Darleaner.'

Katherine drank it all in one go. Alcohol cut the sweetness into delicious ribbons, and the ice chilled it all to perfection. She tipped the cup high, the last drops falling onto her tongue.

'You like it?'

Katherine closed her eyes. If this was only what New Havilah had to offer: roach meat skewers, dumplings and broth, and the Red Darleaner, she was certain she could convince most Subsolumers that life above ground was worth any hardship.

'It's delicious.'

Darleaner clapped, grinning. 'It's a bit of a fusion. I got hold of Subsolumer wheat, my husband fermented it himself, and we made whiskey. The sweetness and redness, that's New Havilah's doing.' She pointed to the machine behind her. 'I built a blender to mash it all up with ice and—'

'Strawberries?'

'That's right.'

'From Quinton al-Zoubi?'

'Unfortunately.' Darleaner sat back on a worktop, the grin disappearing, and crossed her arms. 'I built most of his hydroponics equipment, but the Immortal Man'll still mess you around—he won't pay what he owes.' She waved off Katherine. 'He might be a New Havilian, but he sure acts like a Subsolumer.'

Katherine planted her feet on the ground and pushed off the bench, only to be struck by dizziness and stumble back on her arse. 'I need to find him.'

'Don't we all.'

Twitches ran through her neck. It needed a good cracking, but when she tried to get it to pop, she grimaced and flinched.

'All the New Havilians you could bother, you chose Stone Hands Dragana. You really are your father's daughter.'

'You knew my father?'

'Hated him.' Darleaner bent down and picked up the dirty rag from the floor. 'Let me get more ice, keep this tight around your neck.'

'I'm fine.'

She slapped the rag on the workbench. 'I'd offer you more Red Darleaner, but that's the last of those strawberries.'

'I never knew there were Subsolumers in New Havilah,' Katherine said. Nor did she know about the radiation levels, the abundance of food, and the orderliness. Though, after coming close to the Tunnel Spirits via strangulation, she had her doubts over the orderliness. 'You must have worked above ground.'

'I didn't get a send off? No memorial?'

'How long have you been here?'

Sooty black hands came up and she counted on her fingers,

going around twice. 'Sixteen.'

'You were young when you left.'

'I liked to read.'

Katherine, still rather dizzy and terrified, wasn't sure what to make of that. 'Can I have some water?'

After a nod, Darleaner snatched up the Red Darleaner cup, and carried it over to a basin, where she let the water run clear before filling it. 'You probably bought it all,' she said to Katherine from across the workshop, 'the stories.' She shut off the tap and brought the water over, not before taking a swig herself. 'Here.'

'Thanks.' Katherine gulped the freezing cold water. It softened the twitching in her neck and trickled down through her insides: she shivered. 'I spent a lot of time talking to the Maskirovkas, so I've heard some.'

'No, those are trader stories. I'm talking about the ones the Subsolumer elite feed the rest of us. The lies.'

'My father isn't a liar.'

Darleaner narrowed her eyes. 'He must be up to something,' she said, 'sending his daughter to the surface. Or maybe he's lost his mind. The Maskirovkas haven't been trading much lately. Something's up.'

'It's complicated.'

'You aren't wearing a rad suit or a mask, so you must have seen the rad counts.'

'I have.'

Darleaner clapped her hands again: a cloud of soot shooting out like a ghost. 'And you still believe your father tells the truth.'

'He's trying to protect me.'

'He's trying to control you, honey.'

That sounded like one of Tiffany's lines.

'Can't you see it?' Darleaner pressed, standing taller. 'Subsolum is over. It was over a hundred years ago. The fear of radiation does more damage than the radiation itself. That bunker was never meant to last this long.'

She drank more of the ice cold water. Air recyclers whined above, always present in the awkward pauses in Subsolumer conversation, even in New Havilah. 'The soil was never meant to last this long. I don't know enough about the tunnels to agree.'

'I was an apprentice engineer, at sixteen I could see it. I could feel it. Tunnel collapses, pipe bursts, cable rots, the lot. We slaved away. Round and round—' she made small circles with her head '—fixing things we went. But it was pointless. There's a world out there, I told myself. A world filled with people.'

'A world above our world,' Katherine said.

'You get it. When I wasn't chasing these problems, I was in the archival rooms, reading Old World novels.' She looked up and closed her eyes. 'Oh, the stories of the ocean, of the Sun. I wanted to feel its warmth on my face.'

'They weren't lying about that,' Katherine said. 'There's no Sun, even on the surface.'

'No,' she dropped her head back down, and fixed Katherine with a stare, 'they weren't. So one day, above the surface, working on the tram line, I decided to hitch a ride. I stole onto the back of a Ganymede tram, and rolled right into New Havilah.'

'I never knew.'

'The elites,' Darleaner said, 'would make sure of that.' She crunched the rag up and blew her nose into it. 'They feed you a narrative. The *Stjörnu Farartæki*; the Starship Fables; the Pipeworkers and the agronomists and their mythos. It's all fabricated to keep Subsolumers believing that their progress can only be got through unceasing commitment to life in a bunker.'

'My father's never made up a myth.'

'They don't do it consciously,' Darleaner said. 'They are all so traumatised they indulge in group fiction. And if anyone—' she jabbed her thumb in her mucky overalls '—has an idea that doesn't follow along, they are forgotten.'

'It's changing,' Katherine said. The Pipeworkers want to adapt the fields, grow everything hydroponically. That's why I'm here.'

Darleaner pulled off the goggles tied around her forehead and spat on the lenses. They squeaked as she rubbed them clear. 'Uh huh,' she said, 'and Daniel Marston agreed to that?'

Katherine averted her eyes. 'Yes.'

'I don't really care,' Darleaner said. 'I helped you because you needed help. Sooner or later, Subsolum will either crawl out from its bunker or starve itself to death.'

'I know that,' Katherine said. 'I know it all. I'm an agronomist. The soil is barren and it won't be long before we can't grow a calorie.' She stood, swayed a little, held her fingers to her temple. 'Thank you for the help, and the drink, but I need to leave.'

'Then you know,' Darleaner said, 'that they don't see the truth. They see what they want to see.'

'My father is president because he knows what's right for Subsolum.'

'He's president because he knows how to be a good politician, it has very little to do with how happy Subsolumers are.'

Crossing the workshop, Katherine pawed at dangling chains and pulleys, and headed towards the door. She tried the door handle but it was locked. 'Let me out.'

'Where are you going to go?'

'I'm here to learn from al-Zoubi.'

Darleaner set the goggles back on her forehead. 'And he's let Stone Hands Dragana strangle you. The man's not worth his weight in strawberries.'

Katherine twisted the doorknob until the pain in her neck forced her to stop. 'Just let me go.'

'Do you know where he is?'

'No.'

'Let's both pay him a visit; the man owes me some chocolate.'

BLUE FISTS OF FURY

Black gloop, oily and bubbly, reeking of burning hair and rubberweed oil, singed his eyebrows and the tips of his beard, refusing, no matter where he stuck his nose, to offer up even a faint whiff of chocolate. Where the 'chocolate' had run over the edge of the stainless steel vat, it had cooled and gone as hard as rock. It would take Quinton weeks to scrape it all off.

Six months of cacao beans, gone, rotten.

He jumped from the vat's foot support, and turned off the heating element.

The Black Rot had got his chocolate.

Extractor fans whirled above, sucking the rancid air from the tiny room. He stripped off the over-gown and hat, balled them up, and went to stuff them into the furnace, when the extractor fans caught his attention. Relentlessly sucking. You don't even know if what you're doing is helping. Couldn't you be spreading these particles about? Ejecting the Rot all through our home?

The fan didn't answer.

He rammed his coverings through the furnace trapdoor, and set about furiously washing his hands. The whiffs of soap wrenched him back to the times he'd spent in bomb shelters, bars of RATION SOAP all there were to clean one's self with.

He flicked the water from his hands, wishing he could do the same with the Rot. There must be a way of stopping it. Everything can't end like this. Not after all these years. Hands clean, but soul rather dirty, he went outside, and stood by the production house and smoked his pipe. What he wanted to know was how the Rot had found its way in there. He had never seen it outside the grow houses, except, of course, for what was now on his Flower. It must be the Flower. It must be *me* who's spreading it. There's nowhere else it could have come from. It was as if the thick blanket of stratospheric particles were descending on him: smothering him to death.

As he smoked, the first of the morning's trams rolled through the sleepy Corridor. Traders unfurled their awnings, wiped snow from countertops, and set about laying out their wares. Red lanterns and streamers, flowing sheets of crimson, even a few of Lady Jupiter's candles had reached traders' hands, claws, and tentacles: all of it on proud display, ready and waiting for the Summer Solstice.

He spat into the snowy mush. Perhaps the Flower did have a limited lifespan—after two hundred years, perhaps its life-giving qualities turned dark, became death-giving instead.

Pipe smoke curled out from behind his thin lips: he was leaking, coming apart, no warmth left within him. Clamping the pipe in his mouth, he pulled out his pocket watch, lifted the brass lid, and stared at the photograph of his mother.

That's all it is, Sophia whispered. *All you've got to do is wait for her. It's so simple, Quinton.*

But there was no solace there, in Sophia's words. She had been lying to him. Never telling him she had a daughter. It had to be the reason she never came back. She was only ever a *visitor.*

All he needed now was for his mother to turn out a liar. The Starships could be fiction, too. His whole life nothing more than a vain chase of lies.

He shut the watch, the lid ringing out a high note, and dropped it into his coat pocket.

Pretend all you like, Sophia said, *but those lies have kept you going. You can't surrender now, darling.*

Darling! He almost spat out his pipe.

After padlocking the production house, noting to himself to have Syd and Dobromir seal up the roasting vat and dump the lot on the far side of Gamma Valley, he set off for the nursery.

The closeness of the Solstice had his heart hammering in his chest. Red faced Sun Priests were trekking down the boulevard towards the Sun Church, laden with supplies: baskets of bark beetle powder, jugs of mushroom beer, bindles filled with Brightness knew what swinging on the end of metal poles. I might be growing cold inside, but the rest of New Havilah isn't. He dodged from their path, worried they might be after coffee or chocolate, or some life-giving *Zed,* and kept his head down.

He'd forgotten the taste of *Liphoric Zed,* forgotten what it did to him. That's all this is: I'm running on fumes. And once I'm replenished I'll have an answer for the Rot, I'll find a way through this.

He still wasn't sure what to do with Katherine. And Lady Jupiter wasn't pressing him, at least not yet. Part of him felt guilty for not attending to her this morning, but there was no other way. Her arrival couldn't have come at a worse time, the Flower being in his nursery.

Just as he was about to cross the Corridor, a large blue hand appeared from behind him and yanked him backwards.

'Come with me,' John Ganymede said, the deep voice resonating all the way down the man's arms and into Quinton's chest.

γ

Ganymede's office, at the top of the old parliament building, looked out over the ocean, turning its back on New Havilah. The windows filled one whole side, a huge metal desk parked in front of it, which made little sense to Quinton as it meant whenever you were sitting working at the desk, the view of the ocean was behind you. Lining both of the side walls were ten-foot high bookcases, their shelves bulging under the weight of golden bound tomes. John Ganymede controlled the only printing press in New Havilah and used it, mostly, to reprint the Old World books he thought were on message. *Moby Dick* was a favourite of his: Quinton needed both hands to count the number of times Ganymede had gifted him a copy, but they were easily sold to Maskirovkas, so it never bothered him.

Dead centre of the office stood a stone statue of Ganymede himself: his head inclined, searching the horizon for the next existential threat, bolts of lightning strapped to his back ready to be cast off, and muscles bulging, rendered mid ripple.

Quinton walked over to the statue, knocked his pipe against it to clear the ash, and set about filling the pipe with fresh tobacco. Aren't you so mighty? Lady Jupiter had one way of loving herself, Ganymede another. He sat down at the desk, glaring at the ocean, and lit his pipe. What do you want now, John?

Haze crawled across the ocean obscuring any view of the coast, or the salt makers who would be down there collecting water to boil off. Part of Quinton wondered if one day he would see boats arriving from a distant land. But those images were often obliterated by the Bombs: there was no one left, not on this planet, at least.

Open on the desk was a copy of the latest Subsolum Harvest Report, portions of text marked and noted in the giant's clumsy hand. Not a single picture of his wife. It was always business. He rocked back in the chair, smoking away, trying to visualise the Rot at its molecular level, but giving up.

Footfall soon sounded, and then the door swung open behind. He stood up to meet the source of the noise. It was one of Ganymede's *politsiya* officers, wearing his peaked cap and badge, a pair of arms gripping a Maskirovka trader by the neck.

'Sit down,' the officer said, and gave the trader a harsh shove.

Ganymede entered, nodded at Quinton, and dismissed the officer, who closed the door behind him.

'You've got me wrong,' the Maskirovka said. 'I never took a bit from her.' His false nose dangled off his face by a thread, behind it two narrow slits breathed heavily. The trader's prosthetic eye was smashed to pulp, leaving a single bloodshot eye to scramble about in its socket.

'Al-Zoubi,' Ganymede said, 'you might find this interesting.' Then, addressing the trader, he said, 'Tell him what you know.'

'I don't know anything,' the trader cried. 'I swear.'

Quinton paced over. The trader reeked of sweat and blood. He wore a black Subsolumer suit and tie, stained by the grey paste used to keep his false-face on.

'Are you sure?' Ganymede said.

'I wouldn't lie, Gospodin.'

Bright blue light flared in Ganymede's eyes.

The trader shot up and bolted for the door, struggled at the doorknob, and, when it refused to turn, he started to whimper.

'If you have nothing to fear,' Ganymede said, 'you wouldn't run.'

'Please, Gospodin, by the Sun, I swear I don't know anything.'

Ganymede walked over, grabbed the Maskirovka by his shirt collar, and punched him in the face: a wet crack, then sobs and whimpers.

'John?' Quinton said.

'Al-Zoubi,' the giant said, 'this man stole your blood.'

Between cries the trader said, 'It ain't true! It ain't true!' Snot bubbled from his slitted nose. 'It ain't tru—'

THWACK!

'Stop,' Quinton yelled, running over to hold back Ganymede's arm. 'You'll kill him.'

A meaty mask lay tattered beside the Maskirovka trader, blood soaked: his face had fallen off. The trader's single eye, puffed and bruised, twitched, but did not open. 'I can't see!' the trader cried. 'You've blinded me!'

To Quinton, Ganymede said, 'Juju sent this man up the mountain, carrying two vials of your blood.'

Quinton, chewing furiously at his pipe stem, shook his head. 'This is worth beating a man to death for?'

'Don't you want to know who he gave it to?'

'What does it matter, John?' Bright blue eyes, trapped lightning.

'"What does it matter?"' He kicked the trader's foot, and the trader coughed up blood and spat it over the stone floor. 'My wife is making a deal,' he said, 'and she's used your blood as a gift.'

'It ain't true!' the Maskirovka said. 'I never knew what I was carrying. I did as I was told.' He clawed at the prosthetic mask, stretched it out and pressed it over his face.

'Tell me who you gave the package to,' Ganymede yelled.

The prosthetic face split in two, the trader's face bursting through it. 'You've taken my face!' he cried. 'It'll be months before I can work again!'

Ganymede bundled the trader's shirt collar up, yanked it, and pulled back his other arm to strike.

'You gave it to Daniel Marston,' Quinton said. 'Or his servant.'

'I don't know his name,' the trader said, 'but he was tall and slender and had slicked back hair. I wish I had hair like that. And I *never* knew what I was carrying, I swear it, Brightness me, I swear it!'

Ganymede let the trader go, the lights in his eyes dimming, and called out, 'Take him away.'

The office door opened and the officer, on the threshold, glanced at the blood and gore, swallowed, and reached down to collect the broken and beaten trader.

Once they were alone, Ganymede said, 'Sit, then.'

Quinton shook his head again. 'I don't have time for this, John. I've got a plant nursery to run and a nosey Subsolumer, dropped on me by your wife, to handle.'

'That's my concern, al-Zoubi,' Ganymede pointed at the desk.

208

'So sit and let's talk.'

Relenting, Quinton took his seat again. As Ganymede sat, he slammed the hefty Harvest Report shut and put it away in a desk drawer.

'You know the man the Maskirovka gave your blood to?'

'It's Daniel's servant,' Quinton explained, 'who else?'

'Why does he want your blood? It's useless.'

Quinton laughed. 'Perhaps he knows more than both of us.'

As Ganymede sank deeper into his chair, he said, 'What bothers me are the lies. She never told me about the blood.'

She's stolen my blood to give to Daniel, she's placed Daniel's daughter in my nursery, all while the Flower is Rotten.

'The political situation in Subsolum is volatile,' Ganymede said. 'They are vulnerable, and she's winning favour down there.'

'So what does she want?'

Ganymede looked around the capacious office. Golden-bound tomes glinted on their shelves. 'If I knew that, I should think I'd be a happier man.' Then, after a pause, 'She hasn't spoken with you?'

'Like I told you, John, all she's asked of me is to take the Subsolumer and show her how we grow our food. She wants what I want, to have Subsolum growing everything hydroponically. We would be drawn much closer to them, building all the equipment, no doubt, and providing them with organics.'

Ganymede rubbed his stubble. After a heavy sigh, he slid back his chair and pulled open a drawer. From the drawer he took a small wooden box and set it on the desk. It was a rich dark wood, covered in an intricate pattern of gold, and smelt strongly of tobacco. He lifted the lid, turning the box slightly so Quinton could see its contents: cigars. With his fat fingers, Ganymede pinched one and offered it to Quinton. 'Your fine tobacco,' he said.

Taking it, Quinton said, 'I've not seen it rolled into cigars.'

'It's very good, but very expensive. Requires time and nimble tentacles.' He plucked one himself and shut the box. He snipped his cigar with a shiny cutter, and handed the cutter over to Quinton. 'Ostensibly, her motives make sense. Perhaps she's winning Daniel's favour by giving him your useless blood—'

It was rather useful to me.

'—so she can more easily convince him to abandon the soil.' Holding the cigar in his big blue lips, Ganymede lit the end with a fluid lighter, the scent of the burning roach fat sweet and minty. 'But I don't buy it, al-Zoubi.'

Quinton, lighting his own cigar, the taste remarkably different to his pipe, said, 'So what does she want?'

'She didn't want any fucking strawberries, that's for sure.'

Quinton sensed himself being drawn into an argument he didn't need to be drawn into. 'John, if this is about your failing marriage, I—'

'It isn't failing.'

Quinton let a cloud of cigar smoke go. 'Are you sure?'

'We're very much in love.'

'But you can't go and ask her what she's up to?'

'We don't talk about work. It's a rule.'

'Yours or hers?'

'Hers.'

Quinton shrugged. 'She's a difficult person—' he corrected himself: 'We all are. I don't think you get to the bottom of this speculating on what her motives are. You need to speak with her.'

'And what if...' He turned to one side. The light from behind him bright and clear and blooming through the windows.

'What if what?' Quinton asked.

'What if she is up to something?'

'Then you deal with that,' Quinton said. He rose. 'I'm sorry, John, but I really need to get off. Now we know Daniel has my blood. We know Lady Jupiter gave it to him. But it could be— and most probably is—because she's fighting for our little town.'

Ganymede smoked his cigar until the cherry was as bright as his eyes. 'I sure hope so.'

γ

By the time Quinton made it to the nursery he'd smoked Ganymede's cigar to a nub, and had worked over, in his mind, all the reasons Daniel Marston would want his blood. Perhaps Sophia had told him all about my immortality, told him all about the Flower, too? And now he's in need and is coming for me.

In front of the nursery doors, he brushed snow from his coat, and prepared himself to face the day. He's in trouble and thinks my blood's the way out, has sent his own daughter here to steal it, my blood *or* the Flower. I should keep her from the nursery.

Quinton spat out the cigar end, stuck his key in the nursery door lock, but the door swung open at his touch.

'Bill,' he called out.

'Ahoy,' Billick said, at the bottom of the stairs.

'You're here early,' Quinton said. As he descended the steps, the drying room heat hit him more and more, smelling richly of fresh tobacco. He could never get enough.

'And you're here late,' Billick said.

'You can explain first.' He stripped off his coat and hung it up. His shirt sleeves were stained yellow. All this Rot has had me sweating, he said to himself as he folded the sleeves at the cuffs to hide the stains. I'm melting in my own skin.

'I've moved the strawberry plants to grow house three,' Billick said. 'Had to get in early to beat the traffic on the Corridor.' He ducked through the ribboned doorway into the strawberry room. Quinton followed him through. The growing platform was empty: bare growth media buckets, a few lost petals, and leaky, disconnected nutrient fluid tubes.

'You did all this this morning?'

'Syd and Dobromir helped.'

Groping for his pipe, Quinton said, 'I have a bit of bad news.'

The botanist padded towards the exotics doorway, jutted a long-nailed thumb at the ribbons dangling from the frame, and said, 'Yeah, me too.'

As if Ganymede himself had gut punched him. 'What is it?' Though he had a feeling he knew. I don't know if I can stomach another thing going wrong.

'You, eh, go first.'

Smoothing back his long white hair, Quinton said, 'The Rot got the chocolate. I'm late because I was checking it. The entire vat is black gloop.'

Grimacing, exposing his fangs, Billick shuddered, said, 'All of it?' and nearly collapsed.

Quinton nodded.

In one of those idiosyncratic gestures of his, Billick performed his best approximation for a disbelieving head shake: squeezing his neck-less head into his body and twisting back and forth.

'That's three months of work, six months of crops.'

'I'm sorry, Bill.'

'Sorry?' He hissed, unsquished his head. 'How's the Rot get there in the first place? You dragged it in here.'

Quinton searched about for a stool and sat himself down. His face was hot to the touch, and in the heat of the nursery he was sweating more. 'I've never been so tired in my life,' he said.

Billick hoisted himself into his wheely cart, wheeled it over to Quinton. Looking into the man's eyes, he said to his Cap'n, 'You think now's the time for warmth and sympathies? You've destroyed our money crop.'

With sweaty hands, he greased back his hair. 'I know what I've done.'

There was a hint of forgiveness in Billick's eyes, then a twitch of a smile. 'Sure as the barnacles on my belly, there's never a dull moment.'

'What's your bad news?'

'Follow me.'

They passed through into the exotics room. The ejected pheromones of young tobacco, chocolate, and coffee plants, heavy and earthy, struck him hard. But, as he rounded the central growing platform, never ever did the sweet perfume of his Flower cut through. And he knew, deep down, what he was about to see.

'Cap'n, I don't know what happened.' Billick wheeled closer, yanking himself around with handholds on the worktops. 'It happened over night.'

Standing before the open Flower case, Quinton saw his nightmare vision. The once bright white Flower, now a ghastly grey, limp and lifeless, had lost most of the infected petal. It had melted, black slime drooling from its tip, and wafting forth a rancid scent. He checked the stigma. Dry. However much *Liphoric Zed* he had stored up, it would be his last.

I'm going to die. We're all going to die.

A contorted cry fell out of him. His chin wobbled as if he were a toddler about to burst into tears.

'I didn't know what to do,' Billick said gruffly. And Quinton could hear in his voice the panic. 'I thought I better get the strawberries out of the nursery, before it spreads. We'll lose all this lot.' He swept his narrow arms. 'There's no telling what's infected now.'

Someone had stuffed hempmoss into his mouth. Poured roach fat down his throat. 'I can't breathe,' he muttered. 'Do you have any idea what this means?'

'You didn't get to finish what you were telling me on the tram, Cap'n. Something about us New Havilians being *sick*?'

'Your mutations, passed on through all your generations since the Bombs, are kept from tearing you apart, by the Flower's *Zed*—its sap. Every New Havilian is the same.'

'You're telling me true?'

'I am.'

'This little flower dies, we all die?'

Quinton, shaking, 'That's right.'

'Maybe if we can get through the Solstice, I can charm her, like a mermaid singing to sailors, I'll charm her back to life. Sing her a little song?'

Fretting and panicky. 'You're good, Bill, but not that good.' He ferreted out his pipe, clamped it so hard between his teeth he heard it crack, dropped a nugget of tobacco in the bowl, and shakily held a jet-lighter to it. He breathed the heavy smoke in until he was sure he was going to cough, and let a cloud go.

'Quin,' Billick protested, 'you can't be lighting that th—'

'What does it matter, Bill?' he said, 'we're dead men walking.'

'I can charm her,' Billick said. His wheely cart wheels squeaked—piercing deeply into Quinton's mind.

Tears ran down Quinton's cheeks. He thought he could see his mother. She was right there, waiting for him. He smelt her, the scent of the cedar wood blocks she used to keep the moths from her clothes, the rose perfume she wore, the cocoa butter lip balm, all fading, fading so fast.

'I won't see her,' Quinton said, crying horribly, wailing and sucking on his pipe, 'I won't make it.'

'Nonsense, matey! We've got through—this be only a blunder!' Billick hopped from the cart and hugged Quinton's leg, and Quinton dropped to the floor, where Billick hugged him proper. 'I'm telling you, Quin, we'll figure it out.'

Quinton drew on his pipe, the smoke poured out of him like a volcano close to blowing. 'It's no good,' he said, wiping snot on his sweat-stained sleeve, 'we've had our run and I should think it lo—'

Bangs and thumps from the door.

'Who in Brightness is that?' Quinton said, hoisting himself to
his feet. He craned his head, pointing an ear towards the door.

BANG, BANG, BANG!

'Open this fucking door, you thieving shit-eater!'

The two men stared at each other and said in unison:
'Darleaner.'

FOUND YOU

They rushed from Darleaner's workshop only to linger out front, where Darleaner slid a heavy bolt across the front door, spat on a padlock, and locked the bolt in place.

Over the big marble blocks of the exterior were posters of Lady Jupiter, solemn and serious, a slogan underneath reading, 'New Havilians are Rad Proof, Subsolumers Ain't.'

'What are the posters for?' Katherine said.

Fiddling with keys, Darleaner quickly glanced up at a poster, and said, 'She's a megalomaniac. They both are.'

'Both?'

As Katherine said that, a tram rolled by, blaring its horn at the slow moving slimers on the tracks in front.

'See,' Darleaner said, pointing at the tram. Along its side, glowing blue lights burst from the eyes of a big-headed man on another poster. The heading underneath read: 'Ganymede Manufacturing: It Don't Break.'

She recognised the name from the New Havilian books that found their way into Subsolum, but not the face. Ganymede Publishing. All her New Havilian books had the golden stamp on the inside of the cover.

'That's John Ganymede, New Havilian Domestic Affairs Chair, runs pretty much all the industry in New Havilah. I work for him.' She set off down the path outside the workshop. 'Those two are married.'

217

Katherine managed a few pacey steps before slowing and putting pressure on her neck to try to relieve the tension. 'How far is he?' Katherine asked. 'I don't know if I can walk over snow and ice.'

Darleaner, at the bottom of the path, turned left, a silly grin on her face as she pointed. 'About four or five, that way.'

'Four or five kilometres?'

Then she started up another one of these paths, the one right next to hers, saying, 'No, steps.'

Katherine hobbled to the end of Darleaner's path, wishing for another cup of Red Darleaner, and, when she started up the adjacent one, she saw it, the huge, gaudy sign affixed to the building:

AL-ZOUBI PLANT NURSERY

'Open this fucking door, you thieving shit-eater!' Darleaner hammered on the metal door.

A small crowd took little time to gather behind them, the Corridor so full of shoppers and market vendors. Katherine searched for Stone Hands, and thankfully couldn't spot her. Two Subsolumers threatening to bash down the Immortal Man's front door wasn't the image she wanted to cultivate. It didn't mesh with her ideas of cooperation.

'Can't you keep your voice down?' Katherine said, to which Darleaner paused her onslaught, looked back with a face of pure indignation, and then resumed her thumping.

'I'll give you two *fokking* minutes,' she yelled, 'and then there'll be no door left to keep locked. You pirate wannabes.'

'Maybe they aren't even here.'

They stood there, Katherine perched on a low wall, rubbing at her sore neck, Darleaner panting, swearing between each heavy breath, when a quick pitter-patter of footsteps betrayed all doubt as to whether anyone was home.

'Bill,' Darleaner said. 'I hear you.'

The door unlocked from the inside and came open an inch or so. Bill's string o' pearl eyes peered forth. 'You,' the gruff voice said.

Katherine heaved herself to her feet and hobbled next to Darleaner.

'And you too!?' He slammed the door shut, bolts scrapped against metal, feet pitter-pattered again.

'Look,' Katherine said, 'I'm here to make peace, not start trouble.'

'If you want peace,' Darleaner said, 'you'll have to start a bit of trouble first.' She bashed on the door again. 'Open it up, Bill.'

All this for chocolate. What would Darleaner do for the magic flower?

Heavier footfall, thick snow-boots, and, even from behind the door, the portentous reek of tobacco. 'That's him.'

The door opened. But the face peering through the gap wasn't the face of the man who buried a metal fence pole through the roach that wanted to eat her; this face was of a dejected, tears-crusted-about-the-eyes man, who looked as if he had seen his death, had had words with his maker, where he was told all the secrets of the universe and found them rather disappointing. There is no purpose, Katherine thought, and you've seen it.

219

These thoughts evaporated the moment al-Zoubi, smoke bleeding from his nostrils, said, 'Get inside, the both of you.'

Warmth enveloped them like the heavy New Havilian duvet she had woken with: the air thick with pollen and the sharp, tangy scent of nutrient solution. The stairs went down from the surface, so the nursery sat buried a few metres underground. That, Katherine assumed, was to help it retain heat. Beyond the entranceway, masked by long strips, was another room. The ribbon material wasn't transparent enough to let her see through to the room on the other side. If his magic flower were here—in the nursery—then it would be through that door.

They huddled beside a room housed behind a glass window. Inside, pegged to hempmoss twine, were long leaves of drying tobacco, gold brown and curling at their tips.

Bill came through a ribboned doorway, carrying a steaming mug. He drank it down, glancing up at his boss, and every now and then picking at his fangs. Haggard and lifeless, al-Zoubi stared through the window, his mouth opening and closing, but wordless.

'I don't see any chocolate,' Darleaner said.

'There isn't any,' al-Zoubi finally said, his voice flat. He stuffed his hands into his trouser pockets. Sweat stained his white shirt, as if he hadn't changed it in all his two hundred years. 'All I can offer you is a portion of those.' He nodded at the leaves. Then, meeting Katherine's eyes for the first time, he said, 'I'm sorry I wasn't there to collect you this morning. My hands have been full.'

The words, It's OK, don't worry, almost spilled out, but she stopped herself.

'You're lying,' she said. 'You were never planning on collecting me. I was nearly strangled to death.'

'Brightness. I'm sorry.' But he wouldn't look at her anymore. He just stared limp and lifeless at his tobacco leaves.

'I'd be dead if it wasn't for Darleaner,' Katherine said.

'That's right,' Darleaner said, 'I've done you another favour, Gospodin al-Zoubi.'

The Immortal Man whimpered. His lower lip hung low and his eyeballs bulged from his head.

'This,' Darleaner said to Bill, 'all feels a bit suspect. You've got no chocolate, the Immortal Man is as white as snow, and you're here sipping coffee.'

'I like coffee,' Bill said.

'It's Solstice in two days,' al-Zoubi said, 'and I've not got any chocolate.'

'What happened to the chocolate?' Darleaner said, suffering another bout of indignation.

The forlorn al-Zoubi remained fixated on the tobacco leaves. Eventually, al-Zoubi sighed, and said, 'The Rot got our chocolate.'

Katherine glanced at Darleaner to make sure she was as confused as herself: going by the low hanging brow and the slight pout, she was.

'You can't pay me because of what?' Darleaner said.

Billick's ears literally pricked, their tips erecting and flushing bright red. He pattered over to al-Zoubi. 'We ain't discussed this, Cap.'

'What else is there?' al-Zoubi said.

'You're going to tell the whole of New Havilah?'

'Tell the whole of New Havilah what?' Darleaner said.

The Rot sounded to Katherine like it could be a plant infection. She'd been wrestling those—potato pox, wheat fungus, snow mould, and so on—since she was a kid.

Finally lifting his head, al-Zoubi said, 'Tell the whole of New Havilah that an infectious disease has set itself deeply into our crops, and I've no way to treat it... It's already...' his voice cracked, he plastered a hand against the window of the tobacco room to steady himself. 'It's taken a dear plant of mine.'

The flower.

'I don't give a shit what's been taken from you,' Darleaner said, prodding him in the chest. 'You owe me.'

'And what would you like me to give you—' he grabbed her finger, and thrust her whole hand away—'black mush?'

'The *fokking* truth.'

'He ain't lying, Dee,' Bill said.

Katherine sat down on the bottom steps, rubbed the soreness in her neck. 'Tell me about it, about the Rot.'

'No, no, no.' Darleaner shook her head. 'I don't want to hear any of his stories. I want to hear the truth. You don't want to pay me. You think you can get the better of me. Cheat me.'

'Dee,' Billick said, 'I swear he ain't lying.'

'Ganymede nearly threw me in the Gamma Valley Deeps,' Darleaner said, 'let the rads swell me up, and the roaches eat my *fokking* brains out, all 'cause I stuck my neck out for you.'

'And why didn't he?' al-Zoubi said, but before she could answer he said: 'Because you gave me up! You're a good for nothing cheat yourself.'

'So you are cheating me.'

At that, the Immortal Man charged through the ribboned threshold, furiously shaking his head.

All this reminded Katherine of home.

'That's right, run off! You lying, cheating thief!'

From the room al-Zoubi disappeared into, came bangs and thumps, frustrated groans, and the distinct hiss of a pressurised nutrient tube being disconnected. The three, Bill, Darleaner, and herself, were left in a silence filled by the droning air recyclers: it didn't take much for Katherine to believe she was still in Subsolum, still mediating pointless arguments and fights.

I told you so, Chick.

Bursting back through, al-Zoubi held out a ceramic pot. From it, limply standing about a foot high, its green leaves shrivelled, its many white petals—not like her father had promised—grey and lifeless was the Immortal Man's magic flower.

I've found you.

Al-Zoubi set the flower on a metal stand, next to his extinguished pipe, and rotated the pot. The petal facing them looked as if its tip were liquifying. It dripped a thin line of black gunk that had pooled in the top of the pot. Black motes speckled the petal, and from each mote tiny threads of black grey spread out.

Darleaner, incredulous, glanced from al-Zoubi to the rotting flower and back again. 'What's wrong with it.'

Bill said, 'It's got the Rot.'

'Black Rot,' al-Zoubi clarified. 'All of our crops: mushrooms, coffee, chocolate, tobacco have been more or less infected by it. This flower—' he cleared his throat—'my Flower, does more for New Havilah than you'll ever know. And now it's infected.'

Darleaner drew nearer and went to prod it. Al-Zoubi slapped her mucky gloved hand away.

'No,' he said. 'You can't.'

Katherine rose, not letting the flower from her sight, and said, 'It's a Jaborosa.'

This stopped al-Zoubi in his tracks. Bill eyed her suspiciously too.

'Can't you take that petal off?' she asked him. 'Remove the infection?'

He shook his head. 'Without all ten petals, the flower doesn't produce sap.'

'And it's sap does what?' Katherine said.

Al-Zoubi merely lifted an eyebrow.

'*Oh*.'

Pieces began to fall into place. The Immortal Man's magic flower, like her father seemed to know, must have properties that remove infections and induce growth and repair. That's how he does it. That's how he never dies.

'You must have more flowers,' Katherine said.

'I do not.'

'You can't grow another? Or take a cutting?'

'I've tried, over the years. This flower is as old as me. It's asexual, seeds every so often, but none ever survive after sprouting.'

'At least there's that,' Katherine said. 'If the seeds sprout, it opens up lots of possibilities to change the environment to induce growth.'

A curl formed on his lips. That ghoulish whiteness of a hopeless face had found a shade of pink: a little warmth.

Darleaner stamped her foot down. 'I don't give two bits! I've got work to get back to and I'm not leaving until I'm paid.'

'Then take your payment,' al-Zoubi yelled, thrusting a pointed finger at the tobacco, 'and get out of my nursery.'

Five pounds of that tobacco—in Subsolum at least—would fetch her more than enough food to feed a family for a year, maybe more, if she could find the right buyer. *Helvíti, I know ten people who'd give their cubes for it.* But Darleaner had been in New Havilah too long, had lost all sense of the desperation in her first home.

'I don't want tobacco. I want chocolate.'

'Well there isn't any, the Black Rot has eaten it all.'

'Dee,' Bill pleaded, 'take a kilo, that there's more cash than you've ever had. You'll be buying rounds for us until next Summer Solstice. You'll be the Queen of the Seas, aye?'

She licked her lips. 'What about the strawberries?'

'What about them?' al-Zoubi said.

'Have you got any more?'

'No,' he said.

'Black Rot got them too, huh? You cheats.'

'Eh, we will have more,' Bill said, 'in a month or two. If you've got the patience for that?'

As much as Katherine was grateful for being rescued, treated, fed a fancy drink, and brought here by her, she found herself wishing Darleaner would just leave.

'You can make more Red Darleaners,' Katherine said. 'Tastiest drink I've ever had.'

Taking out the greasy black rag, Darleaner smiled crookedly. She blew her nose, wiped errant bits of snot from her face, then balled the rag back up. 'OK,' she said, 'but I want two *kilos*, not handfuls, of strawberries.'

Bill and al-Zoubi traded glances, both of them sucking their teeth.

'Alright,' al-Zoubi said, holding out his hand for her. As they shook hands, he added, 'Now get out.'

Darleaner's heavy boots clobbered the stairs.

And she was gone.

The three stood there for a time, simply staring at al-Zoubi's rotten flower. Two smells fought each other for Katherine's attention. One: a rancid, festering stench that brought forth sewage, decaying flesh, and old urine, and the other: a delicate, sweet perfume that filled her head with fond memories, as if she could smell her mum smiling as she scooped cabbage soup into bowls for breakfast, those rare few glimpses of the time before she was ill and bed-ridden, before her father had grown cold and absent. It was as if the flower had hooks in her mind, as if it were speaking to her.

'It has its charms,' al-Zoubi said, pulling her from the reverie. He picked up its pot, saying to Bill, 'Let's settle it into the strawberry room, away from the rest of the exotics,' and carried it through the ribboned doorway, Bill and Katherine following.

The air was warmer this side of the doorway. In the centre of the room was a barren metal table. Pipes ran across it, slightly buried in narrow trenches, with shoots running off them to offer up variously sized valves for connecting pots to. Above the table hung an array of lights that gave out a warm and soft yellow tone. These were very old Subsolumer Sun Lamps—first or second generation—that you could find by the thousands, packed away in the damp lower levels, used and forgotten.

Al-Zoubi set the flower down: its healthy petals glinted under the light. He screwed one of the valves into one of the pot's sockets.

'What about the case?' Bill said. He'd hopped into a small cart, which lifted him to the height of the table.

'It doesn't matter anymore. Unless we have to transport it.'

'Case?' Katherine said.

'Why Darleaner has been hassling us. She built a radiation proof casing for the flower. So I could transport and protect it. But since it's already got the Rot—' he shrugged. 'It cost me a lot.'

Pipes groaned as Bill yanked a handle at the edge of the room. Running along the perimeter of the nursery were narrow worktops, on which tools, discarded and broken hydroponic parts, and bags of growth media all sat. There was no order here. Even Katherine's ramshackle setup in the cubby room had more order to it. It was no wonder al-Zoubi had found himself in this position. He was careless.

A film of nutrient solution ran across the flower's growth medium.

'There we are,' al-Zoubi said to the flower, to which it replied by dripping more gunk from its black rotten petal.

The cart Bill carried himself around in squeaked whenever he moved, its bearings clearly in need of oil. So she said, 'Don't you want to get some lubrication on that?'

'On what?' Bill said.

'Your cart?'

'What cart?'

Al-Zoubi's eyes were as wide as could be. He whispered: 'Don't mention the cart.'

'N-no,' Katherine muttered, 'I don't know what I was saying.'

'That's right,' Bill said, rolling over towards the flower, the wheels squeaking terribly, 'you don't know what you're saying.' He whipped out a magnifying glass from his overalls and got to work glaring at the rotten petal.

She stepped away from the central table, towards the other ribboned doorway, covertly stealing glances as to what was on the other side. She still wasn't sure what was going on. Was he lying? Maybe he had many more flowers and was testing her. Trying to work out if I can be trusted.

Bill's forked tongue flickered: it scooped the air over the black petal.

'Why did you abandon me?' She rubbed her neck. 'It's not a good place for a foreigner.'

'No,' he said, 'and I'm sorry.'

'That's all you've got to say?'

Al-Zoubi patted himself down, searching his pockets, only to grow frustrated and exclaim: 'My pipe.'

'Forget about your pipe. Tell me why you left me in the Hotel.'

228

He started and stopped like a broken radio. 'Don't you—' he bit his lip '—don't you think it's a little odd that Daniel Marston, the man who, despite his promises of cooperation and friendship, has been *stealing* my blood, has now, somehow, placed his daughter to work beside me and my botanist in my nursery?'

Katherine, staring open-mouthed at al-Zoubi, shook her head.

Bill, busy with the petal, darted his eyes about, but kept silent.

'You *know* about the blood?' Katherine said.

'My suspicions grew a lot stronger this morning, when Ganymede found the Maskirovka who delivered it.' He pointed a finger at her. 'And you've just confirmed them. So you might forgive me if I'm a little reluctant to let you into my life, when I know your father is after my immortality. He must be sick.'

She looked al-Zoubi dead in the eyes. 'He is.'

'So he's desperate.'

'Yes.'

'And he sends his daughter to come steal my flower?'

'No—' she nearly smacked the table in frustration '—he's trying to do that right thing. Trying to get Subsolumers off the soil.'

Throwing up his hands, al-Zoubi said, 'Well, what's it matter? Look at this mess—' A limp hand gestured at the dying flower. 'If it wasn't for your talk on sensors and microcontrollers and your apparent experience with plant infections, I might have chucked you out. And anyway, you aren't going to steal a rotten flower, are you?'

'I can't make sense of her,' Bill cut in. 'This flower be a demon of the deep. A foul and dark mistress.' He wheeled back from the flower, sliding his magnifying glass back into his pocket. 'It's not saying anything to me.'

Had the hempmoss not lured her through the blizzard, she would have had a hard time believing Bill could communicate with the plants. But she had heard it that day: a soft calling, a warm hand guiding her towards that coated boulder.

'Is that odd?' she asked.

'Not a good sign,' Bill said.

She motioned for his magnifying glass, which he gave up after some protest, and hunched herself over the flower. In the corner of her eye, she saw one of al-Zoubi's legs shaking frantically, so she shuffled until he was out of view. It was a habit of Tiffany's, one of her nervous ticks, and it reminded Katherine of hunger and famine.

Tiny tendrils of blackness ran through the natural grooves in the petal. At the tip, where the petal dissolved into mush, spores were dropping and floating off into the air.

'First,' Katherine said, not taking her eyes from the glass, 'we create a negative pressure environment.'

The two New Havilians, both wearing confused looks, took a step—or, in Bill's case, a roll—backwards and said in unison, 'Eh?'

She needed more magnification to verify it, but it looked very similar to the fungal root rot she'd battled a few years ago. The spores were of similar size and the amount of them too. It all matched up to what she'd seen. If the roots were split and fraying, then there'd be little doubt about it.

I'm back at it. I'm doing what I do. But as she rose upwards from her bent over posture, a rush of dizziness rolled through her. She cursed Stone Hands, cursed al-Zoubi too for abandoning her at the Hotel.

'We need to check the roots,' she said.

Al-Zoubi leapt forwards and grabbed her wrist. It woke up the pain in her neck and she pulled her hand from him in a hurry.

'We can't risk that,' al-Zoubi said. 'I checked the roots two days ago.'

'Was it rotten two days ago?' she said, rubbing her neck. *Helvíti*, what I would give for another Red Darleaner.

The question paused the hydroponicist.

'Because,' she said now, an exhaustion coming on strong, 'it looks to me like fungal rot.' The warm and heavy air, the insidious whiff of rot, and the tension in her neck: she closed her eyes, held them there and breathed steadily. 'W-we treated it with...' but she faltered.

Al-Zoubi must have slipped the glass from her hand and guided her over to a stool.

'Sit, sit,' he said, 'you're not well.'

Squeaks sounded, a tap running. When she dared open her eyes, Bill was holding out a glass of water for her. She drank it, spilling the icy water down her, hands trembling.

'My equipment,' she said, her gaze focused on the floor, 'let me get it and set it up.'

'How's about some fresh air first, eh?'

γ

231

After standing outside and doing nothing much more than breathing, Katherine caught a chill, so Bill led her on a walk through maze-like back alleys. Compared to the Corridor, where the monstrous buildings were placed next to each other in perfect order, these buildings seemed to grow out of each other, like the roots of a plant. Signs and stone markers appeared with little consistency, so it was the shop signs, which protruded from sloping walls that looked close to buckling that Katherine used to orient herself. The closeness and shoulder to—mostly—shoulder contact wasn't doing her head and neck much good.

'Where are we going?' she said.

Bill, doing all this navigating three or so feet from the ground, said, 'You should see a sign, a blue-headed goat.'

'What's a goat?'

'Blow a man down! Keep an eye out for a blue headed *beast*, with horns, and eyes a little like mine.'

About tall enough to look up and over the jostling stream of people, Katherine spotted the sign: a bright blue-headed—horned—*goat*.

'What is it?' she said.

'The pub!'

The walking had done her some good, but it was the ice cold mushroom beer that saved her. It went down easily, not like the beer they had in Subsolum, it was cooler and fresher and tasted like it was made with generations worth of handed down skill.

Low stone walls, bearing the heads of adult roaches, gave the pub—the New Havilian word for bar—a cosy feeling that wasn't

232

so far from the protection her cube offered her.

I can't believe I might actually *miss* that thing. There's so much space up here, I'd never know what to do with it all.

A well polished slab of mineralized tree had been cut and shaped to form the bar area. Behind the bar were bottles and bottles of New Havilian drink, each with their own unique label. The ones catching her eye most were shaped like bark beetles, their labels, many a neon green, all had the word OTPOBA on them. *Otrova*, Bill translated for her, *Venom*—bark beetle venom. 'A shot or two and you'll be rolling about on deck all night.'

Brass stools, coming in different shapes and sizes to suit the many-formed populace, shone softly under dim orange lamps. New Havilah Wireless trickled in through a pair of speakers at the bar's far side.

There was no comparison to be made with Subsolum's canteen—the only place Katherine could think to compare it to. What she saw here was real, authentic culture. It was like something from *The Beautiful and Damned*, an Old World novel she loved so much, where people drank and had parties in a grand city, except here there were a lot more limbs.

At their table, Bill picked at roach-nuts (roach meat pressed into small balls and then made hard by melting bark beetle powder over them) and sipped his stein of Gamma Valley's Best.

'How you feeling?' Bill asked. 'Quin didn't tell me we were planning on giving you the runaround.'

Massaging her neck, she said, 'Better, now that I've had a drink. If Darleaner hadn't found me, I might be dead.'

'You get into a tussle?'

'Stone Hands Dragana.'

Bill's eyes went wide with panic. He shook side to side as he stuffed more roach-nuts into his mouth. 'Blow a man down,' he said. 'I should have said something. Can't let a Subsolumer wander around by herself. I'm sorry.'

Katherine, grateful to at least get an apology, took another swig of her drink, and let a breath go.

Bill slid the plate of nuts across the table. 'You don't have to be polite. I know you're hungry.'

She took a handful and ate. They tasted salty; she had no words for the other flavours; they were far beyond what she knew.

A few drinkers took their seats at the bar, glaring at her for a moment, but then finding themselves chatting to the barman. Those guys won't strangle me—they've got no arms. As she thought this, the two drinkers, slimers (no arms *or* legs), used their antennae to hoist their frothy beers to their long lips.

They'll find a way, Chick.

Bill gulped his beer. Wiping his mouth, he said, 'You sound like you know what you're doing.'

'With his flower?'

'Aye.'

'I'm an agronomist,' she said, the pride making her sit up straighter and putting a smile on her face. 'I've spent a long time dealing with plant infections.'

'Agronomist,' Bill said, narrowed eyes. 'We don't have 'em here.'

Katherine laughed. 'There's no soil.'

And here Bill leaned forwards over the table, whispered,

'Wanna hear a secret?'

She said, 'Yeah.'

He said, 'That's not *entirely* true.'

And she went, 'What?'

And he went, 'Let me take you downstairs. I need a bit of advice.'

So they finished their drinks, and Bill led her downstairs.

What came next, Katherine, even in her most daring of fantasies, could never have imagined.

Bill took her into a room which smelt, unquestionably, of rich loam. Heat and moisture suffused the air in the narrow hallway. A scent she had no words for tickled her nose, not sharp, but sticky.

They came to a doorway, the doorknob down by her knees, about where it ought to be for a person Bill's height. Through a narrow port hole in the door came warm orange light—the exact same colour temperature as the current generation of Subsolum sunlamps set to midday. The absolute best.

'Now,' Bill said, a hand on the doorknob, 'don't you go telling Quin—or *anybody*—what you're about to see, alright?' He pushed open the door.

And what she saw, what she felt, was as close to what the devout followers of the *Fables* described as transcendental as she had ever got.

Bursting up from a deep, two metres or so in diameter, round tub, alive and in full bloom, was a *tree*. Its branches, thicker than Tiff's arms, splintered off in a mesmerising criss-cross, palm-sized leaves growing happily from their tips. The trunk, a near perfect circle wider than her, projected straight up, sturdy, and pale brown, inches from the high, vaulted ceiling.

She dropped to her knees and said, '*Helvíti*, Bill, that's a *tree*.'

Bill, who had hoisted himself up the tub, and now stood on its rim, said, 'She be indeed.'

'It's got to be the only tree on Earth.'

He raised his eyebrows. 'Ain't it just. Got all the soil through the Maskirovkas. When you've plenty of tobacco to trade, it's amazing what you can get.' He placed a palm on the trunk. 'Roots are good and proper, at home in the soil, and when she gets to five metres, I'll have my mast.'

Katherine got to her feet. 'You're going to chop it down?'

'She's teak,' he said, not taking his eyes from the tree. 'She's destined for a mighty fine purpose.'

'But you can't.'

'Oh, I'll take cuttings. I'll grow another. I'll grow many more. But a pirate needs a ship, don't he?'

'You're going to chop this down and make a boat?'

He rapped his knuckles on the trunk. 'That's right. And then I'm going to learn to sail. I'm going to see what's out there.'

There's nothing out there. It's all dead. She bit back the thoughts, said, 'You said you needed my advice?'

He ran his fingers over a leaf. 'Aye,' he said, 'there's a problem and I don't know how best to solve it.' Pulling the leaf from the tree, the healthy branch bending until it snapped back, he made a face, like he was trying to see through the tree. He handed the leaf to Katherine. 'I think the soil is depleted.'

A narrow, bright crimson line ran the edge of the leaf, like a line of rust.

'Your soil is heavy with iron,' she said, stepping forwards to the tub. 'The iron sinks to the bottom, and it's likely the roots have finally grown all the way down. The roots absorb the iron and it travels all the way up to the leaf, where it colours the new growth red.'

'I should be worried?'

'No,' she said, rubbing her fingers over the leaf, sticky, rough, healthy, 'all it'll do is what it's doing, crimsoning the edge.'

Bill hopped down from the tub. 'I like that,' he said. '*Crimson.* Maybe that's what she'll be called? *The Crimson Mistress.*'

Bill said, 'Now you've put my heart to rest, we ought to get back to Quin and *his* beauty, or Stone Hands might make a comeback.'

They went back upstairs, where Bill paid for their drinks, saying, 'It's only a couple of bytes, don't you worry,' and, before getting back to the nursery, they set off on the tram to Hotel du Soleil, where Katherine wanted to fetch her rucksack with all the goodies she'd spent the better part of a year making.

I'll fix his flower.

And then? Tiff said.

And then I'm going to steal it.

γ

They passed through the first ribboned doorway in the nursery. Her fingers tingled at the sight of the flower. Or is that because my neck has had all its nerves squashed?

She swung her rucksack off, placing it on the growing platform.

237

And as she went to unpack it a wail caught her attention.

Al-Zoubi was crying. From all the way at the back of the nursery, the Immortal Man's cries still found them. Not even the whirling extractor fans could suppress the sound.

'Is he…?'

'He's lost at sea,' Bill said. 'This flower means more to him than I'll ever know. Means more to New Havilah than I ever knew, too.'

'What's that supposed to mean?'

'Don't you worry.' Bill wheeled his cart over to a set of metal drawers. 'He'll stop his wallowing sooner or later, and we better have something good to show him.'

I came up here to learn, too, and I'm the one doing all the work.

You really think you can have it both ways, Kath? Don't you remember what I told you? You've got to pick a side.

Katherine unpacked her rucksack: microcontroller, optical transducers, spools of wire, an ancient LED display, and her old soldering iron. 'Have you got any solder?' she said.

Bill pulled open the drawer, fished out its contents and set them all on a worktop: spare wire, a lump of solder, and other miscellany she made a mental note of (pipettes, glass vials, sponges, iodine, etc.)

'All this lot hasn't seen the light of day for years—that wire and metal, I don't even know where it came from. But there's a lot to use.'

As the Immortal Man cried in his office, Katherine and Bill set to work. They sucked the growing pool of Black Rot from the flower's growth media pot, stashed that away in the glass vials, and inserted the first of the transducers into the growth medium. She monologued a tale of phosphorus, potassium, and nitrogen, weaving a narrative to the enraptured Bill. As she spoke, it became clearer to her that he had absolutely no idea about the molecular and atomic worlds. Osmosis, respiration, photosynthesis, and their ilk had no part in Bill's understanding of plants.

He really does all this by intuition. Or maybe he does speak to the plants. And they speak to him. Will they speak to me?

'Quin knows about all that stuff,' he assured her. 'He's tried to get me reading on it.'

Unspooling the copper wire, Katherine said, 'You didn't learn about this in school?'

'School? In New Havilah there are two schools, both along the Corridor, both inaccessible if you lived out in Gamma Valley.'

'You grew up in Gamma Valley?' In New Havilah, she'd heard it mentioned, mostly in the form of a threat: I'll drop you in Gamma Valley and leave you for the roaches! And back in Subsolum, trying her hardest to escape the monotony, she'd let New Havilah Wireless play at all hours, drift off, only to have: 'Gamma Valley, the only place in the world where the crops eat you!' wake her up in the middle of the night-cycle.

All of this mushed together in her subconscious the idea that Gamma Valley was where crooks and no goods got sent.

'Aye,' he said, 'a shining lot better than Radon Ravine.'

She clipped the end of the copper wire to the sensor protruding upwards from the flower's pot.

'It's why I owe him,' Bill went on. 'He knew my parents—

hempmoss farmers—and one evening they were all in the living room, smoking and discussing crop yields, and I wanted to show him a ragweed I'd grown, taller than you.

'"No ragweed grows that high," he'd said. My parents told him I'd grown it from a sapling. He offered to take me to the city, train me as a botanist and assistant, and here I am. But I never went to school.'

They slotted the copper wire through a trench on the growth table and soldered its other end to a pin on the microcontroller.

'Two more wires,' Katherine said, 'and we'll have counts on the big three.'

The flower's petal, now nothing more than a black stub, cut short the faint spur of progress.

Al-Zoubi's right. I can't take it—steal it—all rotten like this. At the rate it was disintegrating though, she imagined not returning with a flower, but with a box of black gloop. I'll fix it, but it could be weeks.

How long until the Solstice? That was how long she had.

Hurriedly, they laid two more copper wires. She showed Bill how to solder the ends to the microcontroller pins, and gave a short explanation that grew into a much longer explanation on embedded systems, assembly language, circle buffers, and even a bit on signal processing.

'But we can't change the microcontroller's programming,' she said. 'Or make any more microcontrollers.'

Bill pressed the iron's tip into a damp sponge until it stopped hissing. He said, 'It won't sense other nutrients.'

'Yes.'

'Why?'

'There are no computers to program them. And to make a microcontroller you need to know how to make semiconductors. Which no one does anymore.'

She plugged the short, ribboned connector dangling from the finger-sized LED display to the microcontroller. The display came to life: flashing a few times, then, in bright neon red: ERROR!

'*Helvíti*,' she exclaimed.

A microcontroller was a sensitive bit of kit. The journey up to New Havilah—filled with roach attacks, falls, bumpy tram rides, and errant radiation emissions—could easily have destroyed it. She wiped the sweat from her palms and pulled the power cable out, counted to five in her head, thought about praying to the Star Ships, then thought better, and stuck the power back in.

Al-Zoubi emerged from his office at the back of the nursery, parting the curtain of ribbons and sticking his head through. 'You're right, you're right,' he was saying, 'but we'll all be dust when the ships return.'

'Ahoy,' Bill said.

The Immortal Man, eyes puffy and red, jolted, as if disturbed from a dream. He passed through the flower room, declaring, 'I'm going to smoke,' and he wouldn't meet Katherine's eyes with his own. 'Don't you dare uproot that flower,' he said.

When the door at the top of the stairs slammed shut, she said, 'I don't know how you put up with him.'

'This, or a life in Gamma Valley. That's how.'

'Was he talking to us?'

'He chatters to himself.'

241

'An immortal's quirk?' Katherine guessed.

'That's more a Quinton al-Zoubi quirk—he's got barnacles on the brain.'

'Look, look, look.' On the LED display, in bright green, was: K 1.1 v. 'That's the potassium intensity, measured in voltage,' she explained.

The cart wheels squeaked as Bill drew closer. He whipped out his magnifying glass and stared fixedly at the now green display. 'K?'

'The elemental symbol for potassium.'

'And 1.1 is good?'

'No,' Katherine said. She cast her chin at the flower. 'For a plant that size, that voltage is indicative of a much too low intensity of potassium. But it's good, we've got a reading.'

Over the next few hours they laid and soldered more copper wires, calibrated the optical transducers, drew up more Black Rot from the flower's pot, and flushed it through with distilled water, ready to mix a new solution based on the data collected from the transducers.

Katherine gave lectures on plant macronutrients. Bill oscillated between fiery and inspired yarns on the *Lucha Libre* and its array of wrestlers, life in Gamma Valley and avoiding Radon Ravine, and how to communicate with the plants.

The pain in her neck was forgotten. She was totally absorbed and motivated, like those early years working her first field. And there was something about Bill—working with him was easy, like she'd been doing it all her life.

On the LED display, she flicked through the sensor outputs: K,

P, N, and the seven micronutrients: boron, zinc, manganese, iron, copper, molybdenum, and chlorine. From these readings they produced a new cocktail of nutrient solution and got that squirting across the flower's roots. She could have sworn she saw it glow, like a long dormant lightbulb flickering back on.

They sat staring at the flower, sharing a beer Bill had stashed.

'Is he going to come back?' Katherine asked.

'I ain't never seen him like this,' Bill said. 'He made a fuss about letting you in here, then he abandons you to it.'

She wanted to ask him more about her mother. Did they know each other? How did he give her the book? All this time she'd had Quinton al-Zoubi's book and never knew that *he* was the Immortal Man.

Bill jumped from his cart. 'It's getting late.'

'The sunlamps will have to be left on overnight,' Katherine said. 'Is that alright?'

'Aye.'

The last part of her wily plan was to culture the Black Rot itself. She set aside her beer, and pipetted drops from one of the vials of the rancid stuff into a petri dish. Bill scrounged up a spare cabinet in which she could store the dish.

'Tomorrow,' she said, 'we'll know if we're *fokked* or not. But tonight, I'm going to sleep.'

'And the plants, lassie, they'll find you in your dreams.'

A MARIONETTIST AND HIS MARIONETTE

Dust motes drifted across the office and scintillated in the cone of light bearing down on Quinton from the ceiling fixture. Dried tears gunked his eyes. His eyelids and nostrils were swollen, red, and painful to the touch. A roughness, brought on by all the pipe smoking, strangled the back of his throat, and forced him to tense with each of his breaths. Every now and then a dreadful cry escaped him.

The pocket watch sat open on his desk, ticking. Inside its lid, the only photograph he had of his mother stared back at him, its corners nibbled by mould. If he were being honest with himself, he had lost count of the years.

I'm alone. Abandoned. Been lied to. Proxima Centauri doesn't even exist. There are no stars. All there is is that bleak, grey sky, all the way to infinity.

Do you hear yourself? Sophia said to him. *I must pick you up and dust you off.*

He wrestled himself in his chair and found a comfortable position. One leg over the other, providing him a surface to fill his pipe on.

You've been lying to me too. Why didn't you come back? All this time, Sophia, I have been waiting, and you never sent me a message? Never told me you had a daughter.

I died, she told him, *didn't you hear what Katherine said? The radiation!*

You aren't really dead, he told her, I can hear your voice. 'Oh what's the point?' he said out loud. 'I'm sitting here crying because it's all over. The Flower is dead.' He got his pipe to his lips.

You'll have Billick and Katherine work away in there, then? For what? If you've given up why let them?

'Because...' he searched himself for an answer.

Because you haven't got done fighting, that's why.

'I've got nothing to lose, Sophia. Not anymore.'

That's right, you don't. So calm down. Let whatever is happening back there, happen.

Smoke drifted into the light and fluttered the dust motes about. 'She has sensors. She's read my book. She'll know what to do.'

So leave them to it. Rest.

Quinton pushed up from the chair and collected the pocket watch. 'I'm coming to see you.' He held the pipe between his lips and pocketed the watch. 'We have the Solstice to prepare for.'

In the exotics room, amongst the low and steady hum of fans and the gurgles of nutrient solution pipes, he pulled the bottle of *Liphoric Zed* from its cabinet, admired the luminescent green liquid, and then made one last check through the logbook.

Billick and Katherine yammered in the other room. Holding the ribbons to one side he stuck his head through, stole a glance at the Flower, at the sensors the Subsolumer had been so quick to stick in its pot.

It's dead, Sophia, it's over. I won't see my mother again and life here is all set to perish. I don't know where the Rot has come from, but I should think it's the Earth, coming to claim what little life is

245

left. We were never meant for it.

You are meant for the Stars, Quinton.

'You're right, you're right,' he said, 'but we'll all be dust when the ships return.'

'Ahoy,' Bill said.

The gruff voice stirred him from his thoughts.

He tore through the room, mumbling, 'I'm going to smoke,' holding his stare on his Flower. On its dead petal.

Pocket weighing heavy, loaded with the bottle of *Liphoric Zed*, Quiton pulled open the nursery door and stepped out. The Corridor's early evening bustle hit him like a sea of crimson: red painted faces; flowing robes and gowns; children sprinting across the tram tracks, blood red streamers tied to their limbs; food stalls packed to bursting with dyed mushroom buns, bark beetle burgers, and red ices.

He slammed the door shut behind him.

All of it's over, he said to Sophia, and I shall enjoy the last in your company.

γ

Home, he toed off his boots, and stashed them neatly by the front door. Orange light from the streetlamps, the usual gloom, tinted every inch of his home. His lover stood at the bay windows: a charcoal silhouette against the murky orange, her hand resting on her hip.

'Sophia,' he said.

'Hello,' she said, not looking round. 'Are you feeling better now?'

'I always feel better when I am with you.'

He sauntered into the kitchen, on his way draping his coat over the back of the sofa. There was a bottle of Radium Dreams— a fine bark beetle venom he'd been waiting to open. He cracked the lid and sniffed: minty, bitter like chocolate, and a hint he could never place. It reminded him, maybe, of oranges, but they had disappeared long before Earth did and he could only guess at their flavour, never having actually eaten one himself.

After pouring a sizable measure into one of his good glasses, he slid open the kitchen window, reached out into the cold, broke an icicle from the ledge, and dropped it into the glass.

Sitting on the sofa, chilled bark beetle venom on the coffee table at his shins, he sank back and smoked. Sophia, fixed in her wrist-on-the-hip pose, didn't move, even as she said to him: *How do you feel now, calm?*

'Very.' He picked up his glass, the icicle sliding around the inside of the rim, and went to sip, when he paused, noticing flecks of black paper on the coffee table.

You must remember not to let go of your faith. Your mother's love travels all across the stars.

But he wasn't listening. The paper shreds had his full attention. He set the glass down and poked at the shreds, sniffed them.

They smelt *rotten*.

A memory gnawed at him; where had the shreds come from? He slid one piece into another. They fit like a jigsaw puzzle.

'You're ignoring me,' Sophia said. 'After all I've done to rouse you up?'

'I'm sorry,' he blurted. Then: 'Can't you smell it? Smell it on these bits of paper?'

'Smell what?' Sophia said.

On the sheet of black paper the first few lines were faintly visible:

Gospodin Quinton al-Zoubi,

The Resource Council requests your

Lady Jupiter's letter, he realised. It had instructed him to go to the Sun Church, but he didn't remember it being black. This was certainly Rot. Hastily, he swept the paper shreds off the edge of the coffee table and into his drink of Radon Dreams. The shreds dissolved and turned the drink into black gloop. 'The Rot's in my rooms,' he said. I mean, I knew it, that it has to have been me. It's following me about. The Flower, the chocolate, the grow houses, everywhere *I* go, it goes too. But the paper? 'I don't understand.' He shut his eyes and pressed his fingertips against them: cast his mind back to when he'd received the letter.

That shining postlady gunking up my letters again! he recalled. In the last few months, all his letters had been gunked up by her.

'The *postlady*?' Sophia said. 'I don't think she's the one seeding our home with the Rot.'

'No,' he said, 'she probably has no idea.'

'Then who?'

At his feet, he found more paper shreds, the bottom of the letter.

'Who else,' he said, tearing the paper up and sprinkling it into his black gloop drink, 'but Lady Jupiter?'

It wasn't the Earth sentencing him—and, unwittingly, the rest of New Havilah—to death: it was her. But could he be sure? Perhaps the letters were stored next to— No, it had to be her. Selling his blood, placing a Subsolumer in his nursery, and smearing rot in his home. It wasn't the sun lamps that had caused the Flower to decay, it was her. It had always been her.

'Can you explain it?' he said to Sophia. He walked across to her, slipped his arms around her waist. 'I can't understand why she wants me gone.'

Red lanterns speckled the streets below, glowing brightly in the dark. The town had emptied out, its people all in their homes, preparing for the next few days.

There must have been many letters. Each sprinkled with Rot. It didn't answer his question, though. Why does she want me gone?

'You're forgetting who she's selling your blood to.'

In his embrace, she warmed. A soft heat.

Lady Jupiter didn't have the knowledge to make a thing like the Rot. Though that assumed the Rot was a made thing, and not a scooping of rancid mould from behind her sofa and slathered on a letter.

'What's it really matter, Sophia? My fate was sealed as soon as the Rot infected the Flower.'

He rested his chin on Sophia's shoulder.

'There's no more fight left in me.'

She became lifeless in his arms: her warmth gone.

He recoiled from her. 'Can't you feel how exhausted I am?' he said.

'You aren't allowed to give up,' she told him.

'This is not giving up,' he said, 'it's…'

… and he ventured back into the kitchen to find the rest of the Radon Dreams. He drank from the bottle, sat on the sofa, and smoked his pipe.

Who cares if Daniel is buying my blood, if Lady Jupiter wants to Rot my plants away. She's destroyed the whole town and not even realised it.

'I'll go out with a bang,' he said. The venom softened him and the pipe smoke sharpened him. 'A drunken bang.'

γ

The telephone in Quinton's rooms rang. It had been ringing all morning and had awoken him from dreams of Sophia. He rolled from the sofa onto the floor, half asleep, half hungover, and belly-crawled until he reached the copperline, where he yanked it from the wall.

He burped and yawned and, in the new found quiet, fell asleep.

Squeaky door, footsteps, creaky floorboards: the sounds came to him filtered through the bark beetle venom haze. His head hurt, and, when he opened his eyes to find the source of these sounds, the cloudlight coming in through the big bay windows forced him into a squint. The pain at the backs of his eyeballs, as if someone were trying to scoop them out with a dull knife, only went away if he kept his eyelids tight shut.

What was odd though was that in those brief moments he had managed to keep his eyes open, to see all that cloudlight pouring in, he noticed *two* silhouettes standing in front of the bay windows.

As he woke more, gathering himself up, patting himself down for his pipe, his other senses came awake too. He heard breathing.

Did I lock the door?

He roused himself, groped about to find something he could put his weight on and pull himself to his feet. Is there someone here, Sophia?

Slumping up against a wall, Quinton heaved himself upright.

'What is this?' a voice asked.

Eyes still shut, he found his balance, and rubbed his head. 'What did you say, Sophia?' He patted himself for his pipe, failed to find it, sighed. The pain behind his eyes let up enough for him to open them one by one: he confirmed what he thought he'd seen earlier: *two* silhouettes in front of the bay windows.

How much did I drink?

'Sophia?' the voice said. 'That was my mother's name.'

At that, Quinton opened his eyes fully, enduring the pain, and blinked until the figure in front of him resolved. *Katherine.*

'What in Brightness are you doing in my rooms!' he snapped. She was standing right beside Sophia, *touching* her, *inspecting* her, *ogling* and *probing* and— 'Get away!'

251

Katherine stepped back, saying, 'You didn't answer your telephone.'

'Perhaps I didn't want to be disturbed.' He reached them both, pushed Katherine away, 'Get out.'

'Did you call this *thing*, Sophia?' Katherine asked.

'*She* isn't a thing, and— Get out!'

Katherine sat down on the big window's ledge. 'You did know her, didn't you. That's how she got the book, you gave it to her.'

Staring hard at his beloved, Quinton said inwardly: All this time you were lying to me—you never told me you had a daughter. I've waited all this time and you were gone.

No words came his way.

'This *thing*,' Katherine said, shock or disgust in her voice, he wasn't sure which, 'you speak to it?'

'Please,' he said, 'please leave.' He lifted an arm and pointed at the door. 'You can't be here. No one can.'

Outside, as the morning light grew, so did the sounds of New Havilians readying themselves for another day's work. Trams rumbled on their tracks. Vendors haggled at their stalls. Street performers danced and sang.

He darted across the room, to the coffee table, and found his pipe. The tobacco worked the tension in his muscles soft, lessened the pain behind his eyes.

Katherine, still seated on the window ledge, never took her stare from Sophia. From *my* Sophia.

'My mother was here, in New Havilah.'

'Yes,' he said. 'Didn't you know?'

'I had no idea. All I ever knew was that book on hydroponics.

She had to have got it from New Havilah.'

If you think you can trust her, Sophia whispered to him, *then trust her. She is my daughter after all.*

He walked across the living room, pipe between his lips, and sat in the armchair that looked out the window. Katherine looked so much like her mother, he almost burst into tears.

Here you are, in front of me, after all these years we've spent apart.

As the Solstice drew nearer and the last time he had drunk *Liphoric Zed* further, he became more and more capricious— I'm all over the place. But there was good reason. Maybe, at last, he might finally get some answers. So he sucked in a large breath and he said, 'Your mother came to New Havilah with the same desire in her heart: to learn the hydroponic method of growing.'

Katherine, learning forwards, 'She kept it all a secret—it didn't change anything.'

'In all my life,' Quinton said, 'I had never met someone so kind, so beautiful, so calm and caring. She drew out of me my absolute best. We were in love.' When he looked over at Sophia, expecting to see her turn from the window and smile at him, like she had done all those years ago, all he saw was a grey, lifeless radiation dummy. 'I couldn't let her go.'

'So you...?' Katherine got to her feet and reached for Sophia.

'Please, don't—don't touch her.'

She hesitated, recoiled. '*Helvíti.*'

'We were in love, you understand? Over the months she was here I taught her everything. I wrote that book for her. I showed her my culture. Told her about the world before the Bombs. Told

253

'every shining detail of my long life.'

'But my father.' Katherine met his eyes, wearing a half scowl, half pleading expression.

'I begged her not to go back to Subsolum. I knew she didn't love him.' He paused, smoked, blinked back the lingering pain behind his eyes. 'What I didn't know was that she had *you*.'

Katherine gulped for air. Her words, no doubt, caught in her throat—her heart, no doubt, skipping beats.

'She promised to return,' Quinton went on, 'but that she had to go back first. And I never understood why, until I met you.' He held his head in his hands. 'I didn't even know that she … that she died.' Fighting back tears, he sat upright in the armchair.

'She died when I was young,' Katherine said. 'I have a handful of memories, that's all I got.'

'I'm sorry,' he said. 'If it means anything, you are so much like her.'

'The radiation gave her cancer.' The last word carried an accusing tone.

'Even all those years ago, Katherine, the radiation levels had fallen. Yes, if she had stayed out on the top of the mountain, or in the valleys, then she would have taken enough radiation to make her sick, but not here, in New Havilah. I showed you the counts.'

'So what made her sick?'

'I don't know,' he said, dropping his head.

'So you created *her*?' A jutting, harsh gesture at Sophia.

'Don't you judge me. When you live as long as I do, you need a reason to keep going. I had found a new reason in your mother, and when she left I couldn't let my love die.'

254

Katherine shook her head slowly. She closed her eyes and lent backwards against the window and rubbed that sore neck of hers. She said, 'A new reason?'

And Quinton said, 'Yes,' hoping that Katherine wasn't about to dredge up any more from his life.

'What was the old reason?' She opened her eyes, spat the words, 'Power? Control?'

Quinton laughed. Maybe she goes there because of Daniel. Power and control? I want *less* responsibility. 'No,' he said, 'that was never my desire.'

'What then?'

He swallowed, slid a shaky hand into his pocket and withdrew his pocket watch. '*My* mother,' he said. The watch lid popped open and he showed her the photograph.

'That's her?' Katherine got up from the ledge and walked over to him in the armchair.

He unclipped the watch and let her take it. The desire to show her it barely beat the impulse to snatch it back.

Katherine said, 'I saw you staring at it on the tram down the mountain.'

On the back of the lid, the shiny brass warped Sophia's reflection, making her something she was not. She isn't distorted or warped or twisted: she is real and alive and here.

I am, Sophia whispered to him.

'What happened to her?'

Quinton, taken from his thoughts, said, 'She is on a Starship, an Evacuee.' I've been here before: said all this before. Trusted like this before. Am I a fool for trying it all again?

255

Katherine, snapping the watch lid closed, looked up at him, squinting. '*You* believe in the Starships? I thought New Havilians had their own religions.'

'Of course I believe in the Starships.'

'Did you see them leave?'

He shook his head.

'Why didn't you go with them?'

Standing now, Quinton walked past Katherine and over to the big bay windows. He rested his hands on the ledge and nodded out to the town. 'Someone needed to stay behind. To keep the world alive as best they could.'

Katherine, shoulder to shoulder with him, offered the pocket watch back, and he took it quickly, clipping it to its chain, placing it back in its right place, patting it down.

'Thank you,' she said, 'for showing me.' She looked out on the town too, and for a time they both stared, not saying a word. The town was so beautiful. Alive and brimming with its people. The rumbles of trams, the banging of steel drums, the gentle whistle of the wind.

'I don't believe,' Katherine said, staring up at the stratospheric dust now, 'that there are any Starships. I think it's a lie.'

'You've been talking to Darleaner.'

'It isn't that, al-Zoubi.'

Why does she call me that? 'Then what is it?' he said.

'It's just a ridiculous idea.'

'Why do you think my mother left? She got a seat because she created the Flower, the longevity drug, *Liphoric Zed*, so she could keep everyone alive long enough to reach Alpha Centauri.'

'And she couldn't get you a seat?'

It stopped him—some—and he had to take a breath before saying, 'She left me here to look after whoever was left.'

Katherine turned from the window, stared him down, saying, 'How old were you?'

He hesitated. 'Six.'

She raised an eyebrow, but held off from pressing him any further. 'I came here to tell you something.' She started walking back to the front door. 'It's your Flower,' she said. 'We've cured it.'

γ

The Flower—his Flower—glinted under the sun lamps. Its nine healthy petals glowed a glorious white. The tenth petal, that had oozed and wept with the Black Rot, now dangled completely unencumbered. Still only half a petal, but free from Rot.

Palms slick and sweaty, Quinton wiped down his coat, shaking his head in disbelief.

She's done it. They've done it.

Two interpretations came to Quinton's mind. The first, that he had got lucky. Very lucky. The Subsolumer agronomist had skills he hadn't, and she had used these skills to help him, in his long fought for cooperation, to save his dying Flower. The second, however, was that this was far too straightforward for her. As if she knew exactly what to do, following a preplanned protocol. One Daniel Marston had orchestrated from afar. She isn't her father, he said to himself, standing there gawping at his Flower, she's here for both our societies.

You do trust her, Sophia whispered. *You trust her like you trusted me.*

And what a fool I was.

Katherine's sensors projected from the Flower's pot: copper wires ran from them like creeping snow vine, following the pipe trenches in the growing table. Billick flicked through the display, showing off the nutrient counts, a toothy grin on his face.

'She's a miracle worker, Cap'n.'

The Flower's stigma though, where the life-giving *Zed* came forth, was barren. The nibbled tenth petal needed to grow fully before secretions could happen.

'It works,' Katherine said. She was chewing a big stick of roach jerky. Getting her own back. 'We're feeding it a new nutrient solution mix. It covers all the plant's deficiencies.'

'It's impressive,' he said, 'but without the petal fully formed, it's hopeless.' And then in a tone that caught not only himself, but Billick and Katherine too, by surprise, he said, 'Is there anything more you can do?'

Katherine slumped onto a stool, cheeks ballooned by roach jerky, and huffed. She took her time chewing, and finally swallowed the great mouthful to say, 'All that's left is to monitor it.'

'You've not checked the roots.'

'You told us not to,' Billick said.

Quinton leant over the growing table and breathed in the Flower's pollen: sweet with hints of the ambrosia. 'Katherine,' he said, 'have you wondered where the Rot comes from?' But before she said a word, he pushed on: 'I've always thought it was a confluence of heat, damp, mould.'

Billick grumbled at this, clearly peeved that only now was Quinton interested in finding the source of the Rot, or daring to experiment, so certain he had been of keeping it under control.

'Can we check the roots?' she said. Her face and eyes became hard, switching to an agronomist mode, no doubt. 'If it is root fungus, then the roots will be swollen and mottled.'

'I did check the roots,' he said, 'not long ago.'

'And how far along was the rest of the infection? It can take time for the root fungus to show.'

Quinton shook his head, shrugging. 'I can't remember. I haven't *exactly* been feeling much like myself lately.'

'Aye,' Billick said. 'We've noticed.'

The three got to work: Billick used a scoop and tweezers to remove the perlite granules from the Flower's pot, slowly exposing the roots. Katherine, between tending to her 'experiment' (explained to Quinton as a culture of the Rot) and stuffing her face with more roach jerky, helped Billick by removing the sensors and keeping them from getting damaged; Quinton, who couldn't bear see his Flower go through all this, hid himself (this time without the crying) in the exotics room, where he prepared the case Darleaner had made to house the Flower once again.

The case had space for Katherine's sensors, and, after a bit of drilling, a routing port for the copper wires.

Once all of this was done, Quinton, off the tram tracks and in no hurry to right himself, smoked his pipe in the Flower room and tried counting the pink dots spread over the Flower's roots.

'Cap'n, I don't know about all this smoking in here.'

Katherine, whose gloved hand held the Flower's roots for all to see, said, 'I rather like it.'

'See, there we are.'

'It'll gunk the extractor fans.'

'Oh, they've had to deal with far worse.' Quinton nodded at the Flower, exhaling a great cloud. 'Besides, don't you notice the mood it puts me in? I could run a confectionary stall on a buzz like this.'

'Shiver me timbers,' Billick exclaimed.

'If we could get to the matter very much at hand,' Quinton said. 'I've not seen those pink dots before.'

'It's fungal root rot,' Katherine said. 'But I've not seen it like this. Usually it's black and slimy, and there's an ash-like consistency to it further up the root.' Using a cottonmoss tip, she prodded the root here and there, explaining how the fungal rot spreads. 'But this is different. Why is it pink? And it's not sticking, you can scrape it off.' Which she did, causing a minor panic and a hasty search around the nursery for the vacuum-pump cleaner.

They brought the Flower's case into the Flower room, ran the copper wires through it, potted the Flower (clean perlite and all), connected up the sensors, and then set the Flower in the case.

Smoking away, gorging himself on the data displayed in bright LED lights, Quinton startled at Katherine's touch.

'Can I try it?' she said, her gaze on the pipe.

Billick, who not long ago had let himself enjoy a short break to read his teak tree book, said, 'Eh, you'll blow yourself through the rafters!'

'I've not smoked before,' Katherine explained.

Quinton brought his lighter to the pipe bowl, mumbled around the pipe stem in his mouth: 'Like this, get the tobacco nice and hot and then take the smoke into your mouth. Don't inhale, and don't feel bad if the bowl goes out, there's an art to it.'

Pipe in hand, Katherine pouted, brought the stem to her lips, and then drew on it softly. Smoke bled from the corners of her mouth: a silky grey line that reached deeply into Quinton's mind, where it plucked a dusty memory. A memory of Sophia: *When you were still flesh. Huddled in a blanket, staring out at the sea, we shared a smoke and tried to imagine what fish looked like as they played.*

I'll never forget it, Quinton.

Katherine's coughing fit ripped Quinton into the present. He snatched the pipe from her and whacked her on the back. Ghostly white and sweating, she looked close to vomiting, but she held herself together enough to push him away, and say, 'You're a mad man, smoking that at all hours!' And then, once she'd settled down some, 'Though I do feel rather good.'

'Yeah, great,' Billick said. 'He'll get you hooked and you'll never stop.' The botanist hopped into his cart, wheeled it over to the Flower in its case. 'We're just gonna let those spores linger on the roots?'

Katherine cleared her throat and explained. 'Plants have their own defensive mechanisms. Now that the Flower is getting what it needs, it should be able to fight off what's left on the roots. It's already proved itself against the spoilage on the petal.'

'So we leave it?'

'I think so.'

A silence fell upon them. Quinton couldn't remember the last time he had worked, really worked, as a team. Of course there were the emergencies that he, Billick, Syd and Dobromir handled. But this was real work. He hadn't explored the Flower in great depths for so long. It was as if Katherine had literally jumped from his past and into his present to remind him where he was heading. The stars!

Breaking the silence, he asked them: 'Have you both got your Summer Solstice dress ready?'

Katherine shot up straight—as if zapped by one of Ganymede's bolts. 'I can go?'

'I don't see why not,' Quinton said. 'You've been working as hard as any New Havilian.' He fumbled around in a pocket and lifted out a couple hundred bytes worth of notes. 'Here—' he handed the money to Katherine '—you and Bill go and buy your outfits. Remember, bright red, and don't cheap out. You two must look your best.'

Two wide smiles on their faces, Billick and Katherine headed right for the stairs. In little time, Bill burst into yarns about the Summer Solstice: the origins of the food and dress, the ceremony itself and the importance of taking Waters. Katherine, unashamedly, gobbled all this up. And the two left.

Leaving me ... *alone.*

γ

Quinton reached the sea.

It always surprised him how few New Havilians made this short walk. The town, its spine the Corridor and its ribs the massive baroque buildings, sat pushed up against the edge of a ten foot granite cliff. As the grow houses went up they, along with the buildings of the Old World, blocked the direct sea views.

And it was all my doing.

Perhaps he was selfish? He wanted the sea for those who really wanted *it*. It wasn't like the sea had been moved, only made harder to get to. But the more he thought about it, the more he realised what a mistake that had been. Making the sea easier to get to would benefit everyone. Its power and charm had a soothing influence on troubled minds.

You showed me the ocean—told me off for not calling it the sea.
He smiled.

A narrow slope, carved into the cliff by the salt makers, ran from the top of the cliff and into a small bay. Only a single salt maker was out today—it being Solstice. They came in all shapes and sizes—saltwater collection one of those few professions that leant itself neatly to varied forms. The single salt worker, a feathered man, whose greying tips and white speckles betrayed a life longly lived, dragged a bucket full of seawater from the waves and up the stony beach. They used a lubricated sheet of metal to reduce the friction. Those that couldn't carry a bucket up the beach, dragged one up the sheet and those that couldn't drag the buckets instead kept the sheet lubricated, fetched lunches, sung songs, and generally made the whole endeavour more enjoyable.

When Quinton reached the bottom of the slope the feathered man noticed him, bobbed his head, his bright red wattle flapping, and then tipped out the salt water into a large kettle.

Quinton hadn't come here to chat. I've come to be with you, Sophia.

But when she gave him no reply, he reluctantly walked across the sand and stones to go and say hello.

'I'll be damned,' the feathered man said, 'the Immortal Man has come to share his presence.'

It was always a fifty-fifty: Quinton either got bitterness or gushing admiration.

He gave no response.

Steam poured from the kettle. The salt maker worked a set of billows with his feet, burning what smelt like dried cottonmoss. 'The steam wants to be thick and opaque,' he said. 'If I can see through it, it's taking too long.'

'Why are you working?' Quinton asked.

The question stopped the salt maker. He took his foot off the bellows and turned to face the sea. Quinton joined him in his stare out towards the horizon. White-tipped waves broke in the middle distance, but only smaller waves rolled on the shore. The bay had a reef—at least that's what Quinton had heard—which stopped waves getting too big on the shore and made the salt makers' lives easier.

'I'm where I want to be,' the salt maker said after a time. 'I'm out here. Listening to the waves break.'

All the time Quinton and Sophia had spent here, laughing, talking, even sometimes being silly, ran through his mind, made a sickly colour by Katherine's existence. All this time he had thought he'd found someone who he could trust, and she had been lying to him. He pressed a hand against his pocket, checking the watch was still there, that his mother was still there.

The two remained silent. The waves, the boiling salt-water, the roaring flames under the kettle, filling the empty space, until the salt maker finally said, 'This place would have been teeming. Gulls squawking, crabs scuttling; prawns, limpets, urchins in the rockpools; grey herons spearing with their beaks for fish; cormorants diving under the water or flapping their wet feathers about in the sun to dry them off.' He gave a little flap of his own feathers. 'Now it's…'

'Lifeless,' Quinton said.

'Apart from me.' The salt maker met Quinton's eyes with a tired glance. 'So maybe that's it, why I don't take days off, it would leave my home lifeless.'

They chatted for a time. His name was Ptitsa, he had three children, seven grandchildren, and a great grandchild on the way. His husband had died two Solstices ago from old age. He lived alone now. He remembered his first Summer Solstice, how good he'd felt after taking Waters, and how it had put an end to his mother's skin infection. A salt maker for five decades, Ptitsa had not once tried his hand at being a Resource Council member, he said Lady Jupiter had good ideas, but thought she was a bad listener and wasn't worth the time. He loved mushroom puffs. His family bought him al-Zoubi tobacco for his birthday and he said every year it always tasted better. He disliked al-Zoubi chocolate, though.

Quinton had come here to process what Katherine had done. She knew the truth about Sophia, his Sophia. He had feared this all his life. Listening to Ptitsa's story, Quinton let all those feelings of shame and embarrassment melt away. *I'm not being judged. I'm not being ostracised. We do what we do.*

Their conversation ended when the salt water boiled off and needed Ptitsa's attention. They said goodbye to each other, and, as Quinton left, he said, 'Don't forget to take Waters.'

To which Ptitsa replied, 'Who forgets to take Waters?' and chuckled.

γ

He walked back up the slope and returned to the Corridor. It heaved with New Havilians all draped in red, chatting and laughing. Billick and Katherine were somewhere in there, scouring all the markets and shops for their Red Threads.

Navigating his way between everyone, keeping his head low, he headed for Ganymede's office, in the Ganymede Manufacturing building.

His theory on the Black Rot, one that he wanted to test on John Ganymede, had fallen into place and needed to be aired out. A slight skip in his step betrayed his better mood: *the Flower is alive.*

The Ganymede Manufacturing building, one of the taller buildings in the Corridor's baroque collection, housed many of New Havilah's brightest minds. The foundry, in the bottom of the building, belched steam at the street level, which made it impractical for market stalls or buskers to set up outside its doors. Ganymede once explained that rerouting the exhausts so they let out from the top of the building cost much more than any vendor might make outside the building's doors, but Quinton knew Ganymede just wanted to keep the riff-raff away.

He went inside, passing through the warm steam, and headed for Ganymede's office. The person at the reception desk said something in bark beetle language—'*Blak blu bo brrif.*'

Which Quinton needed a good few seconds to translate to: He is on roof.

On the roof, he found John Ganymede soaking in a hot pool sunken flush to the ground, steam rising from the water. Arms outstretched and resting behind him, Ganymede opened one eye, and said, 'Al-Zoubi, you've disturbed my peace.'

I'm making it somewhat of a habit, he thought, recalling the salt maker and his initial hostility.

The giant's deep blue skin had a pinkish hue to it. He'd been soaking for a while.

'We need to talk.'

'Yes.' Ganymede rose from the water—exposing himself—and took his time to put on his robe.

Quinton averted his eyes, saying, 'Never a lack of modesty.' There's no moment he won't use for a power play.

Ganymede laughed. He opened his wooden cigar box, plucked out a cigar, and lay back on a reclining chair. Up high on the roof, the winds whipped in easily from the sea and the wind chill put a shiver in Quinton, yet Ganymede seemed as if he were bathing under the sun. He gestured for Quinton to sit on the other chair.

As Quinton sat and struggled to light his pipe, Ganymede said, 'After the other day, I knew we were getting closer to the truth.'

The giant, lying with his head back, sucked on his cigar, and blew smoke. 'Today I tried to speak with Juju.'

Brightness, it's about time. He's more lost than me.

'And?' Quinton had to prompt.

'All the real-time communication between her and Subsolum has been through the official channels. She has been busy organising this paraffin trade. I've had the copperlines tapped for months, and heard nothing sinister.' He adjusted himself on the chair, smoked more. 'What I hadn't been able to read was the post. It falls under the Resource Council's control as it mostly delivers goods to and from Subsolum.'

Which, he thought, backs up my theory: the Black Rot came in the post, from Lady Jupiter.

Ganymede was saying, '…and when I asked her what was going on about Maskirovkas not being able to get power and heat credits—she told me not to worry. So when she left the house I broke into her office and steamed open a few letters.' He sat up now, and, framed by the horizon line, he looked like a deity, like he had the power to float amongst the clouds. 'Her and this man Ólafur have sent many letters back and forth to each other. *For years.*'

'When was the first letter dated?' Quinton asked.

'Four years ago, something like that.'

'Does it match the time you stopped testing my blood?'

At that Ganymede paused. He pinched a fleck of tobacco from his lips.

Quinton re-lit and drew hard on his pipe. They'd run out of tobacco before getting to the end of the conversation at this rate.

'It does,' Ganymede said.

'So she's stolen my blood, lied about it, and sold it to Daniel Marston's servant.'

Ganymede, hunching forwards, 'It seems so. The letters are coded, there's no mention of blood, but it's obvious enough.' He then turned to Quinton. Tiny flickers of lightning flashed in his eyes. Electric blue, dangerous, lethal. It was a rare thing indeed what power Ganymede had trapped inside his eyes. In all Quinton's time, he had never seen another New Havilian that had had a *lethal* mutation—in the sense of it being lethal to others. He'd not seen any working stingers or venomous fangs, but Ganymede had his lightning bolts. And zapped those few who dared cross him. But he couldn't zap her.

Ganymede added, 'Someone, Daniel, I presume, must have a use for your blood. Juju wouldn't go to all this trouble for nothing.'

'You're right, John,' Quinton said, his candour surprising both himself and Ganymede.

The giant stared, unmoving. Smoke rose from the end of his cigar, battered about by the wind, until the cherry faded, extinguished. Eventually he said, 'You've known all this time that your blood *isn't* useless?'

The Flower had been discovered. Sophia—Sophia is gone. She's been gone all along and I never knew. What does keeping this from him get me now? Nothing. 'Yes,' Quinton said. 'My blood holds clues to my immortality—and it appears Daniel and Lady Jupiter are aware of this.'

'You've hidden it all this time? The bits and bytes I've wasted on you, on testing your blood. I could have spent it all on a new brickworks or replaced a line for the trams.' He shook his giant head: the blue light inside his eyes bright. 'All along you've been playing me?'

'I've only kept you in the dark—'

'You can't keep me in the dark'—eyes like blue suns—'I am my own source of light.'

Once Ganymede's eyes cooled, Quinton dared venture to say, 'It's clear Lady Jupiter has made a deal with Daniel, but that isn't all she's done.' He paused, waited to see if Ganymede would react in any way, and when he didn't, Quinton said, 'She's infected my plants.'

'Why?'

'I don't know.' Quinton, shivering now from the wind and the cold, pulled his coat tight around him. 'But I suspect it has something to do with the Subsolumer placed in my nursery. She's helping to cure the plants.'

Ganymede gave no response. He reached behind him to find a lighter and re-lit his cigar.

There's only so much I can tell him—there's no need to bring the Flower into this. Despite what it and I have gone through.

'It could be a coincidence,' Ganymede said from behind his cigar. 'They swapped the Subsolumers at the last moment, if I am remembering right.'

'Hmm.' He still wasn't sure. Do I trust Katherine?

She's my daughter, Sophia whispered.

Changing course, Ganymede said, 'Al-Zoubi, I don't know what is around the bend. Do you understand? I have failed, as a husband and as a leader, and now Juju has had enough.' He sighed, looked off to the horizon, and puffed at the cigar. 'We've fought over and over about expanding the town.' He looked Quinton in the eyes: all the electric blue gone, instead there was void, darkness, exhaustion. 'New Havilah's population is *growing*. The last census put us at 24,434. We are already too big. If the population reaches 30,000, water becomes a problem.'

'Water?' It was the only resource Quinton never thought much about. To him it was endless.

'Yes, al-Zoubi. For drinking, for growing mosses in the valleys, and for power. If the most recent Subsolumer harvest report is correct, the Subsolumers are a bark beetle's width from total collapse. When Subsolum fails, there will be no water, and even if Subsolum doesn't fail now, New Havilah's expansion would strain them enough and force their collapse.'

'I've never thought about this,' Quinton said.

'No, it's not your job.' Ganymede crushed his cigar out on the floor and stood up. 'It's mine.'

And Quinton found himself saying, 'So what should I do?'

'Keep an eye on the Subsolumer. Let her do the work she wants, show her what she wants to see. We must let whatever is going to happen, happen.' As he stepped back into the hot pool, he added, 'Besides, don't you have Summer Solstice to worry about?'

I do.

PART THREE

"'Well,' said my aunt, 'this is his boy—his son. He would be as like his father as it's possible to be, if he was not so like his mother, too.'"

— *David Copperfield*, Charles Dickens

SUMMER SOLSTICE

– NEW HAVILAH –

Kath,

It's been, what, five days? Whenever someone's gone that long it usually means they're dead. I hope you aren't dead, Chick.

How's the weather? That's what I hear Overworlders ask each other a lot. I've been listening to the radio. I brought the one you had in your lab up into my cube. I hope you don't mind. I'm always listening out for news, see if you've had your head bitten off by a roach yet, that sort of thing. I think it's turning me into a jazz fan. You'll come back and find me all cultured. 'How about that, folks?'

I've not been fighting or training. The gym's empty. The grapplers don't even talk anymore. We're all busy working. And when we do see each other, we don't talk about grappling or sparring, we've forgotten what that's all about.

I've never not had a community before. It's all gone, Kath.

Everyone's still on half rations. There's less food than there's ever been. It's not good. There's so much tension. People who don't fight are fighting, some are stealing. Many people think your father has more rations somewhere, that he's hiding them for himself and those that are loyal to him.

I saw him in his office, and he's not doing well, Chick. I'm sorry. I think you need to come back home. He's been coughing blood. My father thinks he's got days left.

Ólafur gives orders and updates.

I wish I could tell you more, Kath. I wasn't even allowed to telephone you over the copperlines. Or actually write. Another grappler works as a station guard and I traded him a few of your potatoes to get this letter to a Maskirovka. I hope it makes its way to you.

I'm trying to figure out the right thing to do. I've been paying attention, you know, and as they say 'the tunnels whisper' so I hear a lot. But it's my dad I hear most. I think the Pipeworkers really are about to take over. People are confused. We were promised to be off the rations, that fields would produce again, and none of it happened. The people are looking more and more to the Pipeworkers for a way out. My father can't ignore them much longer. I don't know what that means, or what's going to happen, but it's desperate. You need to come back and speak to your father. He only listens to you. Before he's gone. Before there's a real fight.

Tiff

Katherine read the letter through again.

In the past few days, she'd nearly forgotten her home entirely. Forgotten her mission. Here she was, dressed in a red, shimmering dress, a plate of mushroom puffs and a cup of al-Zoubi's coffee by her side, wondering if her pair of new earrings really did suit her, when down there, starving and confused, Subsolum slowly split into two and her father lay dying.

A draft blew in from under the kitchen door of her New

Havilian rooms. Bill must have opened the window to fetch ice again for his third late-morning beer.

She quartered the letter and slipped it inside her bra, nibbled on a puff, and slurped coffee.

The last few days, spent working with Bill on the Flower and being shown around New Havilah, had started a turn in her. The feeling, distant at first, but ever drawing closer, that *she* was a New Havilian couldn't be ignored. Stealing the Flower felt like a betrayal, now.

Could I even do it?

Her sensors had done their job. The chances that she would drag the Rot down into Subsolum were firmly in the tolerable range, but getting it out of the nursery, and up the mountain, seemed impossible.

I could borrow it. I don't have to steal it. I could ask him. *Helvíti*, Dad's dying, I've got to try.

All she had to do was cure her father and then bring it back. The trouble, however, stirred when she thought about al-Zoubi actually letting her do it. There wasn't a chance.

But I did save it. Maybe he owes me?

The kitchen door creaked open. Billick stood in the threshold, a scaly hand wrapped around a stein with a large icicle projecting up from it. With his free hand, he doffed his pirate hat, blazoned by a skull and crossbones, and said, 'What do ye think?' in his best pirate voice.

The dark suit, trimmed in crimson, and held together by pearly white buttons, fit him perfectly. A cutlass—a repurposed roachmeater's knife—dangled from his waist. Tall black boots completed the outfit, and even gave him a few inches of height, which he'd claimed meant nothing to him, but she thought otherwise. They had purchased the outfit together, with the 'go away' money al-Zoubi had given them, and at the time Katherine thought they'd left the tailor with an impossible job—a ball shaped man, no neck to speak of, legs as narrow as small gauge water pipes, scaly skin rough and prone to snagging threads—but the tailor had quickly conjured Bill into a suave and charming man, accented by a Seven Seas buccaneer.

'I don't know who I'm looking at,' Katherine said. 'I've never seen such a disarming character before.'

Bill raised his stein and cheersed, a great grin on his face.

'What about me?' she said, standing up and brushing her shimmering dress flat. 'I hope I don't look too bright.'

'Right out of an Old World flick!' he said, hefting Katherine into a blush.

She couldn't remember the last time she felt beautiful, but the dress, the shopping, the success with the flower, and now Billick's big dumb grin: all of it a fine antidote to a lifetime of slugging away in the mud.

They'd had money left over to purchase an item Bill had been eyeing for quite some time. He'd told her, 'I was waiting for one good win on the *Lucha Libre*, but it ain't come yet. Now Quinny boy's gone and lined my pockets, I must have it!' He'd taken her through another twisting alley, further out from the Corridor, where the lanes were much too narrow for trams to get through, and into a tiny trinkets shop.

Most, if not all of it, was Old World: watches, necklaces, and rings; cups and bowls; candlestick holders; lamps and light fixtures; brass and bronze sculptures (clearly lifted from a single collection); raggedly bound books; paintings and prints; and on and on it went, stuffed so tightly the shop could only allow a single customer to walk its ways at once. Bill had sat on top of Katherine's rucksack the entire time.

They reached a silver tray of pocket watches, when Bill told her how envious of al-Zoubi's he was, and wanted one himself. They came in gold, silver, brass, and even a heavily patinated bronze. The proprietor, her head a sprawling mass of finger width tentacles, each ended by a tiny eyeball, convinced Bill, in a good show of salesship, that his green scales best matched the gold watches. To nobody's surprise, these were the most expensive. Forking over the cash, Bill explained that it was vital to accessorise for the Solstice, and that Katherine should pick something out for herself too. Not missing a beat, the proprietor swapped the tray of watches for a tray of jewellery. The fiery red earrings caught the light in a way that reminded Katherine of her father and his glasses, and, for one reason or another, she instinctively picked them up. The proprietor's many eyeballs fixed themselves on Katherine's lobes, and a pair of long, hairy arms raised, took the earrings from Katherine's hands, and clipped them onto her ears. A proffered mirror reflected back a stranger: no longer garbed in the usual agronomists' jumpsuit, no soil stains on her cheeks, and no black bags under her eyes, only a smiling, well rested, and fiery-earring adorned visage.

She had thought to herself, If only mum could see me.

'You really think I'd look the part in an Old World flick?' she said to Billick, taking her seat again beside the puffs and coffee, careful not to crease her dress. 'I look too bright!'

Bill pattered across to her, spilling beer as he went, and blabbering, 'No, no, no, you ain't too bright. I think you look the part. Anyone who says otherwise can taste the steel of my blade.' And he gave his 'cutlass' a rap.

Katherine laughed, only for it to be cut short by a poke from the folded letter inside her bra. Laughing, when they're starving, when my dad's about to die.

'You don't believe me?' Bill said, seating himself next to her on the sofa.

'No,' she said, 'it's not that.' She pinched at a metal sequin on her dress, turned to Bill. 'You've only known me for a week, but would you call me a friend?'

'Ay,' he said, not a moment's hesitation, 'how could I not? Any who the plants speak to has a place at my table.' He drank a big gulp from his stein. The stink of mushroom beer casting her mind back to the red curtained area of the *Stjörnu Farartæki*. The pissing match between Einar and her father.

'When you were in the kitchen,' she said, 'this came for me.' She slipped the letter from her bra and held it out. She unfolded it, saying, 'It's from a friend in Subsolum. It isn't going so well down there.'

Bill, in a gesture of solemnity that wasn't lost on Katherine, set his stein down on the table beside her coffee, and met her gaze.

'And... my father,' she said, 'he's dying.'

Bill's lips curled back ever so, revealing his small, yellowed fangs. And she wasn't sure what to make of the expression—part of her knew that Bill shared the common-ish opinion among New Havilians that Subsolumers were *Dirt Divers*. But he'd never made her feel unwelcome.

She continued uneasily, 'My friend thinks I should go back, before it's too late.'

'And miss Solstice?'

She glanced at the letter. It trembled in her hand. If she could just take the flower back—or better still, extract some *Liphoric Zed*, and bring that back.

'I don't want to miss it.'

Bill reached for his stein, brought it to his lips, tongued the icicle to one side. After a long pull on the drink, he said, 'Then leave after. Leave tomorrow.'

The stench of the mushroom beer put a fear into her. As those stones and bottles crashed around her, as her father coughed and screamed, as Ólafur cried to get them to move on, as the shouting of *Oust! Oust! Oust!* boomed.

'I'll stay,' she said, 'if you make a promise...?'

Bill said, 'Aye, cross my heart.'

She swallowed in a dry mouth. 'Will you help me extract some sap from the flower? That way I can give it to my father, I'll cure him.'

Ear tips crimson, fangs poking out, Bill pulled off his pirate's hat and laid it on the table. He sank back into the sofa and didn't say a word.

I've asked too much. He'll tell al-Zoubi. I'm not a thief or a traitor but al-Zoubi won't see it like that.

She wasn't. She was lost. Stuck between worlds that each gave

279

her what she needed, but only when the other wasn't.

'Bill, I'm sorry, I shouldn't have asked. It's no—'

'No,' he said, 'if it weren't for you there would be no more flower. I'll help you. I promise.' He smiled. And with a wink he said, 'But only *after* Solstice.'

γ

Outside the Sun Church, a swimming river of red ran the entire length of the Corridor and doubled back on itself like a serpent. The New Havilians danced and laughed as they waited to go inside. Roving bands marched up and down the queue, playing songs on steel drums and metal stringed guitars, enlivening the crowd as they came and went. Red coloured smoke Bombs fizzed and burst and enveloped all in crimson haze. It had the energy of the old *Stjörnu Farartæki*. She wished Tiffany were here. If anything could destroy the idea that New Havilah was backwards, it was this.

They were stationed right at the front of the queue, beside the Sun Church's doors. Al-Zoubi, dressed in a dark suit, the only bit of red on him a pocket square, spoke frantically with Lady Jupiter.

'Now isn't the time,' al-Zoubi was saying, 'to get into detail.'

'It never is with you, Gospodin al-Zoubi, is it? But a Solstice without chocolate is hardly a Solstice.'

'I've done my best,' he said.

Lady Jupiter's dress, a mass of frilly cottonmoss, dyed in various shades of red and purple, undulated as she paced backwards and forwards, treading deep footprints into the snow. 'We'll just have to go without.' She prodded him in the chest. 'But you aren't forgiven.'

Cries and cheers erupted.

A tram, shooting jets of flame above it, parted the river of red New Havilians. It crept along its rails until it reached the stop outside the church. The bands all halted their playing, and the crowd grew quiet.

'Forever the showman,' Lady Jupiter spat, and paced over to the church entrance, where the same red-faced, robed figures who had been in Katherine's room on her first morning, promptly escorted her inside.

'Sun Worshippers,' al-Zoubi explained, following Katherine's gaze. 'Once a rather wholesome ideal, I suppose, now nothing much more than Lady Jupiter's personal attaché.'

The tram's doors hissed and opened.

Bill said, 'He does like a spectacle.'

A collection of porters threw a red carpet out the opened tram door, and began unrolling it, brushing aside Katherine, Bill, and al-Zoubi. The Immortal Man's celebrity paled against what was coming next, Katherine gathered.

Trumpets, drums, more shoots of flame: and from the tram's doorway a giant emerged: John Ganymede.

The porters, finished with the red carpet, hurried over to hold up Ganymede's cape. He wore plates of gold metal, like a warrior from ancient history, and a black helmet with a visor that covered most of his face. Blue light poured out from the narrow gaps at his eyes.

The New Havilians whistled and cheered and only grew quiet

when Ganymede lifted both his hands high.

'Let the Solstice begin!' he roared. Lightning blasted from his eyes, high into the sky, accenting the scene in blue.

'Do we go in now or after him?' Katherine said. Trumpets, guitars, steel drums, and singsong rose to a mighty level. The noise hit her chest and heart and she had to grit her teeth to take it. She looked round, thinking al-Zoubi must not have heard her, but he had vanished.

'He does that,' Bill explained, 'on Solstice.' He held out his hand, saying, 'I'll take you to our seats, oh Queen of the Seven Seas! Ganymede likes his time with his devotees.'

Katherine, a little hurt al-Zoubi hadn't said much about her dress, let Bill lead her through.

Where has al-Zoubi gone?

She'd almost forgotten what her father and Ólafur had said to her, back in Subsolum's NÚLL HERBERGI—the Room Zero. There was supposed to be a distraction. I'm supposed to find Ólafur at the mountain tram stop. Will Bill really help me?

Bill led her as they walked over to the Sun Church entrance. Passing through the towering doors, Katherine couldn't quite shake the feeling she was entering Subsolum. The giant basalt slabs of the archway were unmistakably the same colour and texture of those that propped up the Subsolum tunnels and walkways. A keystone, inset at the apex of the arch, bore a many faced New Havilian: one cried, one laughed, one moaned, one yawn, one blew a kiss, but all of them looked like the Tunnel Spirits from the stories of her childhood, those wonderful picture books her mother read to her at bedtime.

Two Sun Priests held open the inner doors and beckoned them on. Bill encouraged her on. 'This,' he said, as they crossed the threshold, 'is the nave.'

The rich scent of mineral oil hit her like a gut punch: at least fifty rows of long—clearly well oiled—wood benches sat before her. 'That's a lot of wood,' Katherine said.

'Ay, you could make a fine vessel from this lot.'

Paraffin candles, burning a soft orange, wisps of grey smoke rising from them, stood on golden candlesticks—like those she'd seen in the trinkets shop—and bracketed each row of benches.

All the way down the aisle, a large limestone plinth acted as, she guessed, a stage. On it was more golden finery: a pair of massive chairs, upholstered in a scarlet fabric, all the joints capped in gold; an array of golden cups and bowls on a hefty wood table; and a silver lectern that stood at least eight feet high, sparkling, waiting for the events to begin.

Hand in hand, they walked down the aisle, her sequin dress glinting in the candle light. Above, the high vaulted ceiling, criss-crossed by swerving wooden arches and pocked by windows of coloured glass, imposed a grandeur, a philosophy so far removed from what Katherine knew as a Subsolumer. It was, without a doubt, style over form. Dangling from lines strung between the arches and pillars, hempmoss quilts, all shades of red, embroidered in swirls of gold and black, much like the ones she'd seen about the town, fluttered and swayed in undetectable currents of air.

They drew nearer to the plinth. Off to one side of the chairs—thrones—stood a bleached white marble water fountain, carved in a tangled mess of tentacles, scales, claws, faces, hands, eyeballs, wings, and all sorts Katherine couldn't quite pin down.

Bill said, 'That's where we take Waters.'

Their seats were in the front row—a special right, Bill explained, for those who headed crop productions. He let go of her hand, unhooked his cutlass from his waist, sat down, and laid the sword over his legs.

'What exactly is Waters?' she said, sitting down. 'I've heard it mentioned.'

'The geothermal water runs through the mountain, sucking down its nutrients and minerals, and gains especial powers.' He shimmied higher up his seat. 'The water collects in an aquifer right below the Sun Church. It takes a year to reach the level where all New Havilians can each have a sip.'

'But all the water comes from the mountain,' she said, 'from the pipes Subsolum runs.'

'This trickle comes from the pipe the first New Havilians tapped. Not enough water to keep us all alive, every day, but enough to take once a year.' He pulled off his skull and crossbones hat, and bowed towards the fountain. 'It'll heal ailments, take a mould infection right off you, put a stop to whooping-cough. Even clear up a cancer or two.'

She flinched at the word cancer.

'But it don't mean you're cured for good,' Bill went on. 'All it means is you've bought yourself a little time.'

'Surely people try to drink from it year round?'

'Oh, aye, but it's only on Solstice that it has its healing properties. New Havilians come all the way out from Gamma

284

Valley and Radon Ravine to drink today.'

After Bill said all this, he went quiet, looking up at Katherine from the corner of his eyes.

Are we both thinking the same thing?

She dared ask, in a hushed whisper, 'And what role does al-Zoubi play in this?'

Bill, wringing his hat as if he'd just been blown overboard and dragged back on deck, said, 'This past week, Katherine, has been one of a grand disillusionment. I— I guess I'm a bit naive.'

She leant closer to him, smelt the mushroom beer and roasted roach meat on his breath. 'It's his doing,' she said, 'isn't it? He's the one who—'

'Kathy—' Bill twisted back and forth '—best not get into it all now, eh? Enjoy the show.'

Is al-Zoubi keeping everyone alive? The question entered her mind and liphored until she thought she might fall off her chair— it would not stop growing. What if he's lying about the rads? What if the radiation really *is* bad and he keeps us all alive by tainting the waters with his *Zed*?

Voices rose in the church as people streamed inside: laughing and cheering, calling out to each other, rushing to find their seats. Not a single person was without their red threads.

Behind the thrones, to gasps and cheers, descended a giant glowing golden ball: twirling and pulsing.

'Ain't it funny,' Bill said, 'we worship the one thing we don't see.'

And she realised that this was a model of the Sun.

'One day,' he said, 'I'll find it. Feel its warmth on my face.'

'No one talks about the Sun in Subsolum,' Katherine said, happy to change subject for the moment. 'We pretend like it never existed.'

'Instead, you lot think a bunch of Starships are coming to save you'—he cackled away—'the shock they'll have when they find us walking the Earth.'

'I never really believed it.'

'I think Quin does,' Bill said. 'It's his people who fled, after all. I've caught him asleep in the nursery more than a few times, muttering about Starships and his mother.' Adjusting the cutlass over his lap, the blade reflecting the golden light pouring out from the 'Sun', he lowered his voice into a whisper: 'But you dare try him on it—he'll chew you out alright. For a New Havilian to believe in Starships— It's ... unlike us.'

'But he isn't really like you.'

'He might look like a Subsolumer, but he's New Havilian. He'd give his life for this town.'

The volume in the Sun Church reached its apex: cries of joy, parents snapping at uncontrollable children, and boundless laughter, all echoed in the high vaulted ceiling, and seemed unstoppable.

The vacant chair beside Katherine, one she'd assumed was for al-Zoubi, got snatched up by a man who snapped his pincers at her. They worked backwards and forwards, spitting tormented syllables, but she couldn't understand a word.

Bill told the man, 'Shut it, no one wants to hear about your shining bark beetles, Barry.'

Barry snapped his pincers at Bill, only for Bill to hold up his cutlass and bellow: 'I'll slice you!'

A beam of electric light shot down onto one of the thrones, putting a quick stop to the confrontation, as well as silencing the rest of the crowd.

'Here we go!' Bill said, rubbing his hands together.

The spotlight over the throne grew brighter, shifted from yellow to red, and began to creep from the throne, passing over the golden cups and bowls, and down towards the aisle. It slid all the way down the aisle, and Katherine, sitting up, watched it track all the way back to the entrance, where it showered Ganymede and Lady Jupiter, arm in arm, in its light. To tremendous applause, the two New Havilian leaders walked down the aisle. Ganymede's golden plated armour, Lady Jupiter's frilly red dress, both set ablaze by light.

Music—a lively band of brass, organ, steel drum, and guitar, stashed away not to be seen, only heard—filled the church and drowned out the applause. The pair held up their hands to the crowd: shook the extended tentacles, hands, and claws of their fellow New Havilians as they strode down the red carpet.

It struck Katherine how different the ceremony was to the *Stjörnu Farartæki*. They honour their leaders. They respect them. There would be no chucking of mushroom beer bottles, no angry jeers, no starved people begging for justice.

The two stepped up onto the plinth, and positioned themselves before their thrones. Ganymede let Lady Jupiter's hand go, and, to more applause, she sat down. He stepped over to the lectern, raised his arms, and the spotlight shut off, the music faded.

'New Havilah,' he boomed, the cavernous Sun Church

287

devouring his words greedily, 'we have another year behind us. Another year, not of survival, not of struggle, not of hardships: but of prosperity, growth, and flourishing!'

The crowd roared and shook the church's foundations. Katherine even found herself clapping and whooping.

'We are a many-faced people, yet we live in harmony with one another. It is the truest form of cooperation. Only together are we strong. Only together do we conquer this unrelenting land. Only together do we survive.'

Raising one hand, he clicked his fingers: a spiral of flame twirled up a column, and from there it ran across a ledge, spiralled down another column, across and then up another, and so on until the whole church was ablaze. Candles burning: Lady Jupiter's—the last of Subsolum's—paraffin, Katherine realised.

The New Havilians burst into applause: whoops and cheers and hollers.

Yet Lady Jupiter, seated behind her husband, a pair of elbows on the armrest of her throne, chin in a hand, looked rather despondent.

Barry's pincers gnashed away next to Katherine. Bill waved his pirate hat, cheering along with everyone else, then threw it high into the air, catching it before it landed on a candle. She wanted to ask him why it wasn't Lady Jupiter, up at the lectern, giving this speech. She had organised so much of this, her and her Sun Priests had decorated the church, lined it with candles and the billowing red sheets. And when Katherine had first arrived, it was Lady Jupiter who had greeted her—threatened her—not Ganymede. She, as far as Katherine could tell, held all the power. So why aren't you centre stage?'

Ganymede raised both hands in a gesture for quiet. And, once he got it, he stepped to one side, the golden spotlight blooming bright over his plate armour, and pointed at the fountain. The spotlight darted over to the fountain. The trickle of water shone and glinted.

'And now,' Ganymede thundered, his eyes an electric blue, 'I give you all... Waters!'

The fountain's trickle sputtered, and then poured in a great flow, streaming out of a beaked mouth.

As the New Havilians cheered: jumping up from their seats to quake the ground; casting hats, gloves, and scarves into the air; snapping claws, slapping fins, and clapping hands, Ganymede lifted one of the golden cups, and carried it over to the fountain. From her front row seat, Katherine saw what she had seen before, intermingled in the Immortal Man's blood, when Ólafur had dribbled it down her father's throat: specks of fluorescent green suspended in liquid.

Ganymede dunked the cup into the rapidly filling fountain basin, brought it to his lips, and drank.

The stream of water stopped.

A deathly silence spread through the crowd, quickly reaching the far rows behind her. Bill, who was standing on his chair, waving his cutlass about, dropped suddenly to his arse.

'Shiver my timbers,' he said.

Lady Jupiter, rising from her stooped posture, smiled.

'Is this,' Katherine whispered, 'is this part of the Solstice?'

A chant—a canticle—filled the silence: 'Ooo, ummm, sttzhz.'

Over and over it went, growing both louder and faster.

'We might have a problem,' Bill whispered back to her.

About the church, either side of the plinth, at the bottom of the candle-spiralled pillars, and beside each row of benches, stood a chanting red faced New Havilian in tatty black robes. The room reverberated with: 'Ooo, ummm, sttzhz.'

Ganymede threw his golden cup—it clattering loudly on the stone floor—and went to storm towards his wife, when three heavy-set robe figures grabbed his arms.

The 'ooo, ummm, sttzhz' reached its crescendo, and died after the last few echoes faded.

'What are you doing?' Ganymede said, struggling, but not fighting the Sun Priests about him.

In hushed tones, Bill said into her ear: 'Quin 'll have a fit.'

'What's going on?' Katherine said. 'Has she shut off the pipe?'

And as Katherine finished the word 'pipe' the electric lighting above the windows, the spotlight, and the lights above the doors, all cut out, leaving the entire Solstice in candle light.

'You've made a deal!' Ganymede said.

During all of this, no one dared move from their seats. Everyone, transfixed, as if this was New Havilah's own fable play. Far more gripping, Katherine thought, than the Stjörnu Farartæki. At least they weren't lobbing bottles.

Clasping the lectern, Lady Jupiter cleared her throat, her bright frilly dress at odds with the distant expression on her face. 'You may be aware,' she said, 'that New Havilah is growing. There are some who think our little nation ought not to grow, ought not to explore, ought not to make allies of foes. But I'—she thumped a palm on the lectern—'think otherwise.'

The New Havilian crowd split almost immediately: some hissed, some cheered.

Sides always get drawn.

She waited for Bill to make a sound, an affirmation or a damnation. But he stood still, gawping, hunched forwards like one of those stone creatures carved into the church walls.

'It does not bring me joy to have to exercise my power,' Lady Jupiter pressed on, once the crowd drew quiet again. 'But I cannot let rot and mould and misery sink any deeper into my home. And that is what this man stands for!' Lady Jupiter thrust out a hand at Ganymede. 'He has ignored our needs for too long.'

'What are you doing, Juju?' Ganymede muttered. His eyes were not blue, there was no lighting there: just soft, brown eyes, totally abandoned. 'Can't we talk?'

'Take him away!' she ordered.

Gasps and hisses and whistles as the Sun Priests led Ganymede from the plinth and out the back way.

Next to Katherine, Barry's gnashing pincers worked up a good rhythm and dribbled yellow spit. He thrust himself up from the chair, fists out in front of him, and charged for the fountain, only for a Sun Priest to crash into him, wrap him up in neon-pink tentacles, and wrestle him to the ground. They rolled and writhed as other pincher-faced onlookers jostled and shouted.

'The bark beetle breeders,' Bill said, 'ain't gonna pick a side quick. But this don't look too good.'

As the two rolled and fought on the floor, eruptions came from behind: New Havilians, the realisation dawning that there was no

Waters this Solstice, wrestling and screaming to get to the front.

'Bill?' Katherine got to her feet. A prayer cushion careened through the air, lobbed from a few rows back, narrowly missed her head, and knocked over the lectern. 'Bill, I think we need to get out of here.'

Is this the distraction Dad had planned? Has he shut off *all* the pipes so I can get out?

Staring dumbfounded at the toppled lectern, Lady Jupiter barked an order to her Sun Priests, who all found a vigour and began pushing and shoving any New Havilian who dared move towards the fountain.

Bill, lost in a trance, held his cutlass high in the air, and yelled, 'She's taking over! It's a mutiny!' and charged at the nearest Sun Priest, swinging wildly. This triggered others to follow. Angry New Havilians barged and shoved and rammed their way to the front. Rows of candles were knocked over; the lower hanging billowing sheets of red were ripped from their arches; paintings, ornaments, anything that wasn't nailed down was heaved and thrown and smashed, chairs toppled, more prayer cushions lobbed: I guess we aren't so different after all.

In the melee, she dove onto the floor, scurried under the rows of seating. There was just enough space for her to squeeze her way back the entire length of the Sun Church: hooves, flippered feet, talons, writhing and slimy tails all tried their hardest to stomp her, but none struck true.

This has got to be it. I need to get out of here, get to his flower. I'll do it without Bill.

Popping out from under the last row of seats, she looked back:

flames licked up the walls and pillars, black smoke belched, Sun Priests and New Havilians fought in earnest. Bill had vanished. That small man consumed by it all. She wondered if leaving him was right. But he charged off.

And if this were her father's distraction, putting the whole town at its own throat, how could she waste it?

The crowd outside—once a long flowing red river, now a dense knot like a lump of congealed blood—waited, still and sickly quiet, every eye and antenna focused on the Sun Church. Katherine, as far as she could tell, was the only one to have left the building, despite it being very much on fire. Through the gaps in poorly sealed windows, various holes and leaks in the rooftop, and the chimney, black smoke poured relentlessly. Snatches of whispered conversation caught her: 'There's never been fire before!' 'What's all the waiting?' 'When's Waters?'

Plodding through snow and sleet in her glamorous dress, she started to shake and shiver, hunted for a tram, only to realise absolutely everyone, tram drivers included, was waiting to go into the Sun Church.

The further along the Corridor she went, the greater her sense of eeriness grew: the usual New Havilian mobs that huddled around food carts and trading stands were now that singular confused mass gawping at the smoking Sun Church. The rest of the town was empty.

She pressed on through the cold: pressed on with her plan.

It hadn't taken her long to reach al-Zoubi's nursery. The icy slush forced a pace on her: if she took a second to stop and breathe,

the coldness soon spurred her forwards. Fantasies of wrapping herself in her thick New Havilian duvet, sipping on coffee, and lying in front of the tobacco drying room seized her strong and hard.

For her shivering self then, the sight of a giant padlock across the nursery's doors might as well have been her own father: You'll never get anywhere, Kathy, you're a silly little girl.

Her fingertips were blue.

She lifted a leg, kicked the door, slipped and crashed on the stone pavement.

What am I doing? Sniffing and shivering, she pulled herself up to her feet. I'm not going to take his flower or his *Zed*. Dad's shut off the pipes. It'll be war. All I wanted was to grow food. Not be a servant to my father.

Echoing up the Corridor: bangs and shouts and screams. Bright flames licked high over the Sun Church tower. A siren warbled. The Sun Priests' canticle lingered in her head like the stench of roach spit, like her father's rotten gin breath.

As the siren rose and fell, Katherine struggled against the padlock. Even if she could break in, draw off as much *Liphoric Zed* as she could, and then run away up the mountain, what good would it do? Her father, healed of cancer, would simply carry on: devoted to soil, to tradition. He won't listen. It's only when he wants something does he pay any attention to me.

He's dying, Chick? Are you going to let him die?

The padlock remained closed no matter how hard she tried. Ice and mushy sleet covered her feet and had frozen them stiff. She pounded and pounded on the nursery door, the feeling in her hands gone. But the door did not budge.

What am I doing? I don't know what's right—I don't think I've ever known. I don't know who to trust. Don't know who to believe.

'You trying to break in?' said a voice behind her.

Katherine, shivering in her red sequin dress, turned: at the far end of the pavement Darleaner stood, holding out a large pair of bolt cutters.

'I'll snip that lock, no problem,' Darleaner said, and snapped the cutters shut. 'It's about time the Immortal Man had trouble come his way.'

γ

Inside the nursery, Katherine found a large coat hung up on a peg. It smelt of mould and rich tobacco and she wasted no time in unhooking it and pulling it on. Reaching all the way to her knees, the coat soon held in her body warmth and slowed her shivering. The tobacco smells reminded her of yesterday, when she dared to take a pull off of al-Zoubi's pipe, certain she wasn't going to steal from him. Stringy bits of old tobacco, hempmoss handkerchiefs, crumbs from some mushroom based pastry: the pockets like an archaeological discovery revealing to her a partial on the life of Quinton al-Zoubi.

Drying room heat radiated out on her: far better than what she had imagined earlier. She closed her eyes and breathed and as best she could squashed any thought that told her what she was about to do was wrong.

Darleaner, quiet, standing on the last step of the stairs, said, 'You set the Sun Church on fire?'

Whatever peace Katherine had found evaporated. 'What?'

'I normally don't read people wrong,' Darleaner said. 'I sort the harmless from the harmful. Never been caught off guard. Except for the Immortal Man. And now I'm second guessing myself about you.'

'Is that why you're helping me, because he cheated you?'

'No,' Darleaner said, 'it's nothing to do with him.'

'I didn't burn down the church. Lady Jupiter shut off the fountain and sent everyone into a panic. All those candles got knocked about and things started burning.'

Darleaner listened but remained as expressionless as Lady Jupiter had when giving her speech.

'Bill's still in there,' Katherine said. 'Everyone's still in there.'

'And you ran away?'

'I have a job to do.'

Darleaner jumped from the step. 'Your *job*, it'll change things down there?'

The starving Subsolumers, her father and his hacking cough, Tiff as she rifled through growth media buckets on the hunt for potatoes, the barren and dead fields: she saw it all, blended together, served up like a gruel.

'It'll change,' Katherine said, 'but good change or bad change? I don't know.'

Through the ribboned doorway came the usual sounds of the nursery: gurgles, drones, hums: doing their best to fill the gaps left by uncomfortable silences.

I don't have time for this. 'If you want to help, help. Otherwise leave.' Katherine parted the ribboned doorway, lingered for a moment as Darleaner made her decision, and then stepped through into the flower room. Intoxicating pollen scents, sweet and soft, tickled the back of her throat. Over on the growing table, al-Zoubi's flower sparkled bright white: beads of fluorescent sap clung to the projecting stigma. Copper wires snaked out through the back of the radiation proof case and then along the shallow trenches in the table, piping voltages to the microcontroller and LED display.

Already the petal that had bled the Black Rot, that had looked as if it were never to come back, half gobbled by a tunnel demon, now hung fully formed: a-glowing, as Bill might say.

Katherine paced over to it, the practicalities of her thievery heavy in her head. All her kit—rad suit, rucksack, rations—was, she realised, stashed away in her rooms in Hotel du Soleil, unreachable. There was no going up the mountain without protection. She didn't even have trousers on. Do roaches eat sequins?

You're hopeless, Chick.

Darleaner, standing at the edge of the growing table, squinting, hands stuffed into mucky overall pockets, said, 'I've run through fields of them in books, but I've never smelt one.'

'It was dying.'

And Darleaner said, 'So the Immortal Man cheats me to get a case to save it?' Then, shaking her head: 'That flower's so beautiful, maybe I would have done the same.'

Gingerly, Katherine tapped one of the petals. Can I take your sap, she whispered to it, feeling only slightly crazy.

Goosebumps rose on her skin.

You may.

It came to her from all around. 'Did you say something?' she said to Darleaner.

'No?'

It spoke to me. It gave me an answer. Hurriedly, Katherine found a washed pipette and a glass vial. And as she drew the sticky sap from the flower, she said to Darleaner, 'How do I get to the mountain stop from here without going down the Corridor?'

'I'll take you there,' the blacksmith said, 'but I'll want paying.'

THE IMMORTAL MAN
– NEW HAVILAH –

Has it really been a year since I was last here?

The church sacristy: damp, dark, cold, but built on New Havilah's main artery, welcomed Quinton inside its mouldy walls once more. Beneath the steel trapdoor came the gushing flow of mountain water on its way to the church fountain. The bottle clinked as he set this year's *Liphoric Zed* on the stone floor. Particles of fluorescent green drifted inside: bound for dilution and then onwards to New Havilian bellies. He thought back through the year. How easy it had gone. No real trouble until the Rot, until Katherine and Lady Jupiter. So much had changed and yet so much remained the same. New Havilah and its people were still here: battling against a sunless world, encircled by radiation and roaches, and forever coming out on top. The conversation with Ganymede came to mind: We're growing. And here Quinton was: tired, bones like chalk, eyes dry and heavy, every aspect of him cut into two: Go on, give up. Go on, give up. Giving up meant letting go of his mother. It meant letting go of what had pulled him through all these years. The Flower should have died. I should have died. But Katherine, from the world beneath his world, had saved it, saved him. Death, however, like mould on warm wet rocks, held fast to him, guiding his ancient self to its ultimate rest. Though now more than ever he had reasons beyond his mother to keep going. Reluctantly, he'd left both of his reasons to themselves—how wonderful Katherine and Billick both looked—and fought back feelings to go rejoin them. And then there was the Black Rot. How had he been so blind to its source: the ever bitter Daniel Marston, influencing Lady Jupiter from afar. He cursed himself, he couldn't be sure, even if the evidence was bordering on the undeniable.

Voices, drifting in from the church, spurred him into action.

That's right, Quinton, it doesn't stop; you don't stop, Sophia whispered to him. Hope swelled in his chest.

And all of it, all his hardships, easily surpassed by the new knowledge Katherine brought to him. Sophia died, years ago. So perhaps she really *did* love me? And that fate had other plans.

He lowered himself into a squat, took the trapdoor's handle, and heaved open the door. The exposed water current roared and danced and enveloped him in soft steam. Straight from the depths of the mountain the stream had come to nourish: its warm waters heavy in minerals, soon to be made heavier. With a sharp exhale, he flipped the trapdoor all the way so it slammed into the ground, turning half a circle on its hinges. Steam had condensed on the bottle of *Zed.* Slippery in his hands. He unstoppered it, sniffed the sweet perfume, toasted the Sun, the Starships, his mother, his friends, life on this rock, and tipped the bottle upside down, pouring the *Zed* out; it fell in a long sticky line, like rope made from guts; the rushing water gobbled it up. Green light mottled the water. The particles swooshed about, beaten into a foam, coursed on to their holy destination.

Once the bottle was half empty, he held it upright, peered at the glowing, gloopy mess inside.

I could go right this minute, go find that boy and give the rest to him; he would go on and live.

'That boy,' he said aloud. 'I've killed him.'

If you die, New Havilah dies too, Sophia told him. *Drink your Zed, Quinton.*

He brought the bottle to his lips. Am I really meant to go on living? Will those Starships ever arrive?

Voices from the church filled the sacristy. Speeches and cheers. The moments before Waters had even the most conservative frothing at the mouth, helicoptering tentacles, or wafting their feathers.

After a few more moments listening to the excitement, the scent of *Zed* right at his nose, he heard the soft music tumble in, and he lingered, listening, letting it take him back to a time when he had been really, truly happy.

'Dancing in your arms,' he said to Sophia. 'Don't you remember?'

But the wet sacristy walls gave him no answer: he was alone, and he knew it.

The music stopped. In its place arrived John Ganymede's booming voice. Cheers erupted. The church foundation shook. Ganymede roused and gave them all hope, until his voice cut off—

All around came, 'Ooo, ummm, sttzhz'.

Quinton startled, stepped back from the rushing water, and stoppered his half-bottle of *Zed*. Slipping the bottle into his suit jacket, he quickly walked around to the trapdoor. As the 'Ooo, ummm, sttzhz' bellows rose and fell, he worked hard lifting the trapdoor and slamming it shut over the rushing water.

Lady Jupiter's voice arrived.

John's right—I'm right—she's had enough.

He sat for a time in the sacristy and listened to Lady Jupiter's speech—Katherine and Billick would be there, front and centre, and he'd no idea what they'd make of this.

At some point in her speech a commotion broke out. Not long after, smoke tinged the air.

He headed outside, the sacristy exit spitting him out on the back alleys.

At the bottom of the alley two Sun Priests stood, like guards, so he carried on up the alley, further from the church. When he turned around for another look, great clouds of black smoke were pouring from the Sun Church.

Panicked cries carried in the evening breeze.

He stood gawking as the smoke rose.

It wasn't long before coughing and hacking New Havilians were running up the alley and past him.

Quinton, not wanting to get trampled, ran over to the edge of the alley and climbed up a wall. More Solstice goers rushed past him. Some clambered up the wall, others stumbled in the snow to be trod and slithered upon.

Smoke bled from the Sun Church windows, the chimney stack.

His hands trembled, his blood roared in his ears, his lungs inflated and deflated like a billows machine.

Stuck.

His thoughts drifted uselessly to Katherine and Billick. They were in there. Or somewhere in the escaping masses. But picking either of them out in the blur of faces was impossible. A siren rose from low pitch to high, warbled up and down. Orange and yellow flames licked up the Church's walls. Flammable insulation, no doubt, catching alight. The bells tolled: started knocking out a steady rhythm, only to fall into a chaotic beat. Flames burst from the bell tower. A bell rope snapped away, ablaze and bright, whipping out like a divine weapon. The bell dropped from the tower, crashed against the lower roof Sun Church tiles, spraying shards all over.

He willed himself down from the wall. Wanted to go charging into the chaos to find his friends, but all he could manage was a twitch.

Those fleeing by running up the alley had thinned out, and following up behind the last of them were Lady Jupiter's Sun Priests. Like roach hunters pushing a roach closer to the edge of a cliff.

A high pitched squeal, his heartbeat in his ears, icy muck in his face. Throbs in his jaw. It took him a moment to realise he'd been knocked off from the wall.

Shards thudded down on the snow and ice around him, on flesh and bone, and when they stopped Quinton dared to look up. The church was gone. New Havilah's heart had been ripped out. Devoured.

He groaned and got to his feet. The Sun Priests had all been blown flat too, some helping others get to their feet or hooves or talons.

He ran as fast as he could and didn't look back.

γ

Darkness hung over New Havilah like a sulphurous cloud vomited up from the bowels of the mountain. Streetlights, house windows, shop fronts: all without power, totally black. A tram sat idle on its tracks in the middle of the Corridor, abandoned.

Everyone's scurried inside, like the roaches Lady Jupiter thinks we are.

In the darkness, the only bit of light coming all the way from the flaming mess of the Sun Church, he stumbled his way to his nursery. If Billick and Katherine hadn't been trampled or exploded or arrested he'd find them there.

This really is a coup. Neither he nor Ganymede had realised how serious this all was. He'd been so focused on the Flower that he'd forgotten to look up. How Ganymede could be so blind, he didn't know. But if what he'd said were true, if New Havilah were growing, perhaps this form of government was no longer fit for purpose.

New Havilah couldn't continue on like this. Couldn't continue surviving on Waters each year. How soon before the Flower finally does die? Or before there's not even enough water to go around? Even Subsolum, in their rocky warren, couldn't keep going if New Havilah fell.

He reached the nursery to find the doors wide open. The padlock lay on the ground, snapped apart.

His heart fluttered. The thought of his Flower stolen, after everything that it's been through, after everything that *he's* been through, after Waters getting interrupted and the Sun Church exploding, after it all, for the Flower to have been taken so easily, without a fight: it crushed him, demoralised him, made a boy out of him.

Feeling his way about, he stepped inside, shut the doors, and carefully stepped down the stairs, where a faint white light soon found him. What little warmth was left in the nursery was like the last breaths of a dying beast.

The heating elements in the tobacco drying room were off. Without power, the tobacco would decay, eaten by mould, all his exotics too, and his Flower— If it's still here.

Through the first ribboned doorway came the source of the white light. He called out, 'Bill?' and stepped through. A sun lamp, its filaments running at much too high a current and burning white, shone over the room. Springy cables ran from the lamp to an old acid battery on the floor. Bill and his motley collection of kit. The Flower case stood tall and proud on the growth table, and, as he went to check on the Flower, a voice said, 'Cap'n, don't you throw me overboard now.' The botanist appeared from the shadows. Quinton reeled at the sight of him: blood and bruises about his eyes, a gash along a cheek. But was soon flooded by a feeling of love.

He's alive, here, well. Thank the Stars.

'Lady Jupiter's shut off the pipes,' Billick said.

Quinton groped himself for his pipe. She's done an awful lot more than shut off the pipes. The smouldering Sun Church remains, the rain of shards and roof tiles, the bell tower collapsing. No one took Waters. Is the *Zed* I poured gone? It was a good thing, then, that he hadn't drunk his half just yet.

He paced around to the Flower, where it glimmered in its case;

its black rotten petal fully formed. Though there wasn't as much sap as he'd hoped. If the Flower was still here, then who had broken into the nursery? And why?

Billick, hopping into his cart, 'You're gonna have to hear this.'

'Hear what?'

He wheeled around until he was beside the Flower. With his knobbly finger, Billick pointed at the stigma, said, 'She's had her lick and gone.'

'Bill, for Brightness' sake.'

'She's taken some sap from it and run off.'

'Who?'

'Our fair Subsolumer, Katherine, that's who.'

'She broke the lock on the door?'

'Aye,' Billick said, 'I assume so.'

'And she's run off where?'

'Back home. Her father is dying.'

Quinton brought his pipe to his lips. 'How do you know it was her?' he said.

'She confided in me, Cap'n. She pulled me aside and asked if I'd help her do it.' He sighed. 'I thought we were friends.'

He'll never make a good pirate, his heart's too soft. 'And why'd you go and do that?'

'There's more,' Billick said, ignoring his question. He dabbed his fingers against a cut. The man looked like a *Lucha Libre* fighter who didn't know when to quit. 'Your Flower,' he went on after inspecting his fingertips, 'tells me it told Kathy it could *have* the sap.'

Holding his jet lighter to the pipe bowl, Quinton narrowed his eyes, stared hard at Billick, and wondered if this was all a joke. *Maybe I've not even woken from my drunken sleep.*

'I ain't lying, Cap'n. Your Flower's one chatty creature.'

Quinton blew smoke. 'Is it speaking to you now?'

Billick said, 'Oh aye, won't shut up, actually. It says, "You've given what is needed, take what is given." It's a poet, your Flower.'

'Does it hear me?' Quinton asked. He dragged a stool over, sat down, elbows on the growing platform, face right up against the Flower. *Please, talk, tell me what you know.*

Billick, rolling his cart to make some space, 'Quin, it don't talk to everyone. It don't listen to everyone either. It calls to those who've got the … *gift.*'

'Alright,' Quinton said sharply, 'I get it. But can you ask it something?'

Billick cracked his knuckles, said, 'Aye.'

'Ask it why my mother left me here.'

The question froze Billick. He broke eye contact, wincing. Then, at length, he said, 'Ain't that a bit personal?'

'Just ask it, please.'

'Erm, sure.' Billick closed his eyes, waited a few moments, then opened them again. 'It says Nancy al-Zoubi always meant to leave you here. It says Nancy al-Zoubi died to do it. It says you've got to keep the world spinning. That you've got to be The Immortal Man.'

And as Quinton's inner self approached supernova, the nursery lights, the extractor fans, the pumps and valves, all of it, sprang to life.

'The power's back on,' Quinton said, trying to run as fast as he could from his thoughts. Then, noticing Billick had his eyes closed again, he asked, 'What's it saying now, Bill?'

'"WACOOH, WACOOH, WACOOH ..."' the botanist said. 'Blimey, what in Brightness does that mean?'

Quinton sat and smoked and stared off into the void. Memories, their tentacles reaching out from beneath dark water, squeezed him, didn't let him go until he'd run them through.

He felt his mother's embrace again, as they huddled in a Bomb shelter, as Bombs exploded above and rumbled the Earth. Broken pipes dripped water, left puddles all over that tried to rot his feet. The sweet scent of dried strawberries hung in the air, barely masking the reek of dead and decaying bodies, but offering him his only escape. He remembered how each morning—they knew morning because that was when the Bombs resumed—his mother would hand him a fistful of dried strawberries, and tell him to eat them slowly, that that was all he was getting. Then one day she was gone—*Evacuated*, leaving him with a pocket watch. And then, a few days later, the Flower appeared.

He broke from his past and looked at Billick. 'Did the Flower really say all that?'

'Aye, Cap'n.'

'It named my mother as Nancy?'

'Aye.'

'You never knew her name?' Quinton asked.

'No.'

'And it told you she died?'

'Aye.'

'My whole life,' Quinton said after a pause, 'has been a lie.' Sitting hunched on the stall, the pipe dangling from his lips, he grabbed tight to the last half—his half—of the *Liphoric Zed* bottle stashed away in his jacket pocket. The red trimmed suit jacket, one he'd got from the tailor nearly twenty years ago, suffocated him, wrung the sweat from his pores.

'Let's get out of here,' he said.

'Where we going, Cap'n?'

'How's about a drink?'

γ

By the dials of his pocket watch, it was near eleven o'clock. Usually at this time on Summer Solstice the Corridor heaved with New Havilians. The people, rejuvenated for the year, their unravelling postponed, would dance and drink and sing until the cloudlight arrived. But tonight, as Quinton and Billick surfaced from the nursery, the Corridor lay bare, empty, only the gloomy orange street lighting left to greet them.

'No chocolate. Rot in my growhouses. My mother's dead. My love, who lied to me about having a daughter, dead too—all along. Brightness me, Bill, it's a catastrophe.'

'You know what's a catastrophe?'

He looked down to meet the botanist's eyes.

'Torn sails a thousand miles from land.'

Quinton laughed.

And maybe I've taken all this too seriously? I've indulged my fantasy of rescue for far too long.

He readied himself from a response from Sophia—any thought that objected to his mission always set right by her words—but he heard none. In fact, as he and Billick walked towards The Blue-Headed Goat, that warming, nourishing feeling of her presence grew fainter. Each step took him further from it. He marched on. And he didn't grow colder.

'And Katherine,' Quinton said, 'I really did trust her.'

'I don't feel great about it.'

'You like her?'

All the way from the mountain, a tram's rumble travelled in the silent night to reach them.

Billick said, 'Yeah, I do. But we ain't the same.'

'Your last girlfriend,' Quinton said, 'the one who always left bite marks on your cheeks, what was her name?'

'Olga,' Billick said.

'How many arms did she have?'

He counted on his hands, paused a moment to ask, 'Are we counting antenna as arms?'

'Sure.'

'*Five*, then.'

'How many have you got?'

'Aye, bucko, I get your point, but Katherine's different, she's a Subsolumer—she's in *God's* image.'

The smouldering wreck of the Sun Church still burned at the bottom of the Corridor. A few firefighters appeared to be out, attempting to tame the blaze with salt-water hoses.

'Don't give me that, Bill. God's image is the reflection of the guy holding all the sticks—you shouldn't worry about it.'

'You think I've got a chance?'

'I'll give you eleven-to-one.'

They both laughed, and continued on to the pub.

Through the pub's windows came a warm flickering light. Rich and homely scents of roasted bark beetle and stewed mushroom hit their noses as they stepped inside. All those who had found themselves stranded in town when the power went out, had gathered here. These were the people of Gamma Valley and Radon Ravine, hemp and cottonmoss collectors, New Havilah's backbone, those who lived amongst danger to forage for life.

Quinton had often thought about how to grow the mosses in areas safe from radiation, had tried numerous times, but the very thing he had fought was the element he relied on. Out in the Valley and Ravine, the mosses thrived *on* the radiation; they soaked it up, harnessed its energies, and grew out in the open under a sunless sky.

If Katherine had stayed, I'm sure she would have found it curious—maybe she even has a trick up her jumpsuit, something we could use to move our fields.

The bartender spotted Billick and gestured for them to come over.

Rows and rows of candles, stuffed into the tops of glass bottles, stood behind the bar, on five or so long shelves. Dotted around the pub were golden ornaments from the Sun Church. It appeared there had been looting. They'd stolen candles, golden finery, hempmoss canvas works, prayer cushions: in fact, wherever Quinton set his eyes, he spotted another piece of *booty*.

Billick clambered up the bar, Quinton stood, every seat taken.

Conversations went on quietly, hurriedly, punctuated every now and then by a laugh.

It will take much more to break these people.

'You look terrible, Bill,' the bartender said. 'You've lost your hat.'

'Aye,' Billick said, 'now why don't you stop blabbering and pour us a few drinkies? We've walked the planks, and yet here we are, still swimming with the sharks.'

As Billick and the bartender spoke, a distinctive smell caught Quinton's attention. Onions. Over in the corner, wrapped around what the slimers called a *lounging poll*, was that poor boy's father, the hempmoss collector. The boy, also wrapped around a lounging poll, sipped at his drink, the sores about his breathing holes terribly red.

Quinton turned back to the bartender and Billick and interrupted their chat on *Lucha Libre* to ask if he could have a jug of warm water.

As soon as this was handed to him, he carried it over to the boy and his father.

'You,' the slimer said, unravelling himself from the pole and projecting his antenna. 'What have you come to do? Rub our faces in it—my son's going to...' He stopped himself, curled down into a small form, whimpered, cried. 'I've tried everything, begged everyone. My boy is going to die and there's nothing I can do. What sort of parent am I? What sort of father can't save his son?'

On the table in front of them, Quinton set the jug of warm water down. He found an empty shot glass and placed that next to the jug.

From his jacket he took out his bottle of *Liphoric Zed*, glanced at the boy, eyeing up how much *Zed* he needed, and then poured some into the shot glass. He diluted this down with the warm water, then held out the glass for the boy.

'Drink,' he said.

The boy, tentatively, flinching as he reached for the glass, finally took it, and, after a shake from his father's antennas, the boy drank down the *Zed* and warm water mix.

The sight of the Immortal Man had drawn onlookers—the shiny, fluorescent particles of the *Zed* held their attention, and the near instant rejuvenation of the boy, the closing of his wounds, the flecking-off of his scabs, drew out their gasps.

'Thank you! Thank you!' the father said as he wrapped Quinton in a hug.

The boy said, 'I can breathe.'

Quinton, free from the hug, sat at the table, and he said, 'Let you all form a line; there is Waters to take, so spread the word.'

The entire Blue-Headed Goat erupted into cheers.

You'll die, Quinton, Sophia whispered to him.

Die like you, die like my mother—die like I ought to.

FAMILY REUNION

The power came back on as Katherine and Darleaner reached the mountain tram stop. The single tram waited at the platform, the interior lights off, but the person, hanging from the open door, was visible in their bright yellow radiation suit. The person—a Subsolumer, going by the number of limbs and the rad suit—gestured for her to hurry. The elegant wave gave Ólafur away easily.

Katherine jogged over, leaving Darleaner behind, slipping through the platform barriers and onto the platform, impressed that Ólafur had made it without getting attacked by roaches.

'Miss Marston,' Ólafur said through his mask, 'it's good to see you.'

'What's going on?' Katherine asked, breathless, the reek of burning Sun Church rubble stinging her nostrils. 'The New Havilian's church exploded.'

'I don't know,' Ólafur said, 'but don't worry.' He looked her up and down. 'Don't you have a suit? A mask? What about the flower?'

'No.' She shook her head. 'I— Has my father done this? Did he plan for all this? Is he okay?'

Ólafur reached to take her hand, but she moved it before he could. 'Miss Marston, I suggest we leave, before we draw unwanted attention.' He stepped back inside the tram. 'Please,' he said.

As Katherine climbed in, Darleaner reached her, put a hand on her shoulder.

'I owe you another thank you,' Katherine said, turning to face her. 'You've saved me twice.'

Darleaner, eyeing Ólafur over Katherine's shoulder, said quietly, 'Don't forget what I told you. They make their own myths.'

I hope it isn't true.

Katherine unclipped her earrings and held them out. 'Is this payment enough? I'd have got lost in those back alleys without you.'

Darleaner took one look at the shiny earrings, sighed. 'This one's free,' she said, and started to walk back down the platform, but stopped a few paces away to add, 'The next one ain't. Hopefully see you around.' And she vanished into the night.

Before Katherine could take her seat, the tram whirled, sparks flew from the power lines above, and Ólafur, in the driver's cabin, sent them on their way up the mountain.

γ

In the darkness, their journey slow and noisy, she kept mistaking the tram's screeches or the wind's howls for hungry roach calls, imagining packs of them burying into the snow and waiting to burst up to attack her again.

Ólafur had the foresight to pack her a change of clothes: agronomist overalls and an Old World radiation suit. She swallowed anti-rad pills, strapped a gas mask on too—all off it, as if she were going *back* into the womb, back to the life before life, where it was warm and she never made any decisions.

The noise, the darkness, the masks, the tension of it all, left the two in a silence. Katherine hadn't had much silence recently, but after a few hours rising up the mountain, she couldn't hold back her questions any longer. She needed to know if her father was well. Why wasn't Ólafur worried about her not having the flower? He wasn't normally *this* quiet.

She slipped off the mask—How much I've changed in a week— and said to her father's servant, 'New Havilah is nothing like what he says it is.' Ólafur, peering out into the darkness, the tram's headlights all there was to light the way, kept quiet. 'Ólafur, listen to me.' She got up and stood right beside him, clinging on to a hand hold that felt like it wasn't designed for her. 'I think we've got it all backwards; I think it's not just my father who has lost his mind. I think we all have. We've spent all this time underground and have been living this life and we've forgotten—our culture has forgotten—what it means to *truly* live.' She waited to see if her words had any effect. The servant stayed quiet, eased on the tram throttle as they came to a flatter portion of track. And then as she was about to go on, he switched on the cabin light and lifted up his mask.

'Katherine,' he said, 'you must forgive me.' He eased on the throttle more.

'What's happened, is Dad okay? Why are you slowing down?'

Ólafur turned to look at her: heavy bags under his red and bloodshot eyes; those hollowed cheeks she had seen on the mothers and their children belonged to him too.

'Look at you,' he said to her, 'you have colour in your face, and your cheeks, they are full; you have been eating. It would make your mother happy.'

They both swayed as the tram came to a complete stop.

Ólafur took his hands from the controls and exhaled—a cloud of white breath left him.

He's already part ghost, part Tunnel Spirit.

'We're not far from the top now.' He stared at her: his ghastly, death-like face so far from who she knew. 'In the week you've been gone, Katherine, your father has only got worse, in more than one dimension. He is sick of body *and* mind.'

'What are you saying?'

'I'm saying that I no longer work for him.'

Katherine paced back from the cabin, sat in a tram seat, and held her hand in her hands. '*Helvíti,*' she muttered. 'And who do you—'

'The Pipeworkers, Miss Marston, that's who, Einar Laxness. He knew this day would come, told me so when I answered the telephone in your father's office that day we were chased from the play.'

'All this time you've known he would take over and you didn't tell us?'

He sighed. 'Your father lost control the day your mother returned from New Havilah.'

Katherine sat up straight. 'My mother— I know about the rads, about New Havilah's lower, liveable levels.'

Ólafur licked his lips. 'Yes—so did your mother.' His narrowed eyes would not meet hers. 'I owe your father my life; it's true— he saved me and my husband from a situation I thought was inescapable. The loyalty and respect I have given your father over the years, the patience, too, he has savagely abused and now I can no longer stand it, not when there's another option. In all those years too, I watched you grow up—grow up to be like her, like your mother. And I can no longer stomach these lies. *His* lies. I thought I did it for peace, to keep Subsolum stable, but I now know I did it out of cowardice, afraid that your father might return myself and Magnús to the lower levels, to have us struggle for breath as we make glass for the bulb makers. So I swallowed the truth down and I watched you wonder about your mother and I said nothing and I collected his spit buckets and gave him his gins—keeping him somewhat drunk made it all easier.'

Ólafur paused, looked up and through the tram's windscreen and onto the brightly lit snow.

'It's the outside,' he said, 'there's a feeling when you are outside that makes it easier for you to think.' Finally, he looked her in the eye, all this time Katherine had no thoughts, she stared and listened, transfixed. He said, 'Your mother died because of him. He killed her.'

The wind swept the snow, blew it around and made it dance, its whistles and howls echoed in her head, a ringing, too. Am I about to collapse? The roaches have found us. They'll burst through the thin tram skin and eat us.

She saw her mum, as she lay dying, blankets covering her. The endless groans, but no complaining. Gasping, Katherine realised she'd left the book in New Havilah. All she had left of her mother.

The tram rumbled back to life. Ólafur, poised, ready to set off and not say another word, avoided her gaze. He's going to make me ask.

'Turn it off,' she said. 'Turn it all off until you've told me everything.'

Again he switched the motors off, again everything fell silent, again the wind and snow rose up around them.

'Your mother came back from New Havilah changed,' he explained. 'Not only had she found a better way to grow food, not only did she have proof the radiation levels were liveable, she also, Katherine, was deeply, desperately, in love.'

'The Immortal Man.'

'Yes,' Ólafur said, with a sharp nod. 'She wanted to take you up here, to live here.'

'You've known all this and you never told me. How could you?' She got to her feet again—she clenched her fists, resisted an urge to scream. 'All this time, Ólafur. How could you?'

Curled forward, he said, 'Your mother made me promise.'

'What?' She walked over to the driver cab, grabbed tight to some part of it, hissed: 'You're lying.'

'Please,' he said, 'please. Take a moment.' Once Katherine had eased her grip on a railing, once she'd slowed her breathing, he added, 'Your mother made me promise I would never tell you how she got ill.' He looked upwards, through the tram windscreen, and into the starless, pitch dark sky. 'Forgive me, Sophia,' he said.

Katherine, 'Tell me. How did she die?'

Ólafur, 'Cancer.'

Katherine, 'I know that! How did he—'

Ólafur, 'All your father had to do was take a radioactive source,

319

have her drink or eat it, explain to the rest of Subsolum that those that left the warren—even your president's wife—will ultimately succumb.'

Katherine, 'You don't *know*, do you? You suspect.'

Ólafur, 'He did it, Katherine. He admitted it to me and forced me to keep his lies. "It's the perfect reminder," he'd said. "It will rid any lingering doubts in Subsolumers' minds. They will know the cost of leaving."'

Darleaner is right. We do make our own myths.

Exhausted, defeated, Katherine strapped her mask over her face, lay across the long row of seats at the back of the tram, and tried her hardest to shut the world out. To cling on to those fast dying *good* memories of her mum, and even of her dad, too.

'We must keep going, Katherine,' Ólafur said, calling back to her. 'Subsolum depends on us.'

γ

The freight lift doors parted, and the wave of Subsolum's stink crashed into Katherine like it were giving her a welcome home hug. A smell she had forgotten quickly, it coursed about her, returning everything she had left behind—her rhythms, habits, gestures—her entire being, even her way of thinking, began to revert back to what it had been before, this slow and heavy awareness, very different to the pacey ease at which her thoughts came in New Havilah. What had evaporated now condensed. She wanted to retreat, to go and hide under her covers and pretend like all this were all a dream.

Ólafur, walking up the three metal steps and into the capacious freight tunnel, beckoned her on.

'Where is everyone?' Katherine asked, so used to seeing this space filled with traders packing up crates of glass bulbs, filaments, and—in more productive days—wheat, cabbage, carrot, and onion, whatever had been grown and harvested and was worth trading.

'Confined to their homes, Miss Marston. These are uncertain times and we cannot risk another riot.'

He led her through the freight tunnel and towards the ramps. Reflexively, she headed down, towards the lower levels where her cube was, but Ólafur was heading up, explaining to her that, 'There is no time to waste, Miss Marston, you must speak to Mister Laxness—he is waiting.'

They walked the ramps to the Pipeworks level in silence. Katherine wondered where her father was—if he'd locked himself up in his office with all the gin or if he had retreated to the glamorous comfort of his home. She hated that home. It must, really, be the biggest in Subsolum. The more time Katherine had spent in other people's homes, the more she realised the grossness of her own. Her friends' homes all had a single toilet; tables, seats, and beds that unfolded from the walls; inventive shelves and cupboards; there were no pianos, bookshelves, L-shaped sofas, chandeliers, bathtubs, dining *and* living rooms.

At the Pipeworks level, Ólafur, again leading the way, headed for the main pipe room, where the master pipe lived, that ten foot diameter monster which bled the geothermal pools and aquifers with little mercy. The pipe room also served as Einar's office.

As they walked, the blue coloured sun lights that lined the tops of most tunnels stopped abruptly, replaced by old style lamps that shone down in cones. Spaced every three or so metres and carved into the tunnel walls were busks of long gone Pipeworkers. The orange light cast on them produced strong shadows which brought the relief work out more than the mock-sun lights could. Which was Katherine's assumption as to why they had taken the sun lights off and replaced them with the bulbs.

The effect of each passing busk, much like Room Zero with its paintings and preserved uniforms, was intimidation. The reverence the Pipeworkers held for themselves far exceeded that of the agronomists.

We've all got giant egos though, don't we?

Einar, the bearded Viking warrior, rose from his desk chair as Ólafur and Katherine entered. Behind Einar, the main pipe chugged away, droning, the beating heart of Subsolum—and, Katherine realised, New Havilah too.

Einar, looking about ready to collapse from exhaustion, walked across the grated metal flooring, below which rested a complex of pipes and valves and shut offs.

'Welcome back, Katherine,' he said, taking her hand into his. He squeezed so hard she nearly reached up with her other to pull away. 'Ólafur has explained the situation?'

'Not really,' Katherine said, her hand free and lacking colour, 'but I've heard a lot.'

More than I really want to admit. Dad couldn't have ... could he? And if he really made Mum sick, could he lie to me all these years—keep me blind to it? No. Ólafur has left him and is trying to turn me against him, I'm sure of it.

'...and we think it's in Subsolum's interest to change leadership,' Ólafur was saying as Katherine came out from her thoughts.

'What?' she said.

Ólafur shuffled nervously.

'Your father is not fit to lead, Katherine.'

'And you are?'

The question's bluntness stifled the Viking man. The glint in his gold teeth seemed to weaken.

'Yes,' Einar said eventually, 'I do.'

'So why am I here? If he is so weak, just announce you are taking over.'

Einar shook his head; Ólafur lifted his hands as if to begin a prepared speech, but was cut off by Einar saying, 'That ... that isn't how leaders in Subsolum are selected. The people have to vote. Daniel must resign, lawfully. This cannot look to be a violent transition.'

Katherine huffed. She was hot and sweaty and stank and wanted to go back to New Havilah and bathe in a hotpool. *Down here we are so enclosed and I never knew it.*

'Convince him to resign.'

Katherine's immediate thought was that he wouldn't listen to her, but Ólafur, as if reading her mind, said, 'He will listen to you, Miss Marston, only you.'

Everyone keeps saying it but I don't think they really know.

'How ill is he? Tell me.'

Einar and Ólafur traded concerned glances.

Einar said, 'He is stable, but the medics can only do so much.'

'Even after, Miss Marston,' Ólafur said, 'even after I gave him all the rest of the Immortal Man's blood—he is still coughing and struggling to breathe. He doesn't have long. But there are those who are still loyal, who, if he dies, will not accept Einar as president. President Marston must resign and tell his people who to vote for.'

After Ólafur had said 'he doesn't have long' Katherine stopped listening. A ringing sounded in her ears and the good memories filtered through her, almost as real as when she had first made them.

'So he'll *fokking* die and you're both trying to make it all easier to take his place.' Katherine waved them off, and started for the exit. 'I won't be some puppet of yours,' she said, gripping tightly onto the small vial of *Zed* in her overall's pocket. 'I want to hear him out.'

'Katherine,' Einar shouted, 'please, listen to us.'

But she forgot them. Left them. She wanted to make up her own mind.

γ

Her father wasn't in his office. In fact it looked as if no one had been there since the cries of *Oust! Oust! Oust!* had chased them into it.

Taking the ramps to the higher level, she tried to think what to say to him. Mum would never love a person like al-Zoubi. But Katherine could easily imagine her mother returning with a love of *New Havilah* in her heart. She saw her mother's desperate attempts to explain that the radiation levels were lower, liveable, that New Havilah wasn't the nightmare Subsolum believed it to be.

And as she walked the narrow, well lit tunnel to her childhood home, she remembered Darleaner's words. They make their own myths.

At the door, she knocked but got no response, so called out and still got nothing. Trying the door, she found it unlocked and slid it open. The house's grand and expansive entrance way sprawled before her, tightening her stomach. The Old World paintings on the wall; the vases, sculptures, rows and rows of books, all of it nothing more than a show of inequality.

I had it better.

Coughs and hacks echoed through the empty house. She went up the spiralling stairs to the landing where more paintings and Old World books covered the walls. A set of photographs she had never seen before, taken by a black and white Subsolumer camera, lay neatly along a waist high brass shelf. The photographs were of her with her mother and father. Maybe her third birthday—she was a giggling toddler in her mother's arms. Her father, in a suit, smiling broadly, but not looking at the camera, and instead gazing at his family.

This is it. This is how he thinks of us. I'm still a baby to him, and Mum's what he wants her to be, and only to be, a mum.

The coughing grew louder and more violent. It came from her parents' room. She paused at the door, again tried to think of words for him, but finding none merely sighed and knocked on the door.

'Get away, you traitor!' a raspy voice said. 'There's nothing here for you.'

'It's me, Dad,' she called back softly.

The coughing stopped, a scuffle, then, 'Kathy? Come to me, Kathy.'

She slid the door open to her father, glistening with sweat, surrounded by bloody tissues, a metal bucket on the floor at his side, ripped open rations packets scattered everywhere. Blood and gin tainted the warm air.

Sitting himself up in the giant bed, her father wiped his bloody mouth. 'You're here,' he said, 'have you got it?'

Katherine, stepping into the room as if the floor might give way at any moment, shook her head. A sweaty hand in the overall's pocket, she gripped the vial of *Zed*, hoping that it would be enough to rouse him fully.

'You don't have his flower?' her father said, his face a rictus. He had become a pale, bloodless monster, unable to understand. 'But you must have it.'

The amount of blood about his face, down his chest, on all the tissues, and in the buckets forced her to wonder how he could still be alive.

Again he wiped his mouth, tried to sit up straighter still. 'You must have it.'

'I don't,' she said. As she reached his bedside his smell reached her too. Days spent in bed, sweating and rotting, had left a stink on him that made it hard to notice anything else.

His worn-out eyes looked up at her. These weren't her father's eyes. These belonged to a desperate man, one who Katherine didn't know, didn't love. But a pressure built behind her, pushed tears to the corners of her eyes, and soon she was so overwhelmed she dropped to her knees and took her father in her arms and cried into him. 'I'm sorry,' she said softly, through the tears, 'I'm sorry. I failed long before any of this started.'

'My Kathy,' he whispered.

And then, as if the sunlight from outside had penetrated Subsolum, she broke her embrace, reeled back from him in horror and said, 'Is it true?'

'Is what true?' Wiping himself, his blood, he said, 'I'm dying, I don't have time for questions.'

'Answer me.'

'Ólafur has tainted you,' he spat. 'He's turned you against me.'

She withdrew the vial from her overalls and held it up towards him. The small amount of *Liphoric Zed* inside shimmered bright green.

'What is that?' He tried to lunge for it, but recoiled in pain. 'Is that the *Lifoorrick Zee?*'

The way he pronounced it, maybe he'd only seen it written. 'It's from al-Zoubi's flower, yes,' she said. And then, finding a sardonic tone, 'How did you think I was going to take a *flower* up the mountain, Father?'

A cough erupted from him, shooting blood spittle from his lips and all over the bed sheets. He mopped at his mouth using a blood-soaked lump of cottonmoss tissue.

That *feeling*, one that rose and fell like the tides she'd only ever read about, again swelled inside her heart. This is my father. My dad. The man who looked after me as Mum died. Who fed me, picked me up from class, taught me all about the soil, how to understand the crops; he is my dad who, no matter what, made sure I was never hungry, never without a book to read, never without a place to go.

Until he wasn't all that.

Now he is a man who is clawing for fresh cottonmoss cloth, soaked in his own filth. Can I still call him Dad? Is he?

Fed up with her father's hapless searching for a clean bit of cloth, Katherine took a fresh one from a bundle that had fallen from the bedside table and handed it to him. He wiped his mouth and face clean, then asked for some warm water in a bowl, which she fetched for him, and he washed himself; she gave him a comb and he combed what little hair he had left; he asked for some cool water to drink so she got him some. And then, saying that he needed strength first to talk, he asked for some dry ration biscuit and she gave him the last piece he had left and he ate it all. He never asked for gin. He didn't think about it.

Fed and watered, her father, somewhat more presentable, said, 'Get the chair from there,' and pointed at the metal armchair in the corner of the bedroom.

Dragging the armchair over to the bed, Katherine wondered if indulging him like this was a relapse. He's prepping me for another one of his mind games. He'll convince me Mum died because of her own actions. That he had nothing to do with it. That he's as lost and loveless as I am.

So as she sat in the armchair, a front row seat to *The Dying of Her Father*, she tried as hard as she could to hold on to what she knew. Which, as she realised to rising heartbeat, was very little. All she had were the rad levels. They *were* lower than what Subsolum liked to believe. She'd seen it.

'They need me to resign,' her father began. 'They need me to tell everyone to vote for Einar.' He spat blood. 'They don't care about you, Kathy; you're an instrument to them.'

She had the vial of *Zed* on her lap. After his words, her father locked his gaze on it, not daring to take his attention elsewhere.

'You gave me a faulty Geiger counter,' she said. 'The radiation levels are liveable in the town. New Havilah is filled with people, not monsters. You're a liar, Dad.'

He coughed and sputtered and pawed at his mouth.

'No?' she said, 'there's nothing you want to say?'

Again, eyes on the vial, he said, 'Give me it.'

She held it up, letting the sap inside run into fine threads from the bottom to the top. 'You'll get it,' she said, 'when you tell me the truth.'

'We do not belong on the surface, Katherine. We have lost. Lost long ago. *They* are the meek. Not us. Our home is gone. The Stars, the *Starship Fables*, the *fokking Stjörnu Farartæki*, all of it a creation to keep us sane, to keep us from suicide. There is no end to our damnation.'

'We aren't damned.'

Groping the bedside table, her father pursed his lips, lost and clueless, as if all this wasn't *his* doing. And not all of it was. Where his cancer came from only the Stars knew. His hand crashed about on the top of the bedside table, aimless.

'What are you looking for?' she asked.

'My glasses.'

'They're on the floor.'

'Can you…?'

She sighed, picked them up, both lenses had small cracks in them, and handed them over.

The moment he put them on, the tightness in her stomach grew worse. He had returned to his dominant form. It was in these glasses that he had bossed her about, raised her, tried to teach her right from wrong. And of course, light caught on them, glinted as he moved.

'Katherine,' he said, resting his head back, but now, with his glasses on, peering deep into her eyes. 'You have been eating. You're flush with colour.'

'There's food in New Havilah.'

He shook his head, a tiny gesture. 'You sound like her.' Coughed into his fist. 'That's what you want to ask me, isn't it? Ólafur threatened me, the nerve; he said if I didn't give in to Einar he would tell you everything.'

'He has.'

'And you believe him?'

'I don't know.'

Al-Zoubi's image resolved in her mind. If you loved someone, were loved by them too, do you make them into a puppet after they leave you? Do you hear their voice as if they were there?

'The Immortal Man knew Mum,' she said. 'He loved her.'

Grimacing, her father said, 'Don't bring him into this. He's nothing. He was being played by your mother. Tricked. She—' he stopped to cough, blood spilling from his lips. 'I didn't want

330

her to go up there. But she insisted.'

'She wanted to change the fields over.'

'Yes,' her father said. He crushed his eyes closed. Behind the cracked lenses, his eyes looked almost New Havilian—like they could see in more than one direction at once. 'And I suppose I thought it wise. The soil is *dead*, after all.'

To hear him say it. He does know. He isn't lost.

'But when your mother came back to me,' he said, 'she no longer believed in Subsolum.'

The blood and filth, his soiled bed sheets, the bed, the armchair, the room, it all vanished; all her attention burnt into him, she saw nothing else, heard nothing else.

'She wanted to go and stay up there?'

'Yes, Kathy,' he said. 'As you have told me today, so did your mother all those years ago: the rad levels are dropping. It's safe—' he looked down, shaking his head in disbelief. 'And I ate it up. I believed her. She wanted to take us all there. We began to plan how to do it. How do you move one culture into another and there not be a clash? How do humans learn to live amongst monsters?'

They aren't monsters.

'It wasn't long,' her father continued, 'before your mother was like I am now, spitting blood, dying, and I knew that she was wrong. There is no place for us up there. If *she* can get a radiation measurement wrong...? We are all doomed to repeat it.'

Katherine, in the armchair, slouched back, exhaling.

'I suppose Ólafur has twisted all that up? Has led you to believe I'm a murderer?'

The room came back into focus. She saw everything again.

Took it all in. As if her father's charm had worn. 'You still let me go up there.'

'So like Sophia. If I hadn't,' he said, gazing at her over his glasses' rims, 'you would have gone anyway. Don't try to tell me otherwise. At least this way it served a purpose.' He held out his hand again, clasping the air for the *Zed*. 'Give it to me, Katherine. Haven't I suffered enough?'

Pinching the vial, dangling it in front of him, she said, 'And what about the Black Rot?'

'Excuse me?'

'This flower, *his* flower, I had to cure it. Remove a fungal root infection that's spread to other plants and crops.'

'What do I care about that man's problems?'

She leant forwards in the armchair, spoke to him like a teacher might a student, 'The infection *has* to have come from Subsolum. I cultured the spores. It's near identical to what took out most of our wheat.'

'You're confused, Kathy, looking for a pattern when there is none.'

Holding up the vail, she said, 'Do you want this? Do you need it?'

He groped the air, flinched at invisible pain, coughed and coughed. 'Please, Kathy,' he managed to say.

She stood. Standing above him, where I ought to be. She demanded the truth. 'Tell me! I don't know what's true and I can't take it anymore. Has all my life been a lie, Dad? Have you tried to keep all this from me—you've tried to cover my eyes in cottonmoss.'

332

Lurching for the vial, her father fell from the bed, landed at her feet. He clawed at her legs, begged her to give him the vial.

She unstoppered it.

'Oh, Kathy, you've saved me, you've cured me of my ills, you—'

And she drank.

Every fibre in her body writhed; her heart pounded, thudded blood and *Liphoric Zed* about her; the taste of the forever was on her tongue—sweet. Already she could feel it passing through her stomach, down into her guts where it reached into her blood. It replenished her.

I have drunk from the fountain of youth.

Her father held to her legs weakly.

'You're a Tunnel Spirit now, Father.'

And she left him there to die.

THE END

EPILOGUE

THE SECULAR AND THE SACRED: A PLAY

PLAY

– NEW HAVILAH –

Characters

Quinton al-Zoubi as *The Immortal Man*

Billick Guenov as *The Pirate Botanist*

Lady 'Juju' Jupiter as *Mother Jupiter*

John Johnny Ganymede as *Sir Ganymede*

Katherine Marston as *The Good Daughter*

And introducing

Johannes 'Slugger' Fehrmehr as *The Saved Boy*

PROLOGUE

Curtains raise and, in the spotlight, *The Saved Boy*, a human sized slug, whose antennae play nervously against a shiny gilded lectern, reads:

> What the water-pipe
> Is made from
>
> Meister Eckhart
> Cannot say
>
> But the water
> Tastes wonderful

Wait for audience applause (if any) and drop the curtains.

ACT THE FIRST

The Blue-Headed Goat's INTERIOR. Our hero, *The Immortal Man,* sits exhausted where we left him in the novel. He pours a healthy measure of *Liphoric Zed* out for a Sun Priest whose tatty Old World robes are half falling off his body.

Sun Priest: Thank the Stars!

The Immortal Man: The Stars? I slaved away to bring you this! Over 200 hundred years! Do you know what that can do to a man? When he's lived more history than anyone ever? You ought to have some respect.

The Sun Priest takes off his robes and presents them to The Immortal Man.

The Immortal Man: Oh, grow up! Put that back on and go and clean your church, or whatever Mother Jupiter has you doing in there. Go on, *get!*

The Sun Priest scurries off the stage.

The Pirate Botanist: He's two nybbles short of a byte, that one.

The Immortal Man sighs.
After wiping sweat from his brow, he relaxes back in his chair.

Over The Blue-Headed Goat's highpass speakers comes *New Havilah Wireless Radio.*

Radio New Havilah: Have you heard the rumours, folks? Word on the boulevard is we've got Waters in the Goat. Why don't you rock out and head over now? Maybe there's something for you?

'Go With The Flow' by Queens of the Stone Age plays

All on stage rock out.

ENTER: *Mother Jupiter*

Music stops with a record scratch.

Mother Jupiter: What's all this?

She's furious, pointing at *The Immortal Man.*
The Pirate Botanist stops his headbanging to look up.

The Pirate Botanist: Brightness me!

Mother Jupiter chases after *The Pirate Botanist and The Immortal Man*
(Classic panto chase ensures)

Over the speakers: 'Two Bugs and a Roach' by Earl Hooker

338

Mother Jupiter grabs a hold of *The Pirate Botanist*. Shakes him with all of her four arms.

(Music stops)

Mother Jupiter (still shaking *The Pirate Botanist*): You imbeciles. I've shut off the pipes for a reason. Closed the tap! Put a stop to this patriarchal endeavour of yours!

The Immortal Man: My what? (realises she's still shaking *The Pirate Botanist*) Stop it! You'll kill him!

The Pirate Botanist (being shaken but smiling): I kinda like it, Cap'n!

Mother Jupiter drops *The Pirate Botanist* in disgust.

Mother Jupiter (wiping her hands): You're both disgusting.

The Immortal Man: That isn't very nice. You stole my blood. *That's* disgusting.

Mother Jupiter: And why did I do that?

The Immortal Man: You want to live forever.

Mother Jupiter (shaking her head): No, Immortal Man, no.

The Immortal Man: Then why?

Mother Jupiter: Because, Immortal Man, I must learn what made *you* live forever. Why is it *you*? Of all the people in the Old World *you* happened to remain. Don't you think that's odd?

The Immortal Man (smiling): You don't trust me.

Mother Jupiter: No, I don't.

The Immortal Man: We don't speak, Mother Jupiter; you are, and always have been, hidden in your Sun Church. Hiding away, controlling those who can't (he pauses here and holds up his index, middle, and ring finger) can't learn to read between the lines.

Mother Jupiter (tutting): You think *I* am the one who controls them? You think little of me.

The Immortal Man: I do, in fact, think little of you. You are like those of the Old World who hoarded like dragons. Only you've done it in the New World, this time prattling your religion.

Mother Jupiter: It isn't religion—what does that word even mean now? Really? It's a *community*. An ordered one. Which is what I, and those who *choose* to follow me, enjoy. Don't stand here and tell me you aren't the same? You and your entourage. You only respect *physical* power. You, sir? You're as bad as my husband.

Over the speakers comes: 'Funny Thing' by Thundercat

ENTER: *Sir Ganymede*

Sir Ganymede is playing the bass guitar (the opening riff from *Funny Thing*). He mouths the words. He doesn't take his eyes off his wife, *Mother Jupiter*.

Mother Jupiter (after the entire song has been played): You're a bunch of boys! The lot of you! (she snatches the bass guitar from him—it's a real funky bass—and she hands it to a member of the Sun Priests, who scurries off stage with it).

Sir Ganymede: Juju, tell me where I've gone wrong.

Mother Jupiter (pausing for two/three beats): You stopped listening to me.

The Pirate Botanist (towards the audience): That's marriage, eh? (might get a bad reaction, so play it cool)

Mother Jupiter: And I, I lost my faith in you. Times are always hard, beloved husband; but times are harder when we stop communicating, when our trust in each other is so broken, we can longer take opinion for what it really is.

The Immortal Man: And what's that?

Mother Jupiter (looks at the audience): A suggestion.

The Pirate Botanist: Ah! Me thinks I know what she's on about.

Sir Ganymede is in deep reflection.

The Immortal Man (to the pirate botanist): Care to enlighten me?

The Pirate Botanist: Alrighty, bucko, here we go … let's put the wax on the felt.

'Start Here' by Damu the Fudgemunk plays on the high pass speakers

The Pirate Botanist (rapping):

It's pretty simple.
Let's tell the people how it should be done
You gotta learn to listen, no need for guns
We gotta make our funky music and don't shun
See the words I rap aren't heard by all
Only those who wish to prevent the fall
Lady Jay knows a way, but she don't know it all
Secular and Sacred are two sides of the same coin
You gotta know both before you burst your loins
Pay attention and get sincere,

remember to listen and never fear.

(drops mic - there's a piped in applause)

Mother Jupiter: Bloody rappers! You think you know it all.

Sir Ganymede (dropping to the floor, clearly distressed): I haven't been listening.
Why!? Why!? (as Shakespearian as we can manage)

'Acid Raindrops' by People Under the Stairs plays

Sir Ganymede begins drumming on bongo drums. He lip syncs the entire first verse and chorus.

(music fades; curtains fall)

END OF ACT THE FIRST

ACT THE SECOND

'Summer Madness' by Kool & The Gang fades in over the high pass speakers

(Geothermal vapour vents onto the boulevard)

Curtains rise on The Goat's EXTERIOR; The Goat's Blue-Headed Goat sign is still in the Summer Solstice air. There's a queue of New Havilians waiting to get in. All are happy, dancing softly to the music.

ENTER (stage right): *The Good Daughter*

'Summer Madness' by Kool & The Gang fades out

The Good Daughter (walking slowly to centre stage): No roaches got me. I'm no roach prey. I'm *good*. But am I? Am I really *good*? What does good even mean? How do I know? I murdered my father, that's not good? Is it? (wait for any audience reaction) I guess not. But ... but sometimes you need to kill your fathers—(looks at the audience)—you kill them dead. Because they become tyrannical. They ... they exercise their power as if they were *divine*. As if they were God given powers. But they're not. No power is God given. God is—well, don't let me tell you what God is, you'll need to figure that one out for yourself. But to me, God is everything we can't understand; but I do understand one thing—(looks at audience again)—and that's that sometimes, sometimes you need to kill your father.

From the orchestral pit comes Thomas Willow's 'Front'

The Good Daughter dances.

Thomas Willow's 'Front' fades softly

The Good Daughter crouches to the floor, crying. For a beat she cries. The door to the Goat swings open. In the threshold is *The Immortal Man*.

'Bam Bam' by Sister Nancy plays

New Havilian steel drummers play along. As the music bumps, *The Immortal Man* bobs his hips.

The Good Daughter notices and comes to her feet. She wipes tears.

The Immortal Man (over the music): You came back.

The Good Daughter: Do you forgive me?

The Immortal Man: For?

The Good Daughter: For stealing some of your *Liphoric Zed*.

The Immortal Man (he comes closer, still bopping): Stealing? My friend tells me you were given permission. That the Flower speaks to you?

'Bam Bam' by Sister Nancy fades out

The Good Daughter (turns to the audience): Why doth thou choose me, O Lord? Choose me over all other potentials? Choose me to take Humanity into the future?

(hold for a beat)

'Cosmic Wheels' by Donovan fades in

The Immortal Man: Silly girl. *You* chose *you*.

They both dance.

In their dance is love. All that can be said is that their love is more than father and daughter; all that can be said is it must be felt, alas, it must be *seen!*

As the song fades, so does the dance.

The Good Daughter and *The Immortal Man* part ways. Each heading off stage. They are happy and sad.

'I Only Want to Sing the Blues' by Dino Dini comes from the orchestral pit

END OF ACT THE SECOND

The Pirate Botanist, *Mother Jupiter*, and *Sir Ganymede* enter the stage through The Goat's door. They are sad, but they shake their 'heads' to the beat.

As the music fades, our three come to the centre of the stage.

Mother Jupiter: You want to know why you can't listen, John?

Sir Ganymede: No!

The Pirate Botanist: There you go, folks! (towards the crowd)

Mother Jupiter: When boys grow up, they always have a choice. Learn how to listen to their mothers, or not. It's *simple*. But for one reason or another, they choose not. Where you, my beloved husband, fell from your father's love I do not know. Don't you understand?

Sir Ganymede: I do have one thing to say, my love. Listen.

Over the highpass speakers comes 'This is Paradise' by Eyedea and Abilities

Sir Ganymede mimes the entire song.

(Curtains lower as some funky bass from the pit plays)

END OF ACT THE SECOND

THE FINAL ACT

Curtains raise to *The Good Daughter*, in the limelight, she is in a sparklingly white dress that scintillates.

'Him' by Lilly Allen fades in over the highpass speakers

The Good Daughter dances.

Once the song is over, curtains come down, and from the pit comes 'Dog Toy' by Speedboat

The entire cast come out from behind the curtains. They take a bow. Another.

There is much applause and ruckus. It is the Solstice and everyone who is alive is happy.

END OF THE FINAL ACT

WACOOH

Whenever Tiffany Guenov was this far from home, she reread *WACOOH*.

She folded up her worn paperback and slid it into her coat. She was often far from home, for she was a sailor, like her father before her, and there were lands ahead and beyond that needed charting. Old World gold that needed finding.

She walked the deck of her vessel, *The Crimson Mistress*, and took the helm. Channelling the energies of the Summer Solstice play, she said to her crew, well-nourished and ready for their next adventure. Nay! She screamed it! 'We're all warm in the centre of our hearts!'

The crew heaved and hoed, and they were off. Sails rippled in the wind. Waves crashed against the bow. Far from the lands of New Havilah. Deeper into the lands of the unknown.

Good luck and God bless ye, ya filthy pirates!

ACKNOWLEDGMENTS

Novel writing is not as lonely as it is made up to be. Over the many years this novel has taken to come together, plenty have helped, inspired, and given it a good shaking down, so I thought I'd try and give these people their much deserved time in the limelight. Without further ado, I give you: Peter Hall, the Vagabond, who I know is out there somewhere, who read the very early drafts of the first few chapters, and who called this novel the 'upstairs downstairs one', and whose words of encouragement kept my belly warm. Eloise McInerney, the Indomitable, whose mastery of storytelling and prose I am ever awed by, who worked me hard and never flinched in doing so, who spent countless hours with me in coffee shops, guiding and teaching. Karen and Pete Vincent-Jones, Alice Ash, and Madeline Denny, the Circus Writers, who opened their homes to me and who encouraged and critiqued. David Whitmarsh, the Blues Hippie, whose many reads of every nook and cranny of this novel, every dead end and cul-de-sac, gave me the insights possible to stitch this world together. Andrey Guenov and his family, the Mighty Bulgars, who welcomed me to their country which inspired so much of New Havilah, whose never ending interest in my haphazard writings spurred me on, and who taught me so much about what family means. Tommy Hardman, the Illustrious Illustrator, whose very fine artwork adorns this novel, and without whose passion this novel would not be in your hands. James Anders Banks, the 8 Bit Codesmith, whose fine editorial work brought this novel into its final state. Simon Fox, Jason

Hazael, and Jamie Ryński-Kelsall, the Beta Readers, who all demonstrated that, yes, this novel was one that could be read, understood, and even enjoyed.

And lastly, Lianne Fox, my wife, whose patience with me has never faltered, who has endured all the lows and shared all the highs, and who I love dearly.

Thank you all, so, so much. And never forget: We're all warm at the centre of our hearts.

ABOUT THE AUTHOR

Harrison is a writer and programmer who lives with his wife, Lianne, and their two kitties Ed and Rex, in the sunny South East of England. He is a graduate of New Writing South's Creative Writing Programme. His fiction has appeared in *After Dinner Conversation* and *Four Star Stories*, as well being longlisted for the *James White Award*. You can find more of his stories, comics, and writings at warpedandtorn.io and also follow his ravings @harrison_perry

Milton Keynes UK
Ingram Content Group UK Ltd.
UKHW042028061123
432092UK00004B/230